MW00365775

Sophie Overett is an award-winning writer, editor, podcaster and cultural producer based in Melbourne, Australia. She won the 2020 Penguin Australia Literary Prize and the 2018 AAWP Emerging Writer Prize. *The Rabbits* is her first novel.

The Rabbits

Sophie Overett

The Rabbits

Sophie Overett

Gallic Books
London

A Gallic Book

Copyright © Sophie Overett 2021
Sophie Overett has asserted her moral right to be identified
as the author of the work.

First published in Austalia in 2021 by Vintage
This edition published in 2023 by
Gallic Books, 12 Eccleston Street, London, SW1W 9LT

This book is copyright under the Berne Convention
No reproduction without permission
All rights reserved

A CIP record for this book is available from the British Library

Typeset Minion Pro by Gallic Books
ISBN 978-1-913547-42-4

Printed in the UK by CPI (CR0 4YY)
2 4 6 8 10 9 7 5 3 1

For my Grandma, who made me love stories, and for my Nona, who knew how to tell them

And now as I disappear, someone else becomes real
— 'Tiniest Seed', Angel Olsen

The night Charlie Rabbit disappears, Delia thinks of her sister.

Not of the last night she'd seen her, when Bo had smiled at her with tea-stained teeth, her cushiony lips pulled fat across them, nor of Bo's brittle bones, burning all those months later in the smoky city crematorium. Rather she remembers the sticky summer nights of their childhood spent at the hospital their mother worked at, where they turned old stretchers into tombs and bandaged each other like Egyptian mummies.

That was before video games and mobile phones, before the cocky, parted knees of boys. A time when Delia was still Del, and Bo was still breathing. A time, a world that was just for them, their small children's bodies contorted into whatever space they'd fit, and their voices lowered, always, because every word felt like a secret and every breath a code. And they'd played, of course they'd played – hopscotch and red rover and tiggy, but nothing more than hide-and-go-seek. Nothing more, because there was nothing Bo was better at than hiding. Folding her body below bed frames and inside vanities, her little feet tucked beneath her, her arms so tightly pressed to her sides she'd seemed like barely a thing at all.

Del was not so good. Del liked to be seen, liked to be found. Liked to catch these moments of discovery, feel her firm skin, hold her own wandering gaze in whatever mirror would have her. She liked to take up space. Of course this meant Bo inevitably found her. *You're no good at this*, she'd tell her, loud, accusatory, and Del was inclined to agree.

So it was through some mix of genetics and luck, both good and bad, that Charlie had come out of Delia so much like Bo, her aptitude for hiding appearing in him just like Delia's green eyes and Ed's gangly limbs. Charlie could hide before he could sit, stand, run, and Delia spent too many hours of too many days pulling him out from below clothing racks and cabinets, or finding him slipped up inside the roof's rafters, his long, skinny legs curled beneath his long, skinny body, his toothy child's grin a reminder of what she had lost.

And she'd felt it, even then. The fear that he was just like Bo and not like her at all. That he'd leave her, just like Bo had.

It startled her, how much she was afraid of it. Because no matter how often their mother had called that coil of spirit in them wanderlust or walkabout, a pair of nomad feet, a *now you see me*, they had all known what it really was.

A little disappearing act.

1

'Turn to the left. Now back to me. Can you describe who's sitting beside you?'

A student three rows from the front raises her hand, and Delia tilts her chin just enough to acknowledge her, but she doesn't call on her. Not yet.

'Can you tell me the shape of her jaw? The curve of his nose? What colour are the eyes? The lips? The cracked skin between their eyebrows? Can you draw them?'

The hand goes down, and the class titters around her, stifled in the stale summer heat of the lecture theatre. Delia steps forwards, her legs sweating in her sheer, glossy stockings, the hair at the base of her neck curling wet. She can hear a student panting, more than one, their heads lolling, mouths open. This drought has left them all parched, stretched the season thin in an unusual way for Brisbane. They're so close to the sea that they typically get tropical storms at this time of year, the Shakespearean sort that boil like godly tempers, and without them the dry broil has left the city brittle, stripped back trees to gothic contortions and baked the earth firm.

Even here, in the bowels of the college, the heat finds them.

Delia leans back against her desk, rolling her shoulders in an effort to shift her polyester shirt from her damp skin. The class looks expectantly at her, bleary eyed and slack jawed after the end-of-year break, the room around them musty from months of disuse. She had come in early that morning to wipe the soft coating of dust from the plastic backs of chairs, and she can still feel it on her fingers, soft as the down on a baby's head.

'Over the next twelve weeks, we will be exploring interdisciplinary drawing, with a particular focus on life drawing. Pay attention, and you'll finish the course with a firm understanding of the nature of visual perception, and how that perception translates to a page or a canvas, essential skills for any artist.'

A girl with an oily forehead and freckles on her lips writes this down.

'Assessment will be folio based, plus a written assignment on the sociocultural history of life drawing, and—'

The far door of the lecture theatre cracks open, throwing light down the linoleum surface of the stairs. A boy walks in, a man, his dark hair tangled, shoulders sloped. He catches her eye and smiles a crooked smile.

And so what if her breath catches? So what if he notices, slinking cat-like into a seat?

'—and an exam.'

Delia clears her throat, turning back to the blackboard and scrawling her name in flaking chalk.

'My name is Delia Rabbit. I have a master's degree in fine art from the QCA. I specialise in pencil work and acrylics and, very occasionally, I see the light and return to my Catholic roots with tempera. I like the work of Hilda Rix Nicholas and Thea Proctor. That's me. Now we're going to go around the room. I want you to introduce yourself, your preferred medium, and an artist who inspires you. Let's start at the back.'

O

Olive's on her second cigarette by the time Lux Robinson stumbles into the loading bay behind the grocery store, last night's make-up shadowing her eyes, her uniform reeking of yesterday's BO, Impulse body spray and vanilla-whipped-cream vape juice.

'Had a big one?' Olive asks, casting her an amused look, and Lux flips her off.

If you were to ask Mindy Chan, she'd tell you that Lux is close to an hour late for her shift, something Olive only really knows because of Mindy's loud ranting earlier, her full, tattooed frame crouched beside Olive's in the stockroom as they pulled rotten fruit out of hot crates, the pulpy, decomposing bodies of pears and peaches catching beneath their nails.

The coldroom motor had croaked the night before – the third time this summer – leaving Mindy's jaw clenched and a hot pressure pulsing behind Olive's eyes. Nothing can beat the heat, she had thought, not even Mindy's uncanny knack for kicking the fridge motor into working again, and she can still smell it, even now, that potent scent of soured fruit and festering, green-tinged meat, glommed to her pores.

'Has Frank noticed I'm late?' Lux asks, and Olive shrugs, flicking the ash from the end of her cigarette.

'Doubt it, but Mindy did.'

'Fuck Mindy. She's such a cunt.'

Olive frowns, which only makes Lux roll her eyes, push out a hip and fumble in her back pocket for her vape pen. She makes a quick motion of the habit, inhales, exhales, the sickly vanilla liquid Olive smelled earlier filling her nose again.

'She can't hear us, dipshit,' Lux says, the smoke still wavering around her stained teeth. She rubs a hand beneath her eyes, smearing her eyeliner into ashy clouds. 'Jesus, it stinks out here.'

And no shit, Olive thinks. It had taken her and Mindy forever to get all the spoiled fruit and meat from the fridges into the heavy industrial bins behind them: brown mangoes, wrinkled apples, melons with their insides sloshing about within hard, pruned skins. The flies had been a nightmare, the ants racing away in lines with tiny parcels of foul meat perched on their backs. Olive had had to pinch her skin till it bruised to quell her nausea at the sight of it. It had been bad enough in the store itself, but out here it's worse, without the fans dispersing the putrid scent and with no tart bite of garlic and balsamic olives from the deli to overwhelm it.

'I don't smell it,' Olive says all the same, shrugging. 'Maybe it's you.'

Lux replies by pursing her lips in a look that says *whatever*, smoke pouring out of her nostrils while the obstructed midday light casts a strange, foreign glow at her back. If Olive were perfectly honest, she'd say there *is* something foreign about Lux Robinson. On paper, she's a lot like Olive. They're both unusually tall, blonde by birth – although Lux dyed her hair vein-blue last spring – with the delicate bones you usually only see on models and mannequins. They are sharp edges in starched shirts, talons behind the checkouts, but while Olive's round cheeks and dollar-coin eyes give her a softer look, Lux is all angles. Fey or alien, depending on who you ask.

'Don't be jealous just because I have a life outside this place,' Lux coos, her tone shifting when she looks back at Olive. 'You could come with tomorrow night. This kid Dom knows is throwing a party out at Kangaroo Point.'

Lux rolls her eyes at her own words, a mockery of the rich kids with the picturesque city views who live out there, and Olive tilts her feet in, stares at her scuffed shoes, at the tattered, dropped hem of her work pants, and frowns.

'I don't know.' She wipes her sweating palms on her shirt and turns back towards the store. 'I don't really like that shit, you know?'

Lux doesn't let her get far. She springs forwards, her clammy fingers wrapping around Olive's wrist.

'Oh, come on, what's stopping you? I think Jude's going.'

The flush finds her cheeks right away, a tension sets her fingers, and *god*, she's embarrassing. She blinks hard, swallows the lump in her throat.

'So?' she bites, keeping her gaze fixed ahead. 'You know he couldn't pick me out of a line-up.'

Behind her, Lux makes a noise like she disagrees, but Olive pretends she doesn't hear her, taking a little breath to ground herself instead and instantly regretting it when she gets a new whiff of rotten fruit.

'Mum's back at work, anyway,' she adds. 'I've got to look after the boys.'

The excuse is an easy one in no small part because it's

not a lie – something Lux knows pretty much as well as Olive at this point – but the other girl groans anyway and something in Olive lurches. A familiar feeling hooking her chest, dragging her down, down, down, and—

No.

Pull yourself together.

Olive sucks in another lungful of rancid air.

'Come *on*. It'll be fun. You need to have fun, Rabbit. Don't pretend you don't.'

Down at the other end of the loading bay, a few of the boys are clocking off from their shifts, one walking backwards while he talks to another, hands high in the air, whether in show or cheer or just to dry the sweat stains at the armpits of his work shirt, Olive can't be sure. His voice carries though when he says something about cleaning up before the pub, and his mate's does too when he laughs, tells him he shouldn't bother, that it's not the pitstains stopping him from picking up. Olive fixes on their wide, confident gaits and lanky limbs, the parched leaves kicked up in their wake, the dirt so dry it doesn't cloud around their feet but instead scrapes against the bitumen. The first guy drops one of his arms to shove his friend, and then they're scrapping, grinning, easy as anything, and before she can stop herself, she wonders if Charlie and Benjamin will be like that when they're older. If her dad was like that when he was young.

As if to reclaim her attention, Lux suddenly leans forwards and shakes the smoke out of her hair, revealing a glimpse of where fresh blue dye has marked the back of her neck like a bruise.

And maybe it's that. Maybe it's the feel of this moment, the promise of Jude, the probability of pills, the heat, or the way the hair dye makes it look as if Lux has been held down. Maybe the look of it makes Olive feel an echo of pressure at her own neck, as if she's been held down too, but finally she says maybe, and tries to ignore the clench in her belly when Lux cheers in reply.

Benjamin curls his long fingers through the wire of the school fence as Charlie crosses the road towards him, his sagging backpack slung over his shoulder, his hair damp and matted to his forehead.

'You're late,' Benjamin says when Charlie reaches him, but Charlie just rolls his eyes, jerking his head down the fence, towards the entrance of the school grounds. That's all it takes for Benjamin to scamper, to grab his schoolbag and Spectacular Man figurine and stumble down the playground alongside his brother, the net-thin fence the only thing left between them.

'I figured you'd still be mucking around with Jodes,' Charlie says when Benjamin catches up, and the name quickly sours in Benjamin's head. He shrugs petulantly, his schoolbag riding up his shoulders. It's answer enough for Charlie, who does a slow whistle, the sort Olive likes to do, and the thought of that only makes Benjamin scowl even harder.

Shepherd Primary School's playground opens onto the street, and, with the fence between them gone, Charlie and

Benjamin start down the winding footpaths leading home. The day is bright, the sun's glare saturating the afternoon, and Benjamin tugs his wide-brimmed school hat further down to shield his eyes from it.

'Did you know lightning doesn't need rain or clouds to strike?'

Benjamin blinks, looking up at his brother. In the last few months, Charlie has grown almost ten whole centimetres. Benjamin knows this because they measured him, just like Charlie measures Benjamin – scribbling the numbers down on post-it notes that he sticks in the scrappy notebook he keeps for these sorts of things. He may have grown, but it's only to stretch – to make his body something elastic like Mr Fantastic – all the way into adulthood, long, angry red marks appearing on his back as if to prove it. It makes Benjamin feel short and compact beside Charlie's shadow, his brother's age only really showing in his thin and sunken chest, and the softness around his jaw.

'That's where that expression comes from, *a bolt from the blue*. Lightning breaking through blue skies. It's more dangerous that way too because thunderstorms make negative lightning, but blue skies make it positive, and positive lightning carries a higher current, so it hurts more when it hits.'

Benjamin looks sceptically up at the brilliant blue sky above them, his lips pursing.

'So we could have lightning right now?'

'Maybe.'

Benjamin scrunches his nose.

'What's the point of lightning if it doesn't mean rain though?'

Charlie doesn't answer that, which isn't exactly unusual for Charlie, and Benjamin shifts his focus to the long walk home and what he'll watch when they get there – *Voltron* or *Avatar* or *Young Justice* or—

There's a mumble beside him, a mutter, and Benjamin looks back to see that Charlie's started talking to himself – those weird, rambling sentences that usually mean he's worrying his way through a theory or a problem or something all in his head. His fingers tap the case in his hands, and Benjamin eyes it carefully.

'Is there a space thing happening?' he asks, and Charlie hums a little, picking up his step until Benjamin has to jog to catch up.

'Kind of. A planetary huddle.'

'A what?'

'Planetary huddle.' Charlie holds up three fingers, spreading them wide. 'It's when a bunch of planets' orbits line up closely enough with each other, and then with Earth, that we can see them all at once.'

As he talks, he moves his fingers closer together, until they settle in a neat line. Benjamin digests this information, turns over the importance of such an image, such a spectacle to Charlie's logical mind, but all he can think of are the interplanetary politics and battles and team-ups that must be involved when aliens are readying themselves for a huddle. He tells Charlie this, and Charlie laughs, the loud one that Benjamin likes the best.

With his warm summer skin and dark features, and his tangle of chocolate curls, Charlie looks more like their mother than Benjamin and Olive do. His uniform is a little off-colour today, and there's an old, unfamiliar bruise at his arm, peeking out from the sleeve of his shirt – brown, grey, purple. Charlie quickly covers it, folding his arms across his chest and gripping his biceps, still laughing.

'You're a weird kid, you know that, Banjo?'

Benjamin hums, refocusing, and thinks of the games he can play at school tomorrow with this new information about the weird antics of space. Wonders if Jodi Baxter would be willing to don a mask again if it meant saving not just one planet but *three*.

They stop outside their front gate, and Charlie heaves it open, the rusted hinges whining as he pushes it back against the high and wild grass of their yard. Mum refuses to do a thing about it until Olive mows, but Benjamin knows she never will. Knows that she likes the way the grass takes over, even in this dry, barren summer, and if he's honest, Benjamin likes it too. Their backyard looks like the jungles in his comic books – thick and mangled and heavy with insects. Sickly weeds coil around the frame of their old, rusted trampoline, and bees try to build a hive in the joints of Charlie's telescope stand. The narrow path leading up to their house – a Queenslander lurching on its stilts – is nearly engulfed by wilted grass, and by the time the sun sets none of them will be able to walk out here without kicking a broad-faced cane toad or tangling themselves in the silky strings of a spider's web. Benjamin mostly just hopes for owls, the frog-mouthed ones with beaks like secret keepers, but the wildness of the yard isn't quite wild enough for them yet.

Heading towards the sagging wooden steps of their house, Benjamin slows to a stop. Charlie isn't beside him anymore, or even behind him. Rather, he's stopped in the middle of the yard, his school hat in his hand, the rim darkened with sweat, and his bag dropped to the grass, almost swallowed by the foliage. Charlie looks up, a hand to his forehead, his gaze fixed on something Benjamin cannot see.

'Charlie?'

'I've got a lot of notes to make, Banjo, if I'm gonna see it.'

Benjamin nods, ignoring the twist of disappointment in his belly at spending the afternoon alone. He's reaching into the pocket of his pants for his keys when Charlie calls again.

'You want to grab my post-its and my star wheel and help?'

Benjamin blinks in surprise, and turns to meet Charlie's toothy smile. He couldn't say no even if he wanted to.

○

Delia ends the class at five to the hour, and the students pack up and file out, their voices echoing as the theatre empties. She collects her things – her flaking chalk, her well-fingered binder, the check-in list now filled with names scratched in a hopeless hand.

'Ms Rabbit.'

The voice is just loud enough to get her attention, and when Delia lifts her head she's met with the dimple-cheeked latecomer, his satchel slung over a bony shoulder.

'Adam.'

Adam Griffith's eyes are a shade of blue-grey that Delia wants on the end of her paintbrush, to smudge thick like pastels between her fingers and smear on a canvas. His skin is sallow, taut and smooth like cotton pulled by a screen printing press, and his lips are like a gash in the fabric. There's a stretcher stud in each of his ears, and his clean black hair flops over his forehead, a mess of loose curls. She thinks about crushing them in her fist, and then she does.

○

'Well, what do you think of them?' he asks her afterwards, and Delia glances back. Adam – no. *Griff*.

He's Griff here.

Like this.

Griff is sprawled on the floor beside her desk, naked except for a pair of gaudy orange socks. His tattoos creep up his side and across his shoulders like moss on some age-old statue. His sketchbook is open in his lap, a gnawed pencil in his mouth like a bad habit (like he isn't one of hers). There are flecks of black paint caught in the grooves between his teeth, from where he's mangled the tool with his mouth, and god, she hates that she likes the picture.

'Of what?' she replies, flippant, still watching his jaw work, and Griff grins, finally plucking the pencil from his mouth, returning his attention to his sketchbook. He draws a line, then another, and talks to them when he answers her.

'Of your new class.'

'I've only known them for two hours.'

Griff's laugh is bright, boyish, and it makes the corner of Delia's mouth tick up despite herself, while Griff crosses his legs and makes himself a little too comfortable.

Takes up a little too much space.

Her office is barely big enough for the desk and bookcase it houses, so it's always messy, but today is worse than others, even without Griff – folders full of the new curriculum spread across the floor, the bookshelves sagging beneath the weight of door-stopper textbooks and the now empty goldfish bowl in the corner.

Still. The office is hers.

Sitting up, Delia reaches for her blouse and slips it back on, tucking it neatly into her unzipped skirt. Smoothing her dark hair back, she gets to her feet, reaching for Griff's underwear, his jeans, his thin Smith Street Band t-shirt, holey and still damp with sweat. She flings them his way, but he fails to catch them, preoccupied with whatever it is he's drawing.

'You want to grab something to eat?'

Delia casts him a sharp look and he shies beneath it, like she knew he would, shedding all of his seductive bravado for something more bashful, something more *Griff*. She zips up her skirt. With her door locked and the blinds pulled down, it could almost be evening, a smudge of charcoal thumbed across the lines of them.

'Pretty sure you have a class to catch up on,' she says, grabbing her phone from her desk and checking for messages from school or home or *the* home. Griff shrugs, little more than the jerk of a shoulder, before he draws another curve.

'I like being with you,' he says. 'That's all.'

The floor beneath her suddenly feels impossibly soft, like she could sink into it – lie down and rest here inside his hopeless want. There's an appeal in the nakedness of his words that tugs at her this afternoon, that reaches gently for her worn and weary heart.

'You know I can't.'

'Yeah.'

He's already standing up, shutting his sketchbook, shoving that pencil back into his mouth as he awkwardly starts to dress. Now that he has his back to her, she can watch him freely, map his tattoos, try to trace them with her eyes instead of her hands for a change. Still fuck-drunk, she imagines them tumbling off his body and into the air around him, like a child drawing with a marker, scribbling outside the lines. Griff turns, catches her gaze, and grins, that small, honest thing.

Delia looks away.

'See you next week,' she says, slipping into her shoes. 'Don't forget the reading.'

O

By the time Olive pushes her bike through the front gate, fighting the thick, tangled grass at her feet, the sun has started its descent, leaving the air slightly cooler, if not exactly cool. The powerlines hang low above her, weighted down by fat, twitching possums, and Olive vaguely remembers childhood games flinging small smooth stones at them, trying to get the animals to bare their sharp teeth and fierce, moonstruck eyes.

Her father had always hated that. Would try to stop her, like he wanted her to do better, *be* better, but her mother would just watch, unbothered, smoking on the back steps while Olive tried her hand at torment. She could never fling the stones high enough anyway, never slice the air so precisely, and for a moment she holds the memory in her hand like one of the pebbles, and then she lets it go. Wets her dry lips and tries to shed all thoughts, rounding the house only to find her brothers stripped down to their jocks in the fading glimmer of the afternoon.

'This is certainly a look,' she says, and the two of them turn to face her in unison, all bright, freckled faces, wide lemur eyes and uneven teeth. Their narrow bodies are pinked from the sun, still only half formed, a fact clearer now than ever as they lurch around the telescope, somehow invisible to the bees trying to build their nest in the base of it.

Olive walks past them, lime-green crickets springing around her every step, and tosses herself carelessly, heavily, onto the trampoline. It's mostly unused these days, and the scorching mat is stretched and ungenerous, the springs tightening it to the frame caked in rust, small flakes coming away like bronze as Olive drags herself across.

She groans almost as loudly as the springs do as the mat burns her skin even through her clothes, but still, she spreads herself thin. She thrusts out her arms and legs like the Vitruvian Man, a snow angel in sweat, leaving her imprint in moisture against the sticky black surface.

Birds call, bringing the evening with them, crows first then kookaburras then the high squawks of parrots, lorikeets and pink-faced galahs. Olive wonders if she's pink faced, like the birds, like her brothers. Probably. Last week's sunburn is still flaking at her chest, coming away in sheets of sorry skin. She sighs, looking up through the drooping branches of jacarandas and the contorted arms of gum trees to the picturesque sky, so clear it looks painted, so cloudless it could almost be cloth.

Then: a dip in the trampoline.

Olive turns her head to see Charlie, still mostly naked, clambering towards her. She watches him move, watches the shifting lines of his neck and shoulders, and she wonders if she could draw them, get them on paper like their mother might. The pull of ligaments, the breaker line of his clavicle. His chapped lips pull tight.

'Did you know lightning can strike even without clouds?'

Olive rolls her eyes and pushes up onto her elbows, the hot mat of the trampoline burning her cracked skin.

'Thanks for the weather update, Bob, now back to our regularly scheduled programming.'

She's met with a frown, and has to bite back a grin, because come on, she thinks, that was pretty funny. Still, she concedes.

'It's not the lightning we need, anyway.'

'That's what Benjamin said.'

Huh. She snorts as her eyes dip sideways to where Benjamin is fiddling with the telescope, before looking back at Charlie.

'Yeah, well, if he was half as dumb as he looked, we'd have to put him down.'

Charlie's frown deepens, and it's instant – the weight, the stone, in Olive's hand again. Saliva builds beneath her tongue, and she sinks deeper on her elbows into the burning trampoline, letting it sting, not quite letting her gaze shift to Benjamin, who must be smarting, because god, she knows just how well voices carry in the nook of their yard.

'Sorry,' she says shortly to Charlie, who opens his mouth to reply, but whatever he intends to say, she never hears. A light flicks on in the kitchen, and they both look up, watching their mother's silhouette through the window, fiddling with the stovetop before unleashing a sack of vegetables onto the kitchen island. Olive hadn't even heard her pull up. She must have come in through the front. Olive keeps her gaze on her, but her mother doesn't meet it, and when Olive looks away she's startled to find Charlie's gaze on her instead.

'*Fuck*,' she bites, and Charlie laughs, exposing his crooked teeth, metal braces running fat across them. Olive reaches out to shove him, but he rolls away from her, disrupting a few mating moths in the process.

'You staying in tonight?' Charlie asks, and she shrugs.

'You?'

'Nah. Chem test next week. I'm going to stay over at Andy's and study.'

'Nerd.'

'At least I don't smell like a hobo's arsehole.'

Olive flips him off, and Charlie laughs again, louder this time, but the sound is interrupted by a screech above them, and they both look up in time to catch the royal-blue head of a lorikeet. The bird settles on one of the tall bottlebrush trees that begins in the neighbour's yard, lurches across the fence and finishes in theirs. There are only a few wilted flowers on it, but they're a brilliant pink as if to make up for their limpness. The bird clambers down the branch, hanging its body upside down to suck out the nectar.

Later, she'll remember the birds. Not just the lorikeet, but the sleek, black feathers of the crows lingering on the slatted tin roof, the beady eyes of the noisy miners, the mottled plume of the nesting pigeons, and the strong-beaked kookaburras fighting over a glossy-shelled beetle. She'll remember the cut of their wings against the cloudless sky, the way they'd seemed able to slice the setting sun in two.

She'll think of these things and wonder if there was anything in this moment she would have played differently. If she'd have hugged him or followed him, or begged him to stay, but that's half the blessing of hindsight, half the curse. As it happens, on this evening, as on so many others, Charlie pulls his uniform back on, grass stains and all, waves goodbye to their mother, to Benjamin, to Olive, grabs his notebook and his schoolbag, and disappears through their rusting, shadowed gate.

2

'You'll never believe it,' the host says, sending her best morning-show smile down the lens of the camera. 'It just wipes the dust clean away! No more streaks, no more lines; this exciting new innovation will put the *ease* back into your clean.'

With these words, the host leans forwards in her tight pencil skirt, discreetly slipping a hand behind her back to smooth out the lines of her body as she thrusts a microfibre cloth across a staged kitchen counter. There's a hint of a grimace behind her expression, wrapped in the guise of good graces and taught manners. The costume of a perfect woman.

As she watches, Delia pushes the iron over Charlie's school shirt, pressing out the creases. Unconsciously, she practises the look from the television – that careful, manufactured smile.

'That's just amazing, Kelly,' the co-anchor chimes, his gaze approving as she folds herself forwards to catch suggestions of dust. 'Just *amazing*. How much can our viewers at home expect to—'

The channel changes abruptly, Kelly and Bryan's faces giving way to a boldly coloured cartoon robot. Lights strobe like a rapid pulse across the screen. Heroes howl while faceless enemies jeer, the sounds echoing around their living room, ricocheting in Delia's tired skull. She switches off the iron.

'Benjamin!' she scolds, but there's not much behind it, and her youngest son turns around on the couch to pout back at her.

'*Mum*.'

In the throes of summer, the sun rises early, bringing a stifling heat with it. Delia can already feel the humid air mouthing at her bare legs, the first dribble of sweat inching down her back. She can see it on Benjamin too, in his flushed cheeks and his damp and ruffled hair, in the noiseless open pant of his boyish mouth.

'I finished my homework,' he says. 'And I'm ready for school.'

Delia arches an eyebrow, and Benjamin dissolves into a fit of giggles, wriggling down into the couch cushions, nestling so deep that the floral pillows sink and squash around him. Delia bites back a grin, sending him an only half-disapproving look as she shakes out Charlie's shirt, slipping it onto a hanger and making for the hallway.

The text had come from Charlie not long after she'd served dinner last night – telling her that he was staying over at Andy's to finish their project, that he'd be home in the morning to get dressed for school – and despite a brief flutter of annoyance, Delia had let it slide. It wasn't exactly unusual for Charlie to get swept up in something, particularly at Andy's place; and well, it's good, she'd thought. That Charlie has friends.

The floorboards are tacky under the balls of her feet as she strides up the hallway and into Charlie and Benjamin's room, hanging the shirt on their closet door before turning around to find herself staring into Olive's room.

Right.

Delia sucks in a dry breath, feeling something in her tighten in anticipation, and, with her best morning-host smile, steps forwards and through the open door.

It's dim in her daughter's room, with the lights off and the curtains drawn, the morning sun left to press its way in like a kiss against a shirt-covered shoulder. Cigarette smoke fills Delia's nose instantly, but worse is the smell of turned fruit, potent as a spell.

She resists the urge to gag.

'You could knock.'

The words are offered without the respect of attention, her daughter sitting in bed facing the curtain-covered windows, already dressed in her O'Malley's uniform, her hair still damp from the shower and sticking to her neck and the sides of her face as she hunches over her phone. It gives her a wraith-like look, and Delia hums a little, knocking her hip into the doorframe.

'Good morning to you too,' she says, folding her arms across her chest. 'You want a ride to work?'

'Nah, it's fine. It's easier to bike it.'

In her head Delia maps out the route. Sketches in the lines of the suburb, shades in the crisp browning grass and the concrete path, dotted bike lanes and undulating roads. Pictures the beat of her daughter's lanky legs on the pedals, her behind rising, falling, rising off the bike seat as she gains momentum, panting as she powers her way up hills and lets gravity propel her down them, and she thinks: *bullshit*.

'It's not any trouble,' Delia says, and Olive's voice is curt when she replies:

'Neither is riding my bike.'

For a moment, Delia just watches the curve of Olive's back as she leans forwards to tie the laces of her scuffed work shoes. Through the thin fabric of her stiff shirt, Delia can see the craggy knobs of her daughter's spine, the peaks and cliff falls, the hard, aggressive shape of her.

Delia exhales.

'Fine,' she says. 'I'm going to be home late, I've got to visit your grandmother. Would you be able to help Benjamin with that project of his tonight? He really needs to get started.'

A low, frustrated sound escapes Olive, and it pulls something in Delia like a guitar string: a firm, tight *pluck*. She straightens up, watches as her daughter flops onto her bed and tilts her head back to meet Delia's eyes for the first time that morning.

The string pulls tight again.

'Can't you visit her tomorrow? I have plans.'

And it releases.

A wave of irritation builds in her chest.

'What plans?'

'Just plans.'

'You want to talk to me like an adult?'

The question sits heavy between them for a moment, and Delia thinks, *right*, the crest of annoyance ebbing out of her. Probably could have handled that better. She can only watch as Olive sits back up, turning silently, sullenly away from her in the process. How did Ed handle her when she was like this?

No. Nothing good waits for her at the end of that line.

Besides, the question's moot. Olive was never like this with Ed.

Delia sighs.

'Fine,' she says again. 'I'll ask Charlie. Have you heard from him this morning? He's supposed to pick up his uniform before school.'

'Him and Andy are probably fucking around on their way over again. He can get himself to school, you know.'

Delia opens her mouth to reply, but promptly closes it when she sees Olive tense in anticipation. Planting a hand at her waist, she licks her teeth.

'I'll leave him a note then, I guess.'

'You do that.'

There are so many words in her mouth, scrambling for purchase, but she traps them there, crossing the hall to Charlie and Benjamin's room. She grabs a post-it note from Charlie's desk, scribbling a message for him to call her when he gets home, sticks it to his shirt and then gets ready for work.

○

'God, your mum's a dick.'

Olive makes a vague noise of agreement as Lux takes one final drag from the cigarette she pinched from Olive, before dropping it to the ground, stepping on it and killing the last bright lick of flame. 'I don't even know how you handle it.

Like, if my mum ever tried that shit with me, I'd go *off*.'

Even the thought of that makes an amused smile tug at the corner of Olive's mouth as she glances down the loading bay, taking a long drag on her own cigarette. It's not that she doesn't think Lux is capable of it, exactly, more that it'd just never happen in the first place. She doesn't know all that much about Lux's parents, but she knows they don't really seem to give a shit about what she does.

Shifting her weight, Olive bites back a wince. The ride to work that morning had been gruelling – had left her ropey calves aching, her thighs chafed, and maybe she should've taken Delia up on the lift, but then again even the thought of twenty minutes trapped in the car with her had left her blood running hot. She shuffles her feet against the dirty concrete.

'It doesn't matter,' Olive says, taking another quick drag. 'I'm moving in with my dad soon anyway.'

Lux instantly perks up.

'Oh yeah? Is he cute?'

Olive coughs before she can help it, spluttering smoke, and when Lux starts cackling Olive rolls her eyes, shoving the other girl into the brick wall of O'Malley's.

'Doesn't he have, like, a total bachelor pad these days?'

The question comes so suddenly that Olive blinks, her mind scrambling to remember where she and Lux left off.

'He has his own apartment,' she counters, because that's not the same as a *bachelor pad*. Hell, he even has a girlfriend living with him now. She takes a shorter, sharper drag at the thought, folding her free arm around her skinny waist. 'Just since my mum kicked him out.'

'Why'd your mum kick him out?'

'Because she's a cunt.'

It leaves her like another flung stone, and there's that dragging feeling again, the heavy one that sinks something in her low, as Lux chokes on a laugh.

'Dad said I could move in once he got settled,' she adds quickly. 'It's not like I'm a kid he's got to watch out for like Banjo or Charlie.'

Lux hums, and it's soft at the edges, placating almost, and Olive watches as she pulls her phone from the back pocket of her work pants and taps out a message to someone. It's just as quick then, the flush that burns up Olive's cheeks. The air around the loading bay suddenly feels swampy, claustrophobic, and she fumbles for a new topic, a better story, one that might keep Lux's attention. But what else has she got to say?

Hey, you know about that sale on avocados?

Do you know lightning doesn't need rain to strike?

Her fingers twitch around her cigarette, and she's opening her mouth to say *something* when the back door cracks open and Mindy's head pokes out, her hand against her forehead to ward off the midday glare, her eyes searching. She brightens when she spots them.

'Olive, can I grab you for a bit?'

'She's on break,' Lux replies loudly, not looking up from her phone, and Mindy gives her an unimpressed look in reply.

'She's on smoko, not break,' Mindy says curtly. Her gaze pivots back to Olive, and she holds the door open a little wider. 'Please, I just need a hand.'

The shrill cries of lorikeets and the rolling warbles of magpies sound overhead, and not for the first time Olive wishes she could see them. She finds her gaze drifting up above the stagnant heat of the loading bay, but the walls are too high, and the trees that house the birds are hidden by the surrounding buildings and a billboard advertising a movie Olive won't see.

She drops her cigarette beside Lux's dead one, stamping it out.

'Yeah, 'course.'

Mindy offers her a grateful smile in reply, pushing the door open a little wider so Olive can slip in behind her. It's too easy to do it then, to nod Lux off, ignoring her irritated look, and maybe it's also a relief to not have to think of a way to keep her attention anymore. To let Mindy hold her own instead with chatter about store politics and the latest dumb idea Frank's come up with to help them compete with bigger, louder chains.

The air conditioning is welcome too. The cool air nipping at Olive's face and neck and licking down the back of her shirt as Mindy leads her down the bland corridor of O'Malley's. The vinyl floor squeaks beneath their rubber soles, and the harsh, unrelenting store fluorescents make Mindy's dark hair shine.

They pass a few open doors – the staffroom, the cleaning cupboard, the bathroom – before Mindy stops in front of one of the coolrooms, pushes it open, and—

God.

Olive gasps at the smell.

'I know,' Mindy groans, stepping inside. 'I hate to ask again, it's just that we got it done so quickly yesterday.'

'How's it all off already?'

It's unmistakable – not just the smell, but the sludge coating the bottom shelves of the fridge – sunken zucchinis and shrivelled green beans, capsicums warped almost beyond recognition. Something tacky gently slaps against her wrist, and Olive glances down to see Mindy offering her a pair of gloves, and *figures*, Olive thinks, snapping them on.

'It's just the heat, that's all.'

With that, Mindy crouches in front of the shelves and Olive promptly follows, resting on her haunches and eyeing off the array of liquifying vegetables. There's something to it – the murky colours, a palette of decay, and she hates that she thinks of her mother. It's just – it's what they paint, isn't it? In art classes? Bowls of fruit? But it wouldn't be this perfect imperfect picture. She blinks, sniffs, the pungent smell finding her nose again, and it's weird, to suddenly feel Mindy's eyes on her.

'So hey, I've kind of been wanting to talk to you about something,' the other woman starts, and Olive tries to focus on the sight in front of her. She leans forwards to reach the back of the shelf, to start pushing the rotten vegetables forwards. 'It's about Lux.'

Olive's fingers pierce the skin of a soft zucchini.

'Like. Okay, I know she can be super charming and stuff, and I'm not your mum or whatever, but—'

'You're really not,' Olive agrees sharply, wrenching her fingers out of the vegetable, her jaw clenching, throat constricting, and Mindy pauses, her gaze still fixed on Olive.

'No, you're right, sorry. Forget I said anything.'

At the words, Olive jerks her head around to look back at Mindy, her gaze skirting her features, her big, dark eyes and cupid's bow lips, but Mindy is carefully avoiding eye contact now, and *no*, that's not what Olive meant, it's not what she wanted, she just—

Olive swallows, looks back at the rotten fruit.

Another stone flung.

O

Benjamin hooks his fingers through the school fence, staring across the road at the high school. From here, it looks big, cavernous and creepy – more Gotham Academy than Xavier's, but Benjamin kind of likes that. Likes the thought that it might hold secrets behind library shelves or in the hooded corners of an attic, that they might brew something magic after-hours in secluded science labs.

He bounds up until he's standing on his tiptoes, not that this changes his view much. The final school bell rang almost half an hour ago, and the flood of students has turned into trickles, girls with their heads pressed close as they chatter in chequered dresses and boys shoving their long socks down to their ankles to cool their calves. A short girl with a sun-bleached hat pushes a double bass almost twice her size out the front entrance, settling it against a wall and pulling out her phone.

The fencing sags, and Benjamin grunts in surprise,

snatching his fingers from the wire to keep from falling forwards.

'What are you looking at?'

The voice comes from a girl who has appeared beside him, her cheeks flushed from the heat and her eyes bright. With a shrug, Benjamin frowns, trying to remember her name as she looks across the road to the high school, fixing on the line of cars with their doors half open. Poppy Dockens, that's it. She's new this term, an odd last-minute transfer before they all cross the road to the high school next year. She has dull blonde hair and an overbite, a pretty face clean as porcelain. Her lips are pink, pinker than normal, and Benjamin knows that means she's only just finished a music lesson, something involving her mouth – the trumpet or flute or clarinet, maybe.

Trumpet, he thinks.

It's Jodi who plays the flute.

'I'm just waiting for my brother.'

Poppy considers this for a moment, puffing up her cheeks like she's still in recital, but not quite letting go of the air.

'He's late,' she offers after a second, and Benjamin nods, looking back out at the high school, a strange little knot forming in his belly.

'Yeah,' he adds, just for something to say, and Poppy hums, tapping her fingers on her instrument case as if on her trumpet valves. After a moment she rocks back, and Benjamin copies her, watching the way her body folds as she grabs her bag off the ground, and he means to ask her why she's there, who she's waiting for, when a car horn blares down the road.

Throwing up her arms, Poppy waves frantically in the

direction of the sound, reaching back to adjust her grip on her bag before pausing and turning to look at Benjamin.

'My dad would drop you home if you wanted.'

Benjamin shakes his head, a strange feeling burrowing into him in a way he can't explain, and he flashes her a tentative grin.

'Charlie will be here soon.'

The nurse fiddles with her name tag as she examines the notes in the binder on top of the nursing station. A wide finger runs across the line next to *Rosemary Rabbit*, through pill intake to complaints and decline, to whatever the fuck it is they check in a place like this.

'Everything's looking pretty good, Mrs Rabbit. Stable. No real changes.'

'Ms,' Delia says mildly, pushing her sweat-damp hair behind her ears, a foot tapping uneasily on the bleached tiles.

The nurse smiles uncomfortably, and Delia paints one on to match, her best morning-show smile, trying to massage the awkwardness out of this moment. She hasn't liked hospitals since she was a girl, not since Bo, at least, but the aged-care home has another level of sterility to it. Clinical, of course it's clinical, but it's the stranger sounds of a broken quiet that tighten Delia's jaw – the static hum of the air conditioning, the metallic rattle of gurney wheels, the rubber soles of the nurse's shoes, squeaking on the bleached ground. Sounds suddenly interrupted by a patient's lone, hoarse howl.

Delia signs in, picks up her handbag and walks down the

long, wide corridor to her mother's room.

Saint Anne's is almost an hour out of town, away from the slump of inner-city suburbs and past the yawn of developing land left ashen in the summer. The building itself is clean but old, with plaster flaking from the ceiling and small colonies of mould creeping out from behind doorframes. Hokey paintings of golden-haloed saints line every wall, and heavy-looking crucifixes hang on every door, inches above patrons' name plates.

There is no cross on Delia's mother's door, and despite all the things Delia does not know about the woman who birthed her, she at least knows that Rosie Rabbit walked away from religion on a nursing rotation in Vietnam and buried the last remnants of her faith with the bones of her teenage daughter.

Delia steels herself at the door, smooths down her skirt and checks the buttons on her shirt, sweaty from the day's teaching, and then steps through.

Her mother's room is modest, small, with a raised hospital bed, a small television embedded in the wall, a mini fridge, a contact-topped table and a cracked vinyl armchair. It's unencumbered by personal belongings, because Rosie has never been particularly sentimental, and this fact now sits stark in every inch of the place.

As it is now, the light barely cuts through the sheltered window overlooking the carpark, though it still somehow manages to cast uneasy shadows on Rosie.

She is standing up, her thin, shrunken body hunched over by the far wall, sorting through baskets of shrink-wrapped syringes, bandages, gauze. Her hooked, arthritic fingers make careful work of unwrapping them, their plastic casings falling like eggshells at her feet. She glances over as Delia steps in, and her body sags with relief.

'Thank Christ. You were supposed to be here hours ago.'

Dropping her handbag on the armchair, Delia leans against it and gives herself a moment, trying to work out how old her mother is today, *who* she is, but all she can smell is the acidic scent of the dying flowers by the window and the sour smell of the piss leaking from her mother's catheter bag, lying disconnected and forgotten on the white-tiled floor.

'Hey, Mum.'

Rosie laughs, that loud sort she'd never spare for Delia if she remembered her better. Her hair is pulled back into the neat twist she's worn almost every day of her life, and the sight of it is a strange comfort, even if the way it stretches her cellophane skin is not. Vaguely, Delia wonders if she could tug at her thin, translucent skin and lay it across her anew, preserving her somehow.

She wonders if she even wants to.

'Cute,' Rosie says, turning her attention back to her work. 'But I prefer "nurse".'

And well, isn't that the truth, Delia thinks, a sardonic grin twitching at her lips as she watches her mother work.

'I bet you do.'

The sound of Rosie's laugh is brighter than this room deserves, and something pulls loose in Delia as a few strands of her mother's thinning hair fall from its twist. Another packet is unwrapped, another part of Rosie presented to her, and Delia shifts her weight off the arm of the chair and busies her restless head with the parts of this she remembers (roll up your sleeves, wash your arms up to your elbows) in the small sink by her mother's bed.

'New to rotation?' Rosie asks, and when Delia nods, the way Rosie smiles is almost kind. 'We'll be nice. The boys can get a little slick, but they're only boys, really. You'll manage. You can call me Nurse Rabbit, by the way. What was your name again? The doctors never pass on the details.'

It's the test, the kicker, the sting. Delia clears her throat.

'My name is Delia.'

Rosie pauses, her hands suddenly stilling. Delia can't see her face, not from here, but she imagines her mother's eyes sharpening, her lips tugging down, the quiver at her lined throat.

And then:

'You know, I always liked that name. How good are you with sutures?'

○

A woman with an *I want to speak to the manager* haircut and a shrill voice cracks it over twenty extra grams in her bacon order, and Olive is almost ready to tell her exactly what she can do with those grams when Mindy interrupts.

'Olive, why don't you take this back to the deli and grab the customer the right order?'

Mindy's voice is deceptively calm, friendly even, as she nudges Olive out from behind the checkout and takes her place, a firm, artificial grin on her round face, and Olive flashes one last forced smile at the customer before grabbing the bacon off the counter and slipping out from behind it.

There's heat in her cheeks and a stiffness to her legs as she strides across the grocery-store floor, and she tries to shake out the tension so as not to be a total dick to the deli staff. Most of them are retirees, after all, their silver hair tucked into fine hairnets, their eyes watery below the store fluorescents. Olive knows, because she knows these staff, feels embarrassingly comfortable around these women who are mostly old enough to be her grandmothers. They usually keep to themselves, in the stockroom or behind the deli counter, feeding tepid, lined meat through the carving machine, but they've always been warmer with Olive, pulling her into their fold like they see something worthwhile in her company.

She's ready to roll her eyes with Ruth or to bitch with Joan, who's insanely tall and still smells faintly of chlorine from thirty years of competitive swimming, but she is not ready for Jude, who lingers, hairnet and all, over a spread of fat, stuffed green olives.

Jude Elber is straight out of a teen soap. He's tall, broad shouldered and oddly swarthy, with deep-set blue eyes, sharp cheekbones and a sharper jawline. Olive slows her steps before reaching the counter, her heart pounding in her throat, but quickly finds her feet again. She steps around the side of the counter with the parcel of bacon still clutched in her spidery hands.

'Customer complaint. This order needs to be redone. Three-seventy-five grams *exactly*.'

Jude blinks at her, his lips pursed, eyes slightly glazed. His brow furrows as he takes her in, and Olive fidgets uneasily, conscious of the smell of bad fruit and rot on her. She glances behind Jude to where she'd hoped Ruth might be lurking over a block of dimpled feta, but there's no one there.

'You new?'

Olive blinks, her gaze finding Jude's again, his expression curious.

'Pretty sure I've been here longer than you.'

He laughs at that, his eyes closing, crow's-feet showing.

'Sorry. I'm shit with faces.'

With that, he reaches forwards, puts a rubber-gloved finger beneath her name badge and flicks it up so he can see it. The metal pin piercing Olive's shirt lies flush at her skin. Warm. Of course it's warm.

'Olive … Rabbit, right?' Jude says, his mouth tugging up into a grin, and Olive clears her throat, nodding as he laughs again.

'I like it,' he says, then repeats it. Her name. At his lips.

Olive Rabbit.

She likes it there, tries to imagine what the words taste like to him. If he likes them on his tongue as much as she likes 'Jude Elber' on hers.

'Any relation to Peter?'

Olive rolls her eyes.

'Haven't heard that one before.' Her lips curl into a smile though, and Jude keeps laughing, some quiet, lazy, honest thing that wriggles pleasantly beneath her skin. She holds the package a little closer to her palpitating heart, rocking back onto her heels. She still can't see Ruth, who she's sure is rostered on, and looks past Jude back out across the store floor, through the aisles, then finally back to Mindy and Lux at the checkouts. The customer is still there, her neck straining with anger, Mindy's unwavering, considered smile still dialled to eleven. Olive resists the urge to roll her eyes again, and her gaze catches on Lux instead, stepping out from behind Olive's checkout, walking towards the store entrance, towards something, or rather, some*one*. Olive squints to better see.

Just in front of the sliding doors stands Benjamin, blotchy and red-faced, his chest heaving. Olive blinks, looking back at Jude, but he's not looking at her anymore, he's turned around too, to watch Benjamin stumbling into the store, his face crumbling when he reaches Lux.

'Looks like a lost kid,' Jude says, and Olive watches him, watches the point of his chin and the line his long neck makes as he takes in Benjamin, his eyes half lidded, considering. She could stay. Stay with Jude, see if she can get him to laugh again, ignore it all until Benjamin comes tugging on her shirt, but then … she exhales, dropping the package onto the counter and ducking around the side. She walks over to her checkout, a lecture on her tongue about how she is *at work*, only Mindy steps out from behind it, abandoning the customer for a moment, and rubs a hand on Benjamin's back as he drops his head, his fingers white knuckled around his Spectacular Man figurine. Olive picks up her step.

'Banjo—' she starts, but she gets no further. Benjamin lifts his face, his cheeks wet with tears, his eyes glassy. His voice quivers when he speaks.

'Charlie didn't pick me up.'

Olive opens her mouth, but nothing comes out.

'Maybe take him to the staffroom,' Mindy says gently. 'Do you want me to call anyone?'

Shaking her head, Olive finds herself grateful for the suggestion. She grabs Benjamin's hand, pulling him across the store floor and then past the silicon blinds to the back of house, down the sweating hallway and into the concrete-walled staffroom, the fan creaking hypnotically above their heads.

'Jesus Christ, Benjamin, I'm *working*,' she hisses, finding her tongue. 'You should've just walked home.'

And dammit, he *should've*, but her chest clenches all the same when she looks at Benjamin's tear-streaked face, wet snuffles escaping his mouth and his nose. Grabbing a box of tissues from the cabinet, Olive wipes his face, unable to stop her gaze from dropping down to his shorts and even less able to quell her relief when she realises they're dry.

'Charlie never doesn't turn up.'

'He's probably gone back to Andy's again.'

'He would've walked me home and *then* gone, like he always does.'

With a sigh, Olive leans back to stare at his pinched expression, at the dribble of snot pooling above his upper lip. She grabs another tissue and wipes it off.

Briefly, she thinks of calling their parents, but – no. Delia will be at Saint Anne's, and that's almost an hour away, and their dad—

Olive bites the inside of her cheek.

No.

She can't call him over this. He'll think she can't handle this sort of thing herself.

'Give me a minute, okay?' she says, passing another handful of tissues to Benjamin. 'I've got to talk to my boss.'

By the time Olive gets back to the checkouts, the customer is finally leaving, packing up her perfectly weighted groceries and heading out through the sliding glass doors. Mindy watches her go, and when she's out of sight, Mindy turns back to Olive and mimes shooting herself in the head.

'Thanks for dealing with her,' Olive says, and Mindy just shrugs, leaning back against the vinyl countertop.

'Your brother okay?'

'A little shaken.'

'You want to take him home? I'll botch the roster, you'll still get paid.'

Olive pauses, watching Mindy watching her, a careful expression on her face that Olive can't quite place.

'Would that be okay?'

Mindy snorts, nodding.

'I wouldn't offer if it wasn't, Rabbit. Consider it your bonus for helping with the coolroom. Just don't tell Lux. I don't have the energy to deal with her faking a family emergency so she can get out early too.'

'Thanks,' she says, and Mindy nods, waving her off.

○

Delia pulls her car up on the road outside home, stealing the last slice of shade from a more or less barren brush-box tree.

Her sleeves are still pushed to her elbows from her visit to her mother, an hour spent sorting nursing equipment like a new grad. She gives herself another minute, lets the last splutter of the air conditioning cool her chest and her neck. Then she yanks the keys out of the ignition, thrusts her door open and grabs her briefcase, her bag of groceries and the loose binder from the morning's class off the back seat.

She's still fumbling with them when she spots her neighbour over the top of their flaking fence, a lean woman, younger than her, with pale skin and hair like ripe oranges, both in colour and in the way it rests, peeling around her face. 'Hi there!' the woman calls, waving her gardening trowel at Delia, her gloved hands heavy with dry earth. The bleeding light behind her casts a long shadow down her form and illuminates her neat dress and neater garden.

Tilting her chin up in acknowledgement, Delia otherwise ignores her, stepping through her own yard and up the chipped steps to her house. Her mind is already ahead of her, organising pans and lighting the stove. On her way home from Saint Anne's, she'd stopped by O'Malley's and been surprised not to find Olive behind the checkout. All the same, she'd bought purple carrots and red onions, built a swatch of colour in her head with red cabbage, radish, the rich coat of an eggplant.

A bit much, she thinks now. Leave the eggplant and cabbage for tomorrow, swap them for spinach, pine nuts and balsamic vinegar. Does she have creamy, pock-marked feta in the fridge? Red and veiny lamb in the freezer?

Delia drops her things on the kitchen counter and stands

back. Her hair is sticking to her neck, matted and thick, and she runs a hand through it to shift it.

The kitchen feels lived-in tonight, with the sink full of half-washed dishes and Benjamin's homework littering the bench. There's a coil of cool air nipping at her legs too, and she turns to see the fridge door wide open, Benjamin sprawled on the tiles below it, his bare, dirty feet pressed against the crisper drawer. He lifts his head and flashes her a lethargic grin, his teeth a near-inhuman white against the curl of his red lips and his flaking, sunburnt cheeks. He's naked barring his Spiderman jocks.

'*Mum*,' he groans, falling back against the floor. Reaching down to grab his legs, Delia hoists them high enough to close the fridge door. His school shorts and shirt are scattered behind him, his schoolbag gaping open and shoved against the kitchen island.

'Everything will melt. All your YoGos will go off,' she tells him, dropping his legs so they thump against the fridge door and stepping over him towards the pantry. Benjamin groans louder, reaching over to grab Spectacular Man and scoop him close to his chest.

'I'm hungry.'

'You've just had your feet all over afternoon tea. Dinner will be in an hour, why don't you go help Charlie with his …' What's the word for it exactly? What he does with his telescope? Game, research, project? She doesn't need to worry about finishing the sentence though, as Benjamin quickly interjects.

'I'm not going to help him *ever again*.'

With a sigh, Delia pulls out what she needs from the pantry and carries it to the kitchen island. Benjamin hasn't moved, and with Spectacular Man clutched to his chest and his forehead creased and burnt, he looks unusually pathetic.

'Well, do you want to stay and help me with dinner instead?'

Immediately perking up, Benjamin clambers to his feet and Delia pulls her apron off the hook by the stove, shrugging it over his frame before placing a peeler and a bunch of purple carrots on the bench.

'We should get an air conditioner,' Benjamin says as he starts to peel the carrots, and Delia nods, taking the lamb out of the freezer.

'Absolutely. When are you thinking of buying that?' Benjamin giggles, puffing out his chest like he's the man of the house, which, Delia supposes with a wry smile, he very nearly is. She fills the sink with hot water, dropping in the wrapped lamb chops to defrost, before pulling out the rest of the ingredients for dinner, playing it casual when she asks:

'So, can I ask why you're never helping Charlie again?'

The look on Benjamin's face darkens. His peeling becomes erratic.

'He didn't wait for me. I had to go get Olive.'

Delia frowns, pausing.

'What do you mean he didn't wait?'

'I waited at school forever, but he didn't come and get me.'

'That's not like him.'

Benjamin just sniffs in response, and Delia bites her lip. She takes a few steps to the window overlooking the backyard.

She's so used to seeing Charlie out there, bent down over a notebook, a stack of post-its in hand, or standing gazing up at the sky, that his absence tugs at a cord inside of her.

Leaving Benjamin at the kitchen sink, Delia pulls her phone out of her pocket, checking for a text message that isn't there as she ducks into the boys' room, lifting her head only to find it as empty as her inbox. She crosses the hall and pushes open Olive's door instead.

Olive is sitting cross-legged on her bed, wearing only her underwear and her too-long O'Malley's shirt, her thumbs tapping at her phone.

'What's happened with Charlie?'

Olive doesn't even look up or stop her busy hands. 'I'm pissed at him, is what. He bailed on Banjo, so I had to take him home before my shift was even over. He hasn't answered any of my texts either, the shit.'

Pursing her lips, Delia looks back down at her phone, dialling Charlie's number and groaning when the call goes straight to voicemail.

'Do you have Andy's number?'

Olive shakes her head, and Delia walks back to the kitchen, pulling out the class directory from the shelf above the oven. She hears Olive's feet thump on the floor, hears her pad out of her room. She finds Andy's mother's number and calls it.

Leaning back against the kitchen counter, her gaze lands on Benjamin dropping carrot skins everywhere as he tries to walk handfuls of them out to the garden compost. With a sigh, she looks down at the opposite counter, where fat black ants are sucking the sweet oil out of her diffuser sticks, their bodies teetering on the narrow poles. Olive calls her name somewhere behind her as Delia reaches across to flick the ants off, one by one.

The phone clicks and Andy's mother picks up.

'Hey, Trish, Delia Rabbit. Just wondering if Charlie is over there again?'

Olive calls her name again, and Delia covers the mouthpiece of the phone with her hand. 'Give me a minute, Olive.'

'Again?' Trish says, surprised. 'Charlie hasn't been over in a couple of weeks. Andrew's been grounded.'

Delia's breath catches, and she blinks one, two, three times. 'What?'

'Mum!' Olive calls again, and Delia turns to find Olive standing behind her, tall in the dull evening light. In one hand she holds Charlie's clean school shirt, the post-it note still stuck to it, and in the other Charlie's mobile phone, the screen cracked, black and dead.

3

Mum's voice shifts. Benjamin can pick it. The exact moment it loses its pretend calm and slips into proper panic. It happens around her fourth phone call. After she's called Andy's mum, then rung the school, then Charlie's debate team coach, then the Amateur Astronomers Society he joined last spring.

There's a shrillness to her voice he remembers from when he was very small and climbing trees or fences, his pillowcase tied around his neck, the mask Grandma Beth made him heavy over his eyes. The movie-mum voice, that's what Charlie always called it, crinkling his forehead and slapping his hands to his cheeks, pulling a face like that screaming boy they'd talked about in art class. That's how they write mums in movies, Charlie would add. Shrill and useless and down on the ground while the heroes are up in space or the sky, or fighting criminals on rooftops.

('Mums can be heroes,' Benjamin had said once, and Charlie had nodded, flipping one of his big books on space open and settling down onto his bed. 'They can,' Charlie had agreed. 'Just not in movies.')

Benjamin and Charlie's bedroom is the biggest in the house, but you wouldn't know it to look at it. With their two beds, desks, Benjamin's toys and Charlie's books, and the computer Charlie only lets Benjamin use if Mum makes him, it filled up quickly. It's too quiet without Charlie there, and Benjamin drops back onto Charlie's unmade bed with its blue plaid doona and lumpy pillows, and twists his fingers in the sheets below. Twists them so hard the circulation goes, short-circuits like a light, and his fingers turn bone-white and ache.

Spectacular Man is on the bed beside him, the paint chipped from his chest and a strange round bubble of glue at his neck from the time when Olive ripped his head off after Benjamin had bugged her, and then later, when she felt bad, tried to fix it with their dad's glue gun and their mum's pliers. Benjamin reaches over for him now, the shiny plastic warm against his skin, and he holds tight with his sore fingers, then tighter still.

'You need to call Dad.'

Olive's voice is firm, loud enough that he can hear it from down the hall.

'We don't need to worry him yet.'

'Jesus, Delia, just *call* him. Charlie's probably *there*.'

She says it as if any of them have stayed at Dad's new place since he moved out last year. As if that's a thing that happens – Dad swinging round to get them, calling them, seeing them. He hadn't even shown up for Benjamin's Year Six barbecue last month, so Benjamin isn't exactly sure why Olive would think Charlie's there now.

He can't see them, of course, can't Superman his vision, but he can picture them: Mum's creased forehead and sad, worried eyes, and Olive, who must be frightened, more frightened than anyone, because everyone knows Charlie's her favourite, but then Charlie is Benjamin's favourite too. The thought of that aches, and Benjamin tries to swallow the dry lump in his throat, but he can't, not even when he hears Olive's footsteps down the hall and her bedroom door slamming shut behind her.

O

They're there within the hour, the blue and red lights flashing through the gap in the curtains, and Olive peers cautiously out her window as two police officers step out of the car: one a woman, shorter, older, with frizzy hair and a crisp uniform, and a man, taller, younger, broader, glancing up at the house with a hand shielding his eyes, against what, Olive's not sure: the sun is long gone now, the night settled like a blanket across the suburbs.

It's not long before she hears the front door crack open and the police officers step inside, hears their quiet, considered words to Delia, and Delia's harried response. The police don't say much, not now at least.

She's so focused on listening that she doesn't see the other light through her window, or hear the other car pull up, though she hears the tug and groan of their gate again and peers out the window to see her father walking up the overgrown path. His body is tall and graceless, thinner than she remembers, his hair greyer, although she saw him not that long ago – perhaps a month or two – okay, maybe three. She could see him more, if she tried, but—

Olive's fingers clench the curtains, jerk them closed as she hears his heavy footsteps on the creaking wooden stairs.

56

She hadn't been home when he'd left.

The thought comes too quickly, tangles in her ribcage like the roots of a fast-growing plant, and she struggles to catch her breath, blinking back a wave of tears as she hears the front door open and the silence that follows, heavy as an unflung stone. Then her dad and the police start talking, the officers' words clipped and careful, somehow soothing and cold all at once. She hears them ask for a photograph, for a list of friends and relatives, if they can speak to the kids, and then she hears their careful steps down the hall, the knock on her door, her name.

Heart in her throat, Olive walks forwards, tries to reclaim herself, and pulls open the door so she is face to face with the woman police officer, her nose hooked and sunburnt, a deep indentation just above her left eye. The man is just half a step behind her, knocking on Benjamin and Charlie's door.

'Olive? Officer Keely. Can we have a chat?'

○

Officer McBride is a big man in a neat blue uniform. He has the wide, stock chest of a comic-book hero, and his skin is brown, which Benjamin thinks might mean he's an Islander. He glances at Benjamin with dark eyes and his lips curled deep and sad, like someone is holding them there with firm fingers. Benjamin scoots further down the bed, folding his arms around his legs.

While McBride is big, the other officer he'd glimpsed was short, like a cartoon sidekick drawn smaller to make the hero look his best. She had mottled white-and-red skin and

Hermione Granger hair, and almost no lips at all, and he half-consciously turns his own in, as if to mirror them.

After a moment of silence, McBride sits beside Benjamin on Charlie's single bed, the mattress dipping beneath his weight.

Benjamin sits up and lets go of the sheets, but keeps Spectacular Man clenched in his fist as McBride looks around the room. Benjamin can see him clocking the poster of Superman above his bed, the bookcase full of comic books and the Marvel Heroes version of Monopoly in a frayed box on top. Sees him looking at the print of the galaxy over Charlie's bed, the mobile of planets, the glow-in-the-dark stars stuck across the room's high ceiling. He wonders if McBride knows that they're right, can see Charlie's meticulous hand in the way he placed them, if he can see the Southern Cross in them, and Orion too. After a moment, McBride turns back to Benjamin, watching him carefully.

'Who's this?' McBride asks, gesturing to Spectacular Man, and Benjamin shrugs, lightly thumbing the bubble of glue at his neck.

'I've got a Black Panther figurine at my place,' McBride says. 'And a Squirrel Girl. Do you know them?'

'I know Black Panther. He's in The Avengers.'

McBride grins, nods his big head. He adjusts his shirt a little, then his position, and the bed creaks beneath his weight. Benjamin scoots further down. Tries to even them out.

'He is. He's pretty awesome. I got Squirrel Girl because she reminds me of my sister.'

'What are her powers?'

'Well, she can talk to squirrels, and she's strong and fast, but not like The Flash or Quicksilver. Just strong and fast for a regular person. Does your brother like superheroes?'

Benjamin sniffs. 'No. Not really. He likes space.'

'Space? Like *The X-Files*?'

'Not pretend space. Real space. Astronauts and big bangs and telescopes and robots on Mars.'

McBride looks around the room again, and he must see it, Benjamin thinks. Everyone does. The shift between Benjamin's things and Charlie's. Bright-coloured figurines and capes and masks giving way to round, dusty planets and cardboard dioramas. McBride shifts back again, like he's just realised they're on Charlie's bed, not Benjamin's.

'That's pretty cool.'

Benjamin shrugs. He doesn't like it so much. What's exciting about big balls of gas or other planets without aliens?

'When'd you last see Charlie?'

'Yesterday, before dinner.'

'How'd he seem?'

'Like normal.' Benjamin looks up, and McBride meets his gaze. His eyes really are very big, like they've been drawn on. 'He was going to study at Andy's. He studies a lot because he wants to go to NASA. There's only been twenty-four astronauts in outer space, did you know that? Charlie wants to be number twenty-five or maybe twenty-six if someone else gets up there before him.'

McBride raises both his eyebrows like he's impressed. Benjamin doesn't think it's that impressive really. Bruce Willis has been to space plenty of times, and Benjamin knows that's only in movies, but still.

'Does Andy want to be an astronaut too?'

Benjamin shrugs. He doesn't know much about Andy except that when he comes over, Charlie gets meaner. That he doesn't want to hang out with Benjamin then – that he starts to look at him the way Olive does, and that's not something Benjamin really likes to think about.

McBride doesn't ask anything else. Not right away, at least, and Benjamin finds himself looking up at the ceiling and the cracks in the plaster between the stick-on stars. He wonders if they tell stories about the house, like lines on palms or tea leaves in chipped cups do about people and their futures. He wonders if the house saw this coming.

'We'll do our best to find him,' McBride says, and Benjamin looks away. In the corner, the desk chair slowly swivels, and Benjamin fixes his gaze on it, wondering briefly where the air's coming from to move it.

'Policemen can't make promises.' He's seen enough police shows (not deliberately – Mum just leaves them on sometimes in the background while she marks assignments on the couch) to know this. He also knows that if children aren't found in the first forty-eight hours they might not be found at all. He grips Spectacular Man tighter.

'We can't,' McBride agrees. 'But have you seen Officer Keely? She's tough. You wouldn't want to face off against her in a dark alley, would you? Tough as all get out, that one.'

A smile fights through, and McBride pats him on the back as if he's a dog or *one of the boys*, and Benjamin thinks that's very nice, but that it won't exactly bring Charlie home.

O

The front door clicks shut behind Keely and McBride, and Ed turns on her, his face blotchy with anger, his voice booming.

'He's been gone since last night?'

Oh, there it is, Delia thinks, fury smudging her thoughts. She strides towards him, thrusts a finger in his face, something stirring awake inside her.

'You don't get to do this, Ed. *Fuck* you, you don't get to do this.'

The words tear from her chest, rush up her throat, as if summoned from the very depths of her, leaving her raw as she turns away from him and walks stiffly back to the kitchen.

Ed sighs, and Delia glances back to see his shoulders curved, eyes glassy. To see him run a trembling hand over his face, and it figures.

He's always been shit in a fight.

His silence is something of a comfort in the moment at least, gives Delia time to gather herself again, to let her hand find the kitchen counter, grip it tight, and try to curb the panic that crashes against her.

The memory comes quickly.

Her own mother in the kitchen, weeping, clawing at her father the night—

No.

She jerks herself out of it, her gaze drifting out the window to the fence that separates their house from the neighbour's, and she wonders if they heard Ed, if they saw the cop cars, if that woman is still hovering in her yard, burying ugly, hungry flowers in their beds, and listening.

Benjamin had been hungry.

'How could this even happen?'

Ed's voice is heavier than Delia cares to think about as she eyes the lamb still defrosting in the sink, the purple carrots half peeled beside it. After a moment, she wrenches open one of the counter drawers and pulls out a stack of faded takeaway menus. She grabs her phone and dials the first one she sees that promises delivery.

The squawking ring of the phone reverberates in her head, and Delia clutches it to her ear, but not for long. Her gaze travels back to Ed, who is watching her from across the kitchen, his face marred, and she thinks, you weren't here, but instead she says:

'I don't know. He walks everywhere. He always has. Andy only lives a few streets away.'

What a fucking joke.

To lie to herself right now.

To lie to *him*, the father of her son, because Andy's been grounded for weeks and Charlie has lied to her, but she can't quite let herself believe it yet.

Charlie's always been so honest, so good, so—

So like Bo.

She adjusts her clammy grip on the phone.

'You can't drop him off?'

Delia's gaze snaps back to Ed's stare, and her smothered anger licks at the back of her mouth. Her fingers clench, loosen, hold fast to the phone, now trilling with special deals instead of hold music.

'He's sixteen, Ed, what do you want me to do? Keep him on a fucking leash?'

Ed looks ready to fight her on that, but she's saved from his reply by the cut of the meal offers and the squeaky voice of a waiter. She orders, she's not quite sure what, and hangs up to see Ed still watching her, his brown eyes unblinking.

Silence hangs between them for a minute, and Ed rubs his jaw, panic bright in his brilliant eyes.

'It's just like Bo,' he tells her, and it works, like she knows he knew it would, sparking like a match in the kindling of her history, and she seethes, because it's not, it *can't be*, Delia won't *let it*.

'It is *nothing* like Bo,' she spits, and Ed's lips thin, but he doesn't pull back, doesn't quite tear his gaze from Delia's until he does.

'*Fuck*,' he bites. He presses the heels of his hands so hard against his eye sockets that he leaves angry red welts there, and Delia blinks rapidly, trying to calm her frayed nerves. Striding back to the living room, she grabs her purse with shaking hands, checks it for cash just for something to do, and then her phone again, in case Charlie has texted, sent something from a stranger's number.

Just forgot my phone, mum. Be home soon.

She should be so lucky.

At the empty inbox, she drops the purse and phone back on the couch, works her jaw, feels herself perspiring through her shirt, her bra, then a brisk sort of cold that sinks through her bones, and maybe that's familiar at least.

The icy hand of shock.

Delia exhales, finally looking back at Ed.

'Go home,' she tells him, her voice low and as firm as she can manage. 'Go tell your girlfriend. I'm sure she's worried. Then go wait by your phone like I will here. We can talk about it in the morning.'

For a brief, tangled moment, Delia doesn't think he'll leave, and she can't quite unclench her fist at the thought. Can't untwist her twisting heart, desperate in equal measures for him to vanish and remain, for his distance and his bright, warming presence, and she can't even begin to get her head around what that means.

And at least Ed seems much the same, if the way he fusses is anything to go by, his eyes red, shoulders stooped, mouth a little open as he pants wetly in the evening heat.

Neither Benjamin nor Olive have come out of their rooms, and she wonders whether, if she listens closely enough, she might be able to hear them, to confirm that they're both still safe in her home.

'Call me first,' Ed tells her, and Delia's gaze jumps back up to meet his. 'If you hear anything. Don't leave it to the fucking police. You call *me*. You call me *first*.'

Delia looks at his broad jaw, his unblinking brown eyes, his thick lashes, matted together with sweat or tears, she doesn't know which. She looks at his throat, bob, quiver, swallow, and she nods.

He leaves.

He just *leaves*.

Those roots in Olive's chest press hard into the walls of her ribs, and she falls awkwardly off her bed, stumbles over to her dresser and pulls out the small, chipped tin in the back of her underwear drawer. She rolls the thin paper skin between her fingers, her mouth filling with saliva and her throat aching in anticipation of the inhale. There's a pressure between her eyebrows that won't budge, won't fucking *move*, and she bites her lip until the iron taste of coins paints her teeth and dribbles down her throat.

She wraps the weed so badly most of it falls out of the skin, and she swears loudly enough that she's sure Benjamin can hear from his room, but she doesn't care, just drops to the floor and tries to scrounge the cuttings with her still-trembling fingers. Tries to remember the mindfulness exercises her high-school counsellor gave her, the one, two, threes, the hold. The mental notebook of *the things you can control* and the things you can't, but the effort to focus on any of it evades her, and she riffles through the catalogue of exercises faster than any of them can work.

The buzz of her phone cuts through the quiet of her room, and could that be—

Olive springs forwards, scrambling across her bed towards her phone, blood rushing in her ears. She thinks of Charlie's frown yesterday at the trampoline, then of his grin as he'd left, and if this is him, she'll—

But it's not.

A weight drops low.

Party at Kanga Point. Final call. In or out?

Lux.

Olive pants, mouth dry, feels light-headed for a beat, reading and re-reading the message, and she shouldn't. She should stay in with her mother, with Benjamin. She should wait for Charlie. She should try to get an early night and not think about him in somebody's white van or basement or morgue and not think about the fact that her dad came over but didn't even talk to her (look at her, think of her, want to be around her). She should try to do a lot of things. Her fingers, still shaking, type quickly.

In. Meet me at shep bus depot?

Lux sends back a thumbs-up emoji and a confetti ball, and Olive climbs unsteadily to her feet, changing into denim shorts and a singlet, tying up her long hair. She takes three breaths, then another three for luck, then tosses her bag over her shoulder.

She's barely out of her bedroom when Delia spots her, still perched at the kitchen island, her hands around a glass of scotch now.

'I ordered pizzas,' Delia says, and Olive shrugs, toeing into a pair of sandals in the hall.

'Enjoy them.'

It takes Delia a second to catch on, to grasp the implication, but when she does, her face turns itself about the way it often does with Olive (never with Charlie, never).

'You're not going out.'

Olive's lips pull thin.

'Yes, I am. I've got plans.'

'*Olive.*'

'I'm a grown-arse woman, Delia, *Jesus.*'

Olive clings desperately to the sudden righteous anger flaring in her gut. Right now, she can do this. She can have this fight. She can thrash against her mother's desire for her to be twelve and forty-two, her child, her peer, her co-fucking-parent.

Olive ducks around her and out the back door, her feet hitting each step with a fury that won't be stamped out. Delia is calling from above her, behind her, her voice loud and desperate above the swell of screeching lorikeets in the trees around their house, the clicking ribbets of the geckos on their walls, but Olive doesn't turn back. She grabs her bike from the back fence and yanks it up over the grass, pushing away settled moths and a scrap of bright paper caught around the handlebar, drought-stiff leaves and scrambling skinks in the wheels.

Passing the gate, she swings a leg over the bike and pedals down the driveway and into the street, thighs already burning. She turns her head back just enough to catch a fleeting glimpse of her mother on the road behind her, her body sagging and shrunken, half formed in the hazy summer night, barely a thing at all.

4

Green eyes, dark hair. Thick lashes.

Long, slightly upturned nose and a crooked, knowing grin.

Braces.

What colour were the bands he got at the orthodontist last week?

Blue, she thinks.

Yes. Blue.

He's had a lot of freckles lately, from not enough sunscreen and those long walks home from school. From the afternoons and the weekends in the yard, fiddling with his telescope, or lying on the trampoline, scribbling in his notebook. Was he sunburnt? Or was that just Benjamin? Either way, Charlie doesn't burn as easily as his brother and sister. Olive and Benjamin both inherited Ed's fair skin, but Charlie is like her. Quick to tan. To darken beneath fine layers of mousy hair.

Her soft, golden boy.

(Can you draw someone from memory?)

How tall is he nowadays? She can't quite remember. They spring up so quickly at Charlie's age. Weedish and ropey. Hollow-boned elfish things with narrow chests and light steps. Delia had no brothers growing up, no cousins, had been sheltered from adolescent boys as a girl, and hadn't been prepared for the oddness of them. The unformedness. As teenagers, Delia and Bo had seemed to step out of their girlish forms and into the suits of women, their bodies swelling and resetting, moulding into something earthy and firm, whereas Charlie and his friends had become more ephemeral – lanky and fragile and untrue.

But then that had been Olive's way too.

Delia frowns, looking over at the still-open front door. She'd chased Olive into the street, but she'd been too slow, and Olive too nimble, too quick, too desperate to get away. It's been hours now, hours of unanswered phone calls and silence.

She takes a long drink from her scotch glass, the cheap sulfuric liquid burning her throat. She folds forwards on the couch, taking care not to disturb Benjamin, who is asleep with his head in her lap, and tries to draw a deeper breath. Then she sits up again, reaching over to the coffee table to grab her phone, checking the time, her empty message box. Checking for anything at all.

At her thigh, Benjamin wriggles further down the couch, snuffling through a snore, and god, she's jealous of his ability to sleep, however fitfully. She pushes a hand through his soft hair then down to his skull, his neck, his throat, until she can feel his light feathery pulse at her fingers. She presses harder than she means to, just to reassure herself, and yanks her hand away when Benjamin coughs in his sleep.

Pull yourself together, she thinks. Her hand trembles as she holds her son and checks her phone again, scrolling through old messages. Trembles even when the hum from the road, the sound of a car pulling up, jerks her from her reading.

The gate creaks open, and staggered steps disrupt the sounds of frogs and insects. The crunch of wayward stones beneath shoes, then the whine of the wooden stairs outside, and finally a heave, a splutter, a groan.

Delia turns on the couch in time to see her daughter stumbling up the front steps, her tall, spindly body in the doorway, the hallway light casting an eerie glow across her drunken form. Olive leans forwards, trying to kick off her shoes, what looks like vomit caked in her hair, her lips stained a lurid pink.

And it happens, of course. Olive looks up and sees Delia watching her, Benjamin asleep on her lap, and she scoffs, pitching sideways, off-kilter. She pushes a hand to the wall to steady herself, using the other to swipe at her make-up-smeared face.

'Well?' Olive slurs, her free arm swinging around, inviting a reply, and Delia stares at her, relief and regret washing over the rocky floor of her anger.

'I'm glad you got home in one piece,' she says, and Olive's expression wavers, just for a second.

'Whatever.'

She pushes off the wall and stumbles up the hall towards her room. The door slams shut behind her, making Benjamin jump in his sleep (is he even asleep?), and Delia bites her hand to keep from screaming.

○

The vivid stream of morning light wakes her, slipping through her blinds. She throws a hand to her face, rubbing her aching eyelids as the already-hot air mouths at her perspiring skin. With a groan, she pulls herself out from beneath Benjamin's damp, gawky body, rising unsteadily to her feet.

Bird chatter and the hum of early-morning traffic greet her in the hallway, as does the smell of a neighbour cooking something savoury for breakfast. Delia lets it enfold her tired senses as she pads down the hallway towards Olive's room, her cotton pyjamas stuck uncomfortably to her legs and belly.

Olive's room is its own sort of disaster, with posters peeling off patchy walls and bras lying rumpled on the floor, an underwire sticking out of one, the sharp edge of it dulled by a ball of Blu Tack. There are books – some dog-eared and open, others crisp and new – from the one semester of university Olive had managed to stomach. Olive herself is tangled in her bedsheets, her fair hair stuck across her face and shoulders. The mop bucket Delia placed there once she was sure Olive was asleep sits at the side of the bed, stinking with muddied pink vomit.

Olive is otherwise nude, her thin, tapered body exposed to her mother's careful eye. They look nothing alike: Delia is shorter, fuller-figured, with thick thighs and swollen, sagging breasts, while Olive has the look of Ed and her brothers – sprawling, gangly limbs and narrow, boyish hips. Her breasts are small, pert and freckled, her nipples a startling pink. Her ribs are vivid beneath her pale skin, like a birdcage covered by a thin cloth. Delia steps forwards to untangle the sheet from between her daughter's legs and stretch it back across her body, enough to hide her from the buttery air.

The movement makes Olive sigh, the sound seeping from her cherry-stained lips. She stretches, turning away from Delia, contorting her slender frame so that Delia can see her every bone: the uneven peaks of her spine, the blades of her ribs, the tectonic plates of her shoulders. The familiar, foreign shape of her.

So like Charlie in that shape, if not in colouring.

The thought wedges in Delia's head, settles like a clot, and she skitters away, retreats to the hallway and lets her back fall against the closed door of Charlie and Benjamin's room. Her fingers grope the chipped wood, resting in the grooves of it, and she finds herself wondering, as if in a dream, if Charlie is inside. If he is there in his bed, burrowed beneath his sheets, his body imprinting on his thin foam mattress. She wonders if he'll groan as she opens the door, like he usually does, pulling the pillow across his face until he is more bed than boy, his body visible only in snatches of tanned skin jutting out from beneath blankets and bedclothes. The thought lodges Delia's heart in her mouth, sits it like a pill on her tongue, catching at her molars, refusing to be swallowed.

'Mum?'

Delia startles, spinning around to see Benjamin standing before her, his cheeks wet with tears, his lips turned down.

'Mum, I did it again.'

Instantly, her gaze falls to his legs, to where his cotton sleep shorts are soaked through with piss, marked from his crotch to the hem, and then down the pale skin of his calves and ankles.

She rests a hand on his cheek, leaning forwards to press a tired kiss to the crown of his head.

'It's okay, Banjo. Come on.'

He cries when she mops him up. When she takes his soiled pants and underwear and pushes him into the shower. He cries harder when she has to pull her own clothes off too, has to wash her own skin, wet from where they'd shared the couch and her bed during the night. She hadn't even noticed it when she'd woken, hadn't noticed the difference between sweat and urine. She wants to ask him why, if he's crying about this lapse after a good few months or if it's about his brother. Mostly she wonders if she could cry too, but right now she doesn't think she could.

○

Her phone is buzzing.

Once, twice, three times, and Olive wakes up to a heavy head and an empty house. Her mother has gone to work, Benjamin to school, and this leaves her free to lurch off her mattress, trip over the stinking mop bucket, and cross the distance to her dresser. She pulls out the small tin of weed and makes a nervous, fumbling job of it, trying to ignore the dull throbbing at the front and back of her head, behind her eyes and in her throat. She inhales sharply when she almost drops the weed, and then, after a roll and a light, sucks in another drag from the joint.

She's still naked, and oddly relieved for it. She runs a humid hand up her arm, across her chest, feels the sweat gathering below her breasts and in the hollow of her collarbone. She wipes it dry.

Her memories of the party are tainted by a haze of goon and sweet raspberry liqueurs and the pills she and Lux broke apart between them. The remnants of powder are still there, embedded beneath Olive's dirty nails, and she resists the urge to plunge her tongue into the crevices and lick oblivion clean from them. Instead she pushes her thumbnail beneath them, letting the fragments flake onto the floor.

With another drag, she reaches for her phone, still half lit on the corner of her mattress, and opens most of her apps – TikTok, Twitter, Tumblr, Instagram, Facebook. Tries to find any memory of the night before that she can reclaim. She skims a few messages from Lux, from *where'd you go?* to *why didn't you tell me?*, scrolling through her feeds until she's jolted to a stop.

It's the crooked grin. That's the thing. The one Charlie has always had. That one that sits lopsided at his big, white teeth. One of her friends from high school has posted it, and another, an amber alert, a *have you seen this boy?* shared from Queensland Police's Facebook page, a smiling vision of her baby brother, his last school photo, before he had braces.

His eyes are so bright.

Olive's breaths turn into gasps, and she drops the joint, stamping out the flicker of light with her foot and revelling in the burn. The pain in her skull has amplified, is knocking about, declaring its presence, and she tilts her body forwards, dropping her phone to the ground. *Put your head between your knees. Count your breaths. Don't let it own you.*

Please, she thinks. Don't own me.

But everyone knows now. Everyone has seen it. Little Charlie Rabbit with his Charlie Rabbit grin, lost for the whole world to find. Her phone buzzes at her feet, and Olive tries to catch and hold and even out her breath, to stamp down her pulse like the ash at her feet.

She tries, she tries, she tries.

○

'Mr Rabbit? Mr Rabbit. Benjamin.'

Benjamin lifts his head to see Miss Kent looking at him sympathetically, her forehead crinkled, her eyes even more watery than normal. The rest of the class turns in their seats, and he flushes when he feels Jodi's eyes on him, her lips set in a little frown.

'Are you okay, Benjamin?'

He must have been asleep again, feels it in his groggy eyes, the pasty remnants of saliva at the corners of his dry lips. He hopes he wasn't snoring. He hopes – panicked, glancing down at his legs – that he didn't have an accident again. To his relief his shorts are dry. The tension in his arms shifts.

It's not until Miss Kent walks over, her shoes neatly clipping the wooden floor, that he realises he hasn't answered her. She crouches beside his desk, young and pretty, like a television teacher, a nice, soft one – a Miss Honey, Miss Frizzle. She smells like flowers, not the dark, wilting ones that grow in the shadows beneath the steps of their house, but the sunny and sweet ones in their neighbour's yard.

'Do you want to see the nurse? I can give you a slip.'

He doesn't, not again, not twice in one day. He'd barely gotten to school that morning before he'd been sent to the nurse's office and made to sit down as she guided him through questions about Charlie, his mum and dad and Olive, about how he was feeling. Questions he didn't have any answers for.

'No, I'm okay.'

Miss Kent doesn't seem convinced, but she gets to her feet anyway, walking back to the whiteboard and scribbling some notes about their English homework. Benjamin slumps uneasily in his seat again, free from the attention of his classmates. It's only Poppy Dockens who looks back, her lips pressed together to make a clasped circle. He tries to smile at her, like he did yesterday, and she tries to smile back, even if her eyes aren't too honest about it.

Benjamin looks away. Away from Poppy and Jodi and Miss Kent, trains his gaze out the window instead, on the high school across the road, big and quiet in the early afternoon. The light cuts strange shadows across it, leaving it oddly eerie, all Gotham Academy all over again. The police car is still parked outside, has been since Mum dropped him at school this morning, and Benjamin wonders if they're having long assemblies or if the student body is being lined up and led in to conversations with Keely and McBride like Benjamin and Olive and their mum and dad were last night.

A girl walks out of the main school doors, dropping cross-legged onto the front steps. It's not long before another car pulls up, parking behind the police car. A woman gets out, walking towards the girl and passing her a notebook, a textbook, forgotten homework, and the girl leans in, kisses the woman on the cheek and darts back inside the building.

He thinks he knows the girl. Thinks she might be a friend of Charlie's, someone he took to the semi-formal or who came to his birthday party at Movie World a couple of years ago. Benjamin watches as she disappears out of sight and suddenly wishes he had Spectacular Man from his bag. He clenches his hands in his shorts instead, firmly enough that the skin across his knuckles pulls tight.

Did the police interview that girl? Did they think to? Know to? Benjamin blinks hard, until the front doors of the high school open and Keely and McBride step out, formal-looking in the bright sunlight. McBride shields his eyes while Keely puts on a heavy-looking pair of sunglasses, and for a second, just a second, Benjamin could swear they are looking right at him.

Delia is on autopilot throughout her lecture, her fingers slick on the chalk as she talks about the form and function of pencil work, about the shapes a body makes and the ways you can recreate them with the right tools and the right eye.

(Can you draw someone from memory?)

She sketches a few quick lines on the board, a stroke of movement – a turning head – down to a sloping pair of shoulders, the curve of a neck, a narrow, freckled chest. This class will have a model next week, but not today, and so for now Delia draws with the practised routine of an old hand, the muscle memory of an artist.

She's relieved, more than anything, when time is up and the class leaves in a cattle-like shuffle of sweating bodies. Only Griff stays behind, shrugging his bag over his shoulder and taking the steps two at a time towards her. She checks her phone, sees a message from Saint Anne's, asking for a meeting, and another telling her to top up her Linkt pass. She's asked one of the master's students to take her afternoon tutorial, stretching the truth about her sick mother in lieu of any talk of her son. It gives her a free afternoon, though she's not sure what she'll do with it. She thinks of going to the police station, then of home, then, briefly, of her mother.

'Need a hand getting back to your office?'

Her resolve falters when she looks up at Griff.

She could – no, she shouldn't. She snaps her briefcase shut.

'Not today. I've got a few errands to run.'

The hum of the air conditioning sounds louder than it should at Griff's silence, the prickling cool like the memory of his breath at her neck. She runs a hand over it, watching Griff watching her. He reaches forwards to pick up some of the equipment on her desk but stops when she shoots him an ugly look.

'Okay,' he says, holding his hands up in surrender. 'I can walk you out at least?'

'I don't think that's a good idea.'

'People will just think I'm asking you about the lecture.'

Delia shakes her head, adjusting her grip on her briefcase as she heads towards the exit. Her fingers itch to check her phone again. It's only when she gets to the lecture theatre door that Griff speaks up.

'Are you alright?'

Delia's step falters, and she turns to be met with Griff's wide-eyed look, his expression open, true, desperately kind. It speaks to a part of her she'd rather forget – a younger Delia, who'd yearned for the sort of honesty that was given freely and didn't have to be pried from a closed fist. For a moment, she thinks of leaning into it, but then again—

She slips on her best morning-show smile.

'Why wouldn't I be?'

With that, she pushes through the door and keeps moving, walking through the college towards the carpark, dodging throngs of languorous students gossiping between classes. She thought Griff would get the hint but she's mistaken; he's only a few paces behind her until they get outside again, and his hand reaches forwards, his long, broad fingers gripping her elbow.

'Ms Rabbit. Delia. Stop.'

And she does, but not because of Griff.

Over in the carpark, leaning against her car, is Ed.

Delia jerks her elbow from Griff's grip, flustered, her throat constricting.

'Go home,' she tells him, her voice leaving no room for argument. 'I'll talk to you later.'

Griff lets her go, his expression wounded, but he doesn't try to follow her as she walks out across the carpark towards Ed, fishing her keys from her briefcase and counting her breaths. She's only a couple of steps from him when he finally sees her, straightening himself and leaning just enough off her car to stand on his own two feet.

'Please tell me he came home,' he says before Delia can say a thing. 'Please tell me he crawled back in through his bedroom window and laughed about how worried he'd gotten everyone.'

There's a desperation to him that reminds her of the home that is waiting for her, of the terror she's forced down. She can't be paralysed now. Paralysis will not help her find her son (another memory: her mother and father, their hands entwined on the couch, Delia spying on their stony faces from the hall as the policeman asked them – *told* them—).

Delia clears her throat.

There's nothing to say now anyway, so she meets his look silently, and it's the only answer Ed needs. His face crumples. She doesn't think he's showered, because he stinks of sweat and someone else's perfume and the same scotch she drank herself last night. She imagines him pacing, swearing, horribly, hopelessly awake, his girlfriend watching him, and she thinks for maybe the first time in years, I'm not in love with you anymore, and then she thinks she wants to remind him of the summer they spent on the beach at Noosa, and knows that the first thought is a lie. She wants to remind him of their group of school friends, each knocking on the door of adulthood to see what was there. Of that summer, when they were younger than they felt and messed around in the surf and drank on the sand until their heads lolled against each other, and the crashing waves and squawking gulls slurred together like the perfect backdrop of everything and nothing. The way he told her he understood her, the way he *had*, the way he held her and kissed her, on her lips and her collarbone and her ribs and her hips and finally between her legs, his lips cracked from the salty sea air and his fingers still hot from the sun. She wants to remind him of how they made love there, their friends across the beach calling and jeering as her bikini bottoms ended up around her ankles, and how she'd never felt so complete or so seen or so perfect.

Oh, she thinks.

Now, though, Ed just sighs, rubbing at his head. He doesn't move, still leaning against her car, and Delia can feel her resolve eroding, her reserves depleting. I don't know where to go next, she thinks. Not to the police or the school, not to Ed's or Griff's, not to her daughter or her son or her slipping mother. She's in an unforgiving sea with only a vague idea of the direction she should be swimming in, and nothing to head for.

'What do you want from me?' she asks, and Ed doesn't reply, but he doesn't leave right away either. Lingers briefly instead, like he's trying to figure out what to say, and when he can't, he goes without another word, clambering into his own car and driving away.

In the end, she does too.

Drives aimlessly, through this suburb and the next, from the high school to the park to the space centre to the cinema to the shopping centre, her gaze catching on every scruffy-haired long-limbed boy she sees through the dusty glass of her windshield, and when her arms are burning and her eyes drooping she drives to the river instead.

She parks there but doesn't get out, just watches the water lapping lower than it should, and not for the first time since Bo she wonders what they might find if they dredged it.

O

By the time she gets home the air is blister-pink, everything hazy edged, a camaïeu of colour. She had felt her knuckles burning beneath the fractious sun as she sat in the car by the river for hours, her bare knees glowing, but it hadn't bothered her, nor had the sweat that had soaked through the back of her shirt, leaving the seat damp behind her. She could've stayed there all night too, but Benjamin was being dropped home by another parent at school, and she wasn't sure if Olive was staying in or leaving them again.

The long grass tickles her calves as she walks through her backyard, feeling the dry earth crack beneath the heel of her shoe, seeing a skink darting away from her.

Above her the light's on, the smell of cigarette smoke escaping one of the windows, and it's strange, the way it makes Delia think not of her daughter but of her own father, the memory of his bright laugh and nicotine-stained teeth unwrapping in her mind like a gift, and she blinks hard, swallows, looks away, out across her garden and—

She blinks again.

And then she squints. Pushes a hand to her forehead and takes a step sideways, because in the middle of her pink-tinged yard there's an unmistakable bolt of blue.

The grass crunches beneath her feet and bees buzz gently as Delia walks towards it, and her heart skips a beat when she realises what it is.

Charlie's notebook.

The one he uses to record constellations and orbits,

rainwater and eyelashes, heights and hive growth and flying-fox populations. It's damp with condensation, with the dew and humidity, and Delia reaches down with a trembling hand to pick it up.

The ink has run, but not so much that it's unreadable, and she flips through the thick and crusty pages layered with scrappy yellow post-it notes, through paragraphs on planetary huddles and bird migrations and height charts to the entry from the day before last. The day Charlie went missing. She snaps the notebook closed, clenching her eyes shut, trying to stopper the grief and desperation bubbling through her body.

Overhead a bird calls, loud and chattering, and she looks up to see a lone lorikeet swoop down and land neatly on Charlie's telescope, its feathers ruffling, its plumage bright emerald, even in the pinkish hue of the afternoon. The bees buzz docilely around it, their hive little more than a skeleton in the joints of the telescope stand. Charlie hadn't let her do a thing about it. Hadn't let her hack it off or lay fine trails of poison for them to take home on their feet and in their glimmering wings. He hadn't let her do a thing.

Delia keeps walking towards the house. It is only when she gets to the steps that she sees the esky. She pushes back the top to reveal container after container of sticky casseroles and gluggy soups, warming winter meals that spoil in the summer. There's a bottle of wine too, and a few lumpy ice packs, working overtime to chill the meals and achieving little more than fogging up the plastic. She drops the lid back down, grabs the handle and lugs it inside with her.

'Guys!' she calls, letting out a breath she hadn't realised

she'd been holding when she sees Olive leaning over the kitchen island, her hair newly washed and still wet, her phone screen lit up in her hands.

'Do you know where this came from?'

Olive looks at the esky and shrugs, turning her attention back to her phone.

'The neighbour was poking around earlier.'

With a blink, Delia looks out the kitchen window and over towards the neighbour's house, with its neat lawn and bright-eyed possums devouring fruit left out for them on the front deck.

'That was nice of her,' Delia says, because it was, her hands still clutching Charlie's notebook.

If Olive thinks a thing about it, she doesn't say a word.

5

'You look like shit.'

Olive turns to flip Lux off with her free hand, her other devoted to tying her hair back into a half-arsed bun. She's still feeling the long tail of her hangover, the snarl of the day before tugging unhappily at her eyelids and stretching itself out in the cavern her skull. It doesn't help that she knows she smells. Her O'Malley's shirt is unwashed, and it tells in the mustardy feel of the armpits and the stench of BO. She doesn't give enough of a shit to do a thing about it though, not this morning and not last night either, when her mother had offered to soak it clean with Benjamin's piss-wet pyjamas.

'Hey, I'd be more worried if you looked good,' Lux says, sitting cross-legged in one of the plastic chairs. They're holed up in the staffroom, Olive just clocking in while Lux is halfway through a long shift.

As if on cue, Olive's eyes slip sideways, fix on the tissue box on the bench, the one she'd half emptied the day before while she mopped up Benjamin after—

Olive's hands work a little more roughly in her hair.

The smell of that vanilla vape juice finds her nose again,

and she glances over to see Lux looking at her, her phone face-up on the table in front of her, her back to the tiny television in the corner of the room (black-screened, it died forever ago). The other girl's focus feels strangely weighted, or maybe not so strangely, Olive supposes, glancing down at the floor, taking in the brown carpet stain from the full can of Coke one of the stockroom boys dropped last week.

Hadn't she wanted Lux's attention?

Her mouth suddenly dry, she inhales, fidgets and finally drops her hands, only to twitch again when Lux rocks in her chair and asks:

'Any news on your brother?'

Olive's breath seizes, and she shakes her head, grabbing her bag from her feet and shoving it gracelessly into her locker. It's been two days now (three?), and there has been nothing. Keely and McBride have been around again and again and again, but they bring only gentle words and the business cards of counsellors with them.

There've been no more visits from Dad, and shit, she's barely even seen Delia, but then maybe that's not a surprise either.

'Fuck,' Lux offers. She swings sideways on the chair, folding her bony arms over her bony chest. Above them, the ceiling fan rotates, blowing streams of humid air back down at them, and Olive can feel it whispering at her neck, beneath her stinking shirt.

'You should come over tonight,' Lux says. 'Get your mind off it. My mum's still in Sydney, so I have the place to myself. We can have a party of two.'

She sing-songs the last line, closes her eyes, purses her lips, and throws up a peace sign in a perfect Instagram pose. It's so normal, so *dumb*, that Olive huffs out an almost-laugh.

'Maybe. I'm supposed to be picking my—' she stops herself, sniffs. 'I've got to pick up Benjamin.'

Lux snorts.

'What, are you his mum or something?'

'No.'

'Then what's the big deal? Leave him to Mrs Rabbit.'

'Ms,' Olive replies, brushing her hands half-heartedly down her shirt. 'It's Ms Rabbit. My parents never got married.'

'Not even Mr Rabbit wanted to lock that shit down, huh?'

Olive opens her mouth to reply, but finds she's not sure what she wants to say to that. That there is no Mr Rabbit, at least not a living one. Just a Mr Tanner. That Dad told her years ago that it was Delia's decision that they never got married, his tone so wistful he'd seemed almost mournful. That it had been Delia's decision that her kids be Rabbits, not Tanners, because—

Well.

She has no idea.

The thought makes her blink, close her mouth and wet her lips, and her gaze shifts back to the television behind Lux's head, and in its reflection she sees the staffroom door crack open and Mindy's head pop through. She casts her eyes about the room before locking them on Olive and jerking her head in the direction from which she came.

'Olive, Frank wants to see you before you start.'

'Frank?'

Lux pulls a face, and Olive turns to Mindy, taking her in, trying to read her.

'What does he want to see me for?'

Mindy just shrugs, wandering into the room, grabbing a magazine from the staff table and flopping down into the seat opposite Lux. It feels like as much of an answer as Olive's likely to get, so she adjusts her shirt and heads out.

Frank's office is only a few doors down from the staffroom: a small, squat room for a small, squat man. Olive hasn't been in there since she was interviewed for the job almost three years ago, but even so she has a stark memory of being surprised by the sterility of the space, by the clinical, determined order Frank had brought to the room to the detriment of any personality. It's barely changed over the years either – his grey desk is still practically bare, and the black-binder-filled shelves behind him look like the backdrop of a stock photograph. The only glimmers of the unordinary are in the water stains on the ceiling and the smell of deli meat that hangs thin in the air.

Frank himself is half a head shorter than Olive, balding, with a hardened paunch. Behind his desk his height is less noticeable, and he looks older than Olive knows he is, between his liver-spotted skull and his dull, watery eyes.

'Mindy said you wanted to see me?'

The words make Frank startle, his head snapping up to blink gormlessly at her, as if he'd entirely forgotten he'd called for her, and Olive aims for something approaching a customer-service smile.

'Yeah, sorry, mate,' he confirms, leaning back from the

glare of his computer screen. 'I just wanted to check in. See how you were.'

'I'm going fine,' she offers, and Frank hums.

'Mindy alerted me to the situation with your brother.'

His voice is weedy, wiry, like it's distorted through a line somehow, and Olive can't help it – the way it drips like petrol into the constant embers of her anger. Her chest suddenly aches, and she wishes she was somewhere else. Somewhere far from here, where the news of Charlie was buried, where she could just *be*, or not be at all. Where she could lie in tall grass and disappear. She clenches her hands into fists, pressing them into her sides.

'If you need to take some leave you can file it with her. Consider it already approved.'

Olive tilts her head forwards, acknowledging his acknowledgement. She should be glad for it, knows she should. She should be grateful that he's thought of her at all. Against her narrow thighs, her fists clench even tighter.

'Thanks, Frank. I'm okay right now.'

Frank looks at her, his gaze firmer, steadier than she's ever seen it, and it's all Olive can do not to leave, not to wilt beneath this strange look and escape somehow. Above him the air conditioner hums, the noise startlingly loud in Olive's ears, and maybe she is in tall grass already because it sounds like cicadas buzzing, their legs stamping at her eardrums.

'Sure. Keep up the good work,' Frank concedes, his considering look refocusing on his computer screen. 'Let us know if you need anything.'

It's as much a dismissal as anything, and Olive promptly

nods, turning on her heel and heading back to the staffroom. Her whole body is rigid, her back straight, her legs working at odd angles, like the hinges of her hips have rusted shut. She pushes back into the staffroom to find only Mindy there, her ankles crossed on the table as she chews on a browning banana. On top of the cabinet, the TV is showing the news, a report about bushfires ripping through the south of the country, and the whole thing makes Olive stop dead.

'You got it working?' she asks, surprise thick in her tone, and Mindy nods in her general direction, her gaze still fixed on the television.

Olive should be working. Her shift has started, well and truly, and she should be out on the floor helping with the restock, but she ends up sitting down in one of the free chairs instead, watching as volunteers fit little knitted gloves onto scalded koala paws. The screen flickers back to the fires, then to the families, standing by the ashes of their homes, weeping on camera.

'Everything okay with Frank?' Mindy asks, leaning back to look at her, and Olive nods as best she can. Her hands are still clenched, and when she opens them up she's surprised to find her fingers purpled with tension and her palms sticky with blood, a line of crescent cuts left by her hard, long nails. A picture of perfect, bloody moons.

○

Benjamin steps outside to watch the crush of parents pulling up to the school, the cars parked for miles either side of the road. There are more than ever, or at least more than there usually are this far into the term. The swell of people reminds him of when he was small, getting lost amid the crowds at the Ekka, his hands searching for Charlie's in the throng.

But it's Charlie who's lost now, and Benjamin's hands have been reaching for days. The thought wriggles unpleasantly in his belly, and he busies himself with adjusting his backpack across his shoulders before ducking down the school steps.

Shepherd Primary School is a short, stocky building, all tan bricks with flaking white paint. Tall, skinny paperbark trees shield its entrance, lurching high above the schoolyard and housing the occasional yawning, fat-bellied koala and scrappy wooden bird boxes made by some of the high-school kids in DT. Benjamin likes it. Likes the droopy green leaves and the bark they can peel off in sheets. Likes that the building is old without looking abandoned or run-down like so many of the old buildings in the city do.

With Spectacular Man in his hand, Benjamin rises up, eyeing the high school through the swarm of parents, and briefly imagines Charlie breaking through the crowd to walk him home.

The thought will do no good, not today, maybe not ever again.

It's Olive who picks him up now.

He takes a deep breath, holding Spectacular Man even tighter. That feeling is back in his belly, wriggling like a hot worm through his gut. He tries to grab the worm and trap it beneath his hands, to just hold it still, make it stop, and he's so focused on this that he jumps when a boy taps him on the shoulder.

'I think she means you,' he says, and Benjamin looks past him to see Poppy darting towards him, her freckled cheeks glowing.

'Ben!' she calls, and going by her tone, it's not the first time she's called it. She picks up her step, her shoes kicking up dust, her socks browning with the force of it. Benjamin looks back to the road, hopes for Olive, but it's no use. He waits for Poppy instead.

'Nobody calls me that,' he says when Poppy reaches him.

'What?'

'Nobody calls me Ben. I'm Benjamin.'

'Isn't Ben short for Benjamin?'

Benjamin scowls. 'Not for me.'

'Okay,' Poppy replies with a shrug. 'Sorry.'

He sucks his lips in, nodding awkwardly, before starting down towards the school's east pick-up point, just in case Olive has forgotten the usual spot. It wouldn't surprise him – Olive never pays attention to what he says. The thought makes him scowl, walk a bit faster, but he's barely made it five steps before Poppy's walking alongside him. She smells like kiwifruit lip balm and sunscreen, and her trumpet case keeps hitting her leg as she walks, making a strange thumping rhythm with her pace.

'Poppy's not short for anything, and there's not really any nicknames you can have with it. I wish I had a nickname. We call my sister Mouse, but that's because she's only a baby, not because it's short for her name. Her real name is Michaela.'

There are even fewer people at the east pick-up point, and most of the kids are younger than Benjamin and Poppy, little things lost beneath floppy school hats and turtle-shell backpacks, playing beneath the watchful gaze of Miss Kent and one of the jowly school administrators. He's pretty sure Olive's picked him up from here before, back when he was smaller. He lifts his free hand to shield his eyes from the sun, to look across the playground for her familiar form, her lurching bike.

'Is your brother still missing?'

It's like a laser beam, the question.

Stirring the hot worm in Benjamin's belly, making it writhe, and he turns, wide-eyed, to look at Poppy, who just stares back at him expectantly.

Adjusting his backpack straps, holding tightly, Benjamin starts walking again.

Maybe Olive went to the high school by mistake, or maybe she's had to work late. Maybe she fell off her bike or got hurt some other way.

Maybe she's missing too.

'He seemed nice. I wish I had a brother. I've only got sisters, and I love them a lot, but there's so many of them. Sometimes I wish I could swap one of them for a brother. Do you have any sisters?'

His fingers tighten, and he has to level out his breathing, to try to stop the hot worm, which has wriggled up to his chest, and the *ba-dum-ba-dum-ba-dum* of his suddenly too-loud heart.

'I bet you do. I can usually tell these things, you know. My mum says I have excellent into— intoosh— intuition.'

When she finally finds the right word, she leans in to

nudge him, and the contact lights up Benjamin's skin like a hundred crackling fireworks. He stops dead in his tracks and spins on the spot to face Poppy, jerking back when her face is so close he can count her freckles, and smell nothing but her sunscreen.

'Why are you following me?' he asks her hotly, firming his ground, and Poppy blinks back at him, her mouth hanging open.

After a minute, she just grins, something small and bashful, scrunches up her nose, and says:

'I don't know.'

Her tone is so shy, her eyes so bright, they startle a disbelieving laugh out of Benjamin, and he starts to reply, only Poppy's gaze is gone from him and focused instead on the way they came.

'That's my dad,' Poppy says. 'I'll see you at school tomorrow, Ben.'

'Benjamin!' he yells after her, but it's too late. She's racing back across the schoolyard towards a minivan, her trumpet case still banging loudly against her leg.

Lux's house is always bigger than Olive remembers. A sleek, modern building in an up-and-coming part of town. An area clean and well maintained, with smooth roads and sprouting trees, pretty things designed to canopy the streets in the years to come. A promise of beauty more than its actuality.

'My mum's away again for the week,' Lux says, dropping her bag onto the kitchen counter and pulling open the large french doors of the fridge. 'She's hosting a charity auction in Sydney for some, like, total arseholes, and my dad's still up north, so basically we have the place to ourselves.'

Even the prospect is foreign to Olive. Despite both her parents working as much as they do, the Rabbit house has never felt empty, at least never for long. A revolving door of chaos, that's what her mum had always called it, her tone dry but something in her look making Olive think she secretly liked it that way. Liked the way Benjamin ran up and down the halls, making the spiderwebs in the high ceiling corners shiver, the way Charlie took up space in the yard and the way Olive used to curl herself up on the couch and watch shitty Netflix movies while painting her toenails or doing her homework.

Liked the way Dad used to come in in the last ten minutes, drape himself behind Olive and try to guess the plot.

There's a memory then, a glimmer.

Dad saying something outlandish, something dumb, and Delia overhearing from the kitchen island, laughing as Olive tries to shove him away, annoyed but grinning and then annoyed she is grinning.

Remembers looking back at Delia – at her mum – seeing her face warm and her eyes twinkling, seeing something *fond* on her face, and then just as suddenly something very far away.

The memory unravels, and Olive finds herself staring at Lux's back.

She clears her throat. 'I thought you'd have Dominic over,' she says, taking the container of melon Lux offers her and dropping it onto the kitchen island, and Lux shrugs, still half inside the fridge, but doesn't say anything else.

The tiles are cool beneath her bare feet, the air conditioning crisp and kind to her clammy skin. It calms her, at least a little, until her gaze catches on the clock above the stove, and she feels her belly twist with guilt. She tries to shake it. To refocus on the cuts on her palms instead, to slot her long nails into them like keys into locks, and when she does she pushes all the harder, until she can feel the thick, sticky ooze of blood against her fingertips all over again.

Fuck, she could use a cigarette.

She takes a deep breath, cheeks hollowing, like she's taking a drag already, and walks out of the room, ignoring Lux's humming from the fridge behind her.

She means to find her bag and her smokes, to go outside, only her steps slow in the hallway as she finds her attention snagged.

Along the wall is a mosaic of photographs. A family tree of sepia-toned wedding pictures of grandparents and great-grandparents, and happy, holidaying families stretched out across golden beaches. Of rainforest retreats and children's shows, reunions and a luau-themed fiftieth, and a girl in clean jodhpurs placing third at gymkhana.

There's a woman who can only be Lux's mother, young and fresh-faced in pink satin, a Miss Mermaid Beach '86 sash clipped across her shoulder. She smiles delicately at the camera, her white teeth crowded in her poised and modest mouth. Beside it is a wedding photograph, then one of little baby Lux outside a suburban chapel, pretty in her baptism best, then, again, older, all cream lace and frills at her holy communion. Another from her high-school formal, yet another from her graduation, then a posed group portrait of the good family Robinson, all stone-washed jeans and bleached shirts, their hair neatly parted, their arms locked.

It's all very perfect, Olive thinks, lifting one from its hook. She rubs her thumb across the edge of the plastic frame, the blood from her fingers marking up the cardboard backing. She swears, tries to rub it off, only to roughly re-hook the picture when she hears Lux approaching.

'Hey, Rabbit,' Lux calls, appearing in the kitchen doorway. She holds up two dusty bottles of champagne.

'Let's get fucked up.'

○

'Can anyone tell me the name of this technique?'

The class looks at her blankly, silent except for one student towards the back whose music they can all hear muffled but loud through poorly hidden headphones. Delia wipes the back of her neck with the collar of her shirt before continuing.

'It's not a trick question.'

The silence doesn't break, and Delia turns back to the blackboard, scribbles *ABC* in blue chalk. On her desk her phone vibrates, the screen flashing in bright pockets of colour. She resists the urge to rush.

'The Angle Based Constructive method, otherwise known as the ABC method. It's about using the science of angles and observation in art to recreate something exactly.'

Shauna – a big, pale girl with thin lips and a sharp, angular nose, good with acrylics – yawns, not even trying to cover it, and Delia feels a bubble of anger bob in her throat.

'CeCe, could you continue with the reading?'

CeCe – a small Korean girl, great with chalk and charcoal, best with anatomy – nods, picking up where Delia left off while Delia slides back into the chair behind her desk, checking her phone about as unsubtly as Shauna yawned. She scrolls through the messages: two from Saint Anne's, one from Ed. Four from Griff. There're none from the police station, and none from anyone resembling Charlie. Leaning back in her chair, she watches blankly as CeCe stumbles through the reading, and thinks about ending the class early when her phone lights up again, Shepherd Primary School's number blazing across the screen.

○

Brisbane sunsets aren't like the slow, sleepy things Benjamin's seen in movies. You can't sit at some make-out point and look into each other's eyes while the sky changes colours like a kaleidoscope being slowly turned. It's blink-and-you-miss-it. Bright sun, no sun. Like someone covering your eyes with both hands.

Blink, sun.

Blink, none.

Benjamin shivers, which is silly because it's not cold, and his fingers curl tighter at the neck of Spectacular Man, thumbing the ball of glue there. Beside him, Miss Kent yawns, folding her arms a little tighter around herself and flashing him a warm, tired smile.

'Not long now,' she tells him again, and Benjamin looks away. Miss Kent gave him a pair of shorts from lost property, but they were too big on him. He'd been so relieved there had been almost no one left at the school when it had happened. That surge of panic, that wet, warm line down the insides of his legs. He tightens his grip on the waistband of his not-his shorts.

The sound of an engine echoes down at the gateway of the schoolyard, a smear of yellow as the sun reflects off a windshield. Benjamin holds his Spectacular Man hand to his head, shielding his eyes and casting a man-shaped shadow across his features. Miss Kent stands up beside him, dropping a soft hand to his shoulder.

The car jerks to a stop in front of them, and the passenger door is thrown open to reveal his mother, a frazzled look on her face.

'Christ,' she says, and he lumbers forwards, clambering into the passenger seat. Miss Kent leans halfway in with him, her short brown hair shielding his face as she moves to buckle him in, her arm heaving forwards with the plastic bag containing his school shorts and underwear.

'Thanks so much,' his mum says, taking the bag from Miss Kent. 'I'm so sorry.'

Miss Kent just nods, gently squeezing Benjamin's shoulder in the process.

'It's okay,' is all she says. 'I'll see you tomorrow, Benjamin.'

She's gone barely a minute when he starts to cry, the

hot worm having grown in his gut from the moment he realised Olive wasn't coming, long after Poppy had left, till now, multiplying until there's lots of them, until they're all crawling beneath his skin and his eyelids. Mum's on him right away, unbuckling his seatbelt and pulling him half into her lap. The gear stick jams between them, digging into his leg, but Mum presses him closer, not caring if his wee gets on her because she's never cared if it gets on her, and Benjamin blubbers all the harder.

'I want Charlie,' he cries, and his mum holds him tighter, until there's almost no room between them.

He doesn't know how long they're there for, but she lets him go after a while and drives them home, the only sound between them Benjamin's uneasy, gasping breath and the faint chatter of talkback radio.

When they get home, his mum takes him straight up those creaky stairs and into the bathroom again, undressing him with a jerky hand before tossing his clothes in the corner and pushing him into the shower. She doesn't leave because she never does. She sits on the closed toilet seat, and he thinks she thinks he can't hear her crying over the noise of the shower, but he can.

O

She mops Benjamin up, and then herself.

Tears and piss and bluster, she rinses it all away for both of them. Off their skin and out of their clothes. Until they're both pinched raw and exhausted, a pair of loose nerves in the hot body of the evening.

Twice in three days is a lot, even for Benjamin, and she drops his soiled shorts into the same sink she'd soaked his other ones in the night before, letting the fabric balloon with water and Dettol. Her fingers knead the scratchy polyester until the stains are swallowed whole, the sour smell of urine subsiding beneath a faux tropical blend.

He'd stopped crying after the shower, but his face had still been blotchy, his capillaries firing with shame or grief or anger or some ugly mix of the three. Something too ugly for a boy so young, and Delia feels her own cheeks flush with a cocktail of the same. A mother should protect her son, but how can she protect him from his sister, from himself, from his missing brother? From the fucked-up leftovers of this fucked-up family? Was she like this when Bo—?

Delia shuts her eyes, fingers gripping the rim of the laundry sink. Inhales shakily, and blinks away the remnants of tears.

Was Rosie—?

Dinner.

She needs to organise dinner.

Standing taller, Delia steps out of the laundry and into the kitchen. She stumbles through it as if in a dream, pausing by the sink to look at the stark image of Charlie's telescope outside, half lit by the little hanging light beneath their raised house. The bees are out again tonight, floating quietly around the long legs of the instrument. She wonders what they've done today. Where they've been. What notes Charlie would've made about them.

It's no good to dwell, not right now. She leans over to flick the kitchen light on. Maybe just one of those casseroles from the neighbour would be enough tonight. Or maybe she should cook the steaks growing grey in the freezer, or the wrinkling eggplant in the crisper. She starts towards the fridge only to stop.

For a moment, she thinks that someone has attempted to make dinner ahead of her, leaving a mess behind in the process. That maybe Olive came home earlier and cooked, or – she thinks for one hopeful, golden second – maybe Charlie did.

She thinks this because there are tiny white flecks all across the floor, the size of grains of rice. So many that she's surprised she didn't see them before, and she's reaching for the broom when she sees one wriggle.

And oh, she thinks, gut clenching.

Maggots.

Once she sees the first, she sees them everywhere. Their lurching little bodies peeling out of the bin, having feasted on the remnants of the uncooked lamb from a few nights before, and across her kitchen floor, through to the hall, the living room, inching towards the bedrooms. The house is hot, bastard hot, and she strides over their wriggling bodies towards the bin, opening the lid with the intention of tearing out the garbage bag, only to have it erupt with fat-bottomed silver flies, their glossy wings catching the evening light, colliding with her raw skin.

Delia staggers backwards, her head throbbing. She drops to the floor, crouching, reaching a finger out to the first maggot she finds. She drops her weight against it until it explodes, its guts splattering across her floor.

'*Fuck*,' she hisses, balling her fist and slamming it into the maggot bodies, crushing them again and again and again. Their carcasses coating her hands, her anger echoing each time she slams her reddening fists against the hardwood floor of her home.

○

Her phone's buzzing. Violently, vibrantly against the floor of Lux's bedroom, against the white faux-fur rug sullied by patches of dust and dirt.

'When was the last time you washed this?' she asks, lifting the edge of the rug with her toes. Lux just shrugs, taking a swig of blush-pink champagne straight from the bottle.

'Like, a few months ago maybe? I don't know.'

The screen of Olive's phone goes black and she counts the beats before it lights back up again with her mother's number. Olive sent her a text a half hour ago – hadn't intended to, just hadn't quite been able to stomach the guilt of not picking Benjamin up. A simple *Something came up. Staying over at Lux's.* Her mother has replied with three phone calls and counting, none of which Olive has answered.

She brings her own champagne bottle to her lips, enjoying the light fizz in her mouth and down her throat, comforted by it in the dull light of Lux's room, which is a far cry from her own. All bright pink bedsheets and lush, soft throws. There are magenta feather boas, twinkling fairy lights and a Miss Pacific Fair sash wrapped around her headboard, a flurry of colour beneath the knotted mosquito net hanging over the top of it. The smell of caramel shortbread, oozing from a scented candle, suffuses the room, and the creamy walls are covered in posters of bug-eyed supermodels, baby-faced boy bands and galloping horses.

Sitting on her desk in the corner, Lux lights a cigarette, taking a long drag before flicking the ash off in a tray marked up with Barbie stickers.

'Are you going to answer that?'

Olive shrugs, pushing herself up on the mattress and taking another swig of champagne. A finger of guilt is twitching at her side, coiling itself around her calves, but she stifles it as best she can, asking Lux instead about the new girl at work.

The phone calls don't stop, though, and every new ring leaves Olive gulping down larger mouthfuls of champagne. Leaves her talking more loudly, more earnestly, tapping her tired foot faster and faster on the floor.

'Fuck, man, just answer,' Lux says after the eighth phone call, and finally Olive grabs her phone and does.

'Hey,' she starts, but her mother's voice cuts over the top. Quick as a slap.

'What were you *thinking*?'

Olive flushes, foot tapping faster still, looking sideways at Lux, who is watching Olive with deceptive disinterest. She gets to her feet, walks to Lux's en suite and closes the door behind her.

'Nothing, I guess.'

'Do you think this is a joke?' Delia hisses, the line crackling between them, and Olive can feel the heat rising through her chest, scratching at the walls of her throat. She drops to the floor of the bathroom, the tiles cool beneath her bare thighs. 'Benjamin could've—Charlie's—'

And she can't say it. None of them can. None of them can pry these words from their mouth, and Olive can feel her hand shaking, the back of her neck damp, making her hair frizz. She can feel the righteous anger, too, an untapped well in the rotting earth of her.

'What, Mum?' Olive asks. 'Charlie's what?'

She's met with a heavy, tense silence, and it quickly makes her lose steam, makes her knock her battered fist once, twice, three times into the tiles beneath her.

'Come home, Olive,' is all her mother says before hanging up. The silence is sudden and louder than it should be, and Olive's fists slow their beating. Her mother is right, of course she's right. Benjamin could've—

Olive throws her phone hard into the wall and the screen splinters into a hundred little pieces. Somewhere in the distance, on the other side of the door, Lux calls her name, but Olive ignores her. She curls up, the champagne churning in her belly, acidic in her throat, her crescent-moon cuts leaving bloody smears on the perfect tiles of Lux's bathroom floor.

O

It takes her a moment to get a hold of herself, her body still caked in maggot remains, the pressure still building behind her tired eyes as she drops her phone back to the kitchen counter.

If Benjamin's heard a thing, he has the sense not to come

out of his bedroom, and she's glad for it. Relieved, at least in the moment, for the privacy of the darkness and quiet.

She knots off the last garbage bag of maggot carcasses and ducks out the back door, heading towards the wheelie bin in the yard. It had taken her the better part of an hour to get rid of all the maggots, and she'd sworn herself blue as she'd crushed them, ridding her kitchen of the infestation as best she could, only to step outside into a new one. The sloping brown shells of beetles glow up at her from the wild grass, the hum of hordes of cicadas thrumming through her head, reminding her there's no corner they aren't waiting behind.

She dumps the bag in the bin and then turns her attention to her hands, scraping the guts out from beneath her nails and flicking them straight into the trash. The birds form a cacophony above her, shrill lorikeets and hooting owls, the eerie cries of bush stone-curlews. Delia searches for them, but all she can see is their effect – the rustling leaves, the swaying branches, the shadows they cast across her untamed yard. It's almost peaceful for a moment, but it's all lost when a dog barks.

Loud, close.

Delia turns to see a heavy-set Alsatian, its long snout pushing through the rotting slats of her garden fence. Its body ripples with strength, and with every bark the birds get louder, fearless beneath the cover of night.

The dog's owner, a slight woman with ropey legs and a sunken chest, tries to pull the beast back, but it's no good. Delia has barely had a chance to yell when the dog breaks free of its owner, forcing its way through the fence and bolting into the yard.

'Jazz!' the girl calls, pushing through behind the dog, and Delia watches her fighting the long grass as she chases after it.

The dog does a wonky lap of the yard before galloping over to Charlie's telescope, barking wildly, its tail swinging in frantic figure eights.

'I'm so sorry, oh my god,' the girl stutters, seeing Delia. She grabs the dog's leash and tries to tug it away, but it's no use – it is growling at something unseen, its dark marble eyes fixed on the back of the house, and Delia closes in behind it, curious, looking at Charlie's telescope, the floating bees, the small, swinging light that hangs beneath the awning.

The dog looks at its owner suddenly, briefly, before turning back to the previous spot, its rumbling growl softening beneath the screeching of the birds.

The girl, still clutching at the dog's leash, looks disturbed, and her free hand hovers in the air uncertainly while Delia walks around to get a better look at the dog. Its teeth are bared, large, sharp things, but in almost a heartbeat it wavers in its resolve. Its eyes slip shut, its tongue lolls, its jaw unclenches. It shivers, turning to look up at its owner again before trotting off back down and out of the yard.

The girl apologises again, desperately earnest, then quickly leaves, and Delia watches her go before turning back to the telescope and the shadowed hollow beneath their house. To the swinging light and the bees and the wide, empty space there. Something in it makes her shiver, as if a whisper of wind has found its way to where she's standing. Pull yourself together, she thinks, scrubbing her maggoty hands on her slacks. The bees drift closer, the bird calls get louder, and she's not sure what makes her do it, but she grabs Charlie's telescope before she can stop herself. She jerks it backwards until it's beneath the house, out of sight, and lowers it to the dusty ground, away from the wild things that would try to claim it.

6

'Do you use grids?'

The girl grimaces and shakes her head, sweat pearling at her hairline in a way that makes Delia too aware of herself, of the way her own hair curls at the back of her neck, the swampy feel at her armpits, her lower back. She clears her throat as a distraction as much as anything, grabbing a sheet of tracing paper and her ruler.

'Here.'

Measuring the page, Delia divides it up – six squares across, six squares down – before placing it neatly over the girl's drawing. It's not a bad sketch, some lonely suburban street, but it lacks depth and the perspective is off. Delia tells her this and watches the colour bleed across the girl's skin, from the point of her nose to the dipping neck of her shirt.

'You've been practising?'

The girl nods, and Delia's pencil makes quick work on the tracing paper, righting the slant, the scale, the shading that angles the lurching gum trees so strangely. It's an easy practice. The shadow of an old habit, and out of the corner of her eye she can see the girl watching with wide eyes, her cheeks flushed, her throat quivering in embarrassment or admiration, Delia doesn't really care to know.

'When you're drawing so precisely from life like this, what you're seeing – what you're trying to capture – it can be distracting. You want your audience to see the whole, so you focus on drawing the whole. You treat the picture like it's one image, but nothing's just one thing. Look.' Delia's pencil traces the tree, shades in the shadows left by twisting branches, fills in the sheets of peeling paperbark. 'No picture starts finished. Forget the final product and home in on the individual details. Think about the look the pebbles have left on the long path, the trees that have been there for years, the saplings just starting to grow. Think about the dry grass and the clear sky. You don't build a picture, try to think of it instead as a scene. Like you're capturing a memory for the person looking at it. Something that might resonate with them.'

Her pencil skirts the sky, flicks lines of motion, a dog's wagging tail and a lip raised to reveal pointed teeth. Shades in a sharp eye and trains it on something nobody else can see.

'Gridding can be a good place to start. To help you break down the picture you want into a series of smaller ones, and—'

There's a sudden movement, and Delia looks up to see the girl's fingers swiping at glassy eyes, her pink cheeks mottling, and oh, Delia thinks.

It was embarrassment after all.

Something in Delia's chest burns in sympathy, and she slips on her most placating smile, pulling off her tracing paper and passing the girl's work back untouched.

'You really are close,' she offers. 'We'll get you there.'

With a nervous hand, the girl takes back her sketch, her pencil, and finds her way back to a clutch of students at the far end of the room, their heads bowed together, mouths working fast. Delia pinches the neck of her blouse, pulling it free from her sweat-slick chest, and lets her gaze return to the dog she's drawn before scrunching up the tracing paper, balling it tight in her fist. Despite herself, she can still feel the crush of the maggots beneath her nails from last night. Can't quite shake the way their worming bodies invaded her home, her space, the memory of them holding fast to her body.

Sitting up a little taller, Delia focuses on the class. The practical workshops are both easier and harder than the lectures – Delia doesn't have to stand before the dead-eyed gazes of her juniors, talking foreshortening and through lines and motion, but instead has to sit and watch many of them do what she hasn't been able to do herself in years. Not really. Has to watch them fumble with pencils, charcoal, paint, impasto. Watch them mark up their skin better than the canvas. Watch them—

A hand slaps down on her desk.

'Hey, could I get you to have a look at something?'

Sometimes, she wonders what it is about Griff.

Wonders now in particular, as he stands boldly in front of her, his shaggy black curls unwashed and his grin a little too knowing, too smug, too *young*.

Wonders what made it so easy that first time, at the end of last term, to fall into this thing with him, but then again maybe the answer isn't that complicated.

Arching an eyebrow, Delia tilts her head, gesturing for him to put his sketchbook down on her desk, and Griff does so eagerly.

'I'm playing with this set for my final folio, but it'd be great to get your opinion now before I commit to it.'

There's an edge to his voice, something baited, and he flips casually through a few pages of strangers on trains and inky musicians and even an alien-looking grevillea bloom, and Delia's not expecting anything but somehow she's unsurprised when he stops on a sketch of a woman.

Barely a woman, really.

A girl a little older than Olive, but different in shape – short and bosomy – and Delia knows her vaguely from one of her second-year classes. She's nude, which is perhaps the least surprising thing of all, pretty in the way Griff has drawn her, all curves, soft shadows and hooded bedroom eyes. Delia sifts her memories for a name, but can't quite nail one down – Marguerite or Marielle, she thinks. Some grandiose French name Pygmalioning a working-class Australian girl.

Raising her eyebrows again, Delia glances back up at Griff, to where his lips are still curved in that smug little grin, only there's a new sort of set to it now. It's matched by inquisitive eyes, searching for a reaction, his fingers drumming on her desk as he waits, and stupid, Delia thinks.

The image of Griff's face when she'd dismissed him the other day forms quickly in her mind, and she resists the urge to bury her face in her hands.

'It's looking pretty good to me,' she tells him dryly instead, and Griff blinks hard, mandible working, eyes darting a little more desperately over her face, and after a minute he leans forwards and drops a finger to the drawn girl's leg.

'You can see it there,' he says, and it *is* there. The strange angle of a knee cap. A joint underdrawn. Something he's better than, and for a brief moment she appreciates the faux sincerity he has come over with.

She watches the way his soft skin catches the light from the open windows, the brief ruffle of hot wind mussing his hair. Behind him, the class titters quietly around the scratching of pencils and the mixing of acrylics, and Delia thinks about home. She thinks about the trip to Saint Anne's she needs to make, the call to Ed, about anxious Benjamin and surly Olive, and she thinks about Charlie. Her gut lurches, her hands twitch. She clears her throat.

'You just need to spend a little more time with it, I think.'

She closes the sketchbook and pushes it back towards him across her desk, adding:

'Maybe take another look at the model and try again.'

She loads the words. Arms them, and she sees it – the exact moment they hit him, break the skin, and it pulls something in her, the way he looks at her. He clenches his jaw, and Delia sets her own in reply.

'Maybe a different model,' he says, and Delia shrugs.

'If you want.'

With that, Griff grabs the sketchbook, walking with hard and heavy steps to the back of the classroom, a few students swapping knowing looks behind him, and right, Delia thinks, heart hammering in her head, glancing down at her hands only to pause. She blinks, turning them over, spotting a

strange lump below one of her nails – a small, white ball –
half a maggot's body, curled there like an omen.

O

The fence sags, lurching Benjamin's body forwards.

'Who's picking you up today?' Poppy asks, tossing her
backpack to the grass at their feet and leaning heavily into the
fence beside him. Her hair's tangled and sunburn glows pink
down her nose, but Benjamin just shrugs, looking back at the
road, the hot worm wriggling between his shoulder blades.

'My sister.'

His voice wobbles a little as he says it, and he can't help it.
Mum had promised Olive would be here today, but he doesn't
think Olive even listens to Mum that much anymore, and
maybe it's better if she doesn't come. Maybe he doesn't want
her to. Or – no. He does. Just maybe if he tells himself she's
not coming then he won't freak out again, and if he doesn't
freak out he won't have an accident, and if he doesn't have an
accident then maybe Mum won't be so upset tonight.

Won't—

He frowns, the sound her fists made on the floor last night
echoing through his head again. The hot worm wriggles into
his chest.

'I *knew* you had a sister,' Poppy crows beside him, and
Benjamin casts her a sideways look. 'I have sisters too! Five of
them. It's a lot, but two of them are twins so sometimes it only
feels like four sisters.'

'That's a lot of sisters,' Benjamin agrees, absent-mindedly.
A cyclist goes by and his gaze lingers.

'Is everyone in your family always late?'

The question makes Benjamin jerk his head back in surprise, to turn on the spot to scowl at Poppy.

'Is everyone in *yours*?'

And his tone is hard, *mean*, but Poppy just shrugs, unbothered, dropping her head into the wire until her hair tangles up there too.

'My dad isn't going to be here for another hour and a half. I'm supposed to be at brass-band practice, but I didn't want to go today.'

A plane veers overhead, drowning out the bustle of the afternoon, but as soon as it's on its way the clamour all comes back. Parents yelling and waving while school kids play on the footpath and show each other TikToks on their phones and YouTube videos on their laptops. A boy plays hacky sack with himself, teetering at the edge of the road, while a teacher storms towards him from the school steps.

'Aren't you going to ask me why I didn't want to go?'

Benjamin sighs, turning around against the fence to meet Poppy's gaze.

'Why didn't you want to go today?'

Poppy's face breaks into a wide, toothy grin.

'It's a secret.'

Groaning, Benjamin turns back towards the road, eyeing the smooth line of it, waiting for the sound of a bike. He rode his own to school today, Mum walking at his side. She'd had a late start, which means she'll have a late finish, which means it'll just be him and Olive. His fingers tighten in the wire fence, and he can feel it, the way Poppy's gaze lingers on his face. He turns his away.

'Is your brother still missing?'

He almost tells her it's a secret, meets her game with more of it, but he's nothing if not honest, and the thought of Charlie sits like a stone in his hollow belly.

'Yeah.'

Poppy seems to take this in, spinning so that she sinks into the wire fence, dipping the meshing backwards and pulling Benjamin forwards in the process.

'Where do you think he is?'

'What?'

'Where do you think he is?' she repeats. 'He's missing, right? Not like – not like stolen or nothing. So he might've run away somewhere close. Sometimes my oldest sister goes away for a couple of days and my dad always *freaks out*, but she's usually got a secret boyfriend, or once she told me she just wanted to go on an adventure. But she's usually close by.'

Benjamin frowns, not quite convinced of Poppy's logic. He turns over her words, considering them. Charlie *could* be close. He could. But he'd tell them – Charlie would. Benjamin *knows* he would.

Wouldn't he?

'I don't know.'

'Well, where have you looked?'

'What?'

Poppy sighs, exasperated, pushing her hands into the air in a big display of frustration. Benjamin can feel the tops of his ears pink.

'Where have you looked?' she repeats, and Benjamin pauses, searching for any inflection or strangeness to Poppy. Any hint of a joke in the question.

'The police are looking,' he tells her, and Poppy huffs.

'What do the police know? You're his brother. I'd know exactly where to look for *all* my sisters. For Tiff, I'd look at Mr Fitz's ice cream place, or the cubby beneath the slide at Minnippi Park, or for Margot I'd look in every bookstore in every town, or Isles – she's my oldest sister – she's usually at Angus's or that place between the powerlines and the pony club on the big road near home.'

Somewhere above them a bird calls. A crow, he thinks, something loud and braying. Charlie would've liked that. Would've tried to find it and written down its location, the time, the sound in the pages of his notebook, and then tried to find the same bird every day after to work out its habits. Benjamin's mouth is suddenly very, very dry.

'What if he's not in any place?'

Poppy considers this, rocking her head from side to side before she stops and looks straight back at him.

'Well, what if he is?'

O

She wakes to the sound of her phone alarm crescendoing in the half-light of Lux's bedroom. A bony hand feebly slaps her chest.

'Oh my god,' Lux groans. 'Olive, turn it *off*.'

Olive makes a vague sound of concession in the back of her dry throat as she blinks awake. The air conditioner has left her chilled, forcing her beneath Lux's heavy doona, and it's a relief to be able to burrow into something instead of trying to burrow out. There's a hangover drumming at her temples already, the mothy aftertaste of champagne and vodka coating the back of her teeth. Her eyes ache, even with the blackout curtains protecting her.

She rolls over, steps out from beneath the warmth of the doona, ducks beneath the mosquito net and stumbles over to the dresser to grab her phone.

'*Fuck*,' she hisses, the words *pick up banjo* blaring at her behind the heavily cracked screen. How's it almost four already?

'Fuck's right,' Lux groans behind her. 'I feel like I've been skull-fucked from the inside.'

Olive ignores her, staggering forwards to pull off the nightshirt Lux lent her and jerk on her work slacks, her O'Malley's shirt, her shoes, while Lux sits up properly on the bed behind her.

'I didn't think you had work today.'

'I don't. I'm supposed to pick up my brother from school.'

'So? You didn't yesterday. He made it home okay.'

And she didn't. Knows that he *did*, but the seed of guilt in her is planted deep, unaffected even by the weed and the vodka. She shakes her head, then her hair, hoping it might get the smell of smoke out.

'You heard my mum over the phone last night,' Olive says. 'She went batshit.'

Lux snorts, flopping back onto the bed. She wriggles down beneath the blankets, and Olive looks at her, feeling a stab of envy deep in her gut. She's turning on her heel to leave when Lux's voice calls out behind her.

'You could stay, you know.'

'No, I can't, I just said—'

'No, I mean, like, you could drop your brother at home and then come back. My parents won't care.'

Olive looks back to see Lux playing with her hair. The blue is vibrant at her fingers, wrapped around her knuckles, and something about it makes Olive want to reach over to untangle Lux's fingers from it. It's an image, is all. The look of Lux in her king-size bed, sprawled in soft pink sheets, her teeth stained from cigarettes, her body sharp and coy all at once.

Something tightens in Olive's belly, and she looks away from Lux, looks over her head to the posters of horses and Harry Styles, to the knotted mosquito net and the twinkling fairy lights, and they look like stars, she thinks, and then she thinks of Charlie.

'Whatever,' Lux says. 'Don't overthink it. I mean, like, I don't care or anything. I just thought you might've wanted a break from the harpy.'

The vibrations echo against the mattress, and Lux flops over and grabs her phone from beneath her pillow. She swipes, her fingers working fast across the screen, and then she's laughing at something someone else has sent her, and typing out a quick reply.

'I'll see you later then,' Olive says, toeing into her shoes and grabbing her bag off the floor. She turns briefly back to Lux, expecting what, she's not sure, and when she gets nothing in reply she disappears out the door.

Griff doesn't talk to her for the rest of the class, which is probably as much of a blessing as Delia can really count for herself right now. It doesn't stop him from looking, though, watching, his pale eyes fixed on her, his lips set into what Delia can only describe as a pout. The friend at his elbow, shorter, fairer, better at capturing motion, leans forwards at one stage to whisper frenetically in Griff's ear, his eyes dogging Delia as she surreptitiously unlocks her phone beneath her desk.

She's rescued by the end of the class, by the scraping of chairs against the floor and the new surge in conversation.

'I'll be checking progress next week,' Delia calls when the back door bangs open, the students starting to leave. 'This is your final year here. You should be starting to gather work for your folios and thinking about a thematic through line. If you're not yet, you're behind.'

No one acknowledges her, not her words, not her tone, so Delia gathers her things, forcing them down into the mouth of her briefcase. When she looks up, it's to see only Griff, lingering in the open doorway, his folio tucked beneath his arm, his eyes fixed, unblinking, on her. She meets his gaze, waits for him to say something, but after a minute he just raps his knuckles against the doorframe and disappears down the hall.

Delia drops her hands to her hips, her chin to her chest, until the tendons in her neck pull tight. The noise from the hallway is muted somehow, stifled by the walls between her and them, and it lends itself to numbness. She pushes a hand to her chest, feels the sag of her ageing skin, the brittle plates of her bones. She feels—

'Delia, would you mind if we had a word?'

Dr Truss, the head of the department, is a stocky woman with a sleek silver pixie cut and a penchant for junk jewellery. She has a quiet look on her face, her thin lips over-lined, her thick-rimmed glasses smudged.

'Of course,' Delia says. 'We can go back to my office.'

'No, here's fine. It's nothing so formal.'

Delia nods, sitting back down behind her desk and watching carefully as Truss pulls up one of the student chairs and sits down opposite her. It takes Truss a while to settle, to stop fidgeting on her seat, crossing and recrossing her legs, enough time for unease to prickle beneath Delia's skin. Truss waves her hands in the air, as if to accompany words she doesn't say, before dropping them down into her lap.

'I don't quite know where to start,' she says after a moment. 'A few things have been brought to my attention in the last couple of days, but none as concerning as the news of your son.'

Delia blinks heavily, until she can feel her sweaty lashes starting to stitch together. Until she can feel that tension pulling at her neck again, even without the stretch.

'I just want you to know that the college is one hundred per cent on board with whatever you need during this time. If you need to take time off—'

'No,' Delia says quickly, curtly, her toes curling in her battered shoes. She deliberately, consciously uncurls them. Takes a breath. Puts on her morning-show smile. 'I'd really rather stay at the school. The distraction, you know …'

Truss looks at her appraisingly, as if Delia's a puzzle she can't quite figure out. Something to work over, time and time again. Out in the hall, Delia hears the squeak of shoes on linoleum, a group of students laugh, a door bang shut, before Truss finally clears her throat.

'Okay,' she says. 'Good. I'm glad the college is able to provide a safe space for you during this difficult time.'

It's the way she says it, *safe space*, that gives Delia pause. That works its way unhappily into her head. Like the memory of the maggots still caught beneath her nails.

She blinks and she sees Charlie.

She blinks and – throat tightening – she sees Bo.

Delia rolls her shoulders back, pushing the images from her mind.

'I appreciate your concern, Sandra, but honestly, I'm okay. As okay as I can be, rather. We're in regular talks with the police still, and they are not *not* positive, even as time's ticking on, so to speak. He's sixteen, you know, so he might've just fallen in with a crowd, it really could be anything at this stage.'

She says it as if she believes it. As if Charlie's ever given her a reason not to trust him (but he *has*, she reminds herself bleakly – Andy had been grounded), and Truss nods again, rising from her chair. She drops a hand to Delia's shoulder across the desk, squeezing until her fingers pinch around the bone, before releasing her. She starts towards the exit, turning briefly at the door.

'Just one more thing, Delia. A couple of the tutors have heard, ah, rumblings, about you and a student. Adam

Griffith. I would not wish to instruct you on how to act in this difficult time, but I would urge you to refamiliarise yourself with the college's code of conduct.'

Huh, Delia thinks wryly, but she nods all the same.

The muggy afternoon is thick with insects – long-legged midges and swollen mosquitoes, tiny fruit flies, all with whirring wings and groping feelers. Benjamin swats them from his sweating neck, beats his legs faster on the pedals to try to hustle through these suburban backstreets. Poppy presses herself against his back, kneeling against the seat while he hovers somewhere above her, pushing forwards on the bike.

This far east of Brisbane, the suburbs start to slope. To blend into each other like a flip book, and Benjamin can only pedal faster on the bike to turn those pages quicker. They've checked the library, the community garden where Charlie likes to collect samples and make notes on birds, snakes or insects, the computer store on Bennett Road, and the corner store near home. Benjamin wants to check the planetarium, but you have to buy a ticket; the museum, but it's too far to go by bike. It means there's only one more place he *can* look.

Behind him, Poppy clings tighter to his shoulders, her bony fingers digging into his joints, and tighter still when he finally slows to a stop. He lets her hop off the bike first, and then drops it, walking quickly up the steep hill of the lookout.

'Where are we?' Poppy asks, and Benjamin bounds up another few steps.

'Hovell lookout. It's supposed to be the best place around here to look at space. It's Charlie's favourite spot, since he decided he wanted to be an astronaut.'

'Did he always want to be an astronaut?'

Benjamin puffs his cheeks out as he walks, his gaze fixed ahead.

'He's wanted to be an astronaut for a long time, I don't know if always though. Like, he doesn't just like space. He likes knowing a lot of things about a lot of things, and he likes knowing things first, and I think that's half the reason he likes space so much. Because there's so much that he can learn before anyone else.'

There's silence from Poppy then, like she's thinking about it, and all Benjamin can hear are her short huffs as she hikes beside him.

'That's a weird thing to like,' she says after a minute.

'What is?'

'Knowing things before anyone else. Do you like that?'

Benjamin shrugs.

'I don't know. I don't really mind. I like knowing things, but I don't think it bothers me when I know it so much.'

Around them, the park is bustling with people. With joggers and dog walkers and mothers and fathers pushing red-faced babies in heavy-looking prams. The smell of sausages on a barbecue meets his nose, then the stagnant creek water, the loose, uneasy smell of whatever flowers are able to bloom in this heat, acidic almost to the taste.

'My mum's like that, you know. Like your brother, I mean. She's a lawyer, and she definitely likes knowing things first.'

Benjamin laughs, scrunching up his nose.

'I think it'd be important if you were a lawyer though.'

'Yeah, I guess. What's your mum do?'

'She's an art teacher at a college. She used to be a painter though. She used to do shows in galleries and win prizes and stuff too, but she doesn't really do it that much anymore.'

Poppy gasps, excitedly grabbing Benjamin's arm so that he has to stop and turn around to face her.

'A painter! As her job?'

Benjamin nods, but shrugs, feeling oddly bashful.

'I don't really remember when she did it. I think I was too little. Like, I can kind of remember her painting, but it was a long time ago. She just teaches now.'

Poppy's quiet for a minute again, that thoughtful look returning to her face.

'I don't think that's something you can un-become though,' she says. 'Like, I think I'll always be a musician because I'll always know how to play the trumpet, even if I don't do it anymore.'

Benjamin considers this, pulling his arm gently from Poppy's grip. They can't be too far from the lookout now. The trees are starting to thicken to the sides, and the people are thinning out. The sounds of the roads are disappearing too, the horns and the traffic giving way to magpie songs and thrumming cicadas and the whistle and lash of a whipbird. It's close. Benjamin's pulse starts to quicken.

'What about your dad?' he asks, trying to slow his rabbit heart, and Poppy looks down, staring at her feet as she walks.

'He used to be an engineer, but he stays home with us now most of the time.'

In the distance, he can see the long neck of a telescope, the lens directed up towards the sky. There's a body there too, fiddling with the focuser, and before Benjamin can get a proper look he's running, heart in his throat, Poppy calling his name behind him. The body is tall, thin, with a tangle of dark curls, and it tugs at the collar of its shirt, like Charlie does, and it stands hunched and shadowed, like Charlie stands, and Benjamin can taste the relief and the excitement and the desperate need and *please, please, please*. He grabs the body's arm, pulling it only to be met with a stranger's face.

Benjamin steps quickly back.

'Sorry,' he says. 'I thought you were someone else.'

The stranger nods, his startled look smoothing over. He looks back at his telescope, and Benjamin just stands there, frozen, unsure of what to do or say or where to go. He wishes he hadn't left Spectacular Man in his bag. He wishes he had him here, in his hands, something to curl his aching fingers around.

It's not long before Poppy is beside him again, and the news that this man is not Charlie must be all over his face, because Poppy strides forwards, tugs on the man's arm, and says, 'We're looking for a boy called Charlie Rabbit.'

The stranger looks just as startled as before, his face riddled with confusion. He tries for a placating smile.

'Sorry. It's just been me today.'

'Thanks anyway,' Poppy says. She walks over to Benjamin, and before she can say a thing he's turning on his heel and running, faster, faster, down the hill, until the momentum propels him forwards as much as his legs. Until the hot wind whips at his face and he can't tell if his eyes are watering from the pressure of it or if it's tears again. All he knows is he wants to leave. Wants to be as far away from all these spots as possible, every dumb and stupid place that holds Charlie in its memory but no Charlie. Somewhere in the distance he can hear Poppy, hear her shouting his name and her quick feet following him, and a better boy would wait for her, would let her catch up, but he's not a better boy, and he cannot find his brother.

The end of the hill comes quickly into view, and he means to slow, he does, but he trips instead, tumbling down the last few steps until his legs are skinned by the hard, drought-ridden ground and the grass stains his skin. He'll have bruises tomorrow, he knows, but he finds it hard to care as he lies down on the grass and tries to catch his winded breath.

A head appears above him, a cape of blonde hair, blisteringly bright beneath the afternoon sun.

'Ben?'

Benjamin rolls over, until he's lying face first in the grass, the undergrowth prickling his sweating skin.

'There are other places he could be. You said before, we could try the museum or the planetarium. I can get my sister to take us on the weekend.'

'This is dumb,' he whispers, his face pressed so hard against the earth he gets a mouthful of grass. 'This is so dumb.'

He rolls back over to see Poppy's earnest, worried face, and he's the one who's dumb. She's been so nice.

'Yeah, we could try that,' he says quietly, aiming for a smile. 'I should probably take you back to school now though. You don't want your dad to worry.'

Poppy tentatively nods before holding out a hand to help Benjamin up.

○

It takes her longer to get to the school than she'd thought. Lux's house is in a suburb beyond Shepherd, but it might as well be another planet to Olive's internal cartographer. She gets lost down foreign roads and causeways, taking wrong turns and exits, before finally finding her way onto the main road leading towards Benjamin's school.

The afternoon sun bleeds out behind the building and peels through the tall paperbark gums. She drops her bike by the entrance and hurries through the gates, eyeing off the remaining school kids, all blustering out the doors and stinking from after-school sports or dance rehearsals. Olive surveys them all, searching their round, moonish faces for any sign of Benjamin. He's not in the main grounds or behind the school with the huddle of teachers, clutched together hiding cigarettes, their eyes locked on the ground. She tries the east pick-up zone, then the south one, her heart starting to thud in her narrow chest.

He's not here. That much is clear. There are only so many spots where a kid can sit and wait in this place, and Olive remembers them all from long afternoons playing tennis or soccer here in her childhood. Remembers every game and dirty, scratched-up knee, but the only games Benjamin plays involve superheroes, and Olive can't think of a friend he might have run off with in the afternoon heat.

So he's gone home, she tells herself, her legs twitching

beneath her as she heads back towards the entrance, picking up her step. He's walked home alone and she'll get there and he'll be mad, but then he'll see that she really did go. That she did mean to pick him up today, and it'll be enough to make him grin up at her, shy and sweet, and it'll be okay. It'll be okay, it'll be okay, it'll be okay.

The hot air whips past her ears as she picks up speed, weaving her bike between the afternoon traffic, hair growing swampy in her helmet. The setting sun singes the back of her neck, her bare arms, the tops of her feet. She's burning up, sheening with sweat, and she wonders if she shines with it.

Her legs are aching by the time she gets home, kicking off her bike and dropping it into the wild grass of their yard. She bounds up the front steps, fumbling with the keys in the back pocket of her slacks and pushing into the house.

With the lights off and most of the curtains drawn, it looks dusky at best, shadowed and untouched. Mum and Benjamin's breakfast dishes are stacked by the sink, but there's a plate of half-eaten leftovers on the counter, covered in flies. The ironing board is still out, a basket of her mother's wrinkled work shirts and Benjamin's school ones propped beneath it. Olive throws her bag onto the kitchen island and calls Benjamin's name.

When no one answers, she calls again, trying to calm her nerves, ducking through the living room and down the hall, all the way to the furthest end. She checks Delia's room, then the bathroom, even her own room, before turning in their narrow corridor to face Benjamin and Charlie's door. With a trembling hand, she pushes it open.

Has she stepped inside since Charlie disappeared? She doesn't think she has, and she's oddly relieved to see that Delia has put away his uniform, and that Benjamin's is gone too (because he's wearing it, she hopes, prays, begs). There's no Charlie here now, of course, and no Benjamin either, she realises with rising anxiety. She takes a slow, hesitant step inside, staring at Charlie's mussed sheets, at his planet diorama and star wheel, at *How the Universe Got Its Spots* left dog-eared and broken-spined on his bedside table. She pulls her gaze away to look over at Benjamin's side instead, at the stacks of comic books and action figures and half-finished homework shoved up around his bed, and she inhales shakily, digs her nails back into those crescent cuts and tries to ignore the ache in her chest.

Then, a touch at her elbow.

Olive's eyes snap open, and she spins around, ready to yell, to lash out, only there's nothing there: not a thing behind her but Charlie's bed and books and styrofoam planets and all those nothing things she never bothered to ask him about. She rubs at her arm, shaking her head, trying to clear her heavy throat. There's a hot pressure building behind her eyes, leaving her lashes damp, and she's got to find Benjamin, *has* to, can't bear the thought of him being gone too.

She's still thinking this when she hears the gate unlatch outside, and she propels herself to the window to look out, and there, coming through the gate, covered in dirt and grass stains, is Benjamin. Relief bellows through her, quick as a shot, followed by a heady chaser of anger, and then she's striding through the house and down the back steps.

Benjamin's only just locking his bike to the fence when she's on him, grabbing his arm hard enough to bruise it, and yanking him towards her.

'Olive!' he yells, but she doesn't care. Not now. Not with the anger or the adrenaline scoring up beneath it. Somewhere in the back of her mind, she thinks about their neighbours. About their mother, who could get out of work early and show up here instead, armed with a whole new stack of reasons to hate Olive, but still. She jerks Benjamin's arm harder, pulling him fully into the yard.

He wriggles free of her, and she lets him.

'Where were you?' she bites, and he stares up at her, his cheeks flushed, his body bruised.

'I was looking for Charlie.'

He says it like it's the most obvious thing in the world, and his voice has never sounded younger.

'*What?*'

'I was looking for Charlie.'

'What?' she repeats, gaze darting over him as she rears back. 'The police are doing that.'

'That doesn't mean we can't too.'

Somewhere above them a bird calls. One Olive doesn't recognise, some low and strident sound. It takes her out of the moment, out of her anger. It's as if she's watching a television show that she thought she was starring in, only to see Benjamin's precocious child star take the lead. She drops her arms, rocks back on her heels, scavenging for that rotting anger she can never quite be rid of.

'You can't go off on your own like that, Benjamin, it's dangerous.'

The hypocrisy isn't lost on her, nor, apparently, is it lost on Benjamin, whose eyes spark dangerously as he stands to his full height.

'And what? Sitting around waiting for you to not show up isn't?'

Olive tears her gaze away, frustration and guilt mixing in her gut. She looks back towards the house, then around to Charlie's telescope, which is only a foot or two away and seems to have been knocked somehow to point right at them. She rubs at her face, looks up at the endless blue sky, tries to calm herself down.

'Where'd you even go?' she asks the world above them, and she means the words for Benjamin, she *does*, but also—

God.

'To the park and the library, and then to the lookout.'

His tone is softer then, and Olive drops her head back to take him in, her eyebrows raised.

'The lookout? What, you think he's sitting somewhere looking at the stars for days?'

'I don't know. Maybe. I don't know where he is.'

Olive scoffs derisively, before she can help it, and it seems to trigger something in Benjamin, leaves him baulking, his throat visibly constricting.

'At least I'm trying to find him,' he growls. 'It's more than you're doing.'

'He's gone!' Olive yells, her arms spread wide, all her bottled anger, her stoppered grief, bubbling over. Because he is, and it's just like *Dad*. Fucked off amid false promises, only it's worse because at least she knows where her dad is, and she turns on the spot, swinging an arm around deliberately to hit the hinge of Charlie's telescope, to make it fold in on itself and collapse against the ground, but the movement doesn't exactly work. The hive in the joint makes the legs stick out at strange angles like broken limbs, the bees erupting from the middle. One stings her leg and she curses, loud over those strange birds, loud enough that had she not been listening she might have missed Benjamin's next words altogether.

'I hate you,' he hisses. 'I wish it was you that went. *I wish it was you.*'

Olive spins back to face him, snapping her mouth open to reply, but she doesn't get the chance: Benjamin is running away from her, up the stairs to the house, and slamming the door shut behind him.

7

He should let it go.

That's what Charlie would do.

Charlie would let this go. He would put on his best Charlie Rabbit grin, complete with an eye roll, with dimples, with the shake of his head. *Olive's just Olive*, that's what he'd say, just as he did when Olive called Benjamin the *save the marriage baby* or whenever she yelled at him for being in her way or in her room or in her space. Whenever Olive found anything in Benjamin that she didn't like.

He growls a little at the thought, swinging back up to his feet, pacing the floor of his bedroom. He can hear Olive in the yard still. Hear her kick Charlie's telescope again, and then he can smell the smoke from her cigarette, lifting through the cracks in his bedroom floorboards.

He feels heavy.

Or maybe it's not just him, because the heaviness is all around him, not just *in* him, and he feels it at his back, at his shoulders, as if someone's leaning on him or against him, and he's left trying to wriggle out from beneath it. From within it. His heart is pounding so loudly he can hear it in his ears, rapid-fire, and he walks. He walks and walks and walks, around in circles, squares, diagonal lines, in this little hollow in their little room, and he scrambles for anything in his head that might make him feel better. Not his mother, not school, not Jodi, not Poppy, not his dad.

Charlie.

It always comes back to Charlie.

Benjamin crosses the imagined line between his own and his brother's half of the room. He walks towards the shelves lined with books on galaxies and outer space and the wild, on the strange, unnatural, natural things that people want to know. He runs a finger across their spines, not sure what he's searching for.

Maybe there's something here. Something in this room that the police missed, that *he* missed. Something that will lead them right to Charlie. Something that was here all along. It's what happens in comics and movies. Those overlooked things that hold all the answers, lost to the margins. Maybe it's what Poppy really meant when she said he should know where to look. He grabs a book at random, riffling through the pages until they blow out like the frantic wings of an insect.

He hears Olive kick the telescope again, and he grabs the next book, faster this time, searching through Charlie's scratchy notes on solar systems and girls he likes and teachers he doesn't and theories he has about all of them. Benjamin looks for ticket stubs, for plans, for anything that might tell him where Charlie is, but all he finds is an old library receipt, a pressed flower, four wriggling silverfish and a post-it note, stuck on the back of the very last book, that says *I promise it'll be okay* in Charlie's too-familiar scrawl.

It's the last that kills him. Or maybe it's all of it. Maybe it's all of those things, stacked on top of each other like a teetering Jenga pile made up of pieces of the boy Charlie was.

Is.

Benjamin lifts the post-it note off the cover, and he holds it so tightly in his hand that it crumples.

○

The Rabbit house is stark in the yawn of dusk tonight.

It strikes Delia especially hard as she pulls onto the kerb. If she were much younger, it's the sort of place she'd be attracted to, and she guesses a part of her still is. Still revels in the old-fashioned vibe of it, the lived-in atmosphere that swallowed her up the first time she and Ed saw it, Olive strapped to her chest like a ticking bomb, and Delia herself still a wide-eyed tourist in family life (and how far away her mother had felt then; how far away any memory of Bo).

How close Ed had felt.

How close he *was.*

The house has always had the look of some average, ancient thing. An ordinary home with an ordinary history, but wasn't that the appeal?

She had faced no loss within its walls back then, not like the house she'd grown up in, which after Bo had felt ripe with traps.

With the teeth of memory.

But now, here, with Charlie, with Ed—

God, she feels it now.

Delia takes in the growing mould on the slatted wooden front, the rusted roof, the loamy, overgrown yard. She knows that what awaits her inside is little better – a mismatch of abstract art from local painters, older artist studies, a modern television, a moth-eaten herringbone sofa, the seams pulled out by a long-dead cat and too many wriggling children's feet.

She's out of the car but barely past the gate before Olive is upon her, or, rather, beside her, slipping beneath her arm as she would when she was a girl.

'Benjamin's upstairs, I'm heading out.'

'What?' Delia says, surprised, turning on the spot to see her daughter's retreating back. 'Where?'

'Just to Lux's place.'

And at least she's telling her tonight.

At least she's brought Benjamin *home*, and that's all that matters, all that *should*, but Delia watches her daughter fiddling with her bike lock and she feels the weight of her mother's disinterest, and she thinks of Griff and the girl he drew, and before she can stop herself, she says:

'Stay in. I'll make something.'

The words sink like a stone in the liquid air of the night, but still. Olive's hands pause on her bike lock, her tongue darts out. Wets her lips.

Maybe they're a picture – the two of them – standing at opposite ends of the untamed yard, and when Olive looks up at her, across it, she just looks so fucking *young*.

Does she always look this young?

No.

Maybe?

'Maybe another night?'

Olive's voice is tentative, her fingers moving on the bike lock, undoing it in a fluid motion, and Delia can only watch.

'I just – I can't be here right now,' Olive says. 'I've got something I have to do.'

If Delia were the perfect mother, she'd ask her daughter what was wrong. She'd ask her why. She'd pull her close. But Olive has never looked more like a stranger, with her long, pointed nose and her patchy make-up, with those piercing blue eyes of hers. It's like looking at someone else's daughter. Someone familiar and foreign all at once.

So she says, 'Okay. Thanks for picking your brother up. Just. Please don't turn off your phone again, and answer, when I call you. I need you to do that for me, Olive. Please.'

Olive stops then, staring up at Delia, and to Delia's surprise, she nods, before turning and disappearing through the back gate. Delia watches her until she's out of sight, the haze of early dusk enveloping her like a better mother, snuffing her matchstick body from view.

O

It's almost a half hour before Benjamin comes out of his bedroom, a sullen pout on his face. He leans against the kitchen island, stealing a slice of cucumber, another of radish from Delia's chopped pile, before darting off to clamber over the back of the couch.

'Your sister's gone out, so it's just you and me again tonight,' Delia says, chopping the last of the carrots. She pushes all the vegetables into a bowl, tossing them with a serve of loose leaf. 'We could watch something, or read together, or play a board game. What do you fancy?'

The cucumber and radish slices crunch loudly between Benjamin's teeth. It takes him so long to respond that Delia opens her mouth to repeat herself, when Benjamin's voice cuts through.

'Good.'

Delia blinks, tearing her gaze away from the salad to where Benjamin's legs are slung over the side of the couch.

'Pardon?'

'Good. That Olive's gone. I don't want her here.'

He says it with such surly certainty that Delia pauses, placing the knife back down on the chopping board. There are sausages spitting in the pan behind her. Potatoes ready to be mashed with butter, cream and chives in the pot beside it. She should stick to dinner. Try to get it on the table before either of them can get bogged down. Before food becomes an afterthought again, a feast for flies.

Delia blinks and she sees her son's skinny legs.

She blinks and she sees Olive, staring at her across the yard.

Her eyes are just like Bo's.

Delia wipes her hands on her pants and walks out of the kitchen and around the couch, until she can see Benjamin's downcast eyes and Spectacular Man, gripped at his belly.

'I know your sister isn't the easiest person,' she starts

delicately, refocusing, and Benjamin scoffs. 'But she tries, in her own way, and she loves you, even if she doesn't always act like it.'

As she says it, she's surprised to find she still mostly believes it.

Or – fuck.

Maybe she just needs to right now.

Either way, Benjamin can't meet her eye anymore. He turns his face so far away from hers, resists her look so much, that it's almost as if he can rotate his head the whole way around, like poor little Regan in *The Exorcist*. Delia bats his legs off the couch so she can sit down beside him.

'Can I ask what she did?'

He shrugs stiffly as he sits up properly, his gaze dropping to Spectacular Man, his fingers running over the plastic body. Biting the inside of her cheek, Delia counts to ten in her head.

Enough to grant her the patience to deal with this.

Benjamin, her sweetest thing.

He wasn't supposed to grow up.

'Okay,' she says, standing back up. She wipes her sweaty palms on her slacks and starts towards the kitchen again.

'She did come to pick me up,' Benjamin says, and Delia hums, inviting him to continue. 'I mean, not yesterday, but today she did. I just wasn't there this time.'

Behind her, the pan spits.

Boiling oil licks up into the humid air, the exhaust fan whirring loudly and uselessly, and for a moment it's all Delia can hear. All she can focus on. The heat on heat on heat. She exhales as she tries to put out the flame of her sudden fury.

'Where were you?'

The voice doesn't sound like her own.

'I was looking for Charlie,' her son says, watching her closely. 'I didn't find him though.'

This time, when Delia blinks, she does not see her daughter.

'Are you mad?' Benjamin asks.

Green eyes, crooked teeth.

'No,' Delia says. 'I'm not mad.'

Del, a voice says.

Mum, another says.

Benjamin nods, looking back down at his action figure, his little face focused, his eyes bright and wet.

'Where'd you look?'

'Everywhere.'

And oh, Delia thinks, looking away, her hand slipping into her shirt, feeling her sweaty chest.

(Feeling the ache in it.)

Her eyes prickle.

'The police are looking, you know that.'

'Why aren't we looking?'

You're no good at this, a voice tells her, and no, Delia thinks, she's not. She wants to tell him she's done this before. That she's been Benjamin and she's been Olive. That she's desperately searched, and been bitterly angry, but none of it brings back someone who won't be found, and sometimes the not knowing is better than the truth, because at least it means there's a chance. Her chest tightens, constricts to such a degree that she feels light-headed, and she leans back, putting her hand on the kitchen island to steady herself.

'The police are looking, and we're doing something equally important. You know in movies, when they say the best way to find someone is to stay where you are? It's kind of like that. That's what we're doing. We're making sure that when Charlie does come home, he's got one to return to.'

Benjamin nods, but from the silence that follows, she knows that neither of them believe it.

By the time she's cycled back to Lux's, Dom's ute is in the driveway. A big, ugly thing with shining rims and a battered tray. She stalls, pushes her feet back on the pedals of her bike, rises from her seat, and stands there awkwardly, teetering on the road outside. She could go into the city on her own, but the thought settles uncomfortably in her stomach. So instead she pushes her bike against Dom's ute, tidies herself up as best she can, and knocks on Lux's front door.

It's quiet out here tonight, too quiet for a Friday, and it leaves Olive strangely uneasy. She stretches her legs, feeling the nip of the mosquitoes and midges floating through the stagnant summer air. The door cracks open, and she's met by Lux, newly showered and in a satin robe, and loose enough in her movements to already be a few drinks in.

'Olive Rabbit!' she cries, reaching out and pulling Olive in with both hands. 'Dom, Olive's here!'

Then, quieter.

'You guys have met, right?'

And they have.

Sort of.

Olive's seen Dom hanging around the back of O'Malley's, waiting for Lux to go on break, or picking her up in his ute. He's a big guy. Tall and wide, with a thick neck and the beginnings of a beer gut. He has a five o'clock shadow and a faded Southern Cross tattoo poking out from the gaping arms of his singlet.

From a few feet away, Dom nods, lifting his beer in acknowledgement. His lips are wet, whether from Lux or the beer Olive can't really be sure, and she waves awkwardly at him from Lux's side. The gesture captures the other girl's full attention, and she gasps, grabbing Olive's waving hand and pulling it towards her face.

'Look!' she says. 'Nicotine stains. Cute!'

She runs a polished thumb across Olive's yellowing fingers, ignoring it when Olive curls them in embarrassment. Dom is getting closer, shuffling to Lux's back and leaning against her, diverting her attention back to him, which only makes Lux's smile grow coy.

'Did I tell you we slept together last night?' Lux purrs, stepping away from Dom to tuck her arm around Olive's waist. 'Almost naked too, coz of the heat.'

Dom just laughs, a throaty sound that ricochets in the emptiness of Lux's house. This place is weird like that. Olive noticed it last night too. The size and scale of it gives a strangely sterile vibe to every room. Like if it weren't for the family photographs and the excess of Lux's bedroom, the place could almost be a display home, just personable enough to appear homey to the casual eye, but not really able to stand up under closer inspection. Olive had preferred it in Lux's room, pink feather boas, boy-band posters and all.

'Dom's offered to drive us, by the way, so we can park in town instead of having to walk like, a million kilometres from the bus,' Lux tells her, before giving her a once-over with a squint. 'You wearing that?'

Olive blinks, ignoring Lux's slight, her gaze fixing on Dom, who takes another swig of his beer in punctuation.

'I thought it would just be the two of us,' she says, lowering her voice, and Lux shrugs, taking a step back.

'Dom's a dormouse. You won't even know he's there. Plus, did you not hear what I said about *not* having to catch a bus with all the street people?'

It's as if it's been settled, Lux's word as good as any order, and Olive bites her lip, glancing sideways at Dom, who meets her gaze wanly, his expression glazed and dim. Sensing Olive's uncertainty, Lux rolls her eyes, reaching out to grab her wrist and tug her down the hall towards her bedroom. When they're out of earshot, she leans towards Olive conspiratorially.

'You know he's mates with Jude, right?'

Olive stares at her in surprise, and Lux laughs, pulling them both into her bedroom and peeling off her robe. She's skinnier than she's ever been, not just lean, but sickly. Her bones look ready to break through her skin, like blunt knives below terrycloth. Olive puts a hand on her own chest, feels the ladder of her ribs, fine and hard at her fingers, as the other girl disappears into her wardrobe.

Before they were friends, back when Lux was just the odd new girl at O'Malley's, Olive had thought she might have been poor or damaged, living a life of fragments and pills and other broken things. The truth was that Lux was rich and spoiled, her father a FIFO miner out Mount Isa way and her mother a retired glamour model who now hosted functions and events as a Personality. The worst Lux had ever really experienced was her father missing her seventh birthday because a dust storm had grounded the planes out west. He'd still made it to town the day after, though, and Olive likes to imagine that his skin was rough and sheened with sand, eyes red from it, as he'd handed Lux a brand-new Barbie Dreamhouse. Tonight, not for the first time, the image drags her down.

'Besides,' Lux says, reappearing newly clothed and tossing a sequined dress in Olive's direction, 'we've got something we want to show you.'

○

They eat dinner in the relative quiet of the dining room, between Benjamin's homework and project supplies and the game he'd abandoned a few days before, action figures and Lego left out in a half-forgotten formation. The only sounds really breaking the silence are those of them chewing, the evening birds, and some nameless, popular crooner singing through the neighbour's radio.

'What's all this for anyway?' Delia asks, picking up one corner of Benjamin's notebook. On it is written *Mum, Dad, Olive, Charlie, me.* And then above that, *Grandpa Tomas, Grandma Beth. Aunt Moira. Uncle Jeff.* She corrects the last one with the left-out pen, crossing it out and writing *Geoff.*

'It's my school project,' he tells her, and right, Delia thinks, she knew about that. Is sure she did. 'We're supposed to talk about our family, and then choose someone to interview.'

Delia considers this, chewing on a forkful of baby spinach as she eyes off the page.

'This is just your dad's family,' she says, and Benjamin nods.

'I just hadn't written yours down yet.'

When Delia makes a face, Benjamin sighs loudly. He grabs the notebook out of her hand and scrawls *Grandma Rosemary*, then *Grandpa*. He pauses.

'Grandpa Robin,' Delia says, and Benjamin flushes, scribbling the name in.

'I did know that,' he promises, and Delia shrugs, unbothered.

'Maybe you didn't. He died a long time ago.'

Well before Benjamin was born, anyway – before any of her children were born.

Not before Bo had gone though, and there's another memory then, clawing to the surface.

Her father sitting on Bo's bed, face in his hands, shoulders shaking. Then later, at the sink washing dishes, his moustache like a tear catcher, glistening and wet.

Delia's gaze flicks between her meal and Benjamin, and it's a relief when he concentrates on his project instead of her. When he's more interested in the name of the grandfather he never knew than in her.

'Robin and Rosemary,' he says, testing it out and wrinkling his nose. 'They sound like they could be on TV.'

Another memory: her mother and father on the seven o'clock news, holding out a photograph of Bo. Her mother

146

had had to do the talking, her father unable to open his mouth without a wail swallowing his words.

Delia thumbs the handle of her fork.

'What would their show be, do you think?'

'Crime fighters,' Benjamin says without missing a beat. 'Robin would be a vigilante, and Rosemary a no-nonsense reporter with an eye for a story.'

'I think I've seen that one before,' Delia hums, and Benjamin giggles.

'Maybe something else then. Maybe she's a police lady and he's in jail, but he's become a police informant, and then they fall in love.'

She laughs at that, and Benjamin grins up at her, pleased.

'What did they really do?' he asks.

'Your grandma was a nurse and your granddad was a carpenter.'

Benjamin considers this, turning it over in his head. After a second he writes it down in his notebook. Across the page, he writes their occupations beneath all their names. *Homemaker* beneath Grandma Beth, *Lawyer* beneath Grandpa Tomas and Aunt Moira and Dad, *Salesman* beneath Uncle Geoff, and finally, after just a second's hesitation, *Artist* underneath Mum.

Something in her plucks taut.

'Oh, no, sweetheart,' she says, sitting up and reaching for the pencil. 'Teacher. I'm a teacher.'

She's met with his big eyes, and before she can think any more of it, she snatches the pencil from his grip, using the eraser on the end to correct the word.

'I know you teach too, but there are all those paintings in the hall closet, and Dad took us ages ago to see the mural you did in town.'

'It's just something I used to do,' she says. 'What you do isn't necessarily what you are, and what you did isn't necessarily who you're always going to be.'

Benjamin opens his mouth to reply, his forehead furrowing, and Delia quickly interjects, changing the subject.

'Who are you picking to do your project on anyway?'

Benjamin sighs at that, flopping back in his chair.

'I was going to do Grandpa Tomas or Aunt Moira, but I don't know.'

And maybe it's because of Charlie, or Bo, or her dad, or because Delia has lost her youthful ability to escape her, but the next words out of her mouth are, 'What about your Grandma Rabbit?'

Benjamin pauses.

'Grandma Rabbit,' he says, like it's the first time he's considered it. 'I thought she was sick.'

'She has her good days and her bad days. She saved a lot of lives, like one of your superheroes. When she was a nurse, she went to the war in Vietnam. She was a tough woman. I bet she'd be pretty interesting to do your project on.'

'Yeah,' Benjamin says, then, surer, 'yeah.'

His face brightens at the prospect, and something in Delia twists, and just – *god*. Why'd she do that?

O

They end up back in Dom's old ute (third-hand, he tells them: his uncle's, his brother's, now his), and Olive shares the passenger seat with Lux, their bare legs pressed together until Olive can feel the prickling stubble of new hairs like a tough wool jumper. Dom's older, but not by much, twenty-four or twenty-five, and he works at a drive-through bottle shop downtown. That's how they met, Olive knows, with Lux bullshitting her way to a cheap bottle of bad gin, hip cocked, her ID forgotten, and Dom rolling his eyes and buying her something better on the condition she shared it with him after work.

It wasn't as creepy as it sounds, Lux had promised, and Dom had proven rough, but not with her, and even now he drops a square hand to her knee, squeezing lightly, but doesn't make the exploratory move upwards like most of the boys Olive knows.

'Where are we even going?' she asks, tearing her gaze away and looking out the window. She's jittery, her gaze catching on every lanky body dodging cars or hailing buses or ducking into corner stores or dive bars. It's stupid, this whole thing is stupid, but Benjamin looked, and Olive can too.

'City,' Dom says, and that much she could've worked out for herself, watching leafy modern properties give way to slumped suburban houses, the land around them dry and beige with drought, and then to sleek new high-rises, gaining height with every street.

Dom ends up parking at South Bank, down by the gallery, and the three of them walk over the Victoria Bridge into the city. It's been a long time since Olive's been out here, preferring the lurch of the suburbs to the bustle and chaos of town, but she's strangely charmed by it tonight. The main pedestrian street is dominated by gold-painted performers and sallow-cheeked men busking for drunken tourists. Some of the Christmas lights are even still up, hanging from building to building like highwire acts, giant polystyrene presents draped between them.

If Dom and Lux notice any of it, they don't show it. Rather they walk with a purpose Olive has rarely seen in either of them, their long bodies driving through the crowds. Olive resists the urge to dig her heels in, turn away, *go home*. Finds herself instead peering into the face of every teenage boy she walks past, a sick feeling hammering away at her gut. This is a good idea, she reminds herself. She'll find him this way, slumped over the handles of his bike and talking to some pretty girl about the moon and stars. About spacesuits and Sally Ride.

Dom and Lux turn. Off a main street and down into a darker alley – a grungier part of town. They're picking up speed, and Olive finds herself having to almost jog to keep up, her attention drifting from the faceless boys on the streets to the sway of Dom's heavy-looking backpack and Lux's shining blue hair.

'Where are we going?' Olive calls when the buzz of the mall has completely given way to tattered apartments and tired houses, to indie coffee shops and dank outer city bars. Lux turns back, a wild grin pulling her lips apart, revealing a row of white teeth, near-luminescent in the gloom.

'We're almost there,' she says, like that's what Olive has

asked, and not long after that Lux and Dom stop, and Olive jogs to catch up.

The house they've stopped in front of is rickety, raised on unsteady stilts, not dissimilar to Olive's own home. Flakes of blue paint, fine as snow, drift down with every breeze, and the windows are already broken, their frames housing only a few splintered shards of dirty glass. Mould cakes its walls, rust its legs, and Olive can only imagine the wild things up there, making themselves at home in the house's skin and bones.

'What a shithole,' Dom says, cracking his knuckles.

'That's kind of the point, dickhead,' Lux replies, and then she says to Olive, 'Come on.'

She takes the sagging steps two at a time, and when she gets to the top throws her backpack through one of the shattered windows before climbing in behind it. Olive follows uneasily, wanting to stay out in the street, to keep looking for Charlie, but finds herself hoisting her body over the decrepit wooden frame just as Lux did, and pushing herself in through the broken window. A bit of jagged glass catches on her stomach, then another at her arm, but she forces herself to keep going, ignoring the spike in her heart at the feel of her breaking skin.

She's barely gotten through before Lux is tossing her a can of spray-paint that she almost misses. She could blame it on the condensation, on the slick aluminium, but before her mouth can form the words, Lux has moved on. She opens the can, fingers the nozzle until she gets the right angle for it, and when she sprays, it's with a hiss of piss-yellow paint.

'Can or bat?' Dom asks, and Olive looks back to see him tearing open his own bag, six or seven cans of spray-paint rolling out, their metal cases glinting in the last winks of light. Bending down, Olive picks one up as it rolls towards her. It's a sleek black can with an algae-green nozzle, and she shakes both cans on instinct, the fine metal balls clanking up and down their middles.

Dom grabs two himself, eyeing off the colours, and finally selects a traffic-cone orange.

'Olive's mum's an artist,' Lux says, reaching for another can, but Dom stops her, offering her a bright pink one instead. He tosses it to her easily, and she makes an *ooo* sound like she's impressed, but there's a twitch at her eyebrow as if she knows she's being ignored.

'Was,' Olive corrects, almost unconsciously. The corridor is thin, out of the way, and Olive thinks if she widened her stance enough she might be able to straddle the entire space.

'Was?' Dom asks, and Olive looks back up at him, surprised to find him meeting her gaze. She clears her throat.

'She hasn't done anything in years. She just teaches now.'

Dom doesn't respond to that, just uncaps a can of paint and sprays a large, hairy cock onto the first wall he can find. He's chewing on something – gum probably – and she wonders if he and Jude actually do know each other or if Lux made it up. She eyes the two cans, and, dropping one, uncaps the other, but then Lux is beside her, shaking her head. Out of Dom's large bag she pulls a small metal bat, passing it to Olive with a sly grin.

'Something better for you.'

Olive takes it uneasily, watching as Lux mimes swinging it, and – god, she can't be serious?

'No,' Olive says, shaking her head, and Lux shrugs, reaching to take it back, only Olive suddenly finds herself unable to release it, her fingers white knuckled around the handle. Lux laughs, rolls her eyes as she shakes her own can of paint, and then she turns to the nearest wall and sprays a little cartoon rabbit, identifiable only by its fluffy tail and long ears.

Olive stares at the bat in her hands and wonders why Lux even brought her here, and then she thinks about Benjamin, who's a little kid and looked for Charlie for longer than she fucking did, and she thinks about his words earlier that night, *I wish it was you*, and no shit, she thinks, so do I, and it's with an anger and a hatred that choke her that she raises the bat, smashes it into the shaky wooden doorway, and watches the frame splinter beneath her weight.

○

Olive steals in through the back of the house sometime in the early hours of the morning, her hands covered with dried blood and the dress Lux lent her marked up with dust and the flaking remnants of paint. She kicks off her shoes by the back door and creeps through the hallway into her bedroom. Cranking the fan, she strides to the window, opening it wide enough that she can stretch her head and torso out of it. She's sticky from the bike ride home from Lux's, and she holds a hand out in front of her, then lets it fall down, cutting through the air like a knife.

She'd hoped the second-storey height would bring with it a

breeze, but it's as stagnant as it is everywhere. The sun has long gone down, but the air is still humid with the memory of it, a pining lover mouthing at her skin. She huffs, scratches at her flat belly and pulls back into her bedroom. Tugging open the top drawer of her dresser, she pushes aside boyleg underwear, sports bras and cigarettes, and finally grips a narrow box with a sweet design, something floral and golden. A gift from Nanna Beth. The lid slips off and she thumbs through foils, skins, a tiny bag of diced-up weed, a lighter that sits bright and blue against the white bottom of the box.

She's running low on everything, but she manages to roll herself a joint, light the thing and stick it between her thin lips. Taking a few steps back, she drops onto her bed, drawing in a deep breath and stretching out with the exhale, closing her eyes and toeing off her socks as she does so.

The hum of distant cicadas and the belly croaks of frogs sound loud in her ears, the low rumble of a bus a few streets over on the main road. It's later than she thought, the traffic at a lull, and after a second she opens her eyes again, reaching down to fumble her phone out of her pocket. She checks for a message from Lux (there's none), from anyone other than her mother (there's none), and then, with a tremble, she types one last text to Charlie, even though she knows his phone is on their mother's bedside table, plugged into a charger. *Come home*, she types, thumbs gliding over the cracked screen, catching fragments of glass, then she drops the phone, pushing the heels of her hands to her eye sockets. The hot swell of tears is building all over again, and she can feel them boiling, stewing, ready for the drop.

Maybe she'll go out again, back to Lux's or to restart her failed search, breaking down strangers' doors instead of somebody's abandoned home.

There's a creak, the sigh of her door handle, and she turns to see Benjamin shuffling through, his pale face luminous in the dark. She leans over, stumping her joint out in the little jewellery dish she uses as an ashtray, and flops back onto her bed. Benjamin shuffles closer, and it's not long before the mattress dips beneath him too.

'Why didn't you pick me up the other day?' he whispers, and Olive feels that familiar pang of guilt, the one she wants to strip off and leave behind. She's so tired of feeling. 'Why'd you leave me behind?'

There's a quiver to his voice that makes Olive groan and rub at her face.

'I said I was sorry.'

'No, you didn't.'

She racks her head for the memory, something she can pull on, pull *up*, but she knows she won't find a thing, and she rolls over to see Benjamin's steadfast gaze still on her, unblinkingly earnest.

Benjamin doesn't look like Charlie. Not quite so crooked in his features. No. Benjamin looks like Olive, looks like their father, more handsome than an eleven-year-old boy should be, both broad shouldered and foxish.

He keeps staring at her, and Olive should say it now, she means to, even opens her mouth to say it, but Benjamin cuts her off.

'I'm sorry I said I hate you. I don't. I'm just mad at you,' he tells her, and she nods, because it's fair. Because she would be too. She kicks the blankets down and then tugs a sheet over herself. It's too hot for it, but it'll do to mop the sweat off them, to soak their bedtime BO. 'I don't want to be, but I am.'

'Is Mum mad too?' she asks, already knowing the answer, and Benjamin wrinkles his forehead, looks suddenly so old that she wonders what they'll be years from now, if Charlie never comes back. If they'll still be this listless, angry family in this listless, angry house. If he does come back. If it'll all be the same.

'You staying?' is all she asks, and Benjamin nods, scooting below the sheet as she pulls it up and lets it fall over them. Outside, the cicadas hum. Just a while longer.

O

Benjamin wakes with a start, as if he's had a bad dream, as if he's died or fallen or suffocated, but the memory is already lost to him and there's nothing to greet his sleep-blurred eyes apart from Olive's wide-open blue ones.

'Don't be a dick, Banjo,' Olive mumbles, but her voice wobbles and her gaze doesn't waver from Benjamin's face, and Benjamin *hasn't* done anything, doesn't think he has, but there's a post-it note stuck to Olive's forehead, and given the way she's studying his he thinks there might be one there too.

'I'm not,' Benjamin says. 'I didn't.'

He blinks and his eyes have that familiar no-sleep burn and it's an effort to open them again, a chore, and when he does, the note is still on Olive's head, and the way her fingers are gripping Benjamin's arm tells him she doesn't think this is a dream.

The post-it on Olive's forehead says:

Tell her I'm sorry. Tell her I'm home.

He says the words aloud, watching Olive's eyes grow glassy, and it's with a shaking hand that he reaches to his own forehead, pulls off the sharp-edged note there and turns it over to read it.

Tell him I never meant to go.

8

Two lizards dart across the wide ceiling above them. Good ones, green ones, not the translucent-skinned invaders but the army camo ones that have been here for as long as time has marked up this earth. Olive likes the green ones, has since she and Charlie were kids and rescued one from a dart-eyed crow, keeping it in her room for almost two weeks until their mother found it and made them release it back into their yard.

She wonders vaguely if one of these geckos came from that one. If the lizard Charlie found all those years ago decided to make their home its home, if it found a family or if it made one, a perfect house of lizards.

'This is awesome,' Benjamin says beside her, and Olive's head lolls sideways to look at him.

'This isn't real,' she says, her fingers curled delicately around the post-it note, her forehead still tacky from it.

It's real, a pen writes on a fresh post-it note. Hovering above it as if on a string.

'You're invisible,' Benjamin says, watching the pen move with the sort of captivation he's rarely been able to manage outside of movies or comic books. 'You're just like Sue Storm.'

He looks back at Olive with sparkling eyes as she tries to fold her body back against the headboard, her make-up a mess.

'This isn't real,' she repeats, looking at the empty space where Charlie apparently is. 'I am, like – I'm tripping out. That's what this is.'

It's the only thing that makes sense to her right now. The only explanation for the way the pen hovers in midair, for the inhabited nothingness in front of her.

With shaky legs, Olive rolls off the bed, staggering over to her dresser drawer and fumbling for her tin of weed. Her heart thrums in her chest, a buzz of anxious energy she wants to capture and still. Her fingers are shaking too hard to work the latch, trembling around the metal until she gives up, dropping the thing back into the drawer and burying her tired face in her hands.

'Fuck.'

She's met only with silence. Or not silence exactly, with the wheeze of her mattress springs as Benjamin bounces lightly on the top of it, and maybe he's all energy too – sparking nerve endings and brilliant rushes.

The thought makes her uncover her face, look at Benjamin's awed expression, at where he's staring, smiling, at the pen, which is writing something out on a new note that makes Benjamin laugh.

'Do something else,' Olive demands before she can think better of it, and she hates that she can sense it. Hates the way a weight seems to lift off her bed, the way she can feel the air shift, the way her drawer is pulled open beside her and the tin is lifted into the air, opened by invisible fingers. The laugh that escapes Olive's lips is hysterical, even to her own ears.

She reaches for the tin and plucks it out of Charlie's grip, rolling up a joint and lighting it. She's promised herself she'd never do this in front of Benjamin, at least not until he was in high school, but these have got to be extenuating circumstances. The ghost of her brother is haunting her.

She doesn't realise she's talking out loud until the pen is picked up again and makes quick work on the post-it note pack on her bed, until the top one is ripped off and thrust in her direction.

Not a ghost. I'm not dead. Invisible (I think).

'That's what I said,' Benjamin squawks behind them, and Olive bites back a laugh.

'Oh, invisible,' she says, the words sharper than she means. 'Of course, sorry.'

Above her, the geckos dart to avoid the smoke, and Benjamin scoots down the bed, hooking his legs at the base of it and reaching out a hand into the space Charlie should be in. He barely gets close before Olive bounds across the room, grabs his wrist and shoves his hand back.

She ignores his shout of protest, and gives him the stink eye over her shoulder.

'How do we even know it's Charlie, Banjo? What if it's some other ghost or invisible boy or what-the-fuck-ever?'

Benjamin frowns up at her, then looks back down at the post-it note crumpled in his free hand.

'It's Charlie's handwriting.'

He says it like there's no possible doubt. Like this is a thing that could happen to anyone, ever, and Olive feels light-headed, spots appearing before her eyes as if she's stared for too long at the sun. Pinching the bridge of her nose, she shakes her head, opening her mouth to reply only to be stopped by the sound of their mother's bedroom door opening and closing.

Something in her shutters.

Something in her tears open.

She stops in her tracks, looking over at the door as she hears Benjamin and Charlie's open and shut across the corridor, and she barely has time to pull her thoughts together before her own door opens and Delia's head pops through.

'Don't smoke in the house, Olive, Jesus,' Delia says in lieu of 'good morning', and Olive releases Benjamin's wrist and drops her joint into the ashtray on top of her dresser. She holds her hands up in a graceless surrender, watching as Delia clocks Benjamin, his legs swinging beneath him on the edge of Olive's bed.

'I'm glad you guys have made up,' she says, and Olive paints on a smile, tugging the thin sleeves of her shirt down over her cut hands.

'Sure,' Olive says curtly. She glances sideways at where Charlie (?) should still be standing, and she tries harder to see him, smell him, get any sense of the shadows and lines of him, and maybe Benjamin clocks her look, or maybe it just takes him that long to react, but he leaps to his feet, his fingers uncurling around the post-it note in his hand.

'Mum!'

And she's not sure what makes her do it.

Why she feels an urgent need to keep this secret, what promise or warning she sees in it, but before she can stop herself she's leaning over to pluck the note from Benjamin's outstretched hand.

'Hey!'

'Benjamin managed not to piss himself last night,' Olive says, tone dry, keeping her eyes fixed on Delia and not on Benjamin, who she can feel promptly shutting down in embarrassment behind her. The air beside her ... *quivers* almost, and she doesn't look, can't look, can't take her gaze away from her mother, and the words are on her tongue and then they're not. They're in her throat, her stomach, tying up her intestines.

Tell her, she thinks, and then, like a newly flung stone, something in her replies: No.

For a moment, Delia just stares at her, and then she nods, flashing a smile at Benjamin before saying something about breakfast and Saint Anne's (it's the weekend, after all), and the second the door clicks shut behind her, Olive spins back to face her youngest brother.

'We can't tell Mum,' she says quickly, and Benjamin opens his mouth in reply, but Olive doesn't give him a chance to speak. 'Not until we know what this is. Imagine if we're wrong. Imagine how much it would hurt her. Please, Banjo.'

She can see the cogs turning in Benjamin's head, see him turning the thought over and over, before finally his mouth closes and, after a long moment, he nods.

○

Mum goes to visit Grandma Rabbit at Saint Anne's, and before he knows it Benjamin's sitting cross-legged on his bed, waiting for the computer to boot up. It was Charlie's idea, of course – to type up the things he wanted to say instead of wasting all his post-it notes on them, and, at least for now, it makes sense.

Benjamin settles back into the mattress as he watches the screen load, the chair in front of it whining as Charlie rests his weight on it. There are a lot of questions in Benjamin's head, but he manages to hold his tongue until Charlie has opened a document and typed a question mark, ready and waiting.

'Was it an experiment?'

It's the first question Benjamin can think of, his body bent forwards eagerly. A lot of comic-book characters come out of experimentation – Wolverine and Captain America, the Incredible Hulk, Ant-Man, Wasp and Cyborg. Charlie's always liked science enough that Benjamin could believe it. He can see Charlie folded over his notebook, his floppy hair curling around his big ears, his hands and school shirt accidentally wet with chemicals he never meant to touch. Then – a flash!

You're a weird kid, you know that? Charlie types, as if he knows what Benjamin has just been imagining, and Benjamin rolls his eyes. Not an experiment then.

'Well, what then?' he asks.

I don't know. I just did it, and then I couldn't turn it off.

So Benjamin will discard his experimental plots for the tragic ones – Batman first of all, then Robin, the Winter Soldier, the Punisher. Then he reconsiders. There is no death in Charlie's origin story, no murder, no big and gaping trauma. Which means he's either a mutant or an alien, or he's …

Benjamin glances at Charlie's chair.

'Have you always been able to do it?'

It takes a moment for Charlie to type again.

Maybe not always. For as long as I can remember. But not like this. He deletes that last sentence. Re-types. *Not for this long before. Not in a way that I couldn't come back from.*

Benjamin gnaws on his lip, watches the barely-there press of keys, just enough to let him know that Charlie's hands are still resting there.

'How come you never told me? How come you never told any of us?'

The little blinking cursor doesn't move for a long while after that, and Benjamin briefly finds himself wondering if Charlie's gone again. The thought seizes his chest, worries his legs in a way he didn't expect, and his frown deepens, until the keys start clicking again.

I don't know.

'That's not a very good answer.'

If Charlie thinks much of that, he doesn't type anything back, and the pressure eases on the keys, as if he's pulled his hands away. There's a bigger question, of course, one that curdles like bad milk in Benjamin's already aching belly. One he doesn't think he really wants to know the answer to, but he asks it anyway.

'Why did you let us think you were missing?'

The pressure is back on the keys, then gone again, then back. Benjamin watches the keyboard with a careful eye.

He wishes he could see Charlie. Could see if his eyes are doing that thing where they dart all around, or if he's scratching at his ear or if his chest is moving faster. Wishes he could see any of the things that help him know Charlie better.

Do you think Olive is mad at me?

Benjamin's mouth tightens, a worm of tension burrowing between his shoulders. If he were more honest, he'd probably say yes, but that's only because Olive always seems to be mad at everyone.

'She'll be okay,' Benjamin says instead. 'She's just been really sad. She was … I mean, we were *all* worried about you. Dad even came over. *Twice.* He thinks I didn't see him the second time because he didn't get out of the car, but I did.'

He's still not entirely sure he didn't dream that, but it feels right to say it now. He'd woken up bleary eyed and tired a couple of nights ago, his shorts wet, and he hadn't wanted to wake Mum, so he'd washed himself off in the bathroom sink with one of the faded handtowels Mum only really uses for cleaning. As he'd tiptoed back to bed, he'd been surprised to see the living room dustily lit up with the beams of a car's headlights. He'd peeked out the window to see his father's Audi on the street outside, and his father too, his head bowed on the steering wheel and his body curved like the outer rim of a shell.

It had been weird, the way the picture had grown in Benjamin's mind.

Sprouted a seed he didn't even know had been planted.

The keys start clicking again.

Are you *mad at me?*

Benjamin wrinkles up his nose, a grin finding his lips. He probably is mad, somewhere deep inside, about the worry and the police and the days without Charlie, but there are more important things right now.

'Charlie, this is *the best*,' he says. 'You're a *superhero*.'

○

Delia's halfway home from Saint Anne's when her phone buzzes, juddering against the plastic cup holder. She casts a sideways glance at it, trying to make out the caller, but the screen is faced the wrong way. Briefly, she entertains the thought of letting it ring out, of dealing with it when she gets home, but she's still at least half an hour away (more, probably, in the afternoon traffic), and so she tosses out an arm, fumbles blindly, eyes back on the road, letting muscle memory hit 'answer', then 'speaker', and she's expecting the college, the school or Officer Keely from the station, so it's a surprise when she hears Ed's voice.

'Hey, you leaving Saint Anne's?'

Delia hums in confirmation, eyeing the turn-off ahead of her, ignoring the way something sparks in her at the knowledge that he still knows her schedule.

'I went into the station this morning,' he says. 'Spoke to Keely. She's ... not hopeful. There're just no fucking leads. How can there be no fucking leads?'

And right, Delia thinks, adjusting her grip on the steering wheel, her vision blurring at the edges, the white noise roaring in her head.

'I know, Ed.'

She instantly regrets it, if only for the way his breath rattles down the line.

For the way it shakes her.

She pulls over into the emergency bay on the side of the highway, parking as cars crawl past her window.

'Do you think there ever will be?'

'What?'

'Leads,' he says. 'A lead.'

Charlie.

Delia shrinks back into her seat, her head pounding, spots of light appearing before her eyes.

'What do you want me to say to that?'

'I don't know. Something. You've been here before.'

It's not callous exactly, the way he says it, or at least he doesn't mean it to be. The exhaustion weighs down his tone like silt in a riverbed.

The thought makes her shudder, grip the steering wheel tighter, and she remembers sitting by the river in her car that day after Charlie went missing, remembers sitting by it before then, over and over, after—

She sucks in a breath.

Pull yourself together.

'I think we need to keep on with our lives and make sure there's something for him when he comes back,' she says, a weak repetition of what she'd told Benjamin the night before, but it's all she's got right now. Everything she has to keep going.

'You believe that?'

Delia opens her mouth, but no words come out. No sound builds in her to cut through this weighted moment, and she *does* believe it, because she has to. Because the alternative is Charlie showing up like Bo did, and that thought alone paralyses her.

You're no good at this, her sister tells her, and no, Delia thinks. She's not.

Down the line, Ed sighs, and she wonders if he heard that thought, if he still thinks of Bo as much as Delia does, if he remembers the quiet stories Delia told him when they were still young and in love and wanted to know every ugly thing about each other.

'You could come over.'

It's an invitation. No – a request.

Delia huffs out a wobbly sound – something between an exhale and a laugh – and she fumbles for her phone, grabbing it out of the cup holder, taking it off speaker and pressing it to her ear.

'What?'

'You could come over,' he repeats, more firmly this time, his voice closer, a whisper, and Delia shivers despite the heat. She could. She could drive to his place, could burrow in there beside him, be the rabbit her name has always said she is. She wonders what he looks like right at this moment, the way he's sitting, leaning, holding himself, what his new apartment's like, some lush thing in the city for lawyers and the girls they take out instead of their wives, no doubt.

(Never married, Delia reminds herself, balling her hand at the wheel. Never husband. Never wife.)

'What about your girlfriend?'

'She's staying with a friend for a while. To give – I needed some space.'

And it's the kicker, the thing that lights that too familiar fire in her. It's what he'd said to her last year, after everything, when the frustration and resentment had found their way into every conversation, every sidelong glance, every fraught silence. She wonders why he's the one who is allowed space, who can carve it out for himself, can choose to leave his kids, leave her, find a new place, a new home, step away from it all, while she is left to carry them. How he gets to turn around and ask her to carry him again too, and that's the answer, isn't it?

'Goodbye, Ed.'

She should go home, of course. Should get home before Olive has to go to work, so Benjamin isn't left on his own in their empty home. Should catch up on marking, or laundry, or start dinner on time for a change. She should do a lot of things.

She raps her knuckles on the hard wooden door, rocking back on her heels when she hears footsteps thumping down the hallway, the metallic click of the lock, and then—

'Hi,' she says, and Griff reaches forwards tentatively, lifting a hand to brush the hair off her face. She leans in before he can.

Olive should go to work. She should. She means to.

She even cycles the whole way to O'Malley's, but instead of stopping she keeps pedalling, as if her legs have taken on a life of their own. She cycles until they burn, until her body throbs, her chest heaves, her throat goes raw and cold. Pushes until she can't anymore, until she tumbles off her bike onto the ground, panting like an animal, her skin sheened with sweat.

Beneath her there's clipped, brown grass, prickly from the drought, and she pushes her hands harder into it, letting the sharpness stab at the crescent-moon cuts at her palms. She lets her eyes shut, her lashes matting together with what might be tears. She doesn't know. Maybe she doesn't know anything.

She catches her breath at last, her throat warming, chest loosening. She pounds the grass with her fists, tightening and relaxing them again and again, trying to slow her fast-beating heart. She works through a few of those exercises from the school therapist, riffles through them, but can't summon the energy to stick to them. Somewhere in front of her a car slows on the road, the window winding down.

'Are you okay, honey?' a voice asks, and Olive blinks, sitting up quickly to be met with a small woman, leaning out the window, her face wrinkled with concern.

'Yeah, thanks,' Olive says, clearing her dry throat. 'I just fell off my bike.'

The woman makes a noise.

'Are you hurt? You want me to drop you somewhere?'

Olive shakes her head.

'No, I'm okay. Just a little winded. Thanks though.'

The woman nods, winding up her window and driving off into the distance. Olive watches the retreating car with a careful eye, her lips turned down, her heart finally swallowed. Her legs are aching all the more now, that dull muscular throb she used to get after soccer or hockey or tennis in school.

She drops her head to her knees, chest shuddering with the weight of it all, and looks down at her cut-up belly from the broken window last night. Her palms are chafed raw from the bat, from the handlebars of her bike, and for a second it grounds her again. Reminds her that she's here, even though she feels as if she's somewhere else. As if she's looking at her life through frosted glass.

Is this how Charlie feels now? she wonders, and she looks out at the open space around her, at the potholed road in front and the rows of narrow townhouses behind, crowded like teeth on the gummy mouth of this street. Somewhere down the road a woman is jogging, pushing a pram in front of her, the music from her headphones thumping a bass into the world around her, and Olive watches her run past, panting through pinked lips.

Olive looks back at her hands, at her skinny circus-stilt legs, at the frayed hem of her frayed pants.

'Charlie?' she says aloud, the name foreign in her mouth somehow, and she doesn't know what she's expecting, but she's disappointed by the lack of an answer all the same. No notes, no weight, no stranger feel to this strange air. He's invisible, not omnipresent, she reminds herself, and the thought creates a bubble of laughter in her, one that rises up from her belly to her dry throat to her aching, mothy mouth, and she laughs and laughs and laughs.

○

It happens like this:

Ed leaves and Delia throws herself into work.

Ed leaves and Delia picks up more classes at the college and loses herself in study plans and marking and guiding the work of her students – the vulnerable new talent and the amateur egos and the kids who want the aesthetic but not the grind, who want awe not help, praise not critique, the ones who aren't up for the challenge and the ones who are, and it works for those first six months.

It works because Delia's been a lot of things, but she's never been the sort to languish for days unoccupied, and it's easy to forget Ed's not at home when she's working or managing the school run or fighting her mother's memories and her own at Saint Anne's, and the nights she can't forget are so few that she doesn't need anything but her own hand or her showerhead or her vibrator to find a peak she can tumble over, and it works.

For six months.

Because Ed left before he leaves, and they hadn't made love in months anyway, and when they had it hadn't felt like them, and he hadn't touched her like she'd wanted him to, and she hadn't kissed him because of that. Because it hadn't felt right.

Because, because, because.

But then it's six months later and Ed has left her, and her daughter feels like somebody else's and her sons are growing up too fast and Ed's cagey about coming over now that he's shacked up with his girlfriend, Vanessa, as if the kids might find out he was fucking her before he stopped fucking Delia, and so Delia works more, and she's helping Griff – a tender talent, not one of those students fantasising about futures that'll never happen – and he's in her office one night and she's just helping him with his second-year folio, and it's not – it's nothing like—

But he kisses her.

He kisses her and oh.

Maybe she'd been lonely after all.

○

'You have kids, right?'

There's no way that story isn't written on Delia's skin, scrawled on it in the fingers of stretch marks wrapping around her hips and clutching at her, the way her breasts sag with old, dead weight, a memory of milk, a mammary of it.

The mattress below her is hard and probably second-hand, and she can faintly feel the ribbing of the springs, enough that she shifts her spine against it and tries to work out when is too soon to leave. But then Griff rolls over, shifts back slightly so he can look at her properly, and when she turns to meet him he seems sort of horribly absorbed, like a child with something new and important.

'Three,' she says. 'Two boys and a girl.'

Griff leans further back into the bed and stretches, arching until his skin pulls firm over his clavicle and the fine bird-bones of his chest. She wants to rush her fingers there, feel where each bone starts and ends.

'Are they little still?'

Delia shrugs, suddenly uncomfortable. They don't talk often. Delia's never particularly wanted to. Likes Griff's company in the moment, like scenes set apart from the reality of her life. Something she enters unconsciously, a slip beneath a structured dress. Something that makes her feel smoother, sexier, but isn't really anything once she pulls it off. To think about her children here is to think about something more, like her skin, her nails, the fine hair she shaves off her legs that only grows back darker and wirier than before.

'Not so young anymore. Benjamin's just eleven, but Charlie's sixteen and Olive's twenty.'

'Olive Rabbit?' he asks, a grin twisting at his lips, his dark eyebrows arched. Delia tilts her head, pulls her own mouth into a loose grin.

'I was obsessed with Olive Cotton at the time,' she says, edging away from him to sit up, pull her underwear back on. 'I thought I was pretty smart, I guess. You know the joke. Cotton tails, rabbits. It's not very good, in hindsight.'

She halts after a second, seeing Griff's blank stare.

'Olive Cotton,' she repeats. 'The photographer? Jesus, do you not do any of the homework I assign?'

Griff laughs at that, but Delia shakes her head, reaching over the bed for her pants.

'She was one of Australia's formative photographers, you know. She had this way of capturing a moment of time and ruining you over it. Making you love and hate the wildness and the tenderness and the human face of it. She was important, but people don't remember women like Olive, they remember men like Dupain and Avedon.'

Outside, a dog barks, and she can hear Griff's flatmate, that pretty girl with the long fingers and the painter's hands, unhook the latch of the gate, talk in long, loping sentences on her phone. This house traps sound, she thinks, catches it and kills it and then lets it haunt the place. Unravel in the walls and scratch beneath the doorjambs.

'I'll do the homework,' Griff says, and Delia glances back at him, and he suddenly looks serious and so heartbreakingly, impossibly young, and it's his honesty that gets her – hook, line, sinker. Like he's never had a reason to tell a lie.

God, she shouldn't have come here.

'Good,' she replies all the same, standing up and sliding on her shoes.

She doesn't look back at him as she leaves.

O

The hallway closet is halfway between Olive's room and the bathroom, and Benjamin opens it with two hands ready to catch anything that might fall on him. He mostly loves the closet, not because he believes in anything so silly as secret worlds beyond them (doesn't believe in fantasy like he believes in superheroes), but because he likes the way it has collected belongings that are so often forgotten. In it, he can find a history of *stuff*, of things that might be junk now but weren't always.

He rummages through the first layer of musty coats, pushes past Mum's old easel, the boxes of their starchy baby clothes, of Olive's long-forgotten soccer gear. The carcasses of powdery moths graze his hands, and the round balls of their droppings or their eggs or both catch beneath his nails. Benjamin doesn't care though, not now, not when he feels so close.

He's sure it's in here. The costume Grandma Beth made for him before she died. He finds it tucked in one of the

175

baby-clothes boxes, the elastic of the mask stretched out and the once shiny blue satin of the cape now muted and pilled. Stumbling back, he pulls it out with him, stripping off his shorts and socks, his damp shirt, and tugging down the costume over his chest. It's too small, way too small, the armholes cutting into his armpits, the torso barely covering his belly.

It's not perfect, but he can make it work.

○

Riffling through yesterday's mail, Delia walks slowly up the front steps of the house, the midafternoon sun blistering like Griff's breath at the back of her neck. The too-near memory of him makes her shift, swallow, leaves her hands a little rougher on the envelopes, so focused on them that she doesn't notice the esky until she almost falls over it.

Delia stares for a beat, taking in the condensation dripping off the blue plastic exterior, before slipping into the house.

'Benjamin!' she calls, pulling her phone out to check the time. She didn't stay long at Griff's, and Olive should only have left for work in the last half hour, but still, she can't quite bite back her relief when she spots her youngest son at the dining-room table, Spectacular Man forgotten beside him as he stares down at a notebook. His face is lined in concentration, but it's not this that takes Delia by surprise, rather it's the fact that he's wearing the superhero costume Beth made him years ago, the one Delia thought they'd gotten rid of after he'd outgrown it. The sight makes her purse her lips.

'You okay?' she asks cautiously, and Benjamin just nods vaguely back at her, his attention still focused on the notebook in front of him. Delia gestures to the front door with the envelopes.

'I think the neighbour might have left us another esky.'

Benjamin nods again, but doesn't so much as glance at her, and Delia strides over to the window and looks out at the house next door. She drums her fingers a little on an envelope, and after a moment says:

'I might go over. Just to say thanks. Put it all in the fridge for me?'

Benjamin nods a third time, and Delia heads out.

Their houses were built around the same time, but their upkeep has been so different that sometimes it's hard to believe they were built in the same town, let alone on the same street. For everything wild and decrepit about Delia's home, the neighbour's is chic and retro. With crisp, white-painted wood, arched windows, clean lines and humming whirlybirds, the house is framed by willowy bottlebrush trees and sighing ferns. Its yard is neatly manicured, and home to pockets of posies and native orchids kept shaded by netting and stately trees. The only insects that seem to float through are bees and butterflies and long-bodied dragonflies, almost vibrating through the sweetly lit yard.

Delia walks up the front steps, knocks, and within seconds the neighbour answers. She's not much taller than Delia, but she's years younger, maybe thirty-one or thirty-two, with the look of a naturally lean woman stretched from childbirth. Her face is bird-like, her lips thin, and a shock of red hair, bright as syrup, startles her features into prettiness.

177

'Hi, I live next door? I think you've been – I mean, I know you've been—' she stumbles over the words, rolls her eyes a little at herself, and smiles at the other woman. 'I just wanted to say thank you. For the food.'

The woman just looks at her, and visibly swallows. A note probably would've sufficed. Delia slips on her best morning-show smile and is turning to leave when the other woman speaks.

'You don't need to thank me,' she says. 'Really. It was the least I could do. I mean, I can't even imagine what you're going through.'

For a moment, Delia wonders how the woman knows a thing about it, but then she thinks of the police cars, and Charlie's photograph in everybody's Facebook feed, on every local news show, his absence from the yard, his telescope folded down and packed beneath the house.

'I'd feel ungrateful if I didn't,' Delia replies, and a silence settles between them that is almost comfortable. She holds out her hand awkwardly to break it. 'I don't know if I've introduced myself before. I'm Delia Rabbit.'

The woman smiles gently, shaking Delia's hand.

'November Herrera.'

They stand in silence again, neither knowing where to go from here, and then—

'Do you want to come in?' November asks suddenly, hesitantly. Her hand is still curled around the handle of her front door, holding it marginally ajar. A large silky grey cat slinks out through the gap and November shifts her body to make way for it.

Delia glances sideways, up at her own house, where Benjamin is playing alone in the dining room, and she thinks of afternoon tea and dinner, and then she thinks of Ed's breath down the line, Griff's at her neck, and before she can stop herself, she's saying *sure*, watching as November offers her a small, hopeful grin in return before pushing the door open and ushering Delia inside.

The house is as different from hers inside as it is outside, with the same bones in its high ceilings, slatted wooden walls and curving doorways, but a different soul in its neat marble countertops and sweetheart sofa, its generous, modern design. Their homes are as similar and as foreign as two sisters growing up side by side.

'Would you like a drink?'

'Please. Nice place,' she says, and November's already at the fridge, pulling out a bottle of pinot grigio and then two glasses from the cupboard beside it.

'Thanks,' November says. 'It was a steal, really. The housing prices are still low out here, even though we're not so far out of town. They'll be up in the next few years. You won't be able to get a place out here for less than seven figures.'

Delia nods but actually has no idea. They've lived next door since she was pregnant with Charlie.

'I used to work in real estate,' November says. 'But Christ, right? Not really for me.'

She pushes a striped bamboo cutting board onto the counter and lays out a wheel of cheese, crackers and olives before immediately cutting off a thick slice of brie and dropping it into her mouth. In an instant, Delia can see it.

November with her hair shorter, flat-ironed straight, and in a prim, brightly coloured suit, maybe something red that would clash with her tangerine curls. She imagines silky, flesh-coloured pantyhose and lipstick on teeth, grins painted on with a side of desperation. It's an unfair image, Delia knows, but it's the one that comes.

'Can't say it seems like inspiring work.'

'Oh, it can be. I mean, you get to help people find a home. That can be pretty magical. I spent most of my time in rentals though, which is – well. Not quite so magical.'

Delia snorts, and November flashes her a toothy grin. It's a good smile, this one, sweet as anything.

'You're an artist, right?'

Delia startles at that, and November shrugs, suddenly embarrassed. 'I saw your easel when we moved in. You had it out in the yard.'

Did she? How long ago was that?

Delia reaches for her glass of wine just for something to do with her hands.

'Art teacher,' she supplies lamely, taking a sip.

'That must be rewarding work.'

'Ah,' she laughs. 'Sometimes. It depends on the class I guess.'

They settle into silence, and Delia wonders if she should finish her drink faster, get home, suddenly fearful of November's judgement. The mother of a missing boy, laughing, drinking. She probably still smells like Griff.

'I mean, it keeps me busy,' she adds, and November nods, picking up her own drink.

'That's a good way to be.'

She can hear the calls and hoots of little girls down the hall, the two daughters she's seen playing tea party and pirates and witches in the backyard. They're close in age, like Bo and Delia were, and they remind her, sometimes, of her and her sister too. The thought makes her heart stutter, and November leans over, reaches a hand out as if to touch her, but then drops it, hides it, as if the closeness is too much.

'We don't have to talk about your son,' November says quietly.

'What?'

'We can,' she adds quickly, 'if you want, I just figured you've probably done a lot of that over the last week, and I mean, we don't know each other, and—'

Has it only been a week? Maybe it has, but that fact is not as surprising as this soft and strange kindness, and she doesn't want to, but she can feel the hot swell of tears in her eyes, and she pushes them back, and she nods. Sharply. Curtly. She smiles as perfectly as she can.

'So, you have daughters?'

9

The costume has changed by the next morning.

It's one of the first things Delia notices while she fixes herself a coffee, one hip pressed into the kitchen counter. Parts have been substituted out – gone are the too-short leggings, tossed aside for a pair of Olive's old ones, the singlet replaced with a Billabong hand-me-down from Charlie – but the cape and mask fit as faithfully as they did when he was a little boy.

Reaching out with her free hand as he tries to bound past her, Delia latches onto the knot at the back of the mask, tugging Benjamin to a stop and then his head back to look at her.

'What are you up to?'

'The times are changing, civilian,' he replies, forcing his expression into a solemn sort of look that leaves her lips twitching.

'Civilian, huh?'

With a cackle, he breaks free of her hold, tearing out the back door and down the steps to their yard. From here, she can see him clambering onto the trampoline, throwing his body down with such velocity he rebounds off it in a way that briefly makes him look like he's flying.

Delia takes a long sip of her coffee, grabs her tablet and follows Benjamin's line of chaos to the back steps of the house.

The calls of late-rising birds colour the morning, the gargles of magpies, the brays of noisy miners and the dulcet squawks of crows. She can see a few pink galahs crowded onto one of the powerlines, their heads bowed and beaks pressed together as if swapping gossip. A kookaburra watches her son bounce about on the rusted trampoline from its vantage point in Ed's weedy and drought-wilted herb garden, its gaze unbothered, even when a particularly brave noisy miner swoops it.

Across the yard, Benjamin leaps sideways off the trampoline, his body hunching into the long grass, poised and eager, before springing forwards again. He has the mobility of a long-jumper, the wingspan for it, and she traces his movements, following the limber lines of him, until he suddenly stops. His mask has slipped to cover his eyes, the cape loosening at his neck to dangle off his shoulder, and he drops Spectacular Man to the ground in an effort to untangle himself.

'Do you need help?' she calls, but Benjamin just holds up a hand in her direction.

'No, ma'am,' he replies, and Delia can't quite bite back the grin. Just like that, he's off again, his mask back in place as he pulls Spectacular Man out of the grass and runs through the yard, his cape now billowing behind him.

'I thought we got rid of that.'

'Me too, actually,' Delia replies easily, unlocking her tablet and opening the news app, even as her shoulders tighten. She rolls them back in an effort to relax them, but it does little good. The steps behind her wheeze as Ed strides down them, and she angles the tablet just enough to see his reflection in the screen, to take in his fixed gaze and broad jaw, freshly shaven, the history she knows too well – his crooked nose, broken during a football match in high school, the chickenpox scar just above his left eyebrow, the tiny, faint birthmark at his chin that people often mistake for a smudge of dirt.

He must have used his key on the front door.

He must have walked through her house. Past the pile of unironed shirts slung over the arm of the couch, the empty esky she still needs to return to November, last night's dishes still sitting in the sink.

She should take the key back. She bites the lip Griff bit raw.

'He's getting too big for this sort of thing,' Ed says now, and at least that much is predictable. She rolls her eyes, grabs her coffee and has a mouthful.

'He's eleven,' she replies. 'What would you have him doing?'

They both know the answer to that, of course: sport – soccer, rugby, tennis, anything Ed can understand, so he can have another Olive, and not another Charlie.

She takes another, longer sip of coffee as Ed folds down onto the step behind her.

'Why are you here, Ed?'

He doesn't reply to that, and Delia won't look back, just keeps her eyes fixed on Benjamin, whose only tell that he's seen his father is the way he skirts closer to the furthest fence.

'Is he talking to himself?' Ed asks, and it looks that way. Benjamin's head is back, laughing, a stack of notepaper clenched in his hands. He bows his head like the galahs, his mouth moving quickly, and Delia sees his gaze travel to meet them through the holes in his mask.

'He's playing. Are you avoiding my question?'

Ed laughs at that, but there's not a lot behind it, and Delia finishes her coffee. With Ed here, so close, it's like Griff has a hold on her, like his touch has found her across the suburbs, is searing at her skin, but then it gives way to the years-old memory of Ed's, and just – god.

What is *wrong* with her?

Delia works her jaw, scrolling down through the headlines on her tablet but not taking any of them in.

'You can't just show up here anymore,' she bites, and she feels Ed shift behind her, exhale, scratch roughly at his jaw.

'I know that,' he tells her, his voice soft, and she blinks and they're here right now, and she blinks and he's walking out, and she blinks and he's fucking her instead of making love to her, and she blinks and he's holding their son, son, daughter, and they're at the beach again, his big hands sandy and warm as they touch her, and she feels so relieved to be so wanted, so needed, so *seen*, and—

Fuck.

She locks the tablet. Gets to her feet and, for the first time in months, really looks at him.

Those brown eyes of his.

And that's a relief too sometimes.

How much he doesn't look like their missing son.

How much easier it makes it.

From the look on his face, she knows she feels the opposite when he sees her.

'How many times do I have to tell you to go home? You're the one who decided this wasn't it anymore.'

With that, she walks back up the steps of her house, ignoring the way his fingers reach, grazing her ankle as she passes.

○

Mum goes back inside, but Dad doesn't.

He settles in against the step, his shoulders stooping forwards like the gargoyles that sit on top of old castles and churches in stories of dancing girls and monsters. For a few moments, Benjamin can feel the hot worm again, only in his back this time, wriggling across his shoulders and then around to his chest. Mum had been smiling. She'd smiled upstairs, and she'd smiled as she'd watched him, and Olive had made him promise not to tell her about Charlie, but it was almost as if she'd known anyway. As if she'd been able to feel him and hear him, just as Benjamin can now – or, at least, see his movements, the grass shifting at his feet, the rotor on his telescope, still propped near the back of the house, moving carefully.

But now Mum has gone again and Dad is standing up, walking down those heavy steps and out into their wild yard, and Benjamin's grip on Spectacular Man is getting so tight that the painted plastic clothes leave indents in his skin.

'Heya, Ben.'

Dad sits on the side of the trampoline, the rusted springs heaving beneath his weight, and Benjamin doesn't reply, can't. The words stick to the roof of his mouth thick as oozy caramel, and so he turns instead to where Charlie is. To where the bees buzz around his invisible legs and a grasshopper bounds, restless, before landing on what looks like nothing.

'How've you been?'

Benjamin shrugs, and Dad reaches out to touch the ratty fabric of his cape.

'Haven't seen this old thing in a while.'

Across the yard, Charlie moves his telescope an inch or two to the side, angling it better to see whatever it is he needs to. For a moment Benjamin wonders if this is what it's been like, all those days when they worried about him. If they'd just never thought to look. *Where would he be?* Poppy had asked him, and maybe Charlie was here all along. Maybe he never left. Maybe he did and came back.

Benjamin should ask him that.

'How's school going? Any tests coming up?' Dad asks, changing the subject, and Benjamin wonders if he could do what Charlie does. If he could become invisible too, blink his eyes or snap his fingers and disappear from this very moment.

'Benjamin.'

At the sound of his full name, Benjamin looks back up at his dad, at his wide, dark eyes and brows that are so similar to his own. It's Benjamin who looks like him the most. Who got all his pieces, all his parts, and right now, Benjamin hates all of it.

'What?' he bites, surly, and Dad just sighs, his mouth set in a strange, unfriendly grimace.

'Nothing, don't worry about it.'

He stands up then, dropping a hand to Benjamin's shoulder and squeezing lightly before starting to walk away, and Benjamin might not be able to disappear, but he can leave, and he does, bounding back through the grass, scores of slippery-bodied skinks and fuzzy-legged crickets fleeing from his every heavy step.

○

Olive's barely three feet in the door when Lux springs forwards, grabbing her arm and tugging her into the staffroom.

'Jesus,' Olive swears as Lux's clammy fingers release her.

'I thought you were going to ditch again,' the other girl moans, moving to lean back against the staffroom table, her arse narrowly missing a pot of ageing hummus someone has left out. Olive shrugs, walking away from Lux to shove her bag in her locker.

'Are they pissed?' Olive asks, and then it's Lux's turn to shrug, shuffling backwards on the table until her legs hang over the edge.

'A little, but you're golden. You've pretty much got a get-out-of-jail-free card right now with everything going on.'

Huh, Olive thinks, turning her attention back to her locker and pulling her name tag out of her bag. She's not sure how long she lay out by the road yesterday, but by the time she got home it was dark and her mum and Benjamin had both been in bed, and Charlie must've been asleep somewhere too, because he'd left a note on her bed but not answered when she'd whispered his name in the dark.

In the end she'd slept fitfully, and then left in the morning before Benjamin or Delia had woken up, and ridden aimlessly around the suburbs, blissfully alone, until her shift had started.

'I'm a little pissed though,' Lux adds with a wry grin and a tilt of her nose. 'I wanted to talk to you about the other night. You were mental. In, like, a good way.'

The memory of the bat in her hands finds her too quickly, and Olive clumsily pins her name tag to her shirt with bruised fingers. There's a gash on her back from where a part of the ceiling fell in as Dom battered the walls, knocking holes into the plaster and disrupting legions of creeping termites, cuts at her arm and stomach from the broken window, a rash on her arm from the cheap spray-paint.

'Guess I had some shit to work out.'

'Obviously. I mean, it's why I took you,' Lux says with a laugh. She stands up again, holding and swinging an imaginary bat, and Olive looks away in embarrassment. It had felt right the other night, before … She clears her throat, tugging at the mouth of her shirt.

'It's hot,' she groans, changing the subject, and Lux nods in agreement, tilting her chin up.

'Fan's busted again.'

And so it is, Olive realises, looking up to see the still blades. Figures. She shakes her head, already itching for a cigarette.

'Can you sign me in? I'm just going for a smoko.'

'I'll come with you.'

Olive shakes her head, more aggressively than she'd meant to.

'No, I need to make a phone call. Come on the next one.'

She's sure Lux can hear the lie, but if she does she doesn't call her on it. Just nods and darts out of the staffroom, heading back to the deli floor. It gives Olive a moment to collect herself, to let the steady hum of the store beyond fill her ears – customers on phones, calling children's names, stunted orders – before she slides out of the room and into the loading bay.

Out here, a long-beaked ibis wades through the garbage, thrusting its head through the trash and guzzling pulpy vegetable remains and off-coloured cold cuts left to rot. A few pigeons and crows lurk on the store roof, ready to see whatever the ibis turns up, and Olive watches them almost unconsciously as she lights her cigarette and takes a drag.

It feels like only a minute before the door is pushed open behind her, and Olive groans, something deep and throaty.

'Fuck off, seriously,' because she needs the break, the quiet, just wants to be alone with an empty head, but she turns to see not Lux but Jude standing in the doorway, an eyebrow raised and his lips gently parted.

'Jesus, sorry,' he says, and moves to go back inside. Olive fumbles for the words, swearing under her breath and reaching out, before pulling her hand away quickly, her body suddenly awkward.

'No, I'm sorry. I thought you were someone else.'

Jude pauses, takes her in, before rocking his head from side to side. He holds up a cigarette.

'Apology accepted if I can steal a light?'

Relieved, Olive fumbles in her back pocket for her lighter and offers it to him, only he doesn't accept it – instead he puts the cigarette between his lips and leans in, waiting for her to light it for him. The air suddenly feels thicker. Hotter. Brighter, and Olive can hear the blood rush in her ears as she flicks the switch.

Leaning back, Jude takes a drag, turning to watch the ibis in the bin.

'I'm guessing the someone else was Lux?'

Olive snorts, shifting her weight, willing the tension out of her awkward body.

'How'd you guess?'

'She can be a lot.'

'She can. She means well, I just … Yeah. Like you said.'

Jude grins, his big blue eyes locked with hers. His gaze, his attention, is enough to make her flush, to send a hot wash through her body, leaving her flustered. Enough to tear her thoughts from Charlie, to place her here, in this moment. She hopes she doesn't look shy, wishes for Lux's confidence, loathes the thought of a blush staining her pale cheeks, but then, glancing back at Jude through her thick blonde lashes, maybe she doesn't.

They pull out onto the highway late in the afternoon, cruising the distance between home and Saint Anne's with ease, the almost-hour filled with Benjamin's endless bored chatter and Delia's wandering mind.

Somewhere past the slump of the suburbs and the grey monotony of industrial estates, Benjamin pushes his head against the window, leaving a smear of sweat across the glass.

'What if she doesn't want to talk?'

Fog clouds the window beneath his mouth, and Delia has to resist the urge to reach out and tug her youngest son away, to resettle him in his seat. After Ed had left that morning Delia had pulled Benjamin back inside and together they had worked through his project, talking about his Grandma Rosie and writing questions that he could ask her. It had left Delia oddly raw, a fact she had blamed on Ed's uninvited appearance.

'Well, then we come back another day,' Delia replies, and Benjamin makes a small noise in the back of his throat, like it isn't quite the answer he wants.

Outside, the sun bleeds across the long road, leaving everything blisteringly bright. She knows the bitumen will be hot underfoot, even through the soles of her worn shoes. Knows how the heat radiates out here, without the shelter of trees and tall, sloping houses, without the shelter of anything at all. She drums her fingers on the steering wheel, casting a sideways glance at Benjamin, but she can only really see the back of his head, his shoulders contorted towards the window, his eyes locked on something out of her line of sight.

'Which question are you going to start with?'

Benjamin shrugs.

'I don't know. Maybe the one about Great-Grandma, or about growing up in Crows Nest.'

'I think the one about Crows Nest would be good.'

Flicking on the indicator, Delia changes lanes and she feels it more than sees it when Benjamin turns in his seat to look at her.

'What if she doesn't remember?'

Delia sighs, fingers tightening around the steering wheel.

'Then she doesn't remember today. The doctors think it's good though, to try to get her to remember more. I think your questions will be great for that – really helpful.'

Pulling off the highway, Delia drives down the few tired roads towards Saint Anne's. It's not so far from the turn-off onto the gateway, as if it's been conveniently dropped from space. A pit stop for loved ones in their daily commute. She shakes her head, parks as close to the doors as she can manage.

Inside Saint Anne's the lights cast an eerie glow and she watches Benjamin examining the building, his careful, considered gaze taking in the sterile walls and the religious paraphernalia, the haggard faces of the nurses, and the patients, some strapped into wheelchairs, IVs in their arms and drip-bags hanging over their heads like notes in an artist's study.

By the time they get to the nurses' station, Benjamin is pressing against her side, and she's wondering if it was a mistake to bring him here after all. He's always been sensitive, more sensitive than Olive and even Charlie, and her belly folds with guilt as she signs them both in.

'Come on,' she says, placing a hand on the back of Benjamin's head and pushing him gently in the direction of Rosie's room, but they've barely made it five steps before they're stopped by a nurse.

'Ms Rabbit?'

The nurse is older than the ones Delia normally meets, her face deeply lined and home to a pair of dark, sunken eyes.

'Yes?'

The woman's face softens.

'Ms Dorothy was hoping to get a word in before you saw your mother.'

'A word?'

The nurse nods, glancing back down the hall, then down at Benjamin, before ushering Delia aside.

'We've had to move your mother. Just for tonight. She's … had a little episode.'

'An episode?' Delia repeats, and the nurse nods, and Delia can barely feel Benjamin's hand gripping her elbow, and she can see the gauzy lights casting long shadows across everything that looms below, and she can feel her heart beating in her throat, and her fingers brittle and aching with the weight of this moment.

'Ms Rabbit?' the nurse repeats, and Delia takes a seat.

10

The clock on the wall has stopped.

Or rather, it's almost stopped, the long hand ticking back a second, then forward one, then back again, in an endless repeating cycle. The sound clicks through the room, rapping against Delia's tired eardrums, drowning out the hum of the air conditioner and the whine the chair makes whenever she adjusts herself. The battery needs to be changed, that's all, and Delia wonders who she should tell, or if she should tell anyone at all.

Across the desk, the aged-care administrator taps her fingers nervously on her wooden desk, clearing her throat in an effort to pull back Delia's attention. When this doesn't work, she finally speaks.

'Mrs Rabbit,' she starts, only for Delia to interrupt.

'Ms. I never married.'

Maybe she should tell her about the clock. It feels like it'd be important for an administrator to know the time, but maybe she doesn't use the clock, only her phone, like Delia does. Has the clock in her office back at the college stopped, she wonders, or has it kept the time across this long, sweltering summer?

'Right.' The woman clears her throat again. She's a thin thing, with the sort of aggressively toned body Delia's only used to seeing in weather women and reality-show hosts, a mass of ropey muscle with no ounce of fat to soften her. 'Your mother's dementia is escalating. She's growing aggressive, uncommunicative, losing her motor functions. What's more, she's spending less and less time *with us*, so to speak.'

'I understand how dementia works, Ms—' Delia fumbles for a name, jerking her gaze away from the clock, and it's only then that the woman shifts forwards, her body tilting towards Delia as if she's going to take her hand. A tangle of nervous energy and misplaced intimacy.

'Portia Dorothy,' the woman says.

'Ms Dorothy. I kind of thought that handling it was what you all did here.'

Portia nods, the movement oddly awkward. She's not a young woman, but for some reason she seems it. Then again, Delia thinks, some women will always be young, ill at ease in the costume of womanhood.

'I understand that this is a difficult time for you,' Portia says, and Delia laughs, the sound like a gunshot in the dark.

'I really don't think you do.'

If it weren't for the clock, Portia's office would be perfect. A sleek, small room void of clutter. There is a wall of uniformly framed qualifications behind her, bracketed by a selection of heavy bound books on rosewood shelves; bright-lipped orchids sit open mouthed in a pot on her desk. Portia leans back in her chair, adjusting her pen just so. She's all lines, Delia thinks, her fingers itching, for a pencil, for chalk, to carve out the woman's veins and ligaments in the dusty pages of her forgotten sketchbook. The itch is so strong it startles her.

'I can't move her,' Delia says after a minute, feeling suddenly merciful, and Portia reels back in her chair.

'That's not what we're talking about.'

Delia blinks, her own head lolling back, her mouth dry.

'Then why the *fuck* am I here?'

○

One of the nurses takes her to see her mother after Portia has explained the situation, but Delia still isn't prepared for the sight of her. Not for her near-translucent skin, or for the drool crusted in the corners of her lips, or for her yellowing teeth, and certainly not for Rosie Rabbit restrained to her hospital bed, thin, padded straps coiled like cotton snakes around her weak wrists.

Delia drops her handbag to the floor and stands at her mother's bedside. She brushes a loose strand of hair away from her mother's cheek.

'Hi, Mum.'

Rosie doesn't even look at her, just keeps her uneasy, foreign gaze on the far wall of her room, her eyes slimy, her body twisted like a prime-time corpse. If Delia were somebody else, anyone else, she might have reached for her. Might have held her hand, pressed her warm fingers to her mother's cold skin, but Delia is not someone else, and so she sits beside her hollowed-out mother and prays for relief instead.

○

The sun has almost set by the time Olive gets home, pushing her bike against the rotting fence and darting up the steps towards the house. The smell of red wine and red meat greets her when she's halfway up, snaking out the open windows to brew in the humid air above the yard. Her stomach rumbles loudly in response, and she can almost taste it – drink it down and feel full with it – when something makes her stop.

Because it's not just the smell that greets her, but also tinkling, childish music and the high-pitched voice of a TV princess. Olive slows her step, letting herself into the house, and has to briefly double-check that it's her home. Sprawled on the couch are two little girls she recognises as the neighbour's daughters and, in the kitchen, the neighbour herself.

'Jesus, you gave me a fright.'

The neighbour clutches a hand to her chest as she says it, and Olive shrugs apologetically before scanning the kitchen. There's a heady smell of beef, thyme and stock weeping out of a pot on the stove, and the neighbour darts back to tend to it, looking oddly at home.

'Where's my mum? And Banjo?'

The neighbour wipes her hands on the waist of her dress.

'Your mum's just been held up with your grandmother at Saint Anne's. She asked me to pick up your brother from there and get you guys settled. I've got dinner on, and your brother's just doing his homework.'

She steps aside then, so that Olive can look past her to where Benjamin is sitting at the kitchen table, poring over his school notebooks and a long sheet of cardboard. He looks up at her briefly, and then scribbles something down. Beside him a pen moves of its own accord, and whatever it writes makes Benjamin grin. The image settles strangely in Olive – appears to her like a story she's been written out of – and there's that feeling again. The one that drags down, down, down.

'Well, thanks,' Olive says, and the neighbour smiles, moving back to stir the meal, the little girls yelping happily on the couch when the princess solves a riddle.

'You don't have to thank me.'

'Kinda feel I should,' Olive replies with a stiff shrug. The neighbour is pretty, really, in an angular sort of way. A long, pointed nose and small eyes and cheekbones you could cut glass with. She looks nothing like Delia. Nothing like any of them, really.

'I can take over.'

The neighbour pauses her stirring and looks up at Olive.

'It's really no trouble at all. Your mum was a little shaken, and I figured making sure there was something on the table for you guys tonight might take a bit off her plate.'

Olive hums, her chest suddenly feeling too tight. She's not sure what it is about this moment, but all she can see is the neighbour, pottering domestically in *her* house, and all she can hear are the giggles of those little girls – too sweet and too young and—

And something happened and her mother called a stranger.

Not Olive.

Not her dad.

Her mother called a stranger and her brother's missing or maybe he's not anymore and there's this other family in her house and suddenly she feels too hot. It's like there are hands on her, pulling her down, pushing at the back of her neck, and she's prickling with tension and everything is too much and not enough and finally she bites:

'Well I'm here now, so you can go.'

The neighbour's head snaps back up to Olive, the shells of her ears pinking in embarrassment, and she nods.

'Right, of course, I don't want to outstay my welcome.'

Olive hums in agreement, the sound drowning out her thrumming heart, and she studiously keeps her gaze away from where she knows Benjamin and Charlie are watching, fixing her eyes instead on the neighbour's face. She gestures towards her in a way she hopes comes off as an apology.

'It's fine. We're fine. That's all I mean.'

It still takes a minute for the neighbour to nod again. To pass off a couple of instructions about finishing the casserole and to mumble a few more apologies that coil guiltily in Olive's gut. To collect her daughters and switch off the TV, and she is barely out the door before a piece of paper is shoved in Olive's face.

That wasn't very nice.

Rolling her eyes, she plucks it out of thin air, balling it up and dumping it into the bin beside the stove. She hates that she already feels better. Hates that the second the other woman left, she finally felt like she could breathe.

'Who cares?'

'I do,' Benjamin says, and Olive fixes him with a deadpan look. The attention flushes his face quickly, and he looks down at his homework with a creased forehead.

'She was nice, is all,' he adds, and Olive sighs.

'Sorry.' She leans her hip against the kitchen counter, knocks her knuckles a few times against the benchtop. 'Is Grandma really sick?'

'I think she might be, yeah.'

The sound of paper tears through the room.

Grandma's tough though. She'll be okay.

She snorts, plucking the paper out of the air again and looking straight through her would-be brother. A part of her wants to reach out, see if she can feel him, grab his shoulder, his elbow. Hold him like she would when they were little kids, sneaking into the living room past midnight to watch scary movies on cable. She turns away instead, pulling the casserole off the hotplate and switching off the stove. It does smell good. Better than they probably deserve.

A hand taps her shoulder, and she looks around to see Benjamin standing at the table, gathering his things, and then a note again, hovering in front of her.

Want to look at the stars with me and Banjo?

She takes the note, looks at Charlie's familiar chicken scratch, and then up at the great wide nothingness in front of her.

'Okay,' she says.

O

They loosen the restraints on her mother sometime around nine, then remove them entirely shortly before midnight. On anyone else, the padded restraints wouldn't leave much of a mark, but on her mother they leave purple bruises, blowing up like ink dropped in water below her cellophane skin.

It does little to soften Rosie – at least, little to soften Rosie to Delia. Nor does her sweating, clammy body, her hair, loose from its twist, curling wet around her sallow face, the tears clinging to her trembling lashes. The lines in her neck, in her skin, are deep trenches from the war her body is fighting – has always fought, against Delia, against her father, and against the raging losses that have marred the thick canvas of her life. Has she always looked this way? Delia knows there was a time when she thought her mother was beautiful, but the memory is coloured by the way she looks now.

(Can you draw someone from memory?)

Rosie writhes, now free of the restraints, forcing her face hard into the pillow, as if she wants to suffocate herself. Delia gets to her feet, leaving the discomfort of the ungiving chair behind her, and pushes a hand gently beneath her mother's neck, easing her head around until her open mouth gapes at the air instead of the wet cotton pillowslip.

'Hey,' she whispers. 'Come on, Mum.'

The machines blip around them, little mechanical gasps in the eerie quiet of the room. Delia thinks that if she listened harder she might be able to hear beyond it – hear the nurses gossiping out by their station, the moans of other patients, writhing in their damp bedclothes, trying to pull out their pinching drips or tugging catheters, just like her mother does.

Rosie blinks her dull, watery eyes at Delia, her face contorting with something between recognition and confusion, as if Delia is something both familiar and foreign, someone she should know, someone who might not even be there at all. She opens her mouth, exposing her pallid gums and the thinness of her lips.

'Did you see the light again last night?'

Her voice is hoarse, as if it hasn't been used in a long time, rasping and dry and deeper than Delia remembers.

'The light?'

Rosie nods, her neck still warm in Delia's hand. She moves her head just slightly, to lean it against Delia's forearm.

'I hadn't seen it in a while, but it was back. Just by the marsh at the corner of the camp. It makes me feel like I'm on another planet sometimes.'

Her mother sighs dreamily, her eyelids fluttering shut.

'I told the sergeant. He thinks I'm crazy, but Anders swears he saw it too, just like we did.'

Her voice is steadier than Delia expects, firmer somehow, even with the quake of the fever in it. Outside, a nurse suddenly calls to another, and Delia looks through the open door into the corridor, but it's dark out there, the hall lights the only thing warding the night off.

'Maybe I *am* crazy,' Rosie adds with a sigh, her eyes flickering beneath the lids. 'Maybe I always have been.'

'I don't think you're crazy,' Delia replies, because what else is there to say, and her mother laughs, low and sweet, the quiver of her eyelids lessening. They stay like that for a moment, until Delia's sure her mother's close to sleep. She starts to slide her hand out from beneath her neck when Rosie's eyes snap open.

Her hands reach, claw-like, scratching at Delia's arm. Her eyes are bright and wild now.

'Where's Bo? Where's my baby?'

Blood rushes to her ears, to the hot space inside her skull. She pulls her arm free as best she can, watches as her mother's eyes grow wider, more desperate, watches her fumble in the sheets, try to get out of bed, only to fall back when the drip tears at her skin. She screams, hoarse, and Delia presses the call button and steps backwards as two nurses swarm in, lower her mother back into the bed and inject a sedative into her drip, loosening Rosie's consciousness and the memory of her most treasured daughter with one sound push.

O

Benjamin loses track of how long they spend outside. It's got to be hours at the very least, with Charlie – or, well, the presence of Charlie – moving around his telescope and readjusting his gait. The air around them is muggy with the memory of the day, their yard alive with warty toads and powdery moths, with creeping midnight birds and the buzzing of long-snouted mosquitoes.

For a while he tries to see what Charlie's doing by watching the things that move around him, before he gives up, drifting out across the yard, hopping over ant nests and kicking up the dusty earth. It's weird, he thinks, that the air can feel this humid, can make them this damp, while, without the rain, everything around them sits parched, crunching underneath their bare feet.

'How do we know this is really you?'

Benjamin spins around to see Olive standing tall in the grass only a few feet from Charlie's telescope, her long hair down for once, and so fair she looks like the pictures of muses and fairies in some of the books Dad used to read him. Her skin is tanned from riding her bike, but her work shirt has left pale lines on her, clearer when she's out here in just a singlet, marking her up like a drawing. He can only half see those lines, even though he knows there are others there, by the glow of the streetlamps and the light at the top of the stairs. It makes everything seem like a fairytale. This strange, half-lit night.

Olive can't be expecting an answer. Charlie's post-it notes and his pens are still upstairs, and there's nothing in their yard for Charlie to type on. And as far as Benjamin can tell, Charlie's invisibility extends to his voice too. Just like …

Benjamin shivers.

'How do we know we're not having, like, a collective hallucination?' Olive continues, her voice growing louder, firmer. She throws out her arms. 'Or, fuck, even if you *are* here, how do we know you're Charlie and not some other kid or monster or whatever? How do we know you're not—'

She stops, and Benjamin looks away, his fingers balling at his sides.

'A ghost,' he finishes, and Olive's head spins quickly around, until she's staring at him, as if she'd forgotten he was even there. Her jaw wired shut.

After a moment, she turns back to face Charlie, and so does Benjamin, but there's no one there, just Charlie's telescope and the little hive of sleeping bees wedged in its joints. A car passes, then another, their headlights blearing between the slots in the fence, creating streaks of brilliant yellow across the yard. Across *them*. Something in Benjamin's chest catches. He wants to see a shadow, he realises, because Olive is right. He wants Charlie's outline to appear, like in comic books and movies, so that the audience knows where the character is.

So that *they* do.

Benjamin looks away, and is surprised when he hears a thud at his feet. Glancing down through the thick wayward grass, he sees Charlie's notebook lying at his toes, its pages frayed, wet with dew, curling post-it notes sticking out of it in fluoro rainbows of colour.

Bending down, he picks it up, glancing at Olive as she walks towards him, her eyes big and tired and sad, and he wonders if he looks like that too.

With shaking hands, he opens the book, finding notes in Charlie's sharp and uneven handwriting scrawled across pages, little observations and equations, algebra scratched in margins, star formations sketched in crusty ink and fading lead.

Something about it makes Benjamin's heart race, and he closes the notebook quickly, but then Olive's there, plucking it out of his grip, and snapping it open again. She flips through the pages faster than him, eyes scanning, until she stops, and Benjamin looks over and sees the date at the top of the page – the date Charlie disappeared. Scribbled in Charlie's familiar hand is *I ghosted half an hour before school. I'm going to try again tonight, if I can get out of the house. I might see how long I can hold it.*

All Benjamin can hear is Olive's rapid breathing, and suddenly she's gesturing with the notebook towards Charlie's telescope.

'Is this a game to you? Another experiment? Turn it *off*, Charlie.'

And it's Benjamin's turn to snatch the notebook, to go back to that page and turn to the next.

Tried to unghost same day at 23.34, nxt day 01.14, 03.46, 03.52, 03.59, 04.10, 04.15, 04.18, 04.19, 04.20, 04.21, 04.22, 04.22.30, 04.22.35, 04.22.41, 04.22.50, 08.52.

The numbers go on like that, long gaps followed by bursts of desperation, over days and days and days. Benjamin turns the page again to where Charlie's started to try to make sense of it, put it into tables, make it clearer, all the times he's tried to turn it off on one side of the page, and on the other all the things Charlie usually records. All of his weirdly specific observations, from the comings and goings of the wildlife in their yard to constellations and finally to them.

O and B fight, 18.56.

Dad over. Same shirt as yesterday. More grey hairs. He and mum talked. Then he and B. 15.45–16.10.

Mum not doing well.

Need to turn it off.

Need to turn it off.

Need to turn it off.

They're all quiet then, and it's Olive who eventually breaks the silence, her voice wobbling like an untuned instrument.

'It really is you, isn't it?' she says, and the telescope nods, the barrel of it jerking up and down in the only gesture Charlie can really make, and just like that, Olive starts to cry.

That night, Delia dreams not of Bo, not of her mother, but of her father.

She dreams of him as she remembers him best – his big hands calloused as he sanded furniture in the garage, the line of his broad shoulders and his little paunch, that quick, sly grin that was so much like Bo's.

She remembers him humming pub rock songs and his thick arms around her mother's waist. The way he'd kiss her shoulder. The way they'd stand together in their backyard, warm and quiet, while Delia painted banners for *The Rabbit Family Theatre* and Bo warmed up her voice on the leftover wooden boards their father put out for them as a stage.

The Rambunctious, Riveting Rabbits, the Most Magical Magicians, the Star-Born Sisters, Bo would declare, and their mother would watch her, a look in her eye Delia never understood, a curl to her lips Delia could never read, and oh, Delia thinks, watching Bo flourish a pillowcase on their little makeshift stage, hearing her sister say *now you see me—*

Maybe the dream was about Bo and Rosie after all.

The morning light smears across Delia's eyes as she blinks awake, groggy and stiff, her body aching, and she shifts uncomfortably in the hospital chair, swallowing the stale taste in her mouth.

'And Sleeping Beauty awakens from her slumber.'

Still clawing at consciousness, Delia turns to find a nurse pulling off her rubber gloves, a coy smile at her lips. She tries to paint one on to match, to sit up a little straighter, to look a little more together, watching as the nurse scribbles something down in her mother's chart. The air feels cleaner somehow this morning, in spite of the potent humidity – a little cooler against Delia's skin. Her blouse has stuck to her back, and she's sure she stinks in that earthy way most people do after a crap night's sleep. She yawns, thinking about getting a coffee before realising that her mother's awake.

Catching her gaze, the nurse smiles at her again, more gently this time.

'She's doing better,' the nurse says, and Delia nods, sitting up straighter and reaching over to the bed. She grabs her mother's hand, holding it firmly in her own.

'Mum?' she says, her voice hoarse even to her. It takes a minute for Rosie to look over, to tear her gaze away from the nurse at her bedside, and when she does it's in that shrewd, familiar way that tightens Delia's chest. Without a word, Rosie pulls her hand from Delia's grip and rolls over in the bed, leaving Delia to stare at her mother's shrunken shoulders and the craggy knobs of her spine, jutting through her hospital gown.

'I'm sure your mother is very tired,' the nurse says, placatingly, and Delia shakes her head, desperate suddenly for air, even just for a moment. She pushes the chair back, grabs her handbag off the floor and stands up.

'No,' she says. 'It's good. She seems like herself again.'

11

Early in the morning, before school, before even Olive wakes up, Benjamin and Charlie open the hallway cupboard and get to work.

Charlie pulls out a few fraying cardboard boxes full of baby clothes, art supplies, old school projects, binders of their mother's college curriculum and her students' uncollected assignments. They're all inched with dust, eaten by moths and mites and wriggling silverfish, and Benjamin pushes a finger across the crumpled lid of one of the boxes, ploughing a line through the dust like a truck through snow.

'I think I saw it close to the front,' he says, and Charlie's hands pause, like he means to say something, but his notebook is a few feet away on the corridor floor, so Benjamin can't really be sure. It was his own idea, after all. To find the photographs of their grandmother and figure her out that way, instead of through the interview he meant to do.

Charlie pushes out another box, and Benjamin lifts his hero mask to watch his brother's actions more carefully, the pull and push of the new no-man's-land of his body. Benjamin huddles closer to his side, gazing into the bottomless cupboard. Above him the air seems to tremble, a laugh echoing as a mouse-chewed shoebox hovers above his head.

The box is completely nondescript, and if it weren't for Charlie's total assurance that it was The Right One, Benjamin would've dropped it with the boxes of old paints and projects below. The label on the outside is faded, after all, the writing on it beyond recognition, and the thing seems to wear dust like Benjamin wears his cape.

The boards beneath them creak, and the lid is pulled off, dropped soundly to the floor, and Charlie makes efficient work of sorting through the box's contents – a green, gold and red scout's patch, a spotty medal, a small gold wedding band, a tiny, ratty stuffed bear, their old school report cards, and finally a musty envelope.

Charlie pulls the thing open, the sticky strip aged brown, and slides out a small stack of photographs. He thumbs through a few, his fingers leaving imprints on their glossy surfaces. After a minute he pulls one out and passes it to Benjamin, face-down so he can see the writing on the back. *Rosie Rabbit, Aged 19. Crows Nest.*

Benjamin turns the photo over. Grandma Rabbit, if he can call her young self that, has her hair twisted up into a beehive, her face polished with make-up and her dress a lurch of vivid colour. She doesn't look a thing like their mother, but there's something there that reminds him of her all the same, and he grins before he can help it.

Charlie passes him another photograph, this one of Grandma Rabbit in her nursing whites, her face already lined, although she can't be much older than she was in the first picture, her thin lips curved into a frown. Her eyes are shadowed.

'She looks so different,' Benjamin says, and the air seems to hum, those invisible hands returning with Charlie's notebook. He flips to a clean page, and writes:

I don't think mum will want you gluing these to the poster board.

'I'm not gonna. I just want to see,' Benjamin says. He looks down at the photos, these two sides of Rosie Rabbit. Like those old drama masks, though not really. More like a coin flip. Heads or tails. Young Rosie and, well, slightly less young Rosie. The scratch of Charlie's pencil breaks the quiet.

We probably shouldn't have done this without mum.

'You'd have to tell her you're here for that,' Benjamin replies, putting the lid back on the box and slipping it into the hallway cupboard.

○

'Your mother has stabilised,' Doctor Tan says. Her voice is firm but not unkind, her face marred with the steep lines of lack of sleep or age or both, and Delia nods, feeling neither relieved nor disappointed. It must show on her own face, as Doctor Tan closes her binder and drops into the seat beside Delia in the waiting room, letting loose a slow, quiet breath.

Down the hall, a nurse quickens her step. A patient wails. The smell of chemical bleach and iodine saturates the air, so heavy, so heady, Delia can almost taste it. The low-hanging fluorescent lights cast a stark glow on everything, and Delia can see the lines on her hands, the ink beneath her nails from marking homework, the sag of her tired body. She shakes her head, leaning back into her seat. Did she leave dinner for the kids last night? Will they have remembered where the emergency credit card is if she didn't?

'I don't think it'll come as a surprise to you that your mother is deteriorating rapidly.'

Who did she even send Benjamin home with? Did she call Ed? Olive? The babysitter? God, she can't even think.

'It wouldn't be premature to start making arrangements,' Doctor Tan continues, her voice softening, her hands moving from her binder to the arm of Delia's chair. A hair's breadth from a real, human touch. 'Both for your mother and for yourself. For your family. Grief is a funny thing, and it can flatten you in ways you might not expect. In my experience, it helps to make arrangements while you can. Takes some of the pressure off, as it were, when the time does come.'

'I'm okay. We weren't close, you know,' Delia says. She waves a hand in Doctor Tan's direction, distracted briefly by the shadows these harsh lights cast across the other woman's features. She wonders if they're doing much to her own. She wonders suddenly why she even cares. 'Not since my sister died. Not even before then really. I just – there was no one else. To take care of her. That's all. It's just me and her.'

The wailing patient's sobs stop with a hiss, and Delia turns to look. She can't see anyone, of course. The patient is shut away in a room far from here, with her own clumsy family or lover or friend. There's a cooing somewhere, then words of comfort that Delia wouldn't be able to make out if not for the cloying tone in the speaker's voice.

'I'm sorry to hear about your sister,' Doctor Tan says carefully, and Delia feels a bubble of laughter in her chest. Feels it rise up her throat and burst out her mouth, a hysterical competition with the wailing woman, and in the early hours of the morning Delia laughs and laughs and laughs.

○

He thinks of the photographs of his grandmother while he eats breakfast and gets ready for school. It's not something he's ever really considered; Grandma Rabbit has always been more of an abstract concept to Benjamin than an actual person, not like Grandma Beth, who made him superhero costumes and could pop out her artificial teeth with the tip of her tongue on command.

Grandma Rabbit is the woman who made his mother, and who Benjamin only remembers meeting a few times at Christmas and once on a particularly gloomy Mother's Day. The trips were always the same. Benjamin, Charlie, Olive and Dad left to sit tensely in front of the ancient television set while Mum swapped clipped words with their sullen grandmother until, one year, they'd just stopped going altogether.

The chair in front of Charlie's desk sags, and Benjamin looks up from the photograph.

'Do you remember Grandma Rabbit?'

The chair tilts from side to side, as if considering the question. After a minute, Charlie's fingers rap along the computer keys.

Yes and no. I remember thinking she always seemed really sad.

Benjamin looks at the photograph again, at this frowning woman with hooded eyes, like little pearls in the wet shells of oysters. Sad doesn't feel like the right word, and not just because of the secret twist to her look. There's something about her that reminds Benjamin of shadows – not just the literal ones. Not dark necessarily, or lesser, but something hollow and unsure and not entirely there.

He's pulled out of his reverie by the sound of the keyboard clacking again, and he glances up to see more words typed out on the computer screen.

I remember the way she and mum would fight without fighting at all. They'd say things that should have sounded nice and friendly, but they never came across that way. There was something underneath them.

The cursor flickers briefly, as if Charlie wants to change something, but he doesn't. Instead, he adds:

Olive used to hate going over. She'd always complain about it.

Benjamin mulls this over, but it's not exactly a surprise. Olive hates going to most places – at least, she hates going with them.

He slides off the bed, leaving Charlie with the computer and padding out of the room and down the hallway. The heat is trapped there, creating a muggy corridor full of lethargic mosquitoes and a few silver-backed flies.

Benjamin ducks into the bathroom to find Olive slouched over the sink as she brushes her teeth. She smells like Olive usually smells these days. That musty scent of dead fruit and sweat and ash and beer and a million other smells that

Benjamin's not sure he'll ever be old enough or Olive-enough to know.

'Do you remember much about Grandma Rabbit?'

Olive spits out a glob of toothpaste before she turns to look at him. She drops her brush back into the jar and wipes the back of her hand against her mouth, smearing the remnants of spit and toothpaste down her cheeks and chin.

'Sure,' she says. 'Her house was creepy as fuck. You know what Charlie and me used to call that place?'

Olive shivers dramatically, reducing her eyes to slits, curling her mouth into an animal maw. 'The morgue.'

Unimpressed with Olive's performance, Benjamin leans sideways into the wall, unable to stop himself from feeling a bit triumphant when Olive drops the act and rolls her eyes. She fixes her attention back on her haggard reflection and mops up the last bits of toothpaste from her face.

'Did you really call it the morgue?'

Olive shrugs.

'Why do you want to know?'

Benjamin works his jaw, leaning back against the doorjamb, his gaze flicking down to the photograph in his hands. A crow caws suddenly, the noise rattling through the bathroom, seeming to graze the mirror, the pigeon-egg-blue tiles, the slippery, slightly mouldy shower curtain, half off its hooks on the rail.

'Forget it,' he says, moving to head back down the hall to his room, but Olive bounds forwards, grabbing the photograph from his grip. He fumbles after it, but Olive is too fast, holding it above her head and tilting her chin up to stare at it.

Her face contorts in surprise, and Benjamin growls, reaching on his tiptoes to pull the picture from her grip.

'Give it back!'

'Where'd you even get this?'

'Charlie gave it to me. It was in the hall closet. Give it back, Olive. Please.'

Olive rolls her eyes, lowering her arm so that Benjamin can reach up and snatch the photograph from her fingers. He holds it close to his chest as she leans back against the sink, her gaze considering. Considering *him*. He squirms beneath it, regretting coming in at all.

'Careful what you wish for. If Mum knows you're interested in Grams, you might just get admitted to the *actual* morgue, sorry, *Saint Anne's*, with her before she croaks.'

Benjamin glowers at his sister before narrowing his eyes, his curiosity winning out over his annoyance.

'Have you even been there?' he asks, and Olive turns back to the mirror, pulling off her hair tie and loosening her braid. It's frizzy in the summer heat, kinky from the plait, and Olive frowns at her reflection.

'Sure have, Banjo,' she says. 'I barely made it out alive. There are open graves all over the place, I almost fell into a few.'

'You're a liar. I was there with Mum yesterday, and there was nothing like that at all.'

'No way. Seriously. They'd pull up the tiles and there'd be these deep pits underneath. When the geriatrics die they just push them in and retile. You're always walking on top of dead people.'

'That's not funny.'

Olive shrugs, like she doesn't care if Benjamin believes her or not, which, really, she probably doesn't. He glances back at the photograph and is surprised to find that the curve of his grandmother's jaw seems suddenly very familiar. Just like Olive's, he thinks, looking back up at his sister, watching as she plays with her hair.

After a moment, she turns to look at him.

'Get dressed, yeah? I'll walk you to school.'

○

Even stabilised, her mother teeters on the edge of consciousness like a spinning top, her filmy eyelids twitching, her dry lips coughing out words and names and half-thought prayers. If this is the new norm, it's one Delia has mixed feelings about, even as the early-morning light warms the room and she packs up her things to go home.

Less active, less conscious, her mother is less likely to hurt herself, to hurt Delia, but there's something discomforting in seeing her so reduced. Seeing her shrunken form nearly lost in the folds of the starchy, too-white sheets.

In her car, Delia buckles her seatbelt, then stops, her hands heavy in her lap, her body tight and aching from sitting for so long in the merciless chair. She cracks her neck, rolls her shoulders, again and again, then hits the base of the steering wheel, her eyes tightly shut.

Now you see me.

She turns the keys.

O

Bzzzztt.

Delia leans back into the rough wall of the apartment building, feeling the exposed brick hard through the thin cotton of her shirt, and this is a mistake. She knows this is a mistake. Knows it's not too late to back out, to turn and go, and it'd be like she was never here at all, but then Ed's voice sounds through the intercom, a hoarse 'Hello?', and Delia swallows, throat tight, tongue too big in her mouth.

'It's me.'

The line goes dead, and then, with a buzzing sound, the door unlocks.

He's waiting in the corridor outside his apartment, and his voice is lowered when he asks:

'What are you doing here? Is it about Charlie?'

'Why are you whispering?'

Ed pauses, and she can almost see it, the mechanical turn of his mind. His eyes don't leave hers, and she tries not to divert her gaze either. Tries to meet him halfway, like she always has.

'Vanessa's asleep. I don't want to wake her. Is it about Charlie?'

'She moved back in?'

'The other day. She had a fight with her friend. So …' he trails off, shaking his head. He's starting to perspire, away from the crisp air conditioning of his apartment, and Delia finds she's glad for it. The ruffling. The way this weather can't leave him unfazed. Can't leave any of them that way.

'I think my mother's going to die,' she says, and Ed blinks down at her. 'Would that make me an orphan, do you think? Or just alone?'

For a moment all Ed does is look at her, his pupils small and focused. They dart between her eyes, her lips. Ed's tongue flicks out to wet his own.

'You've been alone for as long as I've known you,' he says. 'Even when we were together. Even when you loved me, you were alone.'

'I still love you.'

And then he just looks sad, as if he doesn't quite believe it. He reaches out his hand, picks up one of hers, and brushes his smooth fingers over her cracked knuckles.

'Have you slept much?'

'Not since Charlie. Maybe not since Bo, I don't know anymore.'

She laughs, but it sounds weak, even to her own ears. She pulls her hand from his soft grip. The lights in the hallway cast a stranger glow between them, something bold and unforgiving. From the corner of her eye she can see a lone gecko scurrying across the ceiling, its body wriggling against the smooth white lines of the building, its translucent flesh almost camouflaged. A tokay gecko. A foreigner, not like the earthy-green native ones. Delia sighs, looking back at Ed, surprised to find his gaze so intently focused on her.

'Why did you come here?' he asks again, and Delia thinks that if she could look at Ed, really look at him, she might be able to break him down into the sum of his parts. To grid him out to the fleshy tones of his skin, to the soft, too-light brown of his eyes.

'Where else would I go?'

She doesn't know what she expects. If she expects him to lean in and kiss her or to close the door on her, but Ed does what he always does.

Nothing at all.

She drops Benjamin at school and then doubles back home.

The photograph of their grandmother has reminded her of the wall of family portraits in Lux's house – history captured and laid bare for even the most distant of visitors – leaving her with the sudden, stark realisation that they've hung no photos in their own home.

Or maybe that's not true. Benjamin's most recent school photo is stuck to the fridge, and there's a framed one of Olive, Charlie and Benjamin at thirteen, nine and four at Caloundra on top of the bookshelves in the living room, dressed in their togs, sand caked on their legs. The realisation leaves Olive oddly curious, and before she can think better of it, she finds herself at the hallway cupboard.

She fights boxes of baby clothes and the corpses of old hawk moths, their crumbling wings wide as her wrists. The slick flat bodies of silverfish creep at her skin, the needle-thin limbs of daddy-long-legs turn over in their effort to escape her. The boxes are full of her mother's old art things, their rompers and their christening gowns, faded, dusty exercise books filled with neat and arching writing.

And then an envelope stuffed with photographs.

Olive leans back, dropping from her squat to sit on the

floor. Lifting the fold, she slips out the photos, carding through them, catching glimpses of her mother and father, both younger, and Benjamin, Charlie and herself too, all pudgy, grubby children's bodies nude in the bright cut of summer, giggling beneath the spray of the sprinkler.

There are other photographs, of her grandmother mostly, younger, her hair pulled back into her familiar twist, her sharp features closed off somehow, as they are in every memory Olive has of her.

Olive hadn't been lying to Benjamin when she'd said they used to call her place the morgue. Even now she can remember the chill of it, something dated and unused in the feel of it, as if it was never truly a home, least of all to the woman who called it one. Cobwebs collected beneath buffets and couches, in the uppermost corners of the ceilings. Water damage had eroded the bathroom walls, and mould spawned in flushes of green, blue and grey behind the bathtub and in small colonies on the bedroom walls and across the kitchen bench.

In some of Olive's earliest memories, her mother would stop at the corner shops before they went. There she would buy a fruit bun, a bottle of wine and a bottle of bleach, and after depositing the children in the small family room at the back of the house, Delia would clean and clean and clean.

Once, only once, Olive had crept out in her Sunday Best, with Charlie, still toddling, hanging onto her back, and watched from the hallway as her mother furiously scrubbed the walls. Her grandmother had sat, lip curled into a snarl, as Delia worked, her own face twisted with an animal look. They hadn't said anything to each other, but even then, stupid-young, Olive had known they hadn't needed to. Years of harsh words were somehow built into the walls of this house, a canopy over their heads, a taut string between Delia and her mother that they would never quite be able to sever.

In the photographs Olive's grandmother does not look so harsh. The feral ferocity is still there, but it's different somehow. Like a roaming pack animal, instead of the lean, hunted thing she'd become.

She pulls out more photographs, some of a tall, broad man she recognises from conversations as her mother's father – her grandfather. She files through a few more – of her grandfather at the beach, surfboard under a tanned arm, of her grandmother in hospital, new baby daughter in her arms, and then a photo of Delia, a toothless smile curling at her mouth, and then another, of Delia and a second girl, only a few inches taller than Delia, her dark hair a long, loose nest of curls, her eyes bright, a spark in her somehow both familiar and unknowable.

Olive turns the photograph over to find two names written in a looping hand, *Bo and Del, Summer '82.*

The front door cracks open and Olive fumbles, shoving the photographs back into the envelope, then wedging the envelope beside one of the boxes. She steps over the scrambling insects at her feet.

The front door closes. The sound of keys being dropped to the bench. A glass of wine being poured. And then footsteps heading down the hallway towards her. Delia stops in her tracks.

'Hey,' Delia says, voice thick with surprise. 'I thought you had work.'

Olive clears her throat, only then realising that the photographs of her grandmother and of her mother and Bo are still in her hand. She shoves them into the back pocket of her slacks.

'I do. I'm just heading out now. I was helping Benjamin with his school project.'

Delia shoots her a look like she doesn't believe her, but Olive doesn't really care. She adjusts her O'Malley's shirt and ducks around her mother.

'Don't wait up for me. I'm going out after.'

She hurries down the hallway, away from it all, even as the photos burn a hole through her pocket.

O

Benjamin has left his felt-tip pens out on the kitchen table. The cardboard for his presentation on the family is still blank, but the ends have curled up and one corner has torn already. Delia groans internally, thumbs the edge of it and purses her lips. She puts her glass of wine on the counter and grabs Benjamin's pencil case instead, unzips it with the intention of packing up the pens, but, despite herself, stops.

Putting the case back down, she slides quietly into the chair, picking up a pen, a big, black Crayola with a thick tip, and flips to the back of Benjamin's science notebook, scribbles a couple of quick, amateur designs. An apple in a bowl, an outline of a window that she fills with colour – with greens and golds and the bright blues of a morning sky. The perspective isn't great, rusty, but it's been so long since she's done this outside of school, work, other people's studies, and the pen feels welcome between her fingers. She's sketching more before she can stop herself. A mess of cursive lines and soft shadows, shades beneath a sharp jawline, full lips, crooked teeth, eyes full of boyhood. She's halfway through before she realises it's Charlie. She drops the pen, her mouth full of words she can't articulate. Then she pushes her chair in closer to the table, picks the pen up again and keeps drawing.

○

It's not until the next day that she opens up the hall closet and pulls out boxes, a dusty envelope of photos, a pram, an off-yellow highchair. Behind them is her easel, some large, ancient thing with cobwebs tangled at the joints and dust bunnies behind the screws. The carcasses of hawk moths have settled at the feet of the easel, and she pushes their broken wings aside to pull it out from behind all of the clutter, sixteen years of disuse, of life packed up. Beside it is a box of stiff brushes and solid paints, unusable now, but packed up initially with the intent of being returned to. There are jars marked up by dirty water, broken pieces of charcoal and an artists-pencils set that an old friend bought her, back when Delia had friends.

She jerks open the easel there in the hallway, and it skids on the wooden floor like a baby, an infant taking early steps. She cleans it with a rag, fiddles with the screws and sets it at the right height. Stares at it, her rabbit heart thumping in her throat.

'Right,' she mumbles to herself, tracing the wood with her eyes, seeing the places where it's chipped from when they moved house all those years ago, and then she lifts it with unsteady hands, carries it into her bedroom and rests it against the wall. She packs up the baby stuff and tosses out the brushes, salvages what she can of the charcoal, riffles through old sketchpads full of sprawling landscapes and childhood crushes, the smiling faces of friends she hasn't spoken to in years. Pages and pages of Ed's face and Ed's body and the curves of his eyelids when he slept. The last sketchbook is still half empty, and she leaves it out on the top of her chest of drawers and drives to the art store. She has to look it up, the address, and she remembers a time when she knew the way by memory alone.

She buys herself new, softer brushes and a box of acrylics. She spends twenty minutes in the aisles debating colours and brands, tentative and uncertain in a way she hasn't been in years, and the thought of getting it wrong scares her more than she cares to think about.

She gets home and she starts painting. Painting angry, heavy, sad, happy pictures of a son she fears won't be found. She paints Charlie as if this will make him reappear.

(Can you draw someone from memory?)

Her fingers tremble as she presses the bristles into the canvas. She paints and paints and paints, time lost in the brushstrokes, and that's the way Ed finds her, frazzled and dirty, with paint on her hands and her neck and her face.

He looks startled, takes a step forwards and then another, and Delia puts herself between him and the painting, like she's protecting it, and then he kisses her, furious and passionate and full of things she'd forgotten. The brush falls from her hand, splattering the floor between them, her bare feet, his polished leather shoes. For a second she could do it, fuck him by the door he left her through, but then—

She pushes him away. 'You left me,' she says, and he opens his mouth to say something, then slams it shut again. He keeps them there, his secrets, locked inside the cage of his jaw, and without another word he leaves. Delia cleans her palette.

12

Olive wakes up sometime around midday to an orchestral chorus of birds outside her bedroom window, and the soft, stretched limbs of Lux Robinson tangled up among her own.

'Fuck,' Olive hisses, disentangling herself from the other girl and stumbling out of the bed, her hangover making itself known. Above her, her ceiling fan whirs unsteadily, making rickety noises, and she pauses at her dresser to take unhappy swigs of stale water from a glass she's sure has been there for days.

Her gaze catches on something outside, and she's surprised to see her father hurrying down the front steps, beelining for his Audi. He climbs straight in, slamming the door behind him, but it takes him minutes to leave, and she wishes she could see him through the tinted glass, catch his eye, know what he's feeling, why he is here, remind him, somehow, that she's here too.

I haven't told him either.

The words are written in eyeliner at the corner of her window, so small she could easily have missed them, and Olive frowns.

'Then why was he here?'

I think he wanted to see mum. He went into her room. He wasn't here long though.

Olive takes another swig of water before thumbing the rim of the glass, digging it in just enough to feel uncomfortable.

'I don't care,' she says, and when Charlie starts to write something else she plucks the eyeliner pencil from his grip and tosses it to the floor behind her. The air crackles, but Olive's attention is diverted by a groan from her bed.

'What don't you care about?'

'Literally nothing,' Olive says, and Lux grins, stretching out, cat-like, as she kicks off the sheets.

'Talking to yourself?'

'Something like that. Are you working today?'

Lux shakes her head, and Olive grimaces, checking her phone for the time.

'Go back to sleep then?' she offers, and leaves Lux there, sprawled in her bed. Olive showers quickly, changing back into her O'Malley's uniform, but when she gets back to her room Lux is gone, and there are two notes on her dresser, one from Lux, promising she'll see her soon, and another in Charlie's unmistakable scrawl.

Are you mad at me?

And the truth is Olive doesn't know if she's mad at him. She wonders if she can be mad at Charlie when there isn't a Charlie there to be mad at. She can't Benjamin this situation and run around in a cape, using the static of their lives as fodder for the fantastic, or pretending that any part of her can make sense of Charlie's disappearance, this handwriting and this hurt.

It plants something deep in the untenable soil of her. A seed she doesn't know if she wants to dig up or water. So she does the only thing she can. She pretends it was never planted at all.

'I've got to go to work,' she mumbles, and when Charlie's pencil starts to scratch again she leaves before she has a chance to read it.

O

She's expecting nothing, of course, except maybe Mindy, but Jude is standing by the back door of O'Malley's again, his golden hair glinting in the half-light of the alley, his skin radiant and warm. He looks up at the sound of her and grins.

'Olive Rabbit,' he says, and Olive flushes, pushing her bike against the alley wall, something tightening in her gut.

'Jude Elber,' she replies, and there's something off about him today. His wicked grin doesn't quite meet his eyes. Despite herself, she steps closer. 'You okay?'

Jude just snorts.

'Frank's kind of an arsehole,' he says. He shifts suddenly, moving towards the low wall near the staff entry, flicking bottle caps off the top one by one. 'And Min isn't much better.'

'You're only just realising this now?'

'I never said I was quick on the uptake.'

She laughs at that, tilting her body sideways, feeling the edge of her hangover dulling her movements. The rank odour of the bins is potent, as always, and even the birds have abandoned them in favour of the ones behind the fish and chip shop half a street down. She wonders if Jude is waiting for her to reply, but he's barely looking at her. With a little sigh, she starts towards the store entrance, only to be stopped by his fingers around her wrist.

'Bail with me?'

'What?'

'Bail with me. I mean, seriously, fuck this place. Let's go hang out. Even just for a bit. We can just tell them you're late.'

Olive blinks, ignoring the tremor in her legs at the feel of his hand on hers, the warmth of his skin, the soft calluses of his fingertips. She wishes she'd done her make-up properly, that she didn't smell like cigarettes and cheap deodorant, that she didn't look so fucked up, but Jude's asked her, and he's holding her hand, and maybe he doesn't care what she looks or smells like. Maybe he feels this too.

'Yeah, okay,' she says, and Jude grins wide.

○

Delia is washing out paint pots at the tap outside when November pokes her head over the fence, her pale fingers curling around the dark wood.

'I was hoping I'd catch you. How'd everything go with your mother?'

Stretching to her full height, Delia drops the half-cleaned pots on the back step and dries her hands on her shirt.

'She's doing better.' Delia says, clocking November's sympathetic look. 'Thanks again, for bringing Benjamin home and for cooking. It's a … thank you.'

November smiles, a small, gentle thing, tapping her fingers against the fence. She tilts her head back towards her house.

'You want to come in for a drink?'

Delia glances sideways through her wild yard to where Benjamin lurks, still in costume, his voice low and conspiratorial as he murmurs surveillance to his Spectacular Man figurine. She'd more or less finished painting for the day when she'd picked him up from school, her hands and arms aching from it, her back tight. There's a stroke of fleshy peach at her forearm, a splatter of muddy brown on her feet from when she'd dropped the brush when Ed had—

She clears her throat.

'Give me a minute to clean up and get Banjo together? Then we'll come over.'

○

'Have you met my daughters?' November asks, walking over to the fridge. She fixes them both a drink, and gestures out to her backyard where two ginger-haired girls with skinny, tanned bodies are darting about beneath a sprinkler. 'Jane and Briar.'

Delia shakes her head, perched at November's kitchen island.

'No, but I've seen them. Active imaginations.' She chuckles, scratching at her arm, at the paint still there, and November laughs right back, something full of warmth and grace.

'A little too active sometimes.'

Delia glances over at Benjamin, who is spinning on the bar stool, and jerks her head out the window.

'You want to go out and play?'

He frowns, and she knows he doesn't, but he knows a dismissal when he hears one. It doesn't take much more for him to head outside, and Delia's gaze follows him out the window, distracted only briefly by the girls again. It's a beautiful day, hot, as always, and she likes watching the way the light catches the water, the girls' little bodies tangling up in the beams and shadows, the water weighing down their thick red curls and beading at their necks and legs. The younger one has ribbons of grass coating her feet, and she squeals when a wayward dragonfly finds her, darting between the sprinkler's spray and flitting by her wheeling arms.

The old, niggling memory of her grandfather's funeral comes to her then, her mother's father, when Delia and Bo had been too young to understand exactly what it meant and had stripped off their heavy black dresses behind the church and turned on the hose, flicking water at each other while hymns escaped through the stained-glass windows, their mother's voice, clear and beatific, above the rest.

Now Delia shakes her head, clears her throat.

'They're cute kids,' she says, and November smiles.

'I think so. So are yours, of course.'

As soon as she says it, regret crosses her face, as if she hadn't considered the words, and Delia feels something in her gape wide. She clamps at it, forces it back together as best she can.

'Is it just the three of you here, then?' Delia asks, changing the subject. She takes a mouthful from her wine glass and watches as November does the same.

'A lot of the time, unfortunately. I am married though,' November replies. She plays with her wedding ring, rolling it around on her finger, and Delia's surprised that she hasn't noticed it before.

'Oh?'

Were she much younger she might have blushed at her mistake, but she's grown too old to be embarrassed. Become shameless in her marrow. To her credit, November doesn't seem very phased either.

'I suppose it's an easy mistake to make,' November replies. 'José – my husband – he's in the mines out west. FIFO. He's not around as much as I'd like.'

November pauses, her forehead lightly lined. She drains the last of her wine, then puts her empty glass on the counter.

'I can't really complain though. He makes good money, he likes his work. He's a good father.'

Ah, Delia thinks, a wry smile tugging at her lips, because how many times had she said exactly that about Ed? She'd been so unwilling for so long to complain about the hours he'd worked at the firm, about the way she'd so often felt as if she was raising their children alone, about how little time she had left – for friends, who drifted off, for painting, drawing, even for them. How lonely she'd been, even with him beside her.

'But you miss him?'

November laughs at that, her head lolling sideways until her red hair cascades over her shoulder like draped silk.

'But I miss him.'

234

○

The neighbour's yard is so different to their own that it feels almost alien to Benjamin. It's nice, pretty, neat, the grass squelchy with water from the sprinkler, the neighbour's girls bouncing, almost buoyant, beneath the spray. He hears one of them yell something about mermaids, and they both drop to the grass, beating their legs in unison against the damp earth.

Benjamin ends up exploring around the fence, wishing Poppy was here with him as he looks back into their own yard through the thick and battered slats that separate them. From here it looks even worse, feral in its dense grass and slouching weeds. A patch of grass twitches suddenly, and Benjamin cranes up to try to work out what it is – toad or lizard or snake.

A hand touches his shoulder, and he turns back to see nothing.

'Charlie?'

The hand tightens, and Benjamin smiles. He breaks a stick off a nearby tree, running it noisily along the fence. The sound makes the neighbour's girls look over at him, but they lose interest quickly, their focus returning to their muddied feet and the intricacies of their own game, which suits Benjamin just fine. He mucks around for a while longer, kicking up dandelions and planting Spectacular Man in harvested herb patches and in the shade of frangipani trees, but he wants to go back to their yard, to Charlie's notebook, and to the wild things that are written about in it. Getting to his feet, Benjamin dusts himself off and steals into the neighbour's house to tell his mother.

'So there's no word? No clue? Nothing?'

'No,' his mother says, and Benjamin is jerked backwards into the hall by an invisible hand gripped tight in his cape. 'The police rang yesterday. They don't have anything. No leads, no ideas. They've looked everywhere. It's like he just ... vanished. Into thin air. They think he ran away. There's no other real option. Or there is, but ...'

She exhales croakily in a way that reminds Benjamin of the machines Grandma was on in the hospital, and it leaves his own breath caught in his throat.

'I'm losing hope,' he hears her say. 'Isn't that awful? What sort of mother loses hope like this? I should be fighting it all, right? I should be at the station every day, I should be on the news, I should be ... I don't know.'

It's quiet for a moment, and Benjamin hears the blood rushing in his ears, and then a chair scraping across the floor and the sound of the neighbour's voice ringing through it all.

'I think it's very easy to tell someone what they should be doing when you aren't the one going through it. You're doing all you can. You're looking after your family, and I think that's more than enough.'

Mum laughs then, but there's nothing in it, and Benjamin turns abruptly to the air behind him and reaches out.

'You've got to tell Mum,' he whispers. 'You gotta tell her, Charlie,' but Charlie doesn't respond, and it's like he's not even there at all.

O

Jude ends up taking her to a park nestled in one of the river's s-bends, curled up like treasure beneath a dragon's tail. The air mouths at their warm skin, and Jude promises shade beneath poinciana trees, but they've been stripped back by this endless drought, left parched, twisted and gothic.

So they sit on the yellow grass instead, their hands barely touching, the heat thick between them.

'What did Frank even do?' Olive asks as Jude unpacks his satchel, pulling out a plastic bottle wrapped in a tea towel, rubber bands holding it firm. He takes a quick swig before passing it to Olive.

The tang of cheap cider hits her tongue, fizzes in the bowl of her jaw, and she must pull a face because Jude laughs loudly, though not unkindly, braying in the afternoon.

Along the river, a kayaker paddles, the pointed nose of his boat slicing the murky water. It forces sparrows out of its way, red-legged seagulls, swamp hens and moor hens. At the ferry terminal only a few metres up, a fat-lipped pelican settles onto a boating pole.

'He's just been so far up my arse lately it's like he's trying to give me a prostate exam. He wants me to cut my hair. He thinks I don't follow procedure right, when I fucking do. It's all just bullshit, and I told Mindy about it, and she won't go up against him. Her deal's too sweet at the moment.'

'What deal?' Olive says, eyebrow arched. 'She does all of Frank's work for half the pay.'

Jude doesn't reply to that, just takes another drink, his face drawing inwards, like he's turning over her words. A plane flies overhead, closer to the ground than Olive thought they got this far south. It's quick to rattle her, to turn her attention skyward, to the cloudless blue without blemish or relief. He's so close here, like this, and Olive wills her fluttering heart to slow, wills her skin not to flush and her limbs not to shiver. She fixes her gaze upwards, wills herself a distraction, when—

'Hey, so, Lux told me your brother is missing,' he says, and Olive feels something in her throat bob. She takes another swig of the cider to avoid replying.

'It's pretty fucked up,' he adds, his body curled forwards but his head back. Olive drops the bottle to her thigh, toys with the mouth of it instead, feels the sticky wet rim, and just says:

'Yeah.'

'I'm not bringing it up to be a dick or whatever. I just wanted to say, y'know, if you need anything.'

He gestures towards the river, then back towards himself, and Olive's flush deepens, her pulse growing louder, faster, and when she nods Jude laughs kindly, leaning closer and knocking his knee against her own, sending an electric shock through her body.

'Come on then,' he says. 'I should take you back to work.'

But Olive shakes her head. 'No. Let's stay a little longer.'

Delia finds Benjamin sprawled on the trampoline, Spectacular Man clutched to his chest, his eyes closed in the fading light. She navigates the unkempt expanse of their yard and bumps her shins on the low metal frame, still warm from the day, then waves over the fence at where November is wrapping her daughters in fuzzy white towels to dry their damp skin.

'You gotta let me know when you're heading out, Banjo.'

Benjamin cracks open a single eyelid, revealing a watery iris, before closing it again. He takes a deep breath that seems to balloon his frail chest. Around them, the yard yawns awake, the grass swaying and rustling with blue-tongue lizards and dull-eyed toads, with the sleek shells of armoured insects. There's a crow on the fence, battering a cicada against the timber, and another barely visible below the foliage in the corner of the yard. The bees have gone to rest, at least, she thinks, reaching over to tug on Benjamin's skinny ankle.

'You listening to me?'

'Yeah.'

Delia sighs, closing her own eyes lightly. The summer air warms up her skin and she can see it beneath her eyelids, that red heat that knocks on every door out here.

'November's girls are a bit young, huh?' she says, and Benjamin shrugs. 'Sorry to drag you over.'

'That's okay.'

Delia aims for a smile, and Benjamin returns it, sliding across the trampoline to curl his arms around her waist. She brushes a hand through his hair before hooking her chin at his head, feeling his crooked skull beneath her jaw. Her eyes drift shut again, even as the back gate unlatches and Olive pushes her bike in. Delia hears more than sees her wheel it to the far fence, bolt it there and walk over, her body tall and shadowed.

'What's this about?' Olive asks, voice leaden, and Delia

opens her eyes to see her daughter's face, warm and soft, her round eyes so neat they could almost be stencilled. She could draw Olive. She remembers drawing her a thousand years ago, when she was still docile with infancy, her fingers curled into tiny little fists, her small mouth parted to reveal fleshy gums instead of square white teeth.

'It's been a big couple of days, that's all,' Delia says, and she means just with her mother, but it's more than that, of course it's more than that. Her thoughts drift back to Charlie, then to the painting of him in her bedroom, then to Ed's lips on hers and—

Olive nods, looking away almost uncomfortably, and Delia thinks about reaching a hand out for her daughter. Holding her like she's holding Benjamin, but Olive hasn't let her do that since she wasn't much bigger than she was in those vague, half-formed memories (or were they fantasies? Had Olive ever been docile? Ever so soft as to let Delia draw her?). But then – maybe it's the wine, maybe November, maybe the absence of her son – it's suddenly too easy to reach out, to cup her daughter's cheek with her rough, paint-flecked hand. To feel the heat of it, the flutter of her daughter's pulse at her palm, her son's skull below her chin.

Olive shies back a little, but she doesn't remove herself, doesn't pull away. Just parts her lips a touch as if she might say something, but then seems to think better of it.

Delia drops her hand, moving far back enough that Benjamin's arms fall from her waist.

'I should probably start on dinner,' she says, and promptly turns on her heel, walking up the back stairs to the house, feeling her son's and daughter's eyes on her as she leaves them behind.

○

Sometime the next day, a woman in the queue tries to catch Olive's eye, her hand outstretched, her mouth open just enough that Olive can see a row of ivory teeth and the flick of a pink tongue.

'You'll need to grab one of the floor staff,' Olive says, scanning another customer's groceries – long cucumbers, laundry powder, fat, dimpled oranges. She gestures behind them all to where one of the junior staffers is hunched over a display of crunchy bread, hiding her phone as she texts below the fabric of her O'Malley's shirt.

'It's honestly just a quick question. I'm just looking for—'

Olive glowers, even as she tries to smile.

'I'm with another customer right now, ma'am.'

The scanner beeps loudly in her hand, and she looks back at the customer she's serving, some frail-looking, birdish woman with hair so blonde it's nearly white.

'I don't see why you can't just answer my question.'

'I'm serving another customer.'

The woman's nostrils flare, and she storms off across the store floor, and Olive shakes her head, turning her attention back to the current customer, who pays and charges out, before the next one starts piling up her groceries.

'Well, that was super rude. The customer, not you,' the girl clarifies quickly, and then, after a beat, 'oh my God. Olive? Olive Rabbit?'

Olive looks up quickly to see a short, curvy girl roughly the same age as her, with a moon-shaped face and eyelashes so thick they remind her of the fringing on the curtains at her grandmother's old house.

'Lacey?'

Lacey nods frenetically, her plump lips splitting into a gap-toothed grin.

'Jeez, I don't think I've seen you since Megan's eighteenth! I didn't know you still worked here.'

A flush of embarrassment makes its way from Olive's ears to her toes, and she clears her throat, reaching for the first row of Lacey's groceries, her hands clammy on the fruit.

'Yeah, it's … you know. It's a pretty good gig.'

'That's so great, especially while you're studying, right? I've been lucky with my university placement in the lab, and I mean, they know they're getting students, right? So they're chill, but the pay is pretty terrible.'

Olive aims for a grin, but can feel it turn into a grimace. She shrugs, trying to unstick her shirt from the sweat pooling between her shoulder blades.

'You're still at uni then?'

'Yeah! Only a year left. And then freedom, right? Or at least full-time pay. We kind of need it right now for the wedding,' Lacey says, and Olive blinks, starting backwards.

'The wedding?'

'Yeah, you remember Peter?'

'You guys are like, twenty.'

Lacey laughs, scrunching up her pretty little nose.

'I mean like, not right away, but it's on the horizon. I'll have finished my bio degree in two years, and by then Peter will be at his dad's accounting firm. We'll be set up, you know? So we figured we'll have a long engagement, take a bit of the pressure off or whatever. I'll have to make sure to get your address for an invitation, huh? I think I've got you on Facebook?'

Lacey is grinning, not unkindly, because nothing about Lacey is unkind, and this makes Olive feel all the worse.

'We should catch up for real sometime,' Lacey adds, reaching for her plastic bags. 'I miss you, you know. At least now I know you work here still.'

'Yeah,' Olive says, a little blankly, rocking back onto her heels. 'I'm here most of the time.'

Lacey smiles even more widely, openly, and waves as she walks out of the store, and Olive can feel the heat travelling through her again. She rips off her rubber gloves, ignoring Lux's questioning look from the other register as she strides through the store and into the back rooms, her chest constricting, arms aching, the stress and panic beating through her with all the force of a crashing surf. She bursts into the staffroom and she's wishing for Jude, wishing for him to whisk her to the park again, to make everything else in her life melt away until nothing matters but his body beside hers, only it's not Jude at all, it's Mindy, and—

Olive stops dead in her tracks.

Mindy is sitting with her legs crossed in a chair, one of her hands moving around and around at the wrist, the TV blaring, the fan circling overhead, and when she sees Olive she stops dead, the fan slowing, the TV cutting in response.

'Oh,' Olive says, and Mindy drops her legs.

13

'I learned I could do it when I was a kid. My dad would change the channel, you know. Like, me and my sisters would be watching *Round the Twist* and Dad would switch it to the news or the sport and I'd just think about it, and the channel would change back. Dad bought, like, four different TVs in two years. He was convinced it was just fritzing out. It took me a while to even realise it was me.'

Mindy's hand is going again now, having restarted when she realised there wasn't exactly a way out of this conversation, and Olive finds herself strangely hypnotised by the rotations of her wrist, moving perfectly in time with the fan above their heads.

'I can't do much more than this, though. I'm not, like, fucking Magneto or something. Nothing too big. I fizzle out. But I can turn fans on and change radio stations and turn on broken things for a little while.'

She laughs at that, shrugging. 'It's not that impressive, really. My baby sister is better at it. She doesn't have to keep thinking about it. But my other sister can't do shit, so I should probably stop complaining.'

The staffroom is quiet, and Olive finds herself oddly relieved for it. For this little moment to be kept just between Mindy and her. Her palpitating heart has slowed enough that she feels vaguely human again, and it's all she can do to keep it that way.

'My brother's invisible, not missing,' Olive says, and the words sound weird, foreign, even to her. She laughs, the sound bubbling up in her throat, spilling over in a way she doesn't want. 'He can't turn it off. He can't come back right now. He doesn't know how.'

She can feel Mindy's gaze on her, startled and open and honest in a way she isn't used to. Above them, the fan slows to a stop, and the TV startles alive and then almost as quickly cuts out. When Mindy speaks next, it's with a deliberate casualness that Olive is all too familiar with.

'Well, fuck.'

It shocks enough of a laugh out of Olive that she folds back into her chair, a tension she didn't know she had unwinding inside her. She lurches forwards, resting her hot forehead on the staffroom table, still cool from the fan. She taps it there just once before sitting back up to look at Mindy's careful and considered face.

'Did you ever have imaginary friends?' Olive asks, and Mindy shrugs, hand starting to move again, the fan spluttering to life and cutting up the stagnant air.

'I have two sisters,' Mindy says. 'And we're pretty close in age. They took up, like, all my time. We used to have these pretty wild games, all make-believe shit. One of my sisters still does. Like,' Mindy gestures then, fingers splayed, her lips parted, as if she might say something else, but no words come out. Finally she just settles back, distracted. 'I don't know. Like something.'

'I never had imaginary friends,' Olive says. 'Charlie did, and some of my friends at school did, and I was jealous of that. Stupid, right? Why should I be jealous of something entirely imagined? But I feel like that's where I'm at now. Talking to my brother, who I can't see, who can't talk back without a pen, I think maybe I hallucinated this. Maybe I made it all up inside my head. People do weird things in grief, right? Maybe this is me losing my fucking mind.'

It feels almost too good to get this off her chest, and Mindy tilts her head, a look on her face Olive can't read. After a moment, she clicks her fingers, startling the TV back to life.

'Maybe,' Mindy says. 'Or maybe not.'

O

They set Spectacular Man up with Poppy's favourite doll at the base of the fat-bottomed mango tree in her yard after school, letting the toys watch as they disappear into its folds. It takes a while to climb it. Benjamin's mostly out of practice, but Poppy isn't. She is quick as a possum, her legs fast-moving and her hands firm as grappling hooks. It's impressive, to say the least, even if he feels a small curl of jealousy at her limberness.

'I'm doing my project on my sister,' Poppy says from above him in the tree. She's at least three branches ahead, her body manoeuvring through its limbs. He's told her about his grandmother and shown her the photograph, and she was dutifully impressed.

'Don't you have lots of sisters?' Benjamin calls, reaching for the next branch, his bare feet scrambling for purchase against the bark.

'More than you!'

Her voice carries in a way that disturbs a bird, some slack-jawed noisy miner. It bleats at her and Poppy bleats right back.

'Which sister then?'

'All of them. My mum's got lots of sisters too and so does my dad, and my grandma and my grandpa, so I figured my project would be on all the sisters in my family, coz there's so many, and there's not many sisters in books or on TV or in games. I mean, there's some, but like – not as many as brothers, I think.'

Benjamin frowns, reaching for another branch. Through the leaves and the fruit he can see that Poppy's stopped, has turned to straddle a branch, as if she's riding a horse. She looks up above them both, so all he can see is the pale skin of her neck and the dirty soles of her feet.

'I thought we had to do it on just one person,' he says, and Poppy looks back down at him.

'Nobody's just one person, stupid.'

The late-afternoon light rests easy on Poppy's shoulders, and when she offers a hand down to him, Benjamin takes it, letting her help him up to the branch beside her.

The suburb sprawls out beyond them. Tin roofs of old houses, the tiles of newer ones, like a patchwork quilt blanketing the earth. Trees lean in between bursts of green and tan, like tears in the fabric of it.

He turns to look at Poppy, who's not looking at him at all,

but up into the bright afternoon sky, her gaze fixed on the sliver of white moon hanging high above them, miles away from the sun.

'You know there's going to be a planetary huddle,' he says, and Poppy finally looks back at him.

'What's that?'

And huh, Benjamin thinks. He and Charlie never really went over the details. He giggles, dropping his head to look below, at where Spectacular Man and Barbie wait for them at the base of the tree. The smell of mango skins and bark and night and Poppy are all around him, and this moment seems like something important, like something he'll remember when he's old, and he's not really sure what that means.

'I don't know. Charlie knows that stuff.'

Poppy nods, leaning back against the bough of the tree. She watches him thoughtfully, her lips pursed, her hair messy and littered with leaves. She looks like a wild girl. Benjamin wonders if he looks like a wild boy.

'Have you tried to do it?' she asks.

'Tried to do what?'

Poppy sighs, rolling her eyes.

'Go invisible, stupid.'

Benjamin shrugs. He had told her about Charlie that morning at school, nervous that she wouldn't believe him, but Poppy had taken it as easily in her stride as if he'd told her he'd lost a coin and found it later in the folds of the couch.

'Maybe we can try together,' Poppy says now.

'How?'

'I don't know. How did Charlie do it?'

And the thing is, Benjamin doesn't really know that either. It wasn't in Charlie's notebook, and he hadn't thought to ask. Charlie has always been able to do things Benjamin can't, after all. It must be written all over his face, because Poppy taps at her chin.

'Maybe we just gotta think it really hard.'

'Maybe,' he says, and then Poppy clamps her eyes shut until they crinkle at the corners and her nose scrunches up too and her entire face is a tight coil of muscle, and the rest of her body as well, her fingers clenched around the tree branch they're sitting on.

After a minute she relaxes.

'Did it work?'

Benjamin laughs, shaking his head, and Poppy sighs, then thrusts a hand towards him.

'Now you try.'

'Me?'

'Yeah, you. Charlie's your brother. If it's like the X-Men, these things run in families, right?'

'Not the *same* power. It's like, Quicksilver has super speed, and Scarlet Witch can hex people and Polaris has mental powers.'

'So, you might have a different power. Just try it.'

In the half-light of the evening Poppy looks like a beacon, her blonde hair and her sunburnt cheeks like scraps of fire buried deep in the tree. It's a picture he thinks he likes, and it's enough to make him close his eyes, just like Poppy did, to scrunch up his face and clutch the tree branch beneath him. To think take me to where Charlie is, make me what he is before he can think another thought.

After a minute or two, Benjamin opens his eyes to see Poppy leaning close, her forehead creased thoughtfully.

'Maybe you're a squib.'

Benjamin glowers, leaning back.

'That's from Harry Potter, not X-Men.'

Poppy just shrugs.

'I don't make the rules, Ben,' she says, and Benjamin starts to reply, only the back door of Poppy's house is sliding open below them and his mum is stepping out to take him home. Delia shields her face from the glare of the dying sun, staring up at them, and Benjamin is reminded not for the first time of the civilians in movies or comic books, the ones who watch the action from somewhere far away. The ones left out of the hero's story, and, with a sudden twist in his gut, he thinks maybe he *is* a squib, and that he belongs down there with her and not with Charlie at all.

By the time Olive finishes work, Lux is waiting back by the bins, a cigarette in her claw-like grip. She looks like shit, even for Lux. Her chainsmoking has started to grey her teeth, to leave her with a perpetual smell of tobacco, coating her pale skin and her vein-blue hair.

'You didn't tell me you were skiving yesterday when I was leaving yours,' she says, before Olive can so much as mutter a hello.

'That's because I wasn't. I was just late.'

She adjusts her backpack on her shoulders.

'And then you had lunch with Chan today,' Lux continues,

as if Olive hasn't spoken at all. She flicks the ash off the end of her cigarette, and if Olive didn't know any better she'd swear Lux was pouting.

'Not lunch. We were just talking.'

'I didn't realise you guys were so chummy.'

Olive huffs, rolling her eyes as she walks past Lux and out through the alley. She swings a leg over her bike and starts to pedal, slowly enough that Lux can walk beside her if she wants to, and she does. They move in silence for a minute, before the wall against the pavement shortens enough for Lux to jump onto it, making her a half-body taller than Olive, even when she's on her bike.

'Are you jealous then, or what?' Olive says after a moment, and it feels unkind, even to her, but there's something satisfying in the way Lux's expression darkens all the same. 'Anyway, we're not really. Chummy, I mean. She's just been really nice. Because of my brother and all.'

It does little to placate Lux, who, still pouting, says:

'And I haven't?'

''Course you have. It's just … different.'

Lux doesn't reply to that, but then, Olive supposes, what is there to say? That Mindy has something in the bones of her that ties her intrinsically to Olive's brother? That they have almost nothing in common – not gender, race or even age – and yet share something else, something unreal?

Something fantastic.

'Hey, Lux,' she says, and Lux responds with an *mmm*.

'Have you ever …' She stumbles. 'I mean, do you believe …'

She tightens her hands around the handlebars of her bike, pedalling more slowly, making it wobble.

'Spit it out, Rabbit.'

Olive looks up at Lux's spindly body moving slowly across the wall, her spidery legs casting long shadows in the late-afternoon light. She clicks her jaw.

'Have you ever seen something you can't explain?'

'Sure,' Lux says with a shrug, her tone flippant. 'Shooting stars and birthmarks and cell-phone towers and flying foxes. I can't tell you how a plane doesn't drop from the sky or how your fingernails keep growing after you die or why your skin can sometimes heal so quick and other times takes forever. I see things every day that I can't explain.'

Olive huffs.

'That's not exactly what I meant.'

'What?' Lux says with a laugh. 'Don't tell me you're seeing Jesus in your latte foam. It's a fluke, I promise you.'

Olive sighs, feeling suddenly silly, watching Lux jump off the wall as it ends. So maybe it really is some well-kept secret, stored in the mouths of those it affects.

'Oh, come on, Olive. Don't be like that. It was just a joke. What unexplainable thing have you seen?'

'I said forget it,' Olive says, ignoring Lux's laugh of *no you didn't* behind her.

They're not far from Olive's house now anyway, and it tells in the familiar neighbourhood joggers, glistening in their singlets, their work-day make-up caking at their jaws. Half a dozen cars roll through these suburban backstreets, homeward bound.

'Do you want to go out tonight?' Lux asks, changing the subject, and Olive just shrugs. She's not really sure what she wants to do. Maybe tell Charlie about Mindy. Maybe together they could find a way to turn Charlie back on.

'Or maybe we could stay at yours and hang out with that babe.'

Olive jerks her head around in confusion, seeking out whatever Lux is seeing, and stops in surprise. There, standing out the front of the Rabbit house is a man barely older than Olive. He has dark, floppy hair and a mess of intricate rib tattoos visible through the sunken arms of his singlet.

'Who's he?' Lux asks at her side, and Olive shakes her head.

'I don't know. Must be the wrong address.'

As if he's heard, the man looks up, fixing his gaze on them as they draw nearer.

'Hi,' Lux says, her voice warm and deliberate. 'You okay there?'

The man seems to freeze, a trapped expression on his face, as if he's been caught doing something he shouldn't be. Olive paints on the kindest smile she can, sweetening her gaze. She can feel something behind her, and she half-expects Lux, and is surprised when she turns around and sees nothing. She stretches a hand back until she feels Charlie take it, and she can't explain it, but something in her whispers in warning.

'Do the Rabbits live here?'

'Yep,' Lux says. 'You after one of them?'

'Uh, yeah. Delia. I'm her … one of her students.'

Olive takes in his nervous, uncertain look, his bright eyes, his twitching hands.

'Do her students usually come to her house?' Olive asks sceptically, and the guy pinks at the ears.

'Probably not. I just wanted to talk to her, and she's been off all week and hasn't been answering her phone.'

'So you just thought you'd pop round to her house?'

The guy starts to reply, something nonsensical, but thinks better of it. He stops, purses his lips, and when he looks at them next it's with a more considered expression, something careful and open all at once.

'Is one of you Olive, by any chance?'

Before Olive can say a thing, Lux is stepping forwards, nodding. The guy smiles widely and reaches out a hand. Olive means to interject, she does, only she feels Charlie squeeze her hand, trying to pull her back.

'Oh! Awesome! I'm Adam Griffith, but everyone just calls me Griff. Your mum's told me heaps about you.'

'Well, she hasn't said shit about you.'

The guy pauses, his expression closing. He really is handsome, with rich eyes and a startling look about him. He's almost something else, Olive thinks. Almost.

'Well, why would she?' he says, his voice casual. 'I'm just a student. She doesn't seem to be home anyway, so I should probably make tracks.'

'Do you want me to give my mum a message?' Lux asks, and Griff quickly shakes his head.

'It can wait till she's back at the college.'

Lux hums in agreement and she and Olive watch as Griff climbs into his shitbox of a car and takes off down the street.

'Well,' Lux begins, but whatever she intends to say, she never finishes.

O

The drive home from Benjamin's new friend's house isn't long. Maybe five, ten minutes, a few blocks, a few street corners. Still, it's long enough for him to babble in the passenger seat beside her, his voice loud and boyish, skirting the topics of school projects and playground dynamics and whatever it is he does these days with this new friend of his.

Delia's mind is elsewhere.

She spent half the afternoon at the police station, sitting in front of Keely and McBride, going through pictures of Charlie and his friends and teachers, all the people he might be with. Who might have her son. Revisiting old leads. They played at hopefulness, these police officers before her, played at positivity, and all Delia was left to do was pick the flaking paint from her wrist and nod and shake her head on cue.

Now her fingers tighten around the steering wheel as she turns at the traffic lights, the bleeding blue sky growing gold around the edges. It leaves the birds calling, beckoning the cover of evening, and she has to resist the urge to close her eyes, to succumb to the ache in her like a child might.

'Mum?' Benjamin asks, and Delia's eyes snap back open, she hadn't realised she'd even closed them, and she looks over at her son's sunny and earnest face, his big eyes staring up at her.

'Hey, baby,' she says, feeling his fingers at her elbow.

'Are you okay?'

'Yeah, I'm okay. Just … okay,' she finishes, and Benjamin frowns.

She pulls up on the kerb and heads up towards the house,

bags of groceries weighing down her arms. Benjamin springs out in front of her, gripping Spectacular Man tightly as he bounds through their lush yard, beelining for the trampoline, only slowing when he sees Olive and that girl from her work (Alex? Lauren? Something like that) sprawled across it. Delia waves in their direction with her free arm.

'You all in for dinner?' she calls, and the friend leans up, shaking her head.

'I'm going home in a minute, Ms Rabbit. My mum's made a roast.'

'A bit hot for that, isn't it?'

The girl just shrugs, swapping a look with Olive that sends both girls into a fit of giggles, and Delia sighs, heading up the steps. She drops the groceries onto the counter, pulls out the chicken, carrots, spinach and spring beans, and folds forwards over the kitchen island, lowering her head to her hands. She's so tired suddenly, buggered, fucked, whatever. She should call Ed. Tell him about her meeting with Keely and McBride, but the thought sticks like taffy to the walls of her mind.

She grabs the garlic instead, minces it, throws a pan on the stove, olive oil, drops in the garlic. She sautés it, watches the white flesh tan in the heat. It's too hot, she thinks, reaching up to turn the stovetop fan on, only to pause.

There's a post-it note on the fan button, and she frowns as she pulls it off.

I messed up is written in a chicken-scratch scrawl.

In *Charlie's* scrawl.

Delia turns around, her eyes skirting the kitchen, taking in every nook and cranny, every inch of this place that might be wide enough for Charlie to hide in, and she turns again to see another note, hovering in the air without string or rhyme or reason. Delia stumbles back.

It says, *I can explain everything*.

It says, *I promise*.

○

Lux goes home almost as soon as Delia goes inside, leaving Olive to stretch out across the trampoline, to ignore the spring in Benjamin's step as he propels himself across the grass. He darts towards Charlie's telescope, pulling it out from beneath the house and propping it up in an open patch of garden. A few wayward bees fly out from the base, and he bats them uneasily away, watching their furry bodies bob in the evening air. His cheeks are red, whether with the heat or a blush, Olive isn't quite sure.

Somewhere inside she can hear the crackle of oil in a pan and the first waft of heady garlic and salt. It's nice, she thinks, and then her mind slips back to the boy at the gate, and then to the photo of Bo Rabbit, still in her pocket, and then finally to Mindy.

'A girl I work with has electrical powers,' she says, almost in a daze, and Benjamin stops, looking back at Olive.

'What?'

Olive nods, finds herself choking on a laugh.

'Weird, right? I feel like I'm in some sort of fucked-up fever dream.'

Benjamin giggles at that, his fingers itching around the

legs of the telescope. He pulls one out, then tugs at the neck of his cape, repositioning it around him. There's a weird feeling in her belly, something uncertain and unstable, and she's not sure if it's for the boy or for Mindy or Charlie, who she felt before but can't feel now. She licks her teeth, sitting up on the trampoline, and looks for any sign of him, a dip on the mat, some pressed-down grass, something moving on its own that shouldn't be, but she can't see anything.

'Charlie?' she says, but there's no hint that he's heard. She looks back over at Benjamin.

'Is Charlie here?'

Benjamin looks up at her, and then around, squinting in the early-evening light, his cape drooping. He looks pinched suddenly, as if he's focusing too hard. As if he can sense Charlie's presence in a way she can't.

'I don't think so,' he says after a minute. And then, carefully, 'Why?'

Olive just shrugs.

'I was thinking of going out tonight, and I wanted to talk to him before I went,' she says, her voice light. She sniffs, looking up at the house. 'Hey, can you smell something burning?'

They both look up in unison to see reams of dark smoke escaping the kitchen window, the scent of burning garlic filling their nostrils. Benjamin remains frozen in place, but Olive is tearing through their yard and up the back steps before she can think another thought. She doesn't know what she expects to find – her mother in the bathroom, maybe, or on the long-corded landline she still keeps in their hallway – but instead it's *just* her mother, standing naked-faced in the kitchen, her eyes fixed on something Olive can't see.

'Jesus, Delia,' Olive hisses, turning off the stove and dumping the smoking pan full of blackened garlic into the sink. 'What the fuck?'

But her mother doesn't move. It's as if she hasn't heard Olive at all, and for a second Olive wonders if she's suddenly gone herself, disappeared the same way Charlie has.

And then she sees it.

Post-it note after post-it note stuck across their kitchen cabinets. They clutter up the wooden doors, spread over the fridge, a story in Charlie's scratchy hand.

'Mum?' a voice says behind Olive, and she turns to see Benjamin, his face creased with worry, and she fights the urge to shut her eyes. As if, if she closed them, kept them closed, she could wake up from this moment and start this day anew.

'Tell me this is a joke,' Delia says, still staring vacantly at the cabinets. Olive can't see what it says, but she can see Charlie's handwriting, unmistakable with its jagged capitals and uneven letters.

The blood rushes in Olive's ears, drowning out Benjamin's babbling behind her, his story of finding those notes and keeping it a secret because of Charlie, *for* Charlie, and it's not long before Delia turns to face them, her expression hard, and Olive wants to look away, wants to leave, wants to *run*.

Down, down, down.

'Was this some sort of punishment?' Delia asks, and Olive looks up to see her mother suddenly, hopelessly split open.

Excuses burn on Olive's tongue – that they'd kept this from her to protect her, to try to figure it out with Charlie

259

themselves – but the second Olive thinks these things, she knows it was all bullshit. Knows that some ugly part of her was glad Charlie was hers for a while, a secret from their mother.

A stone in her hand.

'I know we don't exactly get along, but what did I do to deserve this? I know you'd force me out of this family if you could, but this is cruel, Olive. To leave me in ignorance.'

Benjamin's crying now, blubbering, trying to explain, and Olive wonders through the white noise in her head if Charlie is here watching this. If he's sitting back on the countertop, swinging his invisible ghost-boy legs and watching them all fall apart.

If he'll put this in his notebook too.

'Look at me,' Delia says, her voice curt, and Olive turns back to face her mother, but her gaze doesn't hold, and it's not long before she's succumbing to the exact thing her body's been begging for, turning on her heel to run.

14

Afterwards, with Benjamin in bed in his room, Delia goes back to her own.

She's still shaking with anger, with the belly-tightening feel of betrayal, shame, and she forces the canvas she'd primed that morning onto her lurching easel. She mixes the drying paints quickly and efficiently, cleaning off the brushes, finding the right one for this work, this canvas, this moment. She's trembling, feels it in her teeth, her bones, the whole shaken foundations of her. Olive kept this from her, convinced Benjamin to, left her to writhe in the grief of her missing son, of her—

She shoves the paint pots into the easel tray, and tries to salvage her wits.

One, two, three, she counts, eyes quivering shut, and when she opens them, it's to the sight of a post-it note stuck to the middle of her stark white canvas.

I knew you missed me.

Delia chokes out a laugh, looking around at the four, five, six other canvases, all thick with paint, capturing Charlie's warm and smiling face, before braces and with them, his head shaggy, clipped, his eyes the same, always, wild, tree-frog green. They're propped against the walls of her tired room, her dresser, her crumpled bed. Delia looks at the post-it note and talks to it like it's her son.

'Yeah, well. I thought we were a team,' she says. Because she had. Because it had always been her and Charlie. It had always been them. 'You quit without telling.'

She can almost hear it, the echo of his laugh, and then another post-it note is placed on her canvas, directly below the other.

I like the first one you did the best.

Her gaze flicks back to the first painting, but then something else is dropped to the easel frame. It's the page from the other night, the Charlie she had scratched in Benjamin's markers, the weird rough silhouette of him in thick block colour.

'Oh, you like *this* one best?' she asks, unable to keep the amusement from her voice as she takes in her scrappy, out-of-practice drawing. 'You should probably stick to the astronomy, kiddo, I don't know if art's your thing.'

And there it is again, the echo of laughter. The memory of it cuts through her, unearths something in the deep cavern of her chest.

'Where are you right now?' she whispers, and he touches her then, the weight of his hand wrapping around her free one, his fingers soft as insect legs against the skin of her wrist. Her eyelids flutter closed, wet, already, with tears. She tries to blink them away.

'How long?' she asks. 'How long have you been able to do this?'

The touch snaps away, and Delia's eyes slip shut again, heavy with exhaustion, with frustration, with the glaring, unmanageable grief of this moment, this day, this year. She opens her eyes and stares at the third new post-it note on her canvas.

Since as long as I can remember. I was always able to flick it off though, like a switch.

And she remembers too. She remembers pulling Charlie out from below clothing racks, and panicking in department stores, grocery stores, at parks and beaches and galleries. Remembers holding his hand and then nothing in the space of seconds, assuming he'd run away from her. His *now you see me* act.

Delia presses the bridge of her nose for a second and tries to focus. Tries to reimagine those disappearing moments now for what *this* one is, but she can't. Not just yet. So she doesn't say a thing, just pulls the post-it notes off her canvas and picks up a pencil instead. Starts to scratch an outline. A round face, some moon-shaped eyes. An arched nose.

The next time a post-it note appears, it's stuck to the back of her drawing hand.

I'm scared, Charlie has written, and Delia bites her lip. She pulls it off the back of her hand and sticks it onto the canvas. Beneath Charlie's words, she writes, *Yeah?*

Yeah, Charlie replies. *What if this is a forever kind of thing?*

'It won't be,' she says. 'Because it can't be. Because I need to wake up and see my son.'

He doesn't reply to that. Not right away, and Delia sits back and waits. Briefly, outside, she hears the screech of a lorikeet.

She hears some indie folk singer crooning out of November's speakers next door. She hears the croaks of geckos and black-eyed frogs.

Paint me again? Before I forget what I look like.

Delia shakes her head, lifting the sketch from her canvas. 'Not today, Charlie.'

O

She runs and then she cycles.

Faster and faster, the wind whipping past her face, until her legs burn and her rabbit heart keens in her chest. She wonders if she can find Lux. If she can catch up with her, and she texts to ask where she is, but Lux doesn't immediately reply. Still, she cycles out to Lux's anyway, even though she knows the family dinner line was a lie, and the place is empty, true to form, and so she texts her again and this time *honey, we're home* lights up her screen, and she knows that means they're at the house. She briefly wonders if she can even remember where it is on her own, or if she'll have to get Lux to send her a pindrop, but weaving through the narrow streets of the city, beneath the hazy glow of car headlights and streetlamps, she finds it.

It looks no different to how they left it, with its mould-crusted walls and sagging steps. With its sloped tin roof and broken windows, its rotting, festering door. She can see shapes and figures inside, hear the bang of a bat, the hiss of a spray can. She drops her bike on the pavement, bounding up the decrepit steps, her legs aching from the force of her ride. At the top, she smooths back her hair, reties it, and is starting to ease herself over the side towards the window when her foot kicks the door and the sounds inside stop. Then, just as quickly, they're replaced by something else. The nimble steps of an attempted escape, what sounds like something metal being dragged across the floor, hushed voices riddled with worry. Olive drops back to the landing and rolls her eyes.

'Guys, it's me,' she calls, her leg jittering, and the steps pick up again, the door is unexpectedly flung open, and there stands Lux, grinning widely and openly back at her.

'You were supposed to text, arsehole.'

'I *did*.'

'I meant when you got here.'

Pushing past Lux, Olive steps into the house. If the outside looked the same as the last time she was here, the inside is decidedly different. The tall walls are covered in graffiti – everything from rounded, inhumanly large breasts to sunsets to flowers to abstract, childish self-portraits. The doorways are smashed, the beams resting at strange angles, splintered wood erupting from their middles like broken bones. Mould is flowering on the ceiling, neat new ecosystems for grass-coloured lizards to camouflage against, an ugly, alien sky above the cracked floorboards, with creeping vines slowly working their way between them.

Olive sucks in a deep breath of musty air. She can almost taste the mould, and she wonders if it's sporing, if the growths will fill her lungs, will make her insides as wild as her outsides are.

'For someone who's on her phone all the time, Lux is

surprisingly good at missing fucking messages,' Dom says, emptying the bag he must have quickly packed when Olive first knocked. He pulls out a few cans of paint, while Lux staggers back to the wall, grabbing the bat and holding it out to Olive. She goes to take it from Lux's painted hand, but suddenly her attention is caught.

Shrouded in the shadows is Jude. No longer in his O'Malley's polo shirt and slacks, he stands in shorts and a loose singlet, the light from the street casting an uneven, almost holy glow on his tanned skin. His eyes are really fucking blue.

In the moment, he looks appealing and yet totally untouchable, as if he exists in a universe foreign to Olive's own, mugging at a camera like one of the pop stars on the posters in Lux's room. A false promise with perfect hair and pouting lips. She clears her throat, reaching for the bat that Lux is holding out for her, ignoring her wry look.

'Jude's a first-timer,' she says. 'Just like you were last time.'

It seems to be permission enough for Jude, who steps forwards, a thoughtful expression on his handsome face.

'So, what?' Jude says, his low tenor shattering the silence. 'You just break shit?'

'That's the idea,' Dom supplies, shaking a can of spray-paint, the metal ball rattling around its insides. Olive tightens her grip on the bat, her body thrumming. She can feel Jude's gaze on her. Feel the sharpness of his look, disguised behind something lazy, astuteness behind a veil of ease. It electrifies her.

'You want to show him what you're made of, baby girl?'

Lux says, her voice dripping with sugar, and Olive grins, and it feels ugly, warped even to her, and she heaves the bat over her shoulder and swings it, smashing straight through one of the walls. Behind her Lux and Dom hoot, and she turns to catch Jude's piercing gaze, and he looks impressed, and like he doesn't know a thing about her, and for the moment that's all that really matters.

O

He feels it, more than anything.

The shift in the air, the warmth. He knows that Charlie's here again. That he's left their mother's side and is here with him instead. Benjamin doesn't need notes, not anymore. He can feel Charlie better. A brotherly bond, like those he reads about in stories and comic books. Something that runs deeper, is felt harder. Just something *more*.

'Is Mum mad?' he asks, and the screen of Charlie's computer lights up across the room. Within a few seconds Charlie's fingers start tapping away on the keyboard.

Yes and no. I think she was mad. I think she's mostly just sad now.

Benjamin considers this, rocking from side to side on his narrow bed. After a moment he sits up, crossing his legs beneath himself.

'I'm glad you told her.'

Me too.

Not for the first time Benjamin tries to see his brother. Thinks that if he can't go invisible, maybe his special thing

267

is something different. The sort of thing that'll cancel out a brother's. Like x-ray vision or the ability to see through someone else's power.

The ability to turn it off.

But he can't. The light from Charlie's computer screen casts no shadows on him, leaves no mark. If it weren't for the windows opening and closing on the monitor and the slight whine of Charlie's chair, it'd be like he wasn't there at all. Benjamin looks away.

'Hey, Charlie?' he says, and Charlie opens up a Word document again.

Yeah?

'How come you can't reappear?'

It takes Charlie a while to reply, and when he does, he types the letters slowly.

I don't know. It's never happened before.

Benjamin bites the inside of his cheek, looking at the space he thinks Charlie might be in.

'How come you never told me you could do it?'

I don't know. I never told anyone.

'But why?'

I guess it was nice having a secret. Something that was just for me.

He can hear his mum swear in the other room, and he wonders if she's heard from Olive. If Olive texted. If anyone knows where she is. He wonders if Charlie knows, but shakes the thought clean from his head.

'Don't you like sharing stuff with people?'

Sometimes, but when you share things, they belong to everyone you share them with. I didn't want to have to explain

268

this, or to explain why you couldn't do it. I don't understand it. I don't know how it happens or how this happened. I guess it was stupid.

'It's not stupid,' Benjamin says reflexively, and he can almost hear Charlie laugh, hear the echo of his voice in the quiet of the evening.

'I hope you reappear soon,' he says, and it's a long time before Charlie writes anything else, and when he does, it's exactly what Benjamin thought he would say.

Me too.

She sketches the face first, then paints the base.

Tries to get the colour right.

(Can you draw someone from memory?)

She'd been pretty tanned, especially in their youth, even during those long summers that Delia had spent with her inside the hospital their mother worked at, playing at Egypt or Nancy Drew, depending on their mood. Delia was tanned too, but it was from long days roughhousing with boys at school below the blistering Queensland sun, throwing them beneath her with thighs strong from swimming lessons at the Chandler pools.

Bo had been bookish and quiet, but a sly sort of quiet, would sit back in a chair and take stock. Would hoard all the little truths of you in the twist of her grin. And it's stupid, Delia thinks, her throat catching as she paints, but maybe she magicked her son back with this paintbrush, and maybe she can magic Bo back too.

She feathers in the hair. How long was it the last time? Had Bo cut it again, or left it wild? Was it bold and untameable then, crumpled as if in a fist, or had she had it relaxed, curled soft and lush around her face?

Does it even matter? she wonders, dropping the brush. After all, Bo is not Charlie.

Bo is dead.

She steps back from the half-finished canvas, clutching her paint-flecked hand to her chest, trying to still her fluttering pulse. She shivers as she feels something pass her.

'Are you here, Charlie Rabbit?' she asks the empty room. The paint is hardening on her fingers, crusting at her knuckles and she flexes them to try to loosen it. That's how she almost misses it, the unseen hand that knocks her brushes and slides the paint palette along the bottom of her easel.

But there's no other reply. Not one, and Delia steps tentatively out of her bedroom, into the darkened hallway, alive with geckos scurrying across the ceiling.

'Charlie,' she calls again, but there's not a word or a shift in the dark.

She walks further down the hall to Benjamin and Charlie's bedroom, and pushes open their door.

Benjamin is fast asleep, curled up in his narrow single bed, his eyelids twitching almost imperceptibly, his lips parted as he snores. Beside him on the bed is the unmistakable weight of another body, the sheet forming a mound in the dark, but where it would usually open to a moonish face or a pair of holey-socked feet, there is only air.

Delia moves into the room, closing the door behind her.

She tiptoes across the floorboards, lowering herself to her son's bed and brushing her hand over Benjamin's cheek. He wriggles a little, his eyes opening blearily, and, without a word, he moves sideways, making room. Next to him the sheet rustles too, the mound moving further back against the wall, and Delia, painted in the colours of her sister, crawls into bed with her sons.

15

The model is a man in his late twenties with a disproportion-
ately broad chest and bowed legs. He is otherwise handsome,
at least to Delia's first-year class, a fact made obvious when he
steps out of his short satin robe and climbs up onto the raised
platform. One girl drops her pencil, and another, two rows
back, neatly crosses her legs.

'You'll have fifteen minutes, and then Evan will change
poses,' Delia says, leaning back against her desk. The model
flashes her a smug, playful smile. He's enjoying this. They
usually do. Delia gives him an arch look in return, keeping
eye contact as he settles into a pose.

A girl close to the front holds up her hand, her face
luminously red.

'Ms Rabbit? Do we need to draw the *whole* form?'

And well, Delia can't quite hide her grin at that.

'Would you prefer to leave a blank space in the middle of
your work?'

The girl drops her gaze from Delia to the model, and Delia
starts the timer, watching him still. Once the class starts to
draw, the quiet sounds of charcoal on paper become almost

meditative, and Delia traces the spine and the long line of this man on the canvas in her mind.

Her own thoughts are interrupted when the door cracks open and Griff steps through. Most of the class haven't seen him, too distracted by the nude man before them, but it won't be long before they do. She shoos him away with a subtle look, but he stands still, his hand curled around the doorframe. Delia turns her attention back to the class.

'Keep going, everyone. I'll be back in a minute.'

She steps out from behind her desk and strides up the stairs towards Griff, pushing him out the door.

'You know the drawing classes are closed,' she says, and Griff nods, gesturing her down the hallway and into an unused classroom. Reluctantly she follows. He must have done his research, or at least been here before, as the room is unlocked but clearly hasn't been used since before the summer. The blackboard is littered with the ghosts of old lessons, and drop-cloths hang like ghouls off chairs and tables. There's a mustiness about the room that Delia oddly delights in, every inch of her yearning to lean back into this old, tired space and make it new again.

'Are you avoiding me?' Griff asks, and isn't that the question she expected? Delia sighs, lets her head loll to the side so she doesn't have to meet Griff's look.

'Griff. Adam.'

She reaches out a hand, but Griff shies away from it.

'No, Delia. You jerk me around. You want me, you don't want me. Dump me if you want, but *dump me*, don't ghost me then show up at my door. Or don't dump me. Show up. Text me back. *Be with me.*'

His eyes are wide and open, and so painfully honest that something in Delia's chest seizes violently. It's as if he's untethered somehow, a buoy bobbing in some restless, reckless sea, and *stupid*, she thinks.

Her skin prickles, and she exhales roughly as he says:

'Don't cut me out. Please.'

Out of what? she wonders. What story has he built for them, what scene has he cast her in? How has he tried to write her part?

But no, that's unfair maybe.

He might have kissed her that first time in her office, but she kissed him back.

She always kisses him back.

'I'm not cutting you out,' she tells him, placating and exhausted. 'Okay, I'm sorry. I am. Look, let's – next Thursday. I'll get the kids out, maybe we can talk then. Figure this out.'

Griff exhales uneasily, closing the distance between them. Stupid, she thinks to herself again, as his arms curl around her waist, his fingers clenching the fabric of her shirt.

So fucking stupid.

O

The heat clamps at Benjamin's legs as he kicks up dust in the playground. A few of the younger kids dart around him, their school hats flung off, hanging from their forms by the strings around their necks.

Benjamin walks out towards the shade offered by the low-hanging jacaranda trees, the ground bare and compacted in the heat. From there, he can see Jodi Baxter sitting cross-legged with her lunch box open in her lap. She's talking to another girl from their class, someone with a small, upturned nose, braces and polished black shoes.

Benjamin pauses, watching them chatter, and startles when Jodi turns to meet his gaze, her eyes holding a curious look he doesn't understand. He flushes and turns away.

His mum had said people grow up fast at his age, but Benjamin knows better than anyone that they don't change overnight. After all, Jodi hadn't. It was as if they'd been playing and she'd fallen, and then fallen again and again, and every time she got back up something about her was different, until finally he didn't recognise her at all. Or maybe it was the other way around, because Jodi's the one who decided she needed new friends. Ones who know this version of her better. Who don't play cops and robbers during little lunch and superheroes during big lunch, but who rather sit with her on the dry grass talking about books and boys and what high school is going to be like when they all move across the road next year.

'She's not even that nice,' Poppy sniffs, appearing beside him, her knees scraped, her school dress grass-stained. She'd had band practice during their last class, and it has left her cheeks flushed and her lips a bitten red. Benjamin looks down at Spectacular Man in his hands and is suddenly, strangely, embarrassed. The heat is pressing into him, low in his belly, and he feels his own cheeks flush, and wishes he had the excuse of an instrument like Poppy does.

'Yes, she is,' he says instead, and Poppy looks at him like he's crazy.

'How would you even know? It's not like you guys talk anymore.'

And he wants to say that that's not true, but it is, and he wonders how someone can go from being so important to nothing at all.

'Are you pissing?'

Benjamin jumps, turning around to see a boy from his class taking a step back from him, his lunch bag in hand, his face contorted in confusion and disbelief, and Benjamin looks down to catch all that heat leaking down the leg of his school shorts.

His breath becomes shallow, the air around him is suddenly suffocating. He looks up to catch Poppy looking at him in surprise, and then past her to where Jodi's watching him now too, her own face a mix of shock and pity, twisted into something awful.

Shoving past Poppy, Benjamin runs. Runs through the kids and up the steps into the school. Runs down the hall, through the throng of people and straight into the boys' bathroom. Tumbles into a stall and locks it behind him.

He crouches down, tries to make himself as small as possible and thinks please let me disappear, just like Charlie, please, please, please, but when he looks down at his hands and his feet, he is still there.

A small pink hand is thrust beneath the stall door, clutching a pair of soccer shorts.

Benjamin hesitates for just a second before reaching down to pull them free, and the hand disappears only to be followed by a loud thump as a sudden pressure cracks down on the door, as if someone has dropped their whole body weight on it.

Benjamin strips quickly out of his school shorts and wipes up the urine as best he can. He wrings his underwear out in the toilet before bundling it up and shoving it down behind the cistern. He'll come back for it later, when afternoon classes have started and the swell of students in the hallways from lunch has subsided.

Cracking open the stall door, he's met with Poppy's sunkissed face.

'You're not supposed to be in here,' he says. 'It's the boy's bathroom.'

Poppy just shrugs, tilting her head and swaying sideways as she pushes off the stall door. The sound of other kids out in the hall echoes through the tiled bathroom, the playful calls and hoots that Benjamin suddenly feels too tired for. He glances down at Spectacular Man, his fingers closing around his middle before loosening again.

'They'll forget,' Poppy says after a minute.

Benjamin just gives her a look, and Poppy laughs, but it's not mean or loud.

'Maybe they won't. I don't know.'

At her honesty Benjamin looks away again, but he can feel her gaze following him, her eyes searching for something in a way that makes him squirm. It's a look Olive gets sometimes, as if she's working on a puzzle and doesn't quite know what the reward for finishing it will be.

'It's just a thing,' Benjamin says, trying to straighten his back. Mum always told him it wasn't something to be ashamed of, and the thought is nice, but it doesn't make the sticky feeling on the insides of his legs any better, and it doesn't cover the uneasy, acidic smell of piss either. 'About me.'

Poppy silently considers this, and Benjamin wishes he could disappear again, wishes the floor would swallow him up, or that Charlie would tap his shoulder and share his secret with him. Benjamin wishes for a lot of things.

'I guess you really can't go invisible,' Poppy says instead, and Benjamin looks up to find a subdued look on her pretty, freckled face.

'I guess not,' he replies.

O

By the time Olive wakes up, the house is empty, and she's mostly glad for it. The bruises on her arms, her chest and her legs are starting to purple, to bloom like orchids beneath her skin. The crescent-moon cuts on her palms are dried with blood again, even though she doesn't remember slotting her nails there, and she has a streak of thick green spray-paint across her nose that Lux did for a lark.

So she showers again. As best she can. Scrubbing away the memories of last night with the rough sponge of a loofah and her mum's rosemary soap. Then she brushes her teeth, her hair, pulls days-old mascara from her lashes in tiny black tubes. She scrubs everything away, until her skin is pinked and raw, smooth and photo-ready, glistening in the afternoon light.

Only she's not completely photo-ready, even this clean.

The bruises are thick, the older ones yellowing at the edges while the new ones bloom blue. There are heavy bags beneath her eyes and her bones poke out at her shoulders, at her ribs, her hips like bookends for the story inside of her. She doesn't remember being this thin.

There's no use thinking about it now though. She throws on clean underwear, an old house dress, kicks open the bathroom door as she grabs her dirty clothes off the floor, and as she bundles them, a picture slips out of the pocket.

Olive picks it up, turning it over in her hands until the face of this familiar stranger imprints itself on the back of her eyelids all over again, some organic negative left in the shadows of herself.

Bo Rabbit.

That's what the writing says. Her grandmother's hand, she's sure, curved neatly in lead at the stark edges of the image.

A breeze gasps somewhere behind her, and despite the heat, goosebumps pimple across her calves and her ankles.

'Do you know who this is?' Olive asks the air in the hallway she knows her brother stands in. It shivers out a *no*. She means to fold the photo back up, to get rid of it, but then Charlie's reaching for her hand and leading her towards their mother's bedroom, and without any hesitation he opens the door and slips them both inside.

Olive has suspected her mother's been painting again – has noticed the scattered paint pots drying outside and the occasional fleck of colour on Delia's arm or temple – but this doesn't prepare her for the sight of her mother's bedroom.

It is covered in paintings – a funhouse of her invisible son.

Pictures of Charlie at all ages, grinning, pensive, sad, of his telescope, of his long, curved back nearly lost in the grass Olive won't mow, of his bright eyes and his smile and that knowing look on his knowing face. Olive wants to see them all, wants to go through them, to remind herself that *this* is Charlie, not this absence of him. That Charlie was a real boy, her real brother, not this haunting, haunted ghost.

But she can't. She can't because Charlie isn't in front of the paintings of him, he's holding up the lone painting of another face, half finished and foreign above their mother's easel. Not as detailed as the pictures of Charlie, not as realised. It's as if Delia couldn't quite decide on the colours, or the shape of the eye, or the angle of the smile. Still, the face is unmistakably the one in the photograph Olive found in the hallway closet. Bo Rabbit.

Do you think she's the same as the girl in the photo?

Olive nods, walking closer to the painting. Most of it's dry, except for a little swatch of colour at the base of the neck. Pinker than the tones Delia has used on the cheeks.

I think she's a secret.

Olive grabs the post-it note from midair and looks at where she thinks Charlie is (can feel him – is getting better at that, really).

'Maybe she's invisible too,' she says. 'It would explain why Mum always seems to know when I've fucked up. If she had her invisible whatever on my back.'

Olive suddenly feels righteous anger bubbling in her belly, and she doesn't even really believe it, but there's something to it all. As if she's always known her mother as a locked door, but something about this photograph – something about *Bo Rabbit* – it's like being able to peer through the keyhole suddenly.

At the thought, she leans back on her heels and looks around the room again, past all the paintings of Charlie, and raises her voice.

'Am I right, Bo Rabbit? Are you here? The Big Brother of the Rabbit house?'

She can feel Charlie's hand on her wrist, on her arm, trying to get her to stop, but she's itching for the bat, for the cans of paint, to ruin this house like she ruins the one in the city. She turns and reaches for the painting of Bo Rabbit, and Charlie grabs her, pulling her backwards, forcefully this time, and she wonders, through the white hot fog in her head, if it'll leave its own orchid bruise.

'Oh, fuck off, Charlie. Stop pretending you're better than this. That you're better than me. You skulk around here because you can, picking and choosing what you reveal when, like some sort of household demigod,' and the words are coming quicker than she can stop them, that festering pit of anger bubbling higher. 'You let us think – you—'

The air is sucked from her lungs, words suddenly too thick to escape her mouth. She feels the room shudder around her, feels the hum and the throb of it. The pain in it. Not for the first time she wonders how much of this is Charlie, and how much of it is not him, might be whatever the fuck Bo Rabbit is, but that thought is unthinkable, and Olive jerks her arm from Charlie's grip and storms out of this gallery of him before he can stop her.

*

'It's sort of romantic though, don't you think?' November says, a wry grin tugging at her lips. There's sweat at her collarbone, beading like drops of paint and running clear down her skin. Delia can feel it on herself too, in the way her hair grows static, curls in on her temples and then out. A cartoon character with a finger in a socket. She tries to smooth it down with flat palms, which coaxes a laugh out of November.

Delia just snorts. 'What? Teacher and student?'

'No, I mean, artist and art student. Him some fresh-faced appreciator, new young talent, and you the old gun.'

There's a bubble of laughter in Delia's throat, edging closer to the surface. She shakes her head, thumbing her wine glass.

'I don't even know why I told you.'

November just shrugs, tongue darting out to wet her still-grinning lips. 'I've been told I have a way with people.'

And Delia's inclined to agree. There's something warm in November, something kind and coaxing that inspires something like confession in return, and it appeals to the part of Delia that's still a child on stage in her backyard, performing for an audience.

When she'd arrived home November had been out the front of her house, pulling mail from her mailbox, and really, it had been a relief.

To tell someone about Griff.

'Can I ask you a personal question?' November asks now, topping up Delia's wine glass. Her wrists are incredibly thin, frail like a child's. Delia locks the image of them tight in her head to call on later when she has a paintbrush in hand.

'Sure.'

She's expecting questions about Griff. About what it's like, fucking a boy your daughter's age. What it's like to cross that line, but what she gets is something else entirely.

'Did you love your husband?'

Delia arches an eyebrow, reels back a little, surprised, and exhales, collecting her thoughts.

'What brought this on?'

November shrugs, leaning back in her chair, taking a sip from her wine glass.

'I spend a lot of time on my own. I get curious. You don't have to answer,' she replies, and Delia just watches her for a moment. Remembers her the other day. *But I miss him.* She licks her teeth.

'Well, first off, he was never my husband,' Delia says flippantly, because it's as easy a place to start as any. 'We never got married, so I don't know what I call him. Boyfriend? That's too immature, right? Partner doesn't sound right either. We never really were. Lovers? Maybe? God, that sounds ridiculous.'

'Why didn't you get married?'

'Ed wanted to. A lot,' Delia says, watching November watching her. She wonders what November's wedding day was like. If it was a lavish affair or something more intimate. If she wore white. She bets she wore white. 'I really didn't though. It was this weird thing. Like getting married would turn us into my parents.'

The lie comes too easily. Something she's told and retold, to old girlfriends and parents in the playground, to colleagues and cousins and the children she and Ed share. Delia sighs, closes her eyes, shakes her head.

'No, that's not true,' she says, and she wonders if it really is November's way with people that's coaxing this out of her, or if she's just too tired to keep up appearances anymore. 'When my sister and I were kids, we'd say we were going to get married together. Double ceremony like in all those classic romance novels. A regular couple of Bennet sisters. But she died, and the thought of getting married without her … it just … and you know, me and my mother weren't close, my dad was dead by the time me and Ed were really together. I had no one to invite, and the thought of standing at the altar with all of Ed's family behind him made me feel ill.'

And it had.

She'd never felt comfortable with his family. His perfect parents, his sister, his brother, all smart, dull, logical people – the sort of family you want on paper, that she'd wanted before she'd been around his and realised they just made her feel all the ways she didn't fit. Made her remember the brilliance of her own, before it all fell apart.

The Rambunctious, Riveting Rabbits.

'Did you tell him that?'

'Yeah, when we were young. It's why he never pushed it. I guess passing on my name was a way to make the kids more my family than his, too. So I'd have someone in my corner. He never pushed that either. Like he knew. He used to joke that if we did get married, he'd change his name to Rabbit too. So he could be a part of my family, but you know. The kids always liked him more.'

'But you *were* a family.'

Delia shrugs, scrunching up her nose. She and Ed were never quite family. They loved each other. Still do, that much at least she knows. Knows that no matter where Ed gets off, no matter what woman he might curl himself around, he'll always love her most of all. The love was never their problem, it was everything else.

'Did I love him? That was the question, right?' Delia says. 'Yes, of course, a million times yes. We just weren't seventeen anymore. We'd changed so much, and I think we resented the way the other was now. We weren't the same, and we knew that, but neither of us had bothered to relearn the other. We didn't let ourselves grow, we just kept trying to trap our child selves and our child love between us, and we didn't realise that wasn't who we were anymore. Maybe it's weird, but for a while you just feel like this jigsaw-puzzle version of the person you used to be, and you're trying to put pieces in the places they used to go, only something's changed, and you realise it's the picture, not the pieces. It's you.'

Delia looks away, then back at November, who's watching her with folded hands. She can hear the girls playing upstairs, calling out about snow queens and superheroes, tea parties and galaxies in need, and Delia should tell her the other truth, but it's hard to find the words.

During The Bad Years, as Ed would forever call them, he had asked if Delia would paint a colleague of his. This colleague had been fascinated by the thought of him being with an artist, he'd told Delia then, and had seen one painting Delia had exhibited at a small gallery in Fortitude Valley. She hadn't painted anything new in years by that point, and it was flattering for someone to want her work again.

But Vanessa Dine had not been what Delia expected. A wisp of a girl, half Delia's age, she had walked into Delia's living room with a sort of ownership that had disconcerted her, toed off her kitten heels by the sofa and dropped her purse by the door. She had poured herself a glass of juice and found the cups as if she'd done it before, and Delia's a lot of things, but she isn't stupid.

'I never wanted either of us to change,' she says, and November hums a little, tilts her head from side to side.

'We all change. It's inevitable. We're not static, we're organic. We erode. Bad weather hurts us.'

They're quiet for a minute.

'I should save it for my memoir,' Delia gestures lavishly, tilts her chin up. '*My Life as a Footnote.*'

November laughs this time, head back and eyes shut. She's got a good laugh, Delia thinks, full and comforting, like uncurling in front of a fire in the coldest months, not rare and thin like Delia's own.

'Please,' November replies, reaching over to pick up Delia's now empty plate. 'You're a body of work if ever I saw one.'

'So what about November then?' Delia asks, changing the subject, and November collects herself, a grin spilling across her face. She scrunches up her nose.

'What do you mean?'

'That can't be your real name. I refuse to believe that anyone is that much of a cunt to name their kid that.'

November barks out a laugh. There's a light flush over her cheekbones already, and she shrugs, her shoulders taut like a canvas stretched over a wooden frame. Still, there's a looseness to the gesture that Delia can't entirely place.

'My father named me,' she says after a minute. 'I was born in the middle of winter. He says I came out with a head full of red hair and reminded him of the start of summer, the end of spring. My birth was this red heat in the middle of my parents' dying relationship, gave them another few years of grace before they separated. I was the season before the autumn, the fall. I don't know. The name stuck though, and my mother loved him too much then to deny him anything.'

'I know what he meant. Sometimes I think that about Benjamin too. That last-ditch child to give you something in common again.'

As soon as Delia says it she cringes, fingers curling on the table.

'Sorry,' she says. 'I didn't mean to make that all about me again, or say that – god – Benjamin was unwanted. He wasn't. I just don't think I've really talked to anyone in a long time.'

'It's okay,' November says with a shrug. She stretches her arms out, eyes the timer on the oven across from them. She's making a Mediterranean casserole for dinner and the smell of it is thick in the air already, all cumin and paprika.

'I don't talk to my parents so much anymore. Whenever I see them apart I try to remember them together, like maybe if I can remember the love they had, they will too. It doesn't work that way though, not really. I don't know if you ever get those feelings back.'

As November says it, Delia writes a list in her head of the paints she'll buy tomorrow. Thick summer reds and startling ambers, some well-watched sunset that cuts the sky open like a wound. Not a sunset though. November. The long line of her neck, the static frizz of her hair in the humid evenings. The way her lips twitch before a smile or a frown, as if she's always uncertain before committing to a feeling, no matter what that may be. It's horribly romantic, unlike Delia to wax so lyrical about anyone, but right now she just sighs, leans back against the bench and feels it warm her skin through her thin shirt. She cups her hands at the ledge to steady herself.

November starts to reply when one of the girls starts crying, those kitten mews that remind Delia of a hundred years ago, when Olive used to make the same sounds.

She's at home, in bed, before she realises November was probably trying to tell her something about her own marriage too.

O

She doesn't know how to go back and ask, so she paints instead. Doesn't have the colours for November at home that night, but she does for the one on the other side of the world. For winter, and so she paints that, the snow-capped peaks she saw as a girl in the Blue Mountains and the chill that embraces them. The icy fingers of Jack Frost holding to windowpanes and the cool hues of a season Delia has rarely seen. She paints blues and whites and thick, storm-cloud greys, icicles and snow and frost-tipped rivers and skaters in little pink coats skirting around the depths of the season.

She's so absorbed in her work that she doesn't hear the car pull up, or the front door open, or even her bedroom door. She doesn't hear the dip in her mattress, or feel the attention of an audience, not until she reaches around for her drink and sees Ed staring at her.

'Fuck,' she hisses, clutching a hand to her chest. She's ready to yell, to get mad, to *be* mad, but Ed is standing up, walking slowly, steadily towards her, and then he's on her again, his body generous, heavy, so fucking warm.

Delia should push away. Should stop, but then her arms are at his neck, her brush in his hair, and there will be smears of paint across him, smears of *her* paint, and the thought sends a thrill through her in ways she wishes it didn't.

His tongue pushes into her mouth as he turns her away from the canvas, away from the ghost of her son and her sister and this winter cold, and lowers her down onto the bed, his body blissfully familiar on top of her, his hands disappearing up the bottom of her shift dress, grasping at her thick, sweating thighs, at the curve of her soft belly. He mumbles words into her mouth that Delia swallows before she can hear, and she imagines them inside her, rattling against her bones for the rest of the night.

And no, she thinks. *No*.

She holds her fingers to the soft curve of his mouth and pushes them gently, *him* gently, away. Ed follows her directions, like he did when they were still young, when this thing between them felt new and fragile, not enduring, like they both know it is. Like they wish it wasn't.

'This can't be a habit, Ed. *We* can't be,' she says, and she watches Ed's face contort. There is paint on him after all. A smudge of blue at his temple. She reaches a hand out to touch it, and it's already hardening there. A strange, foreign form of ownership.

Ed climbs off her, sits up, looks at her long and hard, turns to leave, and it's only then that she sees it. The bright flash of a post-it note, scrunched up in one of his clenched hands.

16

She hears the party before she sees it, from the high back seat of the council bus, sitting between Lux and some guy stinking of patchouli and goon. It's the bone-rattling *thud thud thud* of the music that shakes the road beneath their feet, that seems to palpitate in the air, louder than the cicadas and the croaking frogs and the nighttime birds. Louder than anything.

After that it's the voices, noisy but incoherent, crying out to be heard over the swell of the music. Then the crashes, dropped glasses smashing, bodies thudding into walls, the calls of *taxi*, the *woo* girls, the *nah, just playing, mate*.

Lux hears it at the same time she does, if her wicked, sprawling grin is anything to go by, and she calls the bus to a stop and leads Olive off before either of them can reconsider.

'Where is this thing, anyway?' Olive asks, shucking her jacket over her shoulders despite the heat, just because she likes the cover of it, the armour of it, the way it hides her fat now-yellowing bruises. Around them the houses seem to grow larger and larger, like reverse babushka dolls, swallowing up the smaller homes. The familiar raised structures and long-legged stilts have given way to multi-storey properties with

French doors and arching windows, with Romanesque pillars and electronic blinds.

'Man, some of these places are *nice*,' Lux says, as if she hasn't heard her. She's half a step ahead (always), and she walks with purpose, even without the maps app open on her phone. Then again, it's not hard to find the party by following the sound, each catcall and bassline thud like a fairytale breadcrumb, leading them to their demise.

'Did you ever play Dream House?' Lux continues. 'My mum and I did. Like, whenever we had long drives or whatever. We'd build our fantasy place. Marble countertops, pink feature walls, mohair carpet in the bedrooms and living room, varnished timber in the rest of them, that sort of thing. It was so fun. I bet half these places are like that.'

Olive doesn't quite have the heart to say that that's what Lux's house is like. Big and garish and the picture-perfect example of how money can't buy taste. She also doesn't quite have the heart to say that she doesn't like it, or any of these places really. They look empty, not in the way the abandoned house they vandalise is, but in a deeper way. Like no matter how much stuff you put in them, no matter the size of the mohair rug or the flatscreen TV, they will always be missing something. But then Olive has always liked the lived-in things, the wild, the untamed.

Lux has her *a-ha* moment as they find the party house, the lights flashing across the street outside. Someone must have a strobe light and a smoke machine, and together they succeed in making the house look as if it could take off for another planet. The whole building shakes with the heavy, heaving mass of people, the *duff-duff* of the music vibrating across the grass.

'It's barely eight,' Olive says as they head around back. If the party was obvious out front, here it's hard to make heads or tails of it. The crowd is almost unseeable, unknowable, moving like one body instead of the dozens there are. It looks as if they've been going for a while. The smell of weed is heavy in the air, smothering the space, and Olive inhales deeply, feels herself starting to wander, wonder, her anxiety smoothening out beneath coaxing hands.

Lux grabs her by the arm.

'I think the bar's over there.'

The bar is barely a bar at all, rather a kiddie pool filled with melting ice and beer and the feet of some scabby white guy with a henna sleeve babbling about full moons and auras. Lux doesn't care though – she plunges a hand straight in and pulls out two cans of Little Creatures, throwing one at Olive and gesturing to a set-up of slumped deckchairs and a picnic blanket. They've barely sat down before Lux is digging into the pockets of her dress and pulling out a small bag of coke. Olive's belly folds.

'Isn't it a bit early for that?'

'Look alive, Rabbit. We've got a lot of catching up to do.'

Lux tosses her legs forwards, slinging them ankle over ankle. She's impossibly long like this, the thinness of her limbs starker beneath the violent strobe lights. It reminds Olive vaguely of games of pick-up sticks in the musty hours of her childhood.

Lux drops a line of the coke onto her hand, snorting it with the neat precision of someone with a habit, and Olive watches her with uncertain eyes.

'What?' Lux says, rubbing her nose. She reaches over then, grabbing Olive's hand and pulling it forwards. She mirrors her actions on Olive, dropping a line there too.

'I …' Olive stumbles, her mouth dry. She looks back out at the party, at the heaving, yelling, cajoling bodies. A couple makes out. Another fights. A girl sits alone, crying as she cradles a goon sack. 'Not yet.'

She doesn't want to say that she hasn't done this before, just pills, little low-dose things that sit on her tongue like salvation, and like she knows, like she *judges* her for it, Lux rolls her eyes, leaning forwards in her seat to lick the line of coke from Olive's hand like a dog.

○

Most of the lights are off when Benjamin and Mum get home from Poppy's house – at least all the ones out the front are. Olive's out, that much they both know, but when Mum heads up the stairs to the house, Benjamin pauses, his gaze catching on the distant flicker of citronella candles out the back. He slings his backpack over his shoulder, waving to his mother before ducking out towards the lights.

The night is alive with insects, and they rustle in the long grass like warriors, parting the sea of green as if they're advancing on an enemy. The bees are back in their hives, but the mosquitoes are fighting the candles, buzzing bleakly over warty toads. Benjamin stumbles back to avoid one.

There's a scratching sound, and he glances up to see Charlie's pencil at work, scribbling in his notebook in the dim candlelight.

'Is the light broken again?' he asks, and Charlie flips to the back of his notebook. He writes something and holds it up for Benjamin to see. Benjamin's eyes strain in the dark.

No. The dark's just better for stargazing.

'I know that,' Benjamin replies, rolling his eyes. 'Not for taking notes though.'

If he could see Charlie, he's sure his brother would have just shrugged, but he can only see the telescope tilt slightly, which must mean he's making adjustments.

'Did Olive come home at all?'

Just to get ready. She went to a party with Lux.

Benjamin wrinkles his nose and thrusts his hands into the pockets of his shorts. Olive's hanging out with Lux more and more, and Benjamin can't say that he likes her. There's something cold about her, mean, and she always smells of cigarettes. He's still thinking about this when the notebook is pushed back in his face.

I told dad.

Benjamin blinks.

'Yeah?'

Yeah. It was hard. I couldn't remember his new address and I had to catch the bus, and someone almost sat on me.

Benjamin grins, but it falls away quickly.

'What did he say?'

Nothing really. He didn't believe me right away, and then he cried a lot, and his girlfriend was there, but I didn't want her to know, and dad promised he wouldn't tell her, and then he drove me home and I think something happened with mum, because he went and saw her, but they didn't fight, and then he left really suddenly, and mum was weird all night.

Considering this, Benjamin rocks back on his heels and tries to imagine what his father would have thought. If he'd been mad at Mum for keeping the secret from him, like Mum had been at Olive, or if he'd been excited like Benjamin or disbelieving like Olive, but he can't quite tell. His father's always been a foreigner to him, even more of a foreigner than Olive.

They're both quiet then, while Charlie readjusts his telescope and records things that Benjamin doesn't understand in the thinly drawn margins of his notebook.

'Hey, Charlie?' Benjamin asks, and Charlie's pencil stops scribbling.

Yeah?

'Are you glad it's not a secret anymore?'

Charlie doesn't reply for a moment, and Benjamin looks up at the tarrish sky above them, the stars flecked like paint, like freckles on dark skin. He wonders if there are aliens up there, and he thinks there must be, and he wonders what they might be like if there have been invisible boys down here on Earth all along.

Olive found a photo of a girl called Bo Rabbit. She was standing with mum. They were both little kids. Mum's been painting her too. We don't know who she is. I think they might be sisters though, or cousins. Something.

The thought makes Benjamin's mouth feel dry, his

296

shoulders tight, but still, he shrugs, not seeing Charlie's point.

'So?'

So I think maybe sometimes secrets are just easier. That's all.

○

Lux grabs her arm again, her fingernails digging into Olive's jacket, her pupils wide.

'There's your man,' she croons, and Olive's head jerks sideways until she spots Jude across the fray, leaning heavily on the arm of a friend, his hair pulled back into a messy bun, his skin glowing gold beneath the strobe lights. Olive finishes her beer – her fourth, maybe fifth, of the night, and tries to slow her rabbit heart.

'What are you waiting for?' Lux continues, and Olive turns to reply, then arches an eyebrow.

'Man, I didn't think this would be Mindy's scene.'

'No way!' Lux's head whips around. Mindy stands a few feet away in a gaggle of girls Olive doesn't recognise. It's strange to see her out here, out of uniform, made up in a short, sweet black dress, gold sandals and bold winged eyeliner. She laughs at something one of the other girls says and sips from a plastic cup.

Beside Olive, Lux reaches up, waving an arm at Mindy until the other girl clocks them, tilting her cup their way in acknowledgement. The girl beside her, the one with a shaved head and thick thighs, leans in close to Mindy, whispering something in her ear that makes her roll her eyes.

'I thought you were pissed at her?' Olive says, and Lux

bats her away dismissively, before pointing again at Jude, and right, Olive thinks. The alcohol buzzes through her. She could just say hi. *Should*. What's she got to lose? With that, Olive nods at Lux and wanders through the crowd, swaying in time to the heavy beats of the music as she finds her way to Jude.

'Hey,' she says, awkwardly nudging his side, and he turns, his face splitting into a bleary grin when he sees her.

'Olive Rabbit!' he cries, leaning in close and then closer again until suddenly he's kissing her. He tastes of ash and cheap beer and cheaper mints, and Olive can feel her heart in her throat as he licks his way into her mouth. He leans away after a moment, eyes glazed, then wraps an arm around her tense shoulders.

'Guys, this is Olive, Olive, the guys.'

The Guys are a group of boys on the uneasy cusp of manhood. They're spotty with pimples, lanky with sun-bleached hair. There's a girl among them, her skin thickened with a fake tan and her weighted lashes curtaining sharp eyes. She gives Olive an unimpressed once-over.

And maybe Olive would care, would think more of it, but Jude is there with his heavy arm over her shoulders and the ghost of his tongue in her mouth. She shivers, feels something warm in her chest stretching out, but the moment slips away before she can grasp it. Jude's arm slides off her shoulders to gesture animatedly to one of the guys, his voice growing husky with laughter over a joke Olive's never brought in on. Her fingers curl around her beer can, and she tries to bump affectionately beneath his arm again, but it's awkward, and Olive can't – she—

'Hey,' she says instead, touching his arm, but Jude doesn't turn back, and a couple of the guys give her a look that settles uncomfortably in her stomach, and right, she thinks. Right. 'I should go find Lux, but maybe we can catch up later?'

Jude nods, distracted, waving her off, and Olive shuffles, dragging her feet as she walks back into the crowd. She doesn't feel bad, just kind of *weird*, the taste of Jude still thick on her lips and she hadn't – that wasn't her first kiss or anything, but it was her first with *him*, and it was just sudden and she doesn't think she kissed back well enough and if she could just find Lux, she thinks she'd feel better.

She tries the bar, the clutch of girls by the portaloo out back, the deckchairs slumped against the side of the house, but Lux is nowhere to be found, and that weird feeling's back in Olive's belly, and she's reaching for her phone when she glimpses Mindy through the crowd, and heads towards her instead.

'Rabbit,' Mindy says, tilting her cup at her, only to pause, and Olive must look – something, she doesn't know, because Mindy's next words are, 'You okay?'

'Have you seen Lux?'

The girl next to Mindy gives Olive a pitying look, and Mindy's face is carefully blank, the way it is with difficult customers at O'Malley's, and Olive really doesn't want to think about what that means.

'I'm pretty sure she left with someone. Maybe her boyfriend?'

And he wasn't going to come, that much Olive knows, and she blinks hard, surprised by the heavy tears escaping from her eyes.

'Cool.'

Olive swipes at her cheeks, the beer muting her senses, turning over in her belly, and she can still see Jude through the throng, punching his friend's arm, and she can still see the house, distorted by smoke and people, and she can see herself, her knees bruised and her arms scabby from the broken window, her hands bloody from digging her nails in again, and then Mindy's hand is on her arm, gentle and soft.

'She seemed a bit fucked up, she probably needed to get out of here, you know? I'm sure she tried to find you.'

The girl beside Mindy scoffs, and Mindy sends her a warning look.

'Oh, come on, Min. Fuck her, she's a bitch.'

The girl looks at Olive then, really looks at her, her expression somewhere between pity and contempt. 'You know her name isn't even Lux, right? It's Anna. She just watched *Virgin Suicides* a few too many times and thinks everyone this side of the city wants to fuck her, and you know what? They don't. She's just a slut, and no one has to work for it.'

'Jesus,' Mindy says, throwing her hands up. 'Just back off, Lauren, seriously.'

She refocuses on Olive, pulling something out of her clutch that Olive belatedly realises is a tissue. Leaning in close, Mindy wipes Olive's eyes, her cheeks, pausing suddenly, and Olive realises she must see the bruises peeking out from below her jacket. Mindy sighs.

'Sorry about her. Lauren and Lux were – look, it's complicated.'

Olive sniffs, shrugs, letting Mindy clean her up.

'Everything always is.'

Mindy tries for a grin, but Lauren's started bickering with one of the other girls, and so with an eye roll Mindy shoves the tissue into Olive's hand, and pulls Lauren off and out of the fight, leaving Olive behind, alone. If she tries really hard, she might be able to beat this feeling down. Keep the lapping emotion at bay. Right now, though, it doesn't feel as if she can. It feels like her insides are primed to flood, like the dam of her is cracking, and she has always imagined herself stronger than this, braver than this, her shoulders able to bear more weight, but perhaps she is none of these things after all.

Did you know all along?

The message blears across Delia's phone screen, bright as any accusation. He'd sent it the day before, after he'd kissed her, after she'd kicked him out. She had expected it, really, after she'd had a chance to process the implications of the crumpled post-it note.

She sighs, pushing her phone aside. She should call him. Explain to him that she didn't know. Hadn't. That it has been a long time since Ed has been the first thing she thinks of. Still, she knows the cruelty of her omission. Felt it herself not so long ago.

Her phone buzzes again, and she leans over, picks it up and sees a message from Griff. She doesn't even bother reading it, just thrusts it aside and fixes herself a drink, downs it over the kitchen sink, her body aching, exhausted.

Benjamin's already in bed now, at least, even if Olive hasn't come home yet. She'd had to soak his shorts again after she'd picked him up from his friend's, and it had been a productive way at least of keeping her mind off Ed, off Bo, if just for a little while.

She finishes the last of her scotch before trekking back to her bedroom and standing in front of her canvas.

The image of her sister had come to her starkly the other day, as if it had simply been covered with a cloth. Her impish grin and knowing eyes, her broader body, just a few inches taller than Delia's, her voice surprisingly deep for a girl of sixteen.

Something clenches inside her chest that she can't quite shake loose. It's been so long since she painted – or at least it *had* been. So long since she used these tools as extensions of herself, capturing parts of herself in the grooves of a canvas, with the horse hairs of a brush.

It doesn't feel as natural as it did back at seventeen, at nineteen, at twenty-five, at thirty-two, but there's something there still, something that inches through her veins and works her fingers. Something that moves in her.

Moves *her*.

The back door cracks open and Delia snaps out of her reverie. She hears Olive drop her things in the living room and stumble down the hallway, then spots her daughter through her bedroom door, her legs bruised and her face a mess. She looks flushed, and there's grass stuck to her back. Threaded through her hair. She smells of sweat and smoke and beer, even at this distance.

'What happened to you?' Delia asks, and she intends it

curiously, but it comes out curt, even to her own ears.

Olive jolts, startled. She curls her body protectively into herself, arms cradling her chest, and shrugs.

'Just went to hang out with some friends. I'm going to have a shower,' she mutters, kicking off her shoes, and Delia watches her daughter, her bare feet, her circus-stilt legs walk down the hallway away from her. Before she can stop herself, Delia calls out. 'Olive!'

Olive pauses, halfway down the hall, and Delia leans sideways to get a better look at her.

'Are you okay?' she asks, the words heavy even as she tries to make them light, and Olive looks back at her, her owlish eyes wide and her lips red and swollen like they've been gnawed.

'Why wouldn't I be?' is all she says before she disappears into the bathroom and out of sight.

17

The next week at school, Benjamin tells Poppy everything over Roll-ups and half-melted lamingtons, and Poppy's still licking the chocolate off her fingers when he tells her that Charlie told their dad. She wrinkles her nose at the news.

'He's not great at being a superhero, huh? It can't really be a secret identity if everyone knows.'

Benjamin considers this as he peels off a layer of sticky, make-believe fruit.

'I don't think Charlie wants to *use* his power at all. Like, he's had it forever, and the most he's done with it is do the experiments he does with *everything* and make a whole lot of notes. Maybe it'll be different when he remembers how to turn it off, but I don't know.'

'Man, if I could go invisible, I'd do so much. I'd be The Girl Who Wasn't There, and I'd put bad guys away before they even knew what hit 'em.'

The sun burns up the concrete beneath their feet, so much so that Benjamin can almost feel it through the rubber soles of his school shoes. If Poppy notices she doesn't seem to mind, but then Poppy doesn't seem to mind most things. Sometimes he wonders if there would be any way to shake her. To make her mad or sad or annoyed, but then, he thinks, if there was, he's not sure she'd be Poppy anymore.

She's still chattering about what she'd do with invisibility when Benjamin turns back to look at her, her face pinked with excitement as she talks about her inevitable foe, The Girl Who Was There Too Much. ('We'd be like Batman and the Joker, Wonder Woman and Ares, only we'd both be girls, because girl fights are way scarier than boy fights.') He grins before he can help it.

'Who would I be?' he asks then, and Poppy laughs.

'Who would you be? I can't tell you that! You've got to make it up.'

Her face is so bright, so alive, it stirs a feeling in him that makes him blush shyly, oddly embarrassed that he's asked the question at all. There's something so *nice* about being with her that he's never entirely sure what to do with himself. He looks away, tries to dim his grin so he doesn't seem too intense – but then his gaze catches on Jodi Baxter. She's sitting with her new friends over by the picnic tables, a sandwich clenched in her hands, and looking pointedly at them. He tries to smile, but Jodi turns back to her friends.

He ignores the dig of the worm in his back, his mood darkening, but when he looks at Poppy again it's like she's switched a light back on, and a slow grin slips across his face.

'I think I'd be Spectacular Man.'

O

'She's having a good day today,' the nurse tells Delia as she signs herself in. 'She's lucid, she's sitting up, she ate some lunch. She even had a full conversation with Sandy an hour ago about the medications she's on.'

She laughs as she says the last bit, at the idea of a nurse treating a fading nurse, a certain uneasy respect between carer and patient that Delia almost understands. The words are meant as a comfort, offered in the same way Delia might offer a failing student a *you're talented, but*— and that *but* sits heavy beneath the word *today*.

'Great,' Delia says, slinging her purse back over her shoulder and turning to walk down the hall to her mother's room. She pauses outside the door, smooths down her skirt, tries to slow her stammering heart. Then she pushes through.

Her mother is sitting upright in the starchy hospital bed, her infirm gaze ahead, and before Delia strides over to meet her she's distracted by the acidic smell of dying flowers. Looking around, she spots a wilting bouquet dense with kangaroo paws and protea on the small table by the window, the water slimy in the glass vase that holds them. She drops her bag to the usual chair and moves to kiss her mother's cold temple in lieu of any other greeting.

She's not really expecting her mother to respond, so it's a surprise to hear her voice as Delia heads for the dying flowers.

'Where have you been?'

There's a familiar note of accusation, and Delia's step falters.

'At work, Mum.'

From the bed, Rosie clicks her tongue, makes that deep

animal noise at the back of her throat that Delia remembers from the bad days. A low, roaring sound, as if she's caught something feral in her jaw. Did she make that noise before Dad died? Before Bo did? Fuck, Delia doesn't know, but remembers it at least after the latter, at the funeral, at the wake, Rosie brittle-boned and razor-edged beside her as Delia struggled to breathe through her own sobs.

'The nurse said you were feeling better today,' she says, almost itching with the memory, and she watches her mother's eyes skirt the monitors at her bedside, clock her own vitals. She nods, her gaze finding Delia's again, and Delia aims for a smile but thinks she probably misses the mark.

She can hear the sound of wheels on tiles, and the calls from the kitchens. Somewhere a man howls, a deep caterwauling sound that reminds her of stray cats lurking in the thickest part of the night.

Below the scent of flowers, her mother has the pungent smell of hospital creams and cheap washing powder, the faint scent of urine, of body odour and sweat, in spite of the little fan rolling in the corner. The only window in the room overlooks the carpark and the long, winding road that leads towards it.

'Did someone visit?' Delia asks, looking at the bouquet of flowers, and Rosie just shrugs. They're pretty, really, despite being wilted. The bright, soft smudge of yellow wattle, the curling, alien bloom of waratah. A few are dead, and Delia plucks them out, wiping the slick, filmy coat of old water from their stems as she does so.

She can feel more than see her mother's gaze as she works,

the careful consideration with which Rosie has always watched her. It sends a shiver up her spine.

'I can check the guest book if you want,' she says. 'If you'd like to know. They must be friends, to bring you these.'

Rosie doesn't say anything, doesn't even acknowledge Delia's presence, and it makes her feel thirteen again, as if she's sitting at home waiting for their mother to give a fuck. At least then she'd had Bo, she'd had her dad, at least then she'd—

'Great, Mum. Great conversation,' Delia snaps, pulling out the dead flowers with growing speed. 'I'm glad I *continue* to drive out here twice a week for you to ignore me. You know my life doesn't stop for you. I'm dealing with a lot of shit right now, so—'

'With your divorce?' It's a petty jab, and Delia looks around to catch a familiar sharpness in her mother's eye, a familiar acidity, and it shocks her still, how quickly it steels her.

'I'd have to be married for that, wouldn't I?'

And that's an old wound, a faded bruise, but it sits there always, just beneath the skin. Rosie works her mouth, the lines in her face sinking like trenches, her skin seeming to toughen. It's the old Rosie, the surly one, the one who braved wars and a dead husband and a dead daughter and who somehow still found Delia the hardest thing in her life to bear.

'I can't believe you sometimes,' Delia hisses, her cheeks flushed with heat, with anger, with some deep, underlying shame. She needs to stop, *wants* to stop. Wants to catch this moment and trap it in herself until it wears itself out, but she can't. It claws free of her, and god, she hopes her mother will forget.

'You know your grandkids are having problems, those

grandkids you never bothered to see. You know your granddaughter's – you know your grandson's disappeared?'

And *no*, Delia thinks. This isn't what she wanted, but suddenly the feeling is too much to bear. As if she needs her mother to know that she's been through what she has, like some last naked connecting line. They both lost Bo, they both lost Delia's father, but Delia has lost her son too, or at least she'd thought she had, and god, she never meant to tell Rosie, never wanted to, but the words fall like a weight off her chest and her mother's silence feels like a surrender, and Delia can't work out if that's what she wanted.

Her fingers shake as she dumps the dead flowers in the bin beneath the table, on top of chip packets and bandages Rosie must have unwrapped again when she mistook this impossible heat for the heat forty years ago in Vietnam.

'Disappeared?' Rosie asks suddenly, her voice quivering through the quiet hospital room, and the crack of guilt in Delia's chest starts to gape.

'Yes, Mum. He disappeared on us.' And she doesn't know why she's clinging to this, what she wants from it, because Charlie might have disappeared, but he's still at home, it's not like …

'He's gone.'

She hears her mother sigh in frustration, as if Delia's not paying attention, as if she isn't doing this right. As if *Delia* isn't right.

'No, Del. Is he gone, or is he …' Rosie's tone shifts, and Delia turns around, to look her mother in the eye, and Delia blinks and then the hospital bed is empty.

18

Her mother reappears sometime in the hour that follows, not in the room where she disappeared but outside on the lawn, staring up at the newly setting sky.

It had been very strange, to see the catheter and monitor pulled out of vacant air, then stranger still to feel her mother's hand on her own, to be led out of the room, down the corridor, and into the bright glare of the afternoon.

And then they'd just sat beside each other, watching the after-work traffic in the distance, and the peace of the moment had made Delia's temper fizzle out and her bones ache, exhaustion settling across her like a weighted blanket, and she'd looked sideways often at her invisible mother, and she had felt her there, like she had felt her son.

This time, when she looks, her mother is fully formed again, her cheeks pallid and her chest sunken.

'How long?' Delia asks, and Rosie just shrugs, her body sagging with age and gravity and maybe this moment too, her cellophane skin near-luminous in the fading light.

'For always, I suppose.'

With a frown, Delia looks out over the carpark. Somebody

has left their headlights on, and they cast an eerie glow around them, stretching their shadows long against the dying grass. Delia leans forwards, pulling her knees to her chest.

'Why didn't you ever tell me?'

'I never told anyone. Not even your father. I never even knew there was anyone like me until Vietnam.'

Delia turns, takes in her mother's stark profile, the mosquitoes buzzing around her, seeking skin to draw blood from. A part of Delia wants to say something, wants to accuse or beg, but for once her mother needs no prompting.

'I was only nineteen when I left, you know. They put me on nursing rotation with the Red Cross and I went out there and I don't know what I thought. I think I thought I'd be like my mother was before me in the war before that one, but none of our stories were ever the same. I saw ...'

Rosie's voice quivers, whether with strain or shock or the remnants of a memory, Delia can't be sure. She reaches out a hand, but Rosie pulls her arms in, balls her fingers into fists.

'I was put in a village and took care of our boys, and the American boys and the New Zealand ones, and when we had spare time we took care of the children in the villages, and their fevers and their broken bones and their sick mothers. You think you go into war thinking *us* and *them*, but out there the *us* was all of us, and *them* was everyone who wasn't. That's just the way it was.'

Rosie's eyes wane suddenly, as if lost in a memory or drawing on a well of unforgotten rage. She shakes her head. Clears her throat.

'Me and one of the other girls were called out one night

to another camp. One of our boys had lost everything from his belly down and somehow survived the initial injury. We could really only make him as comfortable as we could. I was washing the bloody rags in the canteen when I saw this … this *light*.'

She holds out her hand, as if reaching to touch something. A fly settles on her temple, but she doesn't bother to bat it off.

'That was the first time I saw it, but I kept seeing it, for as long as I was at that camp. Usually in the middle of the night, seemingly randomly. It would just appear, bright as a star, and then vanish again. I thought it was like the Min Min lights at first, but then I wasn't in the outback, was I? I got relocated and then moved back to that village and then sent home and then shipped back. One night, at that camp, a woman went into labour. She was a wisp of a thing, her teeth broken. It was a troubled birth, and no one else was there who could help her, so I did.'

She turns to face Delia then, lifting her arthritis-hooked hand to her chest and tapping unevenly at her heart.

'I delivered a star, Del. That's what it felt like, what it looked like. This magical bright light pouring out of her. I thought I was dreaming, but there it was, this ball of light in my hands, and then the woman started crying, and smiling, and she became that bright light too. I thought I was out of my mind. That I was seeing things. I'd read about the hallucinations fevers can bring, but then I remembered this thing that I could do, that I hadn't done since I was a girl. And I did it again that night, vanished, and anyone who walked into that hut would've seen two stars and nothing else.'

Her mother shakes her head, finally batting away the fly at her temple.

'It took him days to fade. For his skin to go from shining gold to brown, and I thought it was the strangest thing in the world, to be in this country we were supposed to be at war with and to deliver someone who was just like me. And then I had Bo, and she was too.'

Delia's heart leaps, and her mother turns her glassy eyes on her, and there's something uncurling in them, like a lifetime of grief and regret fumbling for footing in the remnants of this secret.

'Was that why?' Delia asks quietly. 'Because I couldn't. Is that why you never saw me? Just all these things I wasn't. I do that to Olive now, and I don't know how to stop it.'

She looks back towards her, but the moment of clarity is gone, and her mother has once again been reduced to a shell of herself, her voice trembling when she asks Delia if she knows where her husband went.

'I'll go get him,' she says, and walks with wobbly, uncertain legs back up to Saint Anne's for an orderly to collect her.

○

Afterwards she slams the car door with shaking hands, sits in the driver's seat unable to drive just yet, her mother's words reeling around in her head.

She grips the wheel tightly, her leg jittery beneath her, and something is flickering inside her, something like *hope*, and she knows this can't be the case, because they *buried* Bo, but maybe – if—

Her chest aches as she inhales, and she can't stop herself from calling out into the dusky light of her car. 'Bo?'

There's no reply, of course there's no reply, and Delia makes a hoarse noise in her throat, pounds on the steering wheel, throws her body back forcefully into her seat, thrashing, thrashing, thrashing.

Why is it always Bo? Why does it always come back to her?

Stupid. Delia knows why.

Can you scrub grief from your mind, or does it bury you alive? Does it choke the earth of you? Salt your soul until nothing ever grows again?

Delia wipes her face and starts the engine.

O

Poppy's house is bigger than Benjamin's. He thinks this is probably because her family is much bigger, but then he also thinks that they might have more money than his. Not that it really matters – it hasn't changed Poppy, at least, and the wealth only really tells in the number of fancy instruments she and her sisters play and in the gleam of their big kitchen.

And, of course, in the enormous costume box that Poppy's dad pulls out of the garden shed for them. He laughs all the while, tugging out old Halloween shirts marked with fake blood, and a bag of Poppy's oldest sister's faded dancing costumes, exploding with tulle.

He's barely put it down when Poppy practically folds herself in half trying to get into it, riffling around until she pulls out a sequined cape and a feathered mask that looks more masquerade ball than superhero. If Poppy thinks this, she doesn't show it, just slips the cape over her shoulders, the mask over her eyes, and does a twirl.

'That's a lot to make invisible,' Benjamin says, and Poppy laughs, turning around so that Benjamin can tie the ribbon at the back.

'I don't want a *boring* costume,' she replies, and Benjamin grins. He hadn't thought to bring his own costume in his sleepover bag, but Poppy hadn't seemed too concerned. She goes back to the box and pulls out another cape – red this time, and a yellow shirt that's sure to swallow him.

'I know it's not perfect,' she says, watching as Benjamin shrugs the shirt over his school uniform, and Benjamin widens his grin at her in a way he hopes is good. She smiles shyly in reply, and together they cut the bottom off with a pair of kitchen scissors, and then cut some eyeholes into the scrap of fabric, making a perfect matching mask.

He doesn't realise anyone's watching until a voice rings down from the back step.

'What the ever-loving fuck.'

They both spin to see Poppy's eldest sister, Isles, leaning against the back door, a wry smile on her face as Poppy puffs up her chest.

'Ma'am, I'll need to ask you to please show some respect for Spectacular Man and The Girl Who Wasn't There.'

Isles nods with a serious expression.

'Sorry, sorry,' she says, holding up her hands in surrender. 'It's just a look, is all.'

'*You're* a look,' Poppy bites back, and Isles's expression

shifts, closes off in a way that makes Benjamin step closer to Poppy, ready for Isles to say something mean like Olive might, but that's not what happens at all.

'That's no way to talk to Sinestro!' Isles calls, her surrendering hands suddenly pointing into finger guns. She shoots, and Poppy staggers back in horror, clutching her belly. Isles darts back up through the house, laughing maniacally, and Poppy grabs Benjamin's wrist, tugging him forwards.

'Quick!' she says, leaping up the back steps and into the house, and a surge of adrenaline hits him as he bolts up behind her. They can still hear Isles's laughter, cackling through the house, the heavy drops of her feet, and Poppy's dad swears under his breath as Benjamin and Poppy dart past him.

Benjamin loses Poppy somewhere upstairs, the loud steps having stopped, giggling coming from another room like the distorted noise of a dream. He means to follow it, he does, but there's another sound – a different one – down the hall in the other direction, something like a sob behind a closed door, and Benjamin's never been nosy but he's always been curious.

He pushes up his mask as he plods quietly down the hall, his fingers trailing the walls towards the sound. It falters, something gasping and wet, and he lingers by the door for too long, pressing his ear into the warm wood. He should open it, he thinks. He should take a look inside, just to make sure one of Poppy's sisters isn't hurt, and his fingers reach for the handle.

'What are you doing?'

Benjamin jumps, turning quickly on the spot to see Poppy. She's pushed her mask off her face and is looking at

Benjamin with an expression he hasn't seen before. It makes him puff out his cheeks in consideration, look at the closed door again and then back at Poppy.

'I thought I heard something.'

Poppy doesn't reply to that, not right away, and for a second he wonders if she'll say anything else. She paints on a wide grin that Benjamin's starting to recognise as not entirely honest.

'Our house is so old. It makes weird noises sometimes.'

And Benjamin understands that, he does, because his house does the same thing – but the sound he heard wasn't possum feet on the roof or the scratching of mice in the walls or birds nesting in the rafters. It was a human sound, he's sure of it, but before he can think another thing Poppy's slipping her mask back on and running in search of Isles.

○

The car hits the kerb with a thump as Delia pulls up to the house, and any breath she'd hoped to catch is lost to her, because standing by the rusted gate, clutching a bottle of wine, is Griff.

And – right.

Thursday.

It's why she'd organised Benjamin's sleepover, after all, why she'd organised *this*, knowing that Olive would be working and Charlie would be at the lookout. It had made sense the other day, with Griff so distressed at the college. She needed to get a handle on it, needed to *end* things, only the prospect of doing it right now, with her nerves frayed and years of rewritten history weighing on her back, is almost too much to bear.

Still, she slides out of the car, tries to relax her still-tight throat, and Griff smiles when he sees her, a shy edge to it that makes her think – well, what else can she think?

Stupid.

'Hey,' he says, and Delia nods at him, gesturing him towards the house.

○

Taking the wine from him, she leads him up into the kitchen and promptly kicks off her shoes and pours them both a glass, watching carefully as he steps through the room and absorbs himself in the task of looking at her things. She sees him take in the sink stacked with dirty dishes, the school uniforms hanging from a wobbly clothes horse, Benjamin's school shorts still soaking in a bucket by the back door. There are a few pictures on the walls – all small, delicate things in weighted frames. Only one is her own, the rest have come from the brushes of others. There are no photos in her house either, not really. A few of the kids. She thinks perhaps it's a leftover habit from Rosie.

She'd packed everything up after Bo, after all.

'I like this one,' Griff says, cutting through her thoughts, tapping the base of one of the portraits.

It's her favourite too. A simple sketch of a nude woman leaning off a wall, her face hidden and her body shadowed but for a peel of light that curves down her side. It had made all three of her children blush when she'd hung it. She moves to stand beside him, passing him one of the glasses and taking a sip from the other.

'It's Hilda Rix Nicholas. From one of her early London sketchbooks. She didn't do a lot of classic nudes – preferred profiles and landscapes, I guess. I wish she'd done more of them.'

Griff is looking at her with wide eyes now. For a second she thinks he might kiss her, but he doesn't.

'It's weird hearing you talk about art like you like it.'

Delia frowns, glancing down at the glass in her hand. She swirls the wine around a little. Unfocused.

'I like art.'

'No, *I* like art,' he says, smiling. 'You have, like, a bitter marriage with art. I think you fucking hate it sometimes, and you fight with it all the time, but you know it so well, and you're so good at it, and I'm sure you'll be buried with it, but I don't think you like it.'

It takes her a moment to temper her surprise. Her gaze darts over his face, taking in his earnestness, his amusement, and then she takes a slight step away from him.

'I love art, Adam,' she says, and she means it to be light, but it sounds thick, even to her own ears. Briefly, she catches her reflection in the glass behind him. Her lipstick's a mess, virtually gone bar the red that's stuck in the cracks, like dregs in a wine glass. Her lip liner though is still clear, outlining them a brilliant red, making them plumper than they've ever been. There are heavy bags beneath her eyes, smudged black with eyeliner and bloodshot from her tears on the way home from Saint Anne's, but Griff looks at her like he's awe-struck and dazzled, and she wonders what the fuck she did to deserve all of this.

She should break up with him now, but she doesn't.

Instead, they finish their drinks and have another, and she puts on some music, and loses herself in the way he looks at her, the way he *sees* her, not as she is but as something entirely other, and she wonders what that is, but maybe she doesn't care. Maybe she doesn't mind what he projects onto her, just so long as he keeps looking at her.

Leonard Cohen's 'Take This Waltz' croons out through her speakers, and she stands up and sways and then she dances and then there's a memory of her and Bo as girls, her mother's hand in hers, stepping her backwards, sideways, forwards, sideways.

'My mother taught me to waltz,' she says, because Rosie did, and how had she forgotten that? She's forgotten a lot of things, she knows, but the dance is coming back to her, her feet recalling the movements as if someone's pressed the rewind button on her life and she's fourteen again and in her mother's kitten heels in their old living room, the furniture pushed to the sides and her mother, in a flaring summer dress, demonstrating the movements, Bo smiling from the couch. She's surprised that the memory doesn't seem to hurt.

O'Malley's is dead quiet, so Mindy sends her home early.

It's a nice night, at least, the suburb alive around her as Olive cycles down the winding streets towards home. She thinks about maybe going to Lux's, but they haven't spoken or seen each other since Lux ditched her at the party, so she thinks instead she'll go find Charlie at the lookout, smoke a joint and watch the stars blur into a dazzling kaleidoscope of light.

Or maybe neither.

Maybe she's still pissed off at both of them.

Maybe she'll go home and stay there for a change, sprawl in her empty bed, paint her nails, read a book, try to steal another glimpse of the painting her mother's making of Bo Rabbit.

Dropping her bike against the back gate, Olive bounds over the fence and into their wild yard, heading up the steps only to slow when she hears a dry, dark voice warbling out of her mother's speakers. It's unusual – her mum never listens to music, really, much less when she's home alone, and Olive looks up through the window into the living room, to feel her chest suddenly prised open.

Her mother is dancing.

Her mother is dancing with the young man who stopped by all those days ago.

They are dancing and she is leaning into him and it's too close for it to be anything but what it obviously is, and Olive feels the knowledge lick through her like fire along a wick, and she thinks Bo is not her mother's only secret.

She shifts back, that open, hollow feeling growing, and then leans forwards again, close enough that she can hear their voices through the thin walls of the house, just audible over the music.

'How have you never waltzed before?' Delia asks. 'Back when I—'

'Don't say *when I was your age*,' the guy moans, his face half buried in Delia's neck. 'You're not *that* much older than me.'

'I have children your age.'

'Not quite.'

Griff tries to spin her, and Delia stops him, uncertain or drunk. Finding her footing again, she steps forwards, chin raised, her pale neck long and lithe. She meets him. This boy. This man. She entwines her fingers with his.

Olive does not know how to waltz. She's seen it in the films and period dramas that Delia watches late at night while she grades work, and Olive sometimes watches them too from the kitchen island behind her, feigning disinterest, unwilling to sit beside her mother on the couch. This is not quite like the ones in those, but the steps are familiar, and her mother performs them well. One, two. Three.

One, two.

Three.

Griff is much taller than her mother, and he squares his step, his hands gentle on hers, his body pressing closer. One, two.

Three.

Delia tightens her grip, pushes her chest outwards, so it's nearly flush against Griff's own, and it's just like watching from the kitchen island. One, two.

Three.

They kiss.

Of course they kiss.

○

Peeling out of the backyard, Olive runs. She runs and runs, down past the parks, past the cane toads, kicking up dust and crickets and mites. She runs until she doesn't know where she is, and then she circles back and goes to the only place she can.

The heat is trapped in the loading bay behind O'Malley's, exacerbated by the hot air blasting out the back of the air conditioner. She pulls out her cigarettes from her pocket, her fingers trembling as they nudge the sharp edge of the photograph. She could look at it again, but she's done this too many times before. She thinks she knows Bo's face by heart.

Olive lights a cigarette and takes an uneasy drag, letting her eyes flutter shut. Squatting like this in the alley behind the store, she must look a fright. She half expects someone to show up, to confront her, but she's surprised all the same when a voice sounds above her.

'You okay?'

Olive blinks up to find Jude standing, mechanically chewing a stick of gum.

She nods, feeling her cheeks heat, her stomach suck in, her pulse heighten, the memory of his kiss, his distractedness from the night before burning bright. She clears her throat and is moving to stand up when Jude offers her a hand. She takes it.

'You working tonight?' he asks, and Olive shrugs, flicking ash off the end of her cigarette.

'Was. Mindy let me out early for good behaviour. You?'

Jude clicks his tongue. In the hazy light he looks sallow-skinned and tired, and probably still much better than her. His long nose and sharp chin cast low shadows across one side of his face, and a part of her wonders if she could brush those shadows with the back of her hand and rid him of them.

She clears her throat. Takes another drag.

When she looks back up at him, Jude is watching her, his expression considering and unblinking.

'You want to get out of here?'

'What?'

'It's dead tonight. They can manage without me. Come on. Let's go for a walk.'

The shutters of evening have just started lowering, bringing the black night with them. The moon hangs like a fingernail above them, faint in the dusky grey sky. It calls forth the wild screeches of lorikeets and parrots, carrying the first wisps of night on their wings.

'You're going to get me in trouble one of these days,' she says dryly, and Jude laughs, shaking his head, and then his fingers are nudging hers, and when he holds her hand, she lets him.

O

Jude takes her back to the park.

They get there right as the streetlamps come on, their glow a beacon for the flitting moths and insects, and if Olive looks closely enough she can see the luminous sheen of dragonfly wings. There aren't so many people around at this point in the evening, just a few tired joggers and a man walking a hairy mutt, both of them panting in the heat.

Jude takes off his shirt, letting the last of the day's light warm his tanned skin. It makes Olive flush, sends a heat through her cheeks and chest, and she must look hot to the touch.

'I love the river,' Jude says. They're off the path now, plodding through the kept grass of the park. 'I used to row back in high school.'

He imitates the movement for her as they walk, the muscles of his back and shoulders rolling fluidly.

'Sometimes I wish I'd gone to uni so I could have signed up for a team there too, but it's the only reason I would've gone, you know? So there probably wasn't much point.'

'There have to be local clubs you could join?'

Jude just shrugs, and Olive turns away, her gaze fixing on the long stretch of darkness ahead of them. She can see the curl of the river from here, the sluggish heave of it. The water is low in the drought, and a few ducks and black swans wade languidly in the little that's there, their red beaks stark in the evening light. She wonders if that guy's still dancing with her mum. She wonders if – if they're doing something *else*.

'You at uni?' Jude asks, and Olive glances back at him. Her throat suddenly feels dry. Scratchy. She clears it. Her fingers itch for a cigarette.

'I got in. I didn't stick around though. It wasn't for me.'

Jude hums, not unkindly, and gestures to a small patch of grass before the river. They sit down together, knees knocking, and Olive has to resist the urge to get closer or further away.

She can never really tell. Not with Jude. Maybe not with anyone but Lux.

They sit in silence for a while, watching the push and pull of the river. At some point a couple runs by, giggling, pressing drunkenly into one another as they stumble towards the path. Olive doesn't watch, but she feels Jude watching, and the realisation makes something grow hot in her chest and belly.

Jude drops back to his elbows in the grass.

'There's something sad about you, Olive Rabbit.'

Olive turns the words over in her head, tries to work out if there's something underneath them, but she's not sure if there is. She looks at him. Jude suddenly feels very close.

'Maybe I am sad right now,' she says, because it feels like the truth, and she wants to tell him that she doesn't know what the fuck she's doing, and maybe she's an outsider to her own life, her own family. And god, isn't that a fucking cliché? This sadness in her feels like the river, and sometimes it can be dried up for months and other times it can be so full. Can run so deep and so hard it's impossible to see beyond it, and it's just her and her bones trying to hold it in, but they're eroding and she guesses that means she is too.

But how the fuck is she supposed to even say that?

She shrugs half-heartedly instead, looking away.

'You know, shit's happening with my brother and stuff.'

When she looks back at Jude this time his eyes are closed, his fanned lashes covering the puffy bags below. A hot breeze dances between them.

She's not sure if seconds or minutes pass or something longer, but Jude sits up, and then he kisses her.

It's so much better than it was the first time – his lips are soft instead of sticky, and his mouth tastes like gum and a little like sushi from the store next to O'Malley's instead of ash and beer, and his tongue is coaxing instead of pushing, and Olive tries to imagine the future they'd have together. The one where they grow old, fat and grey, where their skin sags and their memories fade. The one where none of it matters, so long as they're by the other's side, but it rings false, even in this moment, so she breaks the kiss, only to have Jude follow her, his hands hot at her hips.

'I haven't done this before,' she whispers, and Jude smiles gently against her mouth.

'That's okay,' he says, leaning back, his eyes generous and warm, drunk on this moment. 'We don't have to do anything.'

But she wants to, and so she kisses him again, and lets him pull her on top of him, and it might not be right, to do this here, now, but with his hands on her everything else seems to disappear. Everything except her and Jude.

19

'Do you have classes tomorrow? Or – shit,' Griff laughs. 'Today, I guess now.'

He's still looking up at her from the living-room floor, his hair a mess and his mouth bruised.

'Not classes. Marking to do though, lesson planning.'

'You could do that in your sleep though, right?'

Delia arches an eyebrow, clocking Griff's loaded expression.

'Doesn't look like it. Certainly haven't gotten much done tonight.'

He clicks his tongue. Through the curtains the moon casts delicate light across the side of his face, illuminating every crease in his skin, every mark her mouth has left on him, every freckle she'd failed to notice. His eyes don't look blue-grey now, but dull, like rainwater caught in a bucket, and she finds she likes that rather more.

'Spend the day with me instead. Not here. Let's go out. I want to go out with you.'

'Griff,' she sighs, pulling her hand away, but it doesn't get far. He reaches out for it, clutches it in his, and entwines their fingers instead.

'Please,' he says. 'Just one day.'

And she should say no. Should stick to the rules that she made for herself when she started this whole thing with him, but too many of them are broken already. He knows about her children, he's here in her home, he knows too much about *her*, and the realisation hits her like a coward's punch.

She needs to end things.

But then she thinks of all the people disappearing in her life, and doesn't think she's quite ready for him to yet.

'Okay,' she says. 'In the morning. I'll meet you at your place.'

O

He forgets the sound – that quiet, hidden sobbing – distracted by Poppy's costume and the adventures of Spectacular Man and The Girl Who Wasn't There and Isles's enthusiastic nemesis. He forgets it over the fish and chips Poppy's dad gets them for dinner, and over the early-evening screening of *The Iron Giant* (Poppy really, really can't believe he's never seen it), and he even forgets it when Poppy's dad makes them turn the lights off and go to sleep.

He doesn't remember it until the next morning, waiting in line with all of Poppy's sisters to use the shower, when he sees Isles slip through the door he hadn't been able to open, and, after minutes, come out with a small, sad look on her face.

Glancing at Poppy, he sees her eyes fixed on her sister, carefully watching the way Isles swipes at glassy eyes and paints on a big, unreal grin as she pulls one of her younger sisters back into a loose hug, and Benjamin's fingers itch for the comforting plastic form of Spectacular Man, or for Charlie, who at least would know what to say.

'Have you talked to your grandma yet?' Poppy asks, and Benjamin turns around, surprised, to meet her gaze.

'What?'

'You're doing your family project on your grandma still, right? Or did you change your mind?'

Benjamin shakes his head.

'I didn't change my mind. She was sick when we went and saw her. Mum said we'll go again soon.'

Poppy nods, a thoughtful expression on her face. Behind the closed bathroom door the shower switches off, and the curtain rings make a loud, metallic sound as they're pushed aside.

'The project's due soon,' she adds. 'What are you going to do if you can't see her in time?'

The thought hasn't really crossed his mind. He frowns.

'I'll see her in time,' he assures her, and Poppy opens her mouth to reply, but then the bathroom door is pushed open and one of Poppy's other sisters tumbles out smelling of orange bodywash, and then it's Poppy's turn to shower.

He thinks about her words when the shower starts up again, and when she comes back out and it's his turn. He thinks about them on the way to school, crushed into Poppy's dad's minivan, and then again when they're sitting in class, Miss Kent talking about fractions and carrying over numbers by the whiteboard.

It's not until lunchtime, though, that he asks her about it.

Not about her words, exactly, but about the door.

'Why didn't you want me to go in there?' he asks, and Poppy blinks at him, eyes wide and head tilted.

'Why didn't I want you to go where?'

'Behind that door, at your house last night.'

'Why don't you want me to go play at your house?'

Benjamin's chest tightens, and he looks briefly away. The thing is he *does* want Poppy to come over to his house, but he doesn't know what that might mean for them. Doesn't know what Olive will be like (definitely not fun like Isles was), or his mum, or if Poppy'll want to meet Charlie, or if Charlie will refuse to see her and then Poppy will think he's been lying. He twists his hands in the hem of his shirt, glancing back towards the school.

'There was nothing there,' she says with a sigh. 'I don't know why you're so obsessed with it all of a sudden.'

'I'm not obsessed,' he says, but maybe he is. He looks up and is surprised to see Poppy looking straight back at him, not sweetly like she usually does, but almost coldly. Almost like Jodi. Almost like Olive. He shivers, diverting his attention away, and Poppy does too.

'Sorry,' he adds, and Poppy just nods curtly, playing with the velcro strap on her lunch bag, and Benjamin grabs his rubbish – the wrappings from the sandwiches Poppy's dad made them and the foil from the carrot sticks – and walks it over to the bin. He's still thinking about the door when he feels the familiar warm trickle down the inside of his leg.

○

Jude is off deli duty by the time Olive's shift starts, and he lingers instead by the back doors, moving crates of stock onto the floor with other strong-armed boys in crisp O'Malley's shirts. Olive watches. She watches the line of his back and the turn of his neck, and she thinks about his weight pressed against hers last night, and the warmth of his breath and the strength of his hands, and saliva builds behind her teeth.

So she sticks around the deli, and Mindy lets her, the day quiet enough that there's no pressure to stay by the checkouts, and she helps to clean the bain-maries and redistribute plump olives and sundried tomatoes and thin slices of dried meats into the displays, all the while trying to catch Jude's eye across the store floor.

She's so distracted by her task that she doesn't hear one of the older deli staff, Ruth, speak until she says something Olive can't *not* hear.

'I heard about your brother,' she says, and Olive looks at her. They're both tucked behind the deli counter, wearing rubber gloves powdery with disinfectant, their hair pulled back beneath thinning nets. 'It must be very hard.'

Olive hums in agreement, looking back at where Jude is disappearing into the stockroom. She wonders if it would be too obvious if she snuck out the side door and met him by the dumpsters. She could take some of the trash from behind the service desk – there's some plastic there, the sticky stuff that the receipt rolls come wrapped in. Lux eats so much candy that there are always fluorescent wrappers pushed between the till drawers, too. She could get them. It wouldn't look so obvious.

'I lost my son, you know.'

Olive turns around to see Ruth's broad back facing her. Her shoulders are stooped, beneath the weight of the words, Olive thinks, until she realises Ruth is fiddling with a leg of ham, pulling it out of paper and rubbing it with her gloved hand, stripping away the sheeny layer of congealed fat. She lines it up with the slicing machine, letting it sag into the metal tray before flicking the machine on. The sound of the meat being cut drowns out everything else in Olive's head for a minute, and then it stops.

'I didn't know that,' Olive says, and Ruth looks around, her watery grey eyes surprised, as if she hadn't realised she'd spoken aloud. She looks at Olive for a moment, and the distance between them feels both firm and uncertain.

'A car. My husband was driving. That's all. Our son was so small. Greg didn't see him in the driveway.'

Ruth is a large woman, not just big, jutting, but taller than any other staffer in the shop. If Olive looks very closely, she can see a pretty woman somewhere in Ruth, and she itches to tear away the years from her and find the girl there, unmarked by life and still sweet. The one she could maybe relate to.

But then Olive thinks that's a strange thought, for the pretty things in Ruth are the things that have lived to the fullest. The crosshatching on her hands from work, and her sagging jowls, which are somehow, strangely, joyful. As if they have swallowed much of the world's sorrow and still come away from it laughing.

'I'm sorry,' Olive says, her voice hoarse even to her, and Ruth turns back to the ham, now sliced, and settles it onto a clean tray for the deli display.

'There's nothing to be sorry for. You weren't behind the wheel. You weren't then, and you aren't now, with your brother. That's all I wanted to say.'

The words strike a chord in a way Olive isn't expecting, and she feels something in her lurch as she looks back at Ruth.

'Thank you.'

Ruth smiles, but there is nothing in it.

○

The student nurse doesn't clean Benjamin up like his mum would, but she's still kind as she hands him first a wet cloth, and then a pair of shorts from the lost-and-found bin.

'They're clean,' she promises, and Benjamin takes them, stumbling back into the bathroom as he does so. He doesn't think anyone really noticed this time, at least. Thinks he got away with his awkward shuffle to the student office, his legs pressed tightly together and his lunch bag strategically placed, but he'd still had to tell the lady at the desk.

He'd still had to say it.

He bites back a bitter sob as he slips out of his soiled shorts and underwear and into another boy's shorts. He catches a glimpse of himself in the mirror, face mottled and cheeks wet, and he shudders and thinks, now, if I can do this; if I can do what Charlie can do, let it be now, but when he opens his eyes he's still there, wet and stinking of piss in the school bathroom.

There's a knock at the door, and he hears Miss Kent's voice trickle through.

'We couldn't get a hold of your mum,' she says softly. 'But your dad's here. Just talking to the counsellor now. Then he'll take you home.'

For a moment, it's like everything stops. Like the whirr of the air conditioner and the chaos of the kids in the hallway and playground and the busywork of the school administration team have all frozen, and Benjamin's left to stare out into the office where his dad stands, staring right back.

Then – as if fast-forwarded:

Dad signs him out.

Dad walks over, awkward, crouches down, puts a hand on his shoulder.

Dad says:

'Hey, mate, you alright?'

And *no*, Benjamin thinks, he's not alright. He wants to go home, with Mum or with Charlie or even with *Olive*.

He doesn't want to go anywhere with his dad.

Still, he nods, and Dad stands up, taking the plastic bag containing Benjamin's soiled clothes from Miss Kent and leading him out of the office, out of the school, and into the carpark. They pile into his car – nicer, he knows, than his mum's – only for Dad to stop before starting the ignition.

'Your mum's not home,' he says gently. 'I went to hers first to grab you some clothes, but she wasn't there. She must be at the college, I guess.'

Benjamin pauses, watching the nervous bob of his father's Adam's apple, and looks at his own fingers, curled so tightly in the legs of his shorts they're almost white. He loosens them and yearns for Spectacular Man. Maybe he can reach into his bag and grab him.

'I thought you still had a key,' Benjamin replies, and Dad huffs a little laugh.

'I do, I … I'm trying to be better with boundaries. For your mum's sake.'

Benjamin nods and slides further down in the leather seat, ignoring the tacky feel of it under his bare legs, until he can barely see over the dashboard. Until the school is little more than a roof and some tall bristly trees housing puffed-up pigeons and yellow-eyed miners. Beside him, Dad drops his hands from the steering wheel.

'Is it Charlie?' he asks, and Benjamin reels.

'What?'

'You were doing really well. You hadn't …' Dad sighs, rubs his face, and that's all it takes for Benjamin to know that Charlie's not the question at all.

'No,' he says. 'I don't think so. I don't think it's because you left either. I just think it's me. I think it's how I am sometimes.'

It's instant – the way relief spreads across Dad's face, and Benjamin watches it, not sure what to make of it. Not sure how to tell his dad that just because he's not the reason for *this* doesn't mean he's not the reason for other things, or at least part of the reason for them, like why Mum gets so sad or Charlie takes more notes than ever or why Olive's *Olive*. And just – why does *he* get to feel relieved? Why does *he* get to be the one who feels better?

Why didn't Dad try to talk to him or even Olive, that night Charlie disappeared?

Outside, a jogger runs past. A dog barks. A car backfires. Dad scratches his ear.

'You all got your mum's name, you know,' he says suddenly, and Benjamin stares.

'She wanted you to be Rabbits, and I guess I wasn't so attached to Tanner. It didn't seem like a big deal back then, to not have the same last name as my wife and kids.'

Benjamin wonders if Charlie's here right now. He hopes Charlie is here.

'You guys never got married,' Benjamin parrots. 'Mum's not your wife.'

'Have you ever wanted to be a Tanner?' Dad asks, as if he hasn't heard, and Benjamin works his jaw. His father's is unshaven again – the hair on his face as bristly and uneven as television static.

'I'm a Rabbit,' Benjamin says. 'I don't know how to be a Tanner.'

And Dad laughs a little at that, drumming his hands on the base of the steering wheel. He looks very young suddenly, and Benjamin has always known he took after his dad. That he's always looked like him in the set of his skull and the muddy puddles of his eyes, but he feels it now most of all.

'You know, I think about you guys all the time. You and Charlie and Olive. I know it's not easy, this thing with me and your mum, but you know it's not you guys. You know that right?'

And the words are nice, but they don't mean anything, because at the end of the day Dad can think about them all he likes, but what does thinking matter when you don't see someone at all?

'Can you take me somewhere?'

337

So they go to a gallery.

Delia and Griff.

She leads him down the airy exhibits and stands him before the paintings, the photographs, the sculptures she likes best. The ones she hates, to see if he can guess why, and he doesn't ever guess right, because he doesn't really know her, and still. Delia doesn't really mind. She likes watching him look at her, likes watching him play at love with an image in his head, hold it to her and pretend she fits it, and it's not right, but it feels good to be seen, even in the abstract.

Afterwards they get burgers from the gallery café, and she kisses the sauce from the corners of his lips, and she lets him lead her back to his shitbox car with a hand on her lower back, and she lets him kiss down her neck at the red lights, and his hand disappear up her skirt at give-way signs, and maybe it's romantic, but Delia doesn't think she's ever truly wanted romance.

Not like she wants release.

○

'You look funny,' Benjamin says, walking down the hallway of Saint Anne's. Beside him, Dad shrugs.

'I just can't say this is where I thought I'd be going when I woke up this morning.'

To be fair, it's not where Benjamin thought he'd be going either – visiting his mother's mother with his father, in a stranger's clothes. Still, it's not exactly the weirdest turn his short life has taken in the last few weeks. He shucks his bag further up his shoulder and stops outside the nurses' station.

'Hi,' he says, and a nurse turns around, casting her gaze down at him. 'We're here to see Rosemary Rabbit. I'm her grandson.'

The nurse nods, gesturing his dad forwards to fill out the sign-in book before directing them up the hall. Benjamin can hear his dad's breaths growing shaky, sense his body tensing, but Benjamin himself feels oddly loose, glad, somehow, to finally be here, doing this. To be creating a memory of his grandmother that's not built from other people's. He grins the whole way to her door, and all the way through it too.

It's weird to be here again so soon after coming with Mum, and it feels different. The place is blisteringly pale, all white walls and white light, sheets, furniture, floors. The only pops of colour are in the flowers, half dead on the windowsill.

She's frail-looking, but she doesn't seem as breakable as Benjamin expected. He reaches a hand out to touch the skin at her ankle, just to see how firm it is.

Rosie's eyes snap open, roll around in their sockets until they find him. She looks confused, but then she doesn't, her gaze focusing on him and softening.

'Hey, Grandma,' he says, and Rosie's face splits into an almost-grin beneath her nasal tube.

'Hello, my sweet boy,' she says, and Benjamin smiles, crawling up the bed to kiss her sallow cheek.

'I'm doing a project on you, did Mum tell you?'

Rosie shakes her head, pushing her body back a little in

the bed to prop herself up. It's only then that she looks over Benjamin's head and locks her eyes on Ed. It's like time stops, like it's pulsing between them, and Rosie starts to cry.

'Oh, Ed,' she says. 'It's been a while.'

Benjamin looks back at his father, and he's surprised to see him crying too.

'It has, Rosie. You look good.'

She doesn't, of course, but Dad presses close, kisses her forehead, and Benjamin suddenly thinks that his parents have been together a really long time, since they weren't so much older than him when they met, and he wonders what that would be like. How it would feel maybe if he knew Poppy's dad that long, and then saw him like this, but the thought is beyond him.

They talk only a little about Benjamin's project, because Rosie gets distracted easily, and sometimes asking her questions confuses her in a way Benjamin can't understand, and so instead he talks about himself. About school and superheroes, and he lets Rosie's eyes glaze over until it seems like only a part of her is there. She tires quickly, and Dad darts out to get her a drink of water and then she reaches out, her brittle fingers tightening around Benjamin's wrist, and when she leans in her breath is warm on his cheek, and it smells of butter and weak, milky tea.

'Was Ed my husband?' she asks, her voice quaking. 'Was he mine or was he Del's?'

She's still trembling, and Benjamin pulls his wrist out from her hand and then turns her hand over, to hold it in earnest.

'He was Del's husband,' Benjamin whispers. 'He's my dad.'

The words make his grandmother jerk her head back in shock, her watery eyes widening as she looks at him for what feels like the first time, and then her gaze drops sideways, to the space beside him, like she can see something he can't.

'Is it true, Charlie?' she says. 'Are you just like me too? You've got to come back, you know. Don't do to your mother what Bo did to me. You've got to …' She shudders. 'Oh, god, I'm tired.'

Dad's hand drops to Benjamin's shoulder.

'I think we should let your grandma rest, mate,' he says, and they do.

O

Olive's only just getting off her bike at home when her dad's car pulls up on the side of the road and Benjamin slides out of the passenger seat. They both look haggard, lost somehow, and Olive is surprised by the deep, resilient jealousy that uncurls in her belly.

'Dad?' she says, and Ed looks up to wave at her.

'Hey, love. Just dropping your brother home.'

He pulls Benjamin's schoolbag from the boot, along with a plastic bag Olive can only assume is filled with clothes Benjamin's pissed himself in. They trundle through the gate and towards the stairs to the back door.

'Mum's not home,' Olive calls, and Ed turns and blinks at her, shrugging, watching as Benjamin fumbles with his own keys and pushes into the house. The two disappear inside briefly, and Olive moves slowly through the yard, feeling her heart hammering against the cage of her ribs.

It's not long before Ed comes back out, taking the steps two at a time. He looks good, she thinks, but her dad usually looks good. Charming and spirited, albeit with a little more than a five o'clock shadow and his usually clean suit creased from the day.

'You and Benjamin having bonding time now?' she asks when he passes her, and Ed barely stops, car keys already in his hand.

'He just needed me today. There was an accident at school.'

'No shit,' she says dryly.

The afternoon is bright and bold, the evening birds just starting their migration. The day is alive in a way it wasn't earlier, a wild city thrumming inside a man-made one.

'Will your mum be home soon?' he asks, and Olive shrugs.

'Who knows?'

He makes a sort of clicking noise, taps his keys against his thigh, glancing out towards the car, and there's something in his look that ignites a bitter and biting flame in her. His dismissal, it's just – fuck, she doesn't get why he *does* this.

Doesn't get how easily he can unsee her.

'You know she's fucking someone else, right?'

And at least that gets his attention, and Olive feels her throat bob, worse, feels Charlie's hand at her elbow, gripping it, telling her to stop. Olive doesn't stop.

'Yeah, some kid. He's, like, barely older than me.'

The words cut him, she can see it, hurt him in a way she hasn't seen her father hurt in a long time, and she ignores the clamp of guilt in her belly.

'Olive, your mother and me—'

She wants to hear him out, she does, means to, but the next words slip out before she can hold them back.

'Who's Bo?'

It's instant, the way her father's eyes widen, his face turning a funny colour, something ashen and gaunt, and he rubs his jaw, flounders briefly, before saying:

'What?'

'Who's Bo?'

She reaches into the back pocket of her jeans to pull the crumpled photograph out, and she thrusts it in her father's face, makes him take it, look at it, *see* it.

And he's gentle with it. More careful than she's ever seen him with anything, his forehead creasing, his lips tugging down, down, down, and god, she doesn't know what that means, what she's supposed to *do* with that, and she just stands there, useless, until he passes the photograph back to her.

'Bo was your mother's sister. She died a long time ago,' he says. 'Before I even met your mum. Did she show you that?'

Olive stiffens, squaring her jaw at him, and it must be an answer, because Ed sighs, low and hoarse.

'Don't go through her stuff, Olive. It's not fair.'

'She goes through my stuff.'

Ed opens his mouth to reply, but he doesn't get a word out before his name sounds, and they both turn to see Delia standing at the garden gate. In old photos and, as much as Olive would like to deny it, in person now, her mother is beautiful. An unsettling kind of beauty. It should be Olive,

343

of course, who is nearly a foot taller than her mother, with the limber legs of a fawn. It's Olive who has the lush blonde hair and the near-chemical blue eyes and the cherub face. But there's something unseemly in Olive, something unkind, she knows it, has seen it in herself. Like barbed wire caught in sweet, rich silk.

(She thinks her dad sees it too.)

Delia is overweight, with heavy, dark hair and eyes a murky pond green. Delia has soft, sagging sun-kissed skin mottled at her shoulders and back from old acne scars. She shouldn't draw the looks she does.

'I was just bringing Benjamin home,' Ed says, and Olive can see it, can feel it, the way the air seems to shift around her mother and her father. The way it becomes thick and heavy with history, and not for the first time she thinks she doesn't really know all that much about her parents. Not who they were together, or who they are now, apart. They stand there like the centres of each other's orbits, forever and fucking always, and she wants to scream, over and over and over again, *see me, see me, see me.* But they don't, and they won't, not now, and not when Ed leaves, turning back only briefly to cast one last look at Delia.

O

Her phone's ringing. Buzzing in the bowels of her handbag. It goes once, twice, three times, before the caller gives up, the screen dimming in the half-light of her bedroom.

Delia rocks out of the bed, shoving a hand across her

bleary eyes, and pulls her phone from her bag. It lights up –
5.06 am – and she opens her missed-call log when the phone
starts to ring again. After a weighted pause, she answers.

'Hello?'

'Ms Rabbit?'

'Speaking.'

The voice pauses, gathers itself, and when it speaks again,
it's solemn.

'It's Portia Dorothy. From Saint Anne's. I'm calling
regarding your mother.'

Outside, the morning birds are starting to yawn awake,
their chatter mingling with the distant sounds of traffic,
and the sun is just starting to raise its head against the hills,
fanning its golden locks across the sheets of the suburbs. Even
through the window the light is bold, brilliant, and Delia
vaguely remembers the story her mother told her two days
ago about stars here in the world, living inside of people, and
she wonders what it must have been like, to have held one
in the cup of your hands. She thinks of those golden girls
and the women who birth them, who build them inside the
sewing rooms of their wombs. She thinks of her invisible son
and the fairytales she'd always passed off as fantasy as a girl –
songs of sirens and selkies and the earth-eyed nymphs that
her father would read her stories of, and she thinks about the
last time she spoke to her vanishing mother, which would, as
it turns out, be the last time she ever spoke to her at all.

20

'You were the last to see her alive, you know,' Olive says, and yeah, Benjamin thinks. He knows.

He has Spectacular Man clutched between his hands, the glob of glue bulging from his neck like a tumour. Benjamin digs his nails into the fat of it, until they leave crescent-moon scars for him to rub the smooth pad of his thumb across later. He imagines Olive grimacing at the sight, but he's not sure if she really would.

There's the sound of paper tearing, and Benjamin knows Charlie has thrust a note in Olive's face, but it does little to curb the swell in his belly or the hot worm wriggling in his back. He crosses his legs, squirms up the bed, until he can half see the new bits of paper in the air, and Olive's face crinkled as if in a fist. He looks back at Spectacular Man in his lap.

The truth is Benjamin doesn't feel guilty, or sad, and this only makes him feel guiltier and sadder. The truth is that Benjamin thought little of his grandmother before she died, and now that she's gone his thoughts only turn to her when he feels badly for not thinking of her more. Instead, his thoughts stray still to Poppy and the strange sounds in her strange house, and to his father, who asked Benjamin Rabbit if he'd like to not be a Rabbit at all, and to his brother, who stands formless in this room somewhere, scribbling arguments on post-it notes.

He's so lost in thought he doesn't realise that Olive has stopped her terse words and left, and that Charlie's pen has stopped its scratching. Doesn't realise that Charlie has moved until the springs of his mattress whine, and his bed dips dramatically forwards.

You know it's not you, right?

The post-it note is laid on his knee and Benjamin blinks.

'What's not?'

Grandma. Or Olive.

He frowns, leg growing jittery.

'Were you there?' he asks. 'When Dad and I visited her?'

No. Maybe I should have been.

Benjamin considers this. Despite himself, he'd known even then that Charlie couldn't have been there. Had been ready for his grip, or his lean, or the strange, nervous energy that he'd never before been able to detect. It hadn't come, but still. The memory of the way Grandma had looked beside him in her room and talked to Charlie, like he was right there. The way she'd told Charlie to come back …

Benjamin tugs at his ear.

What was it she said when she talked about Bo Rabbit?

O

Her brothers curve away from her.

Like their spines are set that way. Long and lean and

without pretext. She should be used to it, she figures, but she leaves them all the same, and prays one of them might follow, knowing the slimness of the chance.

She means to go to her bedroom, but she ends up outside, in their wild yard. The grass is taller than it's ever been, skirting her knees, gunning for her chest. It lets the insects, the lean-bodied lizards, the squat toads chase her every step, lunge towards her then away again, like not a thing here matters. She ignores it all, flopping onto the trampoline, letting the warmth of the mat soak up through her clothes.

She wishes she had a cigarette.

A drink.

A joint.

A pill.

Anything, really, to loosen her grip on herself. She reaches for her phone and flicks off a text to Lux, something about staying over, about sourcing a party, vague and specific enough that she hopes the other girl picks up on the meaning, and then one to Jude as well. It's only been two days since they fucked in the park, but she's yet to hear from him. Or, at least, he's yet to reply.

Olive drops her phone below her, hears it rattle on the metal base of the trampoline, crumple to the grass below, and lets her eyes flutter shut.

It shouldn't matter, of course. Not Lux or Jude, not the fact that neither of them have spared a thought for her in days. Nothing should consume her more than her grandmother, who she never saw after they moved her into Saint Anne's in the first place. Why should she have seen her? Seeing Rosie had always been a trial. An effort or an affect that had felt wrong on some fundamental level. Delia had obviously hated Rosie, so why had Olive been forced to sit there, opposite the two of them, and talk benignly about schoolwork and boys, a lamb caught between two sets of teeth?

She grimaces, pounds her fists onto the mat a few times and then knocks them against her head.

Oh, fuck this, she thinks.

Fuck it, fuck it, fuck it.

Three boxes. That's all of it. All the earthly possessions of Rosie Rabbit.

'We thought it might be easier,' Portia titters, a jumble of nerves at Delia's side. Delia nods, the movement tense in the long muscles of her neck.

'She didn't bring a lot here in the first place.'

And she didn't. When they'd brought Rosie to Saint Anne's, they'd had to clean out her house. Condense her mother's three-bedroom home and seventy-odd years into whatever could fit in this small room. They'd sold her furniture and thrown away her clothes, passed her cookware, books and linen on to relatives and neighbours, scattered the accumulations of Rosie's life across the state. The few things they'd kept were the things Rosie had insisted on. A few photographs, a ratty bear she'd had since she was a girl, her old stethoscope, the dress Bo was going to wear to her high-school graduation. Delia's mother had packed these things with slow, trembling hands, and now Delia returns the favour, unpacking them with her own set of tremors to see what little of her mother's life Rosie had wanted at the end of it.

After Bo had died, her mother had taken all the photos and put them some place where Delia, only fourteen at the time, hadn't been able to find them. Bo was removed from their lives in a way that Delia and Bo's father hadn't been. Every frame removed, every remnant of her sister packed and kept away, shut into the furthest reaches of their home and their thoughts. Like if Rosie hadn't been able to see Bo, if she couldn't remember the look of her smiling girl, she might have been able to purge the memory of the last time she saw her too.

So it was a surprise to open that box and find a photo of herself and Bo, prepubescent and glowing, their bodies pressed tightly together, intimate in that way only sisters really can be. Bo's dark, night-time hair caught in a pale blue scarf, her big blue eyes wicked in the shadowed light of the photo. Delia racks her head, tries to remember the night it was taken, but the memory is buried, marked up with dirt and earth and time, tainted by a hundred other memories, by a hundred other imaginations.

She clears her throat, slipping the photograph back into the envelope and pushing through the old medical equipment and a wedding ring too big to be her mother's (her father's?) looped around the leg of the stethoscope. She sorts the postcards from friends she doesn't know, and the recipe cards from her own grandmother. She sorts through clippings, and scraps of pretty scarves, and jewellery, until she stops at a small, tattered notebook. The sight of it makes her pause. Of all the things in the box, this is perhaps the only thing she hasn't seen before. She opens it expecting a diary or her mother's nursing notes, but what's inside instead seems to be, at first, gibberish. A list of dates and places. For a moment, she thinks it's like Charlie's notebook – a record of Rosie's invisibility – but she recognises one, and then another, and then another.

She turns the page, heart hammering in her throat, finds clippings from local newspapers and pamphlets. All of her – of Delia. Of her art, her exhibits, every show, listed neatly in her mother's cursive scrawl, and it's only then that the tears start.

'Oh, fuck you,' Delia whispers, turning the page.

'Oh, *fuck* you, fuck you, fuck you.'

21

They bury Grandma Rabbit on a Thursday, in a tiny roadside chapel just outside of Shepherd. Mum had said it was where she'd gone as a girl, back when Grandma still liked church, but it feels foreign to Benjamin to see his mother do the sign of the cross as she steps through the arched door, her black shift dress neatly ironed and her shoes clipping on the stone floor.

The chapel is almost delicate, at least, more delicate than the few other chapels he's been in. It has a high roof and wooden beams that sit like a ribcage around the heavy lungs of the organ. The stained-glass windows cast a severe glow across the procession, illuminating the priest's white robes and lending an air of the fantastic to his droning, ministerial voice. He talks about Benjamin's grandmother like a teacher might about any historical figure – a whole lifetime boiled down to tent-pole moments, timestamps on a YouTube video, a summarised version of her. He wonders if he'd feel better if it had been his mother delivering the eulogy, but she hadn't wanted to. Had told them that, even as Olive had huffed out something that sounded like *of course you don't*, and Charlie had written secret notes and pressed them into their mother's hand.

The thought makes him shift uncomfortably in the pew, pressed tightly between an invisible Charlie and Olive, who is fidgeting in her black dress. He wonders what they must look like to the few people here, the big gap of Charlie making it look for all the world as if their mother is sitting alone. Benjamin trembles, presses his spine into the hard wooden back of the pew, his feet kicking the prayer cushion until Olive hisses at him to stop.

And he does. Locks his body in a tight mental cage. He wishes he had Spectacular Man. Wishes he could hold him quick and smart in his hands, or could lean over and grab Charlie's, but he can't. Not here, not like this. He shivers, thrusting his hands behind him, through the gap in the back of the pew, and he means to just hold the seat, that's all, only clammy fingers are entwining with his, and he turns to see Poppy sitting behind him, holding his hand so tightly he can't feel anything but her.

○

The chapel is hot.

Too hot, really, the heat settling heavy on her drawn shoulders. Her dress sticks to her back, her thighs, her stockings to her sweating shoes. She readjusts herself but can't quite get enough air. Charlie is close to her, Benjamin and Olive on the other side of him, blocking out any chance of cool air.

All the while, the priest drones, his words slow and sluggish, as if melting beneath the heat in this holy place. She needs to stay. To sit tight, keep herself together, for her kids, if not her mother, but then … Her eyelids flutter shut.

Delia slips up from the pew, avoiding the gaze of the minister, of her children, walking quickly, quietly down the aisle and out of the chapel. The gravel crunches beneath her heels as she rounds the back of the building, and she takes a deep breath, her lungs throbbing, the dry, claustrophobic summer heat branding her inside and out. She trembles. Steps forwards then back, her heart hammering against her bones, her blood running, rushing, hot.

'Del?'

She turns around, and it's Ed. Of course it's Ed.

'Hey,' he says, his voice soft, and Delia shakes her head, stares down at the floor, at her polished black court shoes. She curls her toes in them.

'You didn't have to come.'

Ed doesn't reply to that, but she can feel him shuffling towards her. Thinks maybe she feels people's movements better now, since Charlie. Since her mother.

'I have no one,' she says sharply. 'You know that, right? This is the end of my family. My dad, Bo, my mother. I'm it now.'

'The last man standing,' Ed agrees, leaning sideways against the wall. There's a gentle, sing-song tone to his voice, but when she looks at him his expression is riddled with grief. 'You always were, even in a packed room.'

Delia huffs out a dry sound, fumbling in her bag for one of Olive's cigarettes. She lights it with all the extravagance of an addict. A quick, habitual motion that reminds her of the girl she was. She grimaces at the thought, even as she lights up, taps off and takes a deep drag.

'You have family,' Ed adds with a sigh. 'More than you know. You have Olive and Charlie and Ben.'

She snorts, and Ed moves a little closer, gets near enough that the smoke from her cigarette clings to his jaw and his shoulders.

'You have me,' he adds quietly, as if in realisation, and Delia turns back to face him. To look at him, truly. For the first time, she regrets it. Never getting married. To have nothing on paper acknowledging the history between herself and this man – the father of her children, and maybe he was her partner after all – in crime, in life, in sorrow, for so long. For now, still, no matter how hard they try to disentangle.

'Oh, fuck you,' she says, and before she can say another word, he kisses her.

If she were any smarter she'd push him away, but then Ed's hands are on her again, and they just fit, *feel*, so fucking right.

He looks at her through the delicate fringing of his thick blond lashes, and she kisses him on his forehead, his nose, his lips, and in his mouth she hopes to find the man he was and she discovers him too easily, his tongue moving against hers the way it did all those years ago, back before it felt wrong, back when it felt too *right*. Back when they were both young and stupid and reckless and hopeful.

She pulls away, lets her breath drag across his face, and then he's breathing on her neck as he kisses her throat, her collarbone, pressing his lips to the opening of her dress, the no-man's land between her aching breasts.

'It's never like this,' he murmurs. 'Not with anyone else.'

And it should make her pull away, the memory of the girl

he'd brought home and fucked in their bed, but right now it just feels like another chapter in the tome of their past, and she tries to curb the anger that bubbles in her chest when he presses his lips there.

'You believe that?'

'Yes,' he says, moving his hands from her hips to her waist, to the back of her neck. 'It's always you, Delia. I wish it wasn't, but it is.'

A long breath escapes her now, and he hitches her up until her legs wrap around his waist, until he can use the wall to leverage her weight. Her hands clutch at his neck, his shoulders, his broad, strong back, his belt, while he tears into her stockings, ripping the seam, pushing her underwear aside, and they fuck that way, against the wall of the chapel, her mother's funeral droning on inside, their children sitting in wait. Ed's girlfriend sitting alone. And it's sweaty and ugly, she knows, but she lets him shudder into her anyway, his teeth hooked into her shoulder like an anchor in sand, her legs tangled around his waist, her mouth panting wet into the side of his face. He climaxes first, pushing a hand to her clit, and he gets her off quickly, easily, a practised habit, and she trembles against him as she comes.

He doesn't let her down right away, won't, can't, whatever. Just holds her, and it's not until she forces one of her legs to the floor that he lets the rest of her go too.

'We can't do this again,' Delia says quietly, adjusting her underwear, ignoring their uncomfortable dampness.

'We can't?'

He pulls his pants back up, flushed and boyish, his eyes

round, a sated look to his mouth, and Delia groans.

'You cheated on me,' she reminds him. 'You fucked that girl in our bed. You got me to draw her for you.'

The words have Ed shaking his head rapidly, his mouth open, a hoarse, defensive tone in his quick reply.

'No, Del, that was – that was for her. She really did – *does* – love your stuff, and – we weren't together yet. Me and Vanessa. We were just—'

In the chapel behind them a hymn starts, and Delia remembers her father's funeral.

She remembers Bo's.

'We hadn't fucked yet,' Ed clarifies. 'But – yeah. We were – something. More than we should've been. I felt like you'd left me already. I was lonely, and she was – *is* – just – easy. Everything's easier with her.'

'And I'm not?'

Ed laughs, the sound a bark in the small space. The hymn grows louder.

'You are a lot of things, Del Rabbit, but easy is not one of them.'

And what the fuck does she do with that? she wonders, staring back at him, taking in every ageing line of him, the freckles at his cheekbones, his clean-shaven jaw. She probably is a difficult woman, but she comes from a line of them, her mother and Bo, and Olive too. Maybe that's part of what it means to be a Rabbit woman (*The Rambunctious, Riveting Rabbits* – and god, it's still Bo's voice in her head that says it). Maybe that's part of what it means to be a lot of women.

'No,' Delia says. 'That's not fair. It's not *good enough*. You

357

knew. You knew everything about me. You knew about Bo and my mother, you knew what I was when we got together. When we had three fucking children together, *you* picked *me*.'

'I know that, but—'

'And *easy*?' Delia bites, something red-hot licking up her veins. 'Did I not make your life easy? I raised our children, I let you do whatever the fuck you wanted, and I asked for *nothing* from you except your company and your fidelity.'

'I never said you didn't make my life easy,' he snaps back, redness creeping up below the collar of his shirt, rounding the shells of his ears. 'I know you did, I know you still do, fuck. I was just *tired*, Delia. You *exhaust* me.'

'Yeah? Funny, because I don't think you were exactly *resting* with Vanessa.'

'And I don't think you're just teaching one of your students.'

Delia reels back at that, eyes darting across his face, and how does he even *know* that – but, fuck, does it matter? She throws her hands up instead, then drops them heavily to her sides.

'Sure,' she says. 'At least I waited until we were broken up.'

Ed lets loose a bitter laugh. 'Yeah,' he says, honestly, dryly. 'You win.'

There's something about the way he says it – exasperated and the right side of honest – that startles a laugh out of Delia too. That makes her groan, shift her sweaty, sticky legs, that doesn't snuff her anger but at least diffuses it, like kindling kicked across a campsite, and Delia thinks – she thinks—

She should go back into the chapel.

Although she also wonders if there's any point – if she'd

be able to sit with her children, play doting daughter and martyred mother. If she could do any of that. She fumbles instead in her purse, pulls out another cigarette and lights it.

'I don't even know why I've stayed with Vanessa. Why we're living together,' Ed adds. 'Half the time I don't want her around. She's too young.'

Delia arches an eyebrow and takes a drag.

'Thought she was easy.'

'Yeah. But who wants that?'

And Delia laughs again, this time in disbelief, but before she can tell him to fuck off, he adds:

'Her body has no story to it. I like your body. I miss your body. I like how it's changed. I like that I've known it, and *how* I've known it, and how its story is yours but I've gotten to … annotate parts.'

Delia gives him an unimpressed look.

'Oh, please,' she says, and Ed chuckles, embarrassed, burying his face in his hands. When he looks back up at her his face softens.

'I like *you*,' he says. 'I love you, but that's complicated, and I don't know how to talk about that, but I could talk about how much I like you forever. How I liked you when we were seventeen, and how I liked you at forty, and how I liked you when we were fucking us up, and how I like you now, and I don't know what that means for us, but I know it's there, and I don't think it's going to change.'

'You wish you didn't, though,' she says coyly, eyebrow arched, and Ed just shakes his head.

'No, of all the things I wish had and hadn't happened

between us, liking you is not something I regret.'

Like, is that what's kept them circling back to one another? She looks at him, takes in his earnest face, and in the moment, she knows that Ed might always be honest, but sometimes honesty isn't enough. And if honesty isn't, can *like* ever be? She sighs, offers him her cigarette by way of reply and tries not to let her heart lurch when he kisses her again instead.

The car ride home is dull, as if they hadn't seen their mother leave halfway through their grandmother's service, their father on her heels. As if their parents hadn't come back in stinking of sweat and sex and the cigarettes Delia's always on her back about. It leaves her surly, even after Ed goes and she is slumped in the passenger seat of the car, listening to talkshow hosts jabbering on the radio and Benjamin and Charlie scribbling notes in the back seat.

'I was thinking takeaway for dinner,' Delia says, clearing her throat, and Olive shrugs, pushing further down into the seat. She sends another text to Lux but is hardly expecting a reply. The other girl's been AWOL for days, and their shifts haven't overlapped enough for Olive to be able to ask her if she somehow fucked up.

'Maybe Thai? Or there's that new Lebanese place off Ophelia Street we could try?'

'Thai,' Benjamin calls from the back seat, and then, 'Charlie agrees.'

There's a flurry of pencil then, a sure sign that Charlie does not, in fact, agree, and Olive rolls her eyes.

'I'm going out,' she says, and watches as Delia's hands tighten on the steering wheel.

'*Olive* – where?'

'Just to a friend's place. She invited me before Grandma died, and I forgot, and it'd be rude to bail now.'

The lie feels black on her tongue, but she swallows it all the same. She wonders, offhand, if Lux and Dom could take her to the house again, if she could find solace in a bat, or in Jude, who might fuck her in the park again, in front of an audience of insects.

She looks over at her mother then, sees the familiar, unfamiliar shape of her, the twist to her grimace that means she's thinking things she won't say, that she's trying to hold herself together, keep herself that way, and she wonders if there's any part of her mother in herself, and she's not sure what she wants the answer to be. Olive turns back to the window, watches the road pass her by, the suburban houses, hospices, shrubbery blending into one thick brushstroke.

○

She pedals her bike around the city for an hour, maybe two, until the sun is low in the sky and her vacant message bank means no one's going to call her. That Lux and Jude will continue their absence in force. So she goes to the park instead, hearing the distant thrum of mid-week parties and foregoing them for the company of insects and the conversation of evening birds. She drops her bike by the footpath and disappears into the fields, the air thick around her, dense with relentless humidity.

So it's a complete surprise when Mindy stumbles across her.

'Rabbit?'

'Jesus Christ.'

Mindy lets loose a self-deprecating grin. 'No need to be so formal.'

She flops down beside Olive in the grass.

'What are you doing here alone? Didn't you have a funeral or something?'

Olive nods, gesturing to her ugly, starched black dress, and Mindy's mouth opens into a neat little O. She reaches into her tote bag and pulls out a bottle of wine and a picnic cup, pouring generously.

'What are you doing here anyway?'

'Friend's picnic,' Mindy shrugs, gesturing behind them, and Olive turns to see a large group of people sprawled across the grass, talking loudly, laughing louder. One girl drapes herself over the back of a friend, while a guy lies back on a picnic rug, head in the lap of another.

'Why are you hanging with me then?'

'Looks like you might need the company more than they do.'

Olive looks down to pull out a few blades of grass, but despite herself, she's grateful.

'You sure you're okay?'

Olive leaves it a moment, thinks of saying *sure*, saying *remember the funeral?* Saying *is Lux mad at me? Or Jude?* But what comes out is—

'I don't understand her. My mum. She doesn't understand

me either. *I* don't understand me, maybe. Which one of us gets to be the normal one then? The reasonable one? Because I think I am, and I know she thinks she is, so one of us has to be wrong. One of us has to be fucking this up. Fucking *us* up.'

Mindy sighs, a long hissing sound weighed down by cheap cleanskin wine.

'Is it the magic thing?' Olive asks, turning quickly, suddenly, to Mindy. 'Is it my brother? Is that what's done this to us? Do you have this? With your family? With the un-ness of the normals and all the *ness* of whatever it is you are?'

Mindy frowns, puffs out her cheeks, glances back at her friends before finally sighing again. For a second Olive thinks Mindy might reach out and hold her hand, but she never does.

'I have a theory,' Mindy says instead, interlacing her fingers in her lap. 'I have a theory that a person spends half their life thinking they're the normal one, but the reality is that normal doesn't exist. People are complicated, and they make the wrong choice all the fucking time. They've had chicken-shit parents or punchy boyfriends or long, long lives, no matter how many years they've lived, and those things make them cowards or they make them strong and they make them care about other people too much or not enough or not at all, and they give them this weird, warped sense of self-preservation, and it can't be navigated by you or me, because we might see where a person is right now on a map, but we haven't seen the route they've taken to get there. All you can control is *you*, and what's yours, and the choices that you make, not anyone else's.'

In the distance one of Mindy's friends yells, something shrill that sets off a flock of screeching lorikeets.

'Or maybe I'm full of shit,' Mindy says with a laugh, folding herself back against the dry grass. The crickets hum around them, the cicadas too, and Olive can't see them, but she can picture them. Imagine glossy backs and strong legs and whizzing feelers. She looks at Mindy, takes her in, and she exhales.

'I don't think you're full of shit,' she says, and she's surprised to find she means it. The words have Mindy peeling an eye back open, a coy grin tugging at her mouth.

'Careful, Rabbit, anyone might think you actually like me.'

Olive scoffs, bringing her knees up to her chest.

'Don't get ahead of yourself, Chan.'

Mindy laughs at that, a loud sound that makes a dim streetlight at the edge of the park flicker bright.

'So not a magic thing?' Olive murmurs, watching it, and Mindy shakes her head.

'I don't think so,' she says. 'But magic can do this.'

And she catches the light from the streetlamp and pulls it out, this humming ball of electricity, makes it flutter towards them in a wobbly little arc, and finally suspends it, burning, between them, and Olive cups her hands around it, letting it warm her pallid, tired skin.

22

She's sweating through her blouse by the third student meeting, leaving her swampy to the touch. Pinching the neckline, she billows it at her chest to try to push some cool air down it, but it's no use. The ceiling fan above her is near-useless, and at least the students don't look much better, with their damp faces and their dull, glazed eyes.

One by one, she talks through themes and throughlines, techniques and rationales, and it's after a particularly gruelling conversation with a red-eyed, baby-faced girl that Delia finally has a chance to drop back in her seat, to try to clear her foggy head. She has to fight the urge to pull off her shirt, her pants, and sit naked on the floor of her office, and she's so distracted, so desperate for relief, that she doesn't even hear the door open again.

'I swear it's getting worse,' a voice says, and Delia glances up to see Griff, his folio under his arm, looking for all the world as if the heat hasn't touched him. Delia shakes her head.

'We should be glad for it. A storm's coming. Can't you feel it?'

Griff laughs, sliding into the seat opposite her.

'Can you?'

Delia nods. 'Always could. In my skin and in my bones. It whispers at your neck, lets you know it's coming. This one has been taking long strides towards us for months. I think it's getting close.'

'There's not one forecast.'

She hums a little, watching him lazily. These tropical storms feel beyond weather apps and meteorology. They brew in the witch's cauldron of the north and rumble like a deity, prowl across the river until they explode above the city. Vitriolic and howling. It feels like so long since they've had one.

Delia holds out a hand, waiting for Griff to pass over his folio, which he does with a nervous, buzzing energy.

'I'm sure it'll be fine,' she says, her reassurance for every anxious student, every baby artist, but she flips it open to the first page and knows immediately that it won't be.

She wonders if this is what it feels like for Ed, or for Charlie, for anyone whose image she's picked up and run with. If the desperate need to catch their forms on the page at various points in her life has invited the same discomfort and dread, but then the situations don't entirely feel the same. There are pages after pages of her, months' worth of drawing, images of her from last week and last semester too, in charcoal, in acrylics, in watercolours, nude and well-fucked, or still done up from work, with paint on her chest and her fingers, her expression mostly guarded but sometimes too open, and she feels it then, what she's always known. All the ways this has been a huge fucking mistake.

She can feel him looking at her, feel him taking her in, his anxiousness like a new skin. She tries to think of what to say but the words won't come. Won't rise from the cold floor of her mouth, and instead she remembers the last time he was in here, before Charlie, before her mother, when he was her biggest mess. She remembers his neon socks and his body over hers, inside hers. She remembers him in her living room. She shakes her head.

'This can't be your folio, you know that, right? You can't keep drawing me like this. I'll lose my job.'

Griff at least has the ability to look bashful.

'I figured. I'm working on something else too. I'm just. This is what I *would* submit. If I could.'

Delia looks up at him, and she doesn't know what expression she's wearing, but it must say whatever it is she can't. Griff's face splits in two.

'We had a nice day, the other day,' he says, and Delia nods.

'We did.'

'We could—'

'We couldn't.'

His hopeful expression is dashed, almost as quickly as it arrived. She wonders, briefly, if this is the wrong choice. If there's a future in the nook of Griff's neck for her, in the lean strength of his back.

'This is it then,' he says, and she nods, handing him back the folio.

'I think you should change classes. Professor Kasinger teaches the same one on Wednesdays. I'll talk to him for you.'

Griff nods, taking his folio back with gentle hands, and when he goes, he closes the door behind him.

○

'Olive, you're on checkouts,' Frank says, gliding a hand down the roster sheet, the store lights casting an alien glow on the orb of his head.

Olive mock-salutes, but Frank doesn't even look up. It shouldn't matter, she thinks, and it doesn't, but she slinks off to the registers anyway, pulling off the *this till is closed* sign and logging in. It's quiet enough today that she almost wishes she could be on the floor instead, lurking around the freezers for the gasping cold air. Not that she should really complain. At least O'Malley's is air-conditioned.

She fumbles her phone out of her pocket, sending off a quick message to Lux again, before looking out over the floor at where Mindy is directing the stock boys, and then across at Ruth and Charlotte behind the deli counter, stern faced and sallow cheeked, their lined bodies hovering over vats of plump olives and pink ham.

She's so distracted she almost doesn't see the doors open to a portly older woman and her teenage daughter, who duck through the aisles and beeline for Frank. This'll be good, she thinks, expecting a complaint. Expecting the fierceness of someone who's gotten the wrong goods, but the woman doesn't get mad, doesn't yell or fuss. Rather she leans in and kisses him, Frank's thin body opening up to her, holding her, and the girl – his daughter, Olive realises – is grinning, laughing with him, slapping his wrist and pulling faces at her parents' love, and suddenly Olive has to turn away, rotate her body until Frank is gone from her view.

She knew that he had a family, his cheap-looking wedding band dull on his finger, just as she knew Ruth had a life, even if she hadn't always known about her dead son, but there's something in this that twists at her insides. That rears to be heard.

Because she didn't know her mum even had a sister.

Because she didn't realise her parents' relationship was so fucked her dad was going to leave.

She didn't even realise that her mum had a boyfriend.

All these people all around her are like books written in foreign tongues, and she doesn't know how to read any of them, can't, maybe, and she doesn't understand people, she doesn't even understand herself, and grow up, Olive thinks, digging her fists into her thighs. Grow up, grow up, grow up.

○

The branch snaps, and Benjamin fumbles, gripping the one below it with urgency.

Above him Poppy laughs, wrapping her arms around the trunk and looking down at him.

'Careful, Ben,' she sing-songs, turning to sit herself on one of the fatter branches. She swings her legs out, making neat lines in the afternoon sun. She's still in her school dress, like Benjamin is in his shorts, and the cotton will be marked up with sap and bark by the evening. He grins, flexing his bare feet around one of the lower branches and pushing up to hold on to Poppy's branch.

He settles himself beside her, glancing out over the

horizon. They're higher than they've ever been, or at least higher than *he's* ever been. Poppy had known exactly where to stand, which branch to hold, which path to take, but then Poppy seems to know most things.

'We can't all be part monkey,' he replies, and Poppy laughs, before making *oo-oo-ah-ah* sounds and scratching at her sides. The light catches her hair, turning it copper and illuminating her freckles, her skin tanned from the summer. He looks down at his own tanned arms to see the effect of the light there too.

'Funerals are weird,' she says suddenly, and Benjamin puffs out a breath in agreement, looking up in time to see Poppy nod, a considering look crossing her face. Mum had let him invite Poppy to Grandma's funeral the other day, and he'd been glad for it, to see her familiar face, hold her familiar hand. Now, though, Benjamin waits for her to continue, but she doesn't, so instead he looks out at the view. Over the small, shackled roofs of the suburb and the long stretches of road, like the tracks of a maze in the land beyond.

'Oh, no!'

Benjamin blinks sideways at Poppy, whose pursed lips have turned into a pout.

'What?'

'I left my mask in my room.'

'I didn't think we were playing hero?'

Poppy shrugs, pressing her side into the tree trunk, and Benjamin rolls his eyes.

'I can go get it.'

'You don't have to! It's okay.'

Benjamin pushes a hand up, looking dramatically away.

'It is okay, ma'am. Spectacular Man is here to help.'

At that, Poppy laughs, and Benjamin grins, dropping his legs to the branch below and climbing down the tree to the garden floor. He darts up through the house, dashing around Poppy's little sisters and heading straight for her bedroom. The mask is where it always is – hanging off the back of her bedroom door, and he grabs it, looping it over his arm and heading back out into the hallway.

And he means to go straight back outside. He *does*, but the door down the hall, the one next to the bathroom, is half open, and Benjamin's curiosity itches like an insect in his chest. He looks up the hallway then back down, searching for any sign of Poppy or her sisters, but there are none, so he creeps forwards, glancing through the open door.

He's not entirely sure what he expects – the more imaginative part of his brain hopes, perhaps, for a monster or a hidden Dockens sister, fanged or glowing or both, but the room is like many others – a neat little thing with floral wallpaper and the heady smell of incense covering the noxious scent of disinfectant. At the centre of the room is a bed, and in it a woman. When she sees him she sits up a little straighter, adjusts the cannula in her nose, her skin as white as the sheets she lies on. She tilts her bald head sideways, her big green eyes taking him in.

'Hi,' she says. 'You're a new face.'

Benjamin pauses, shuffles, tightens his grip on Poppy's mask, still looped over his shoulder. He should say something, should reply, but it's like the curious insect in his chest has climbed into his throat and lodged itself there, catching words before Benjamin can get them out.

'Let me guess,' the woman says. 'Benjamin Rabbit? Did I get it right?'

He rocks back in the doorway, and the woman grins, some big, sweet thing.

'Thought so. I've seen you and her playing.'

She reaches a pale hand up, gesturing above her bed to where a window overlooks the backyard.

'Don't worry, she hasn't told me too much about you. Most of it I've gotten from her sisters. They're all pretty taken with you. My name is Andi. I'm Poppy's mum.'

Andi clears her throat, her voice hoarse.

'Do you guys play together at school? Is she settling in okay?'

Benjamin nods, glancing out at the long hallway behind him, and when he sees that it's empty he takes a small step into the room.

'I'm so glad. I was worried, with the move. We had to – that's not for you to worry about. What games do you play?'

Benjamin shrugs. 'Lots of things. We play superheroes sometimes, but mostly we just talk.'

Andi's eyes are hungry, desperate.

'Yeah, what do you talk about?' Then, quickly, her lips part, she wets them, a quiver at her throat. 'You don't have to tell me. I'm glad she's got someone to talk to. You guys look like you have fun together.'

'We do,' Benjamin says, and he does, even when they're not playing. He never thought just talking was fun before Poppy.

'Is she okay?' Andi asks. 'I just – we've had a tough little while. And she doesn't really come in here too much with—' Andi gestures vaguely to herself, then to the room. 'It's just been a bit of a challenging time.'

Benjamin nods, unsure of what to do. He shuffles on the spot, hand curling in his shirt.

'I'm glad she has you,' Andi says. 'I'm glad she's making friends.'

And Benjamin blushes, he doesn't know why, his eyes skirting the hall, and his heart stammers when he sees Poppy there this time, wide eyed and pale faced, and when he tries to talk to her, to explain, Poppy runs.

She's barely out of the car when November pops up over the garden fence, brandishing a bottle of wine.

'How's it been going? How was the funeral?' she asks, and Delia groans, stepping around the fence and following November into her house.

'That good, huh?'

And she doesn't really mean to say anything, but she ends up telling November most of it. She tells her about her slipping mother, and about Olive, and about the box in her mother's room, and fucking Ed halfway through her mother's funeral, and November listens, and Delia knows she'll regret it, but she can't quite stop herself.

'So maybe I'm just a shitty teacher and a shitty daughter and a worse mother,' she finishes with a shrug, watching November frown. It's not a pretty thing to say, she supposes, but then again true things rarely are, and the true thing is that Delia has never felt much attachment to motherhood or to her mother. Not a natural parent or a natural daughter, not doting or loving or kind. At least she knows it. Sees it in herself.

She remembers too well nights when she'd stayed up with Olive and Charlie and Benjamin, nestling them into her chest and praying them to sleep or death, whichever would provide her with relief first. She had cared for them. Raised them, wiped their tears, kissed their scrapes, which is more than Ed can claim, too bogged down with work, and too awkward in the costume of fatherhood, maybe finding it as unwieldy as she did motherhood. She loved them, but god, she loved space from them too. She could work and not miss them, even when they were babies, and she had told a friend this one drunken night at thirty and she'd looked at her in shock.

November does not look at her in shock.

'Or maybe I'm just not a natural mother,' she supplies, finishing her drink.

To her surprise, November laughs.

'No one is. I feel like that's the great deception we're born into. We learn it, like anything else. Like men do, but then men aren't held to the same standard. You know a father can do nothing but show up for one soccer game, and he's somehow number-one dad, but there's no such thing as a good mother. She always works too much or not enough or she's shrill and demanding and she's trying to put good values in kids who don't want them and she's still a fucking bitch, right?'

Delia stares at her, her throat raw, and she means to say something else, but what comes out is:

'Olive hates me.'

'Do you believe that?'

'No. Sometimes. I don't know. She was always hard work in a way the boys weren't. Even as a kid. She was so angry, and it was like she was hurt in ways I couldn't work out. I was afraid of her, I guess. Am.'

Delia drops her head to her hands. She thinks of clutching Olive, that first time, of the strangeness between the two of them in that moment, thinks of holding her, crying, when she was a girl, of the way Olive pounded her fists against Delia's chest and forced her away. She shakes her head.

'What are you afraid of?' November asks, and this, at least, Delia knows.

'I'm terrified that when she doesn't have to see me anymore, she won't.'

November's face shifts at that, into something honest and sympathetic, the look almost tangible, so much so that Delia feels she could reach out and smudge the expression beneath the rugged tips of her thumbs.

'I don't think people are like that,' November says. 'Daughters need their mothers.'

Delia hums around her mouthful of wine. She swallows and she thinks of her mother, her daughter, her sister.

'I wasn't even that much older than Olive is now when I got pregnant with her. And I loved her, man I did, and I did it all – I went to the mothers' groups, and I took her to swimming lessons and fed her and read to her. I *talked* to her. All the time. I wanted to be different to my mum, but I couldn't do it. Not well enough. I don't think I knew how.

And now she's … something's happening with her, more than just her brother and her dead grandma, but I don't have any fucking clue where to start, and she doesn't let me try. I feel like I have one shot at it, and that is … impossible for me. And you know, I'm not exactly a good example anyway. I'm a shit teacher, you know? I've been fucking Griff, and he gave me this – *collection* of me, and so that's … I don't know. I just … I'm a cliché? A failed artist, a failed almost-wife, a failed girlfriend, a failed mother, hell, a failed daughter, and there's nothing I can do about that now. People give me their love and I don't know what the fuck to do with it.'

Delia snorts, pushes back into her chair and takes a long, slow drink.

'Bullshit.'

She glances up at November, raising her eyebrows.

'Excuse me?'

'Bullshit,' November repeats, sitting up a little taller. 'You're right, you're not perfect, but you're not a failure, Delia, because failing is a temporary state, not a permanent one. If it was, I'd be fucked.'

'Please,' Delia says with a scoff, and November waves her off.

'I'm serious,' she replies. 'Do you know why I left real estate?'

'Because you had kids.'

'Because I didn't like it anymore,' and oh, Delia thinks. November had said that way back when they first met. 'I was miserable, and I felt like I was just going through the motions and doing enough to get by, but I wasn't happy, and I wasn't living any part of my life well because of it, and I felt like I'd completely fucked up my career by choosing one that didn't work for me, and I had the girls, and I was still working. I didn't quit until last year, and I know that I'm lucky that José works a job that can let me stay at home for a bit, but I still felt like a failure, but I'm not, and neither are you. It's something *my* mum said to me once. You haven't failed. You just haven't finished yet.'

○

Poppy is standing halfway down the street, so still it's as if she's been sketched there, a panel in a comic book, and Benjamin slows his steps behind her. The afternoon air feels leaden. Heavier than he's been used to lately, and clammy. His mum always says that you can feel the rain in Brisbane before the clouds even think to gather. That you can smell it in the air, taste it on the wide, flat surface of your tongue, and he thinks maybe he can taste it now.

He stops at Poppy's side, and he means to ask her something nice, about the game maybe, or school. Something to distract her, but he is tired of secrets, and when he opens his mouth, he says:

'Your mum's not at work.'

It comes out accusatory, and he tries to bite it back, but the words are out there now, spilled between them.

'She's not my mum.'

'Oh,' he replies, uncertain. He brushes a hand through his hair, tugs at it a little. 'Sorry, I just …'

Poppy shakes her head.

'No, I mean. She used to be my mum. Now she's just sick.'

He wishes he could see her face. Wishes she'd turn around, that she'd grin at him in all the ways she usually does. Wickedly or sadly or happily or anything. He'd settle for any of her smiles. As if on cue, Poppy flops down onto the pavement, hugging her knees into her chest and dropping her head to them. A car goes by, then another, and Benjamin sits down beside her. He keeps his distance, close enough that she can reach for him if she wants to but not close enough that he might scare her. He wishes he had Spectacular Man or his mask, and then he doesn't.

He just wishes Poppy would talk to him.

'I think she's still your mum,' he says gently. 'Even if she is sick.'

'No,' Poppy says. 'My mum is smart, and she's funny. My mum is a lawyer and she wears the best things and practises arguing in the car with us when she drops us at school. My mum makes ice cream spiders for us for lunch when she's home on the weekends, and she's the best, fastest swimmer I know, but she gets angry sometimes for no reason, and she always wants to win and she gets so mad when she doesn't, and sometimes she doesn't come home from work until after me and my sisters have gone to sleep, and she always thinks her tuna bake is the best in the world, when it is really, really gross, and sometimes she forgets important things, like the time she promised she'd come on my Year Four camp, but she worked instead, but she was my mum, so it was okay. Now everyone lets her win everything, like they think if she wins at

378

Uno or Ticket to Ride she might win whatever is happening inside of her. Even Daddy lets her win, and he used to laugh so hard whenever Mum's face went all red when she lost. He never laughs anymore, especially never at Mum.'

A magpie lands on the pavement a few feet in front of them, its long body sleek, its beady eyes black. It tilts its head at them before hopping along to the grass in search of insects. Benjamin watches it for a long minute before he turns back to Poppy, surprised to find her head tipped up to look at him, her forehead red from resting on her knees, her eyes dark.

'Is that why you won't talk to her?' he asks, and he thinks maybe that's not fair. Not to Poppy, who tells him to look for the things he's lost, and who holds his hand after he's had an accident, or when he's mad at Olive or Charlie or his dad, or in the church, with his grandmother's small body closed in a glossy wood coffin.

But maybe it is fair. Maybe sometimes seeing someone, really seeing someone, is the only thing that matters.

'Maybe,' Poppy says. 'Or maybe—'

Whatever she was going to say Benjamin will never hear. Poppy starts to cry, and she doesn't stop until the sun dips below the skyline and her dad comes out to carry her back inside.

O

'Again?' Olive groans, and Mindy nods, her face painted with disgust. The storeroom reeks of rotting fruit, their sludgy insides growing colonies of gluttonous ants across the base of the vats. Mindy snaps on a pair of rubber gloves before passing Olive a pair.

They crouch down, eyeing off the crumpled bodies of mangoes and pears, the sunken heads of carrots, cauliflower, broccoli. The smell is invasive, snakes up Olive's skin, hovers just below her nose.

'Can't you magic this fridge colder or something?' Olive asks, pulling a handful of plums out and thrusting them deep into the garbage bag at her side. 'So that this shit doesn't rot?'

'I can't hold it long enough,' Mindy says, forcing the fruit down further into the bag. 'Plus I have to really focus, and believe it or not, I don't *actually* want to have to think about this place all day, every day.'

Olive fake gasps, and it earns her an eye roll and a nudge from Mindy, even as the other girl grins. They work together in silence for a few minutes, focused on the task at hand, and Olive tries not to itch for a joint or a cigarette, for anything that might replace the smell of spoiled fruit in her nose. She works her jaw, her thoughts drifting back to Frank earlier.

'I didn't know Frank had a daughter,' she says quietly, and Mindy blinks sideways at her.

'Oh?'

Olive doesn't reply to that, and Mindy shrugs, reaching deeper for a particularly sad-looking carrot.

'Yeah, he's got a son as well. He's in the army. Working out of the NT at the moment, but he was in Afghanistan for a while.'

The thought presents itself in Olive's head like a drop of ink in water, changing the colour there, or – no – rather changing the image of Frank himself. Her old picture of him bleeding anew.

'Why do you bring it up?'

'I don't know,' she says quietly. 'I mean, I didn't know. It's weird to think about.'

'People *do* have lives outside of this dump,' Mindy says with a laugh. 'We don't all, like, boot up or boot down with our shifts.'

'I know that. I just didn't think, I guess.'

Mindy rolls her eyes again, but it's not malicious or mean, more gently exasperated, but then she makes a sudden loud noise in the back of her throat, as if she's just remembered something.

'Oh, god, speaking of lives outside O'Malley's – did you hear Jude and Lux are doing it?'

Olive jerks her head up to look at Mindy.

'What?'

Mindy nods, reaching down to knot off the garbage bag.

'Yeah, Trini caught them making out in the staffroom the other day. Apparently Lux's shirt was like, bunched up around her pits and Jude's pants were half off, so you can do the math. What a mess, right?'

The blood is rushing in Olive's ears, curdling in her head, and she stands up quickly, jerkily.

'I've got to go.'

And before Mindy can say a thing about it, she's gone.

23

How do you solve a problem like Lux Robinson?

That's what Olive thinks, cycling at breakneck speed through the backstreets of Brisbane, dodging honking cars and the glare of the midafternoon sun. She feels stiff, her bones crushing her chest, a nutcracker to her walnut heart, and she trembles, tightening her grip on the handlebars to anchor herself, to keep herself present, her legs pumping wildly beneath her.

She can already see Lux's house in the distance, see its tall, pristine walls and the angular roof. See the neatly tended yard, the wide, waxed deck, the whirlybirds on top, spinning in the midsummer air. A perfect house on a perfect street. She thinks briefly of stopping. Of calling Lux for what feels like the hundredth time this week, but she knows there will be no answer. She hops off her bike and lets it fall gracelessly to the grass, striding up to the door and banging a closed fist against it.

'Lux!' she calls, her eyes screwing shut. She bangs on the door again, hard enough that she's sure there will be bruises tomorrow. '*Lux!*'

It's only after the third shout that the door cracks open, and Olive stumbles back, words stuck to the floor of her mouth. It's not Lux who stands before her, but Dom, rubbing the sleep out of his lazy eyes.

'She's not here,' he says, his voice little more than a low rumble. He looks down at her, considering. 'She left for work an hour or so ago.'

Olive pauses, feels the fight seeping out of her. Her head lolls back involuntarily, and Dom reaches out a hand to steady her, but she doesn't quite let him. He leans into the doorframe instead, staring at her curiously.

'Figured you two'd be sick of each other.'

Olive blinks.

'What?'

'She's been staying at yours so much, that's all I mean.'

And of course Lux would say that. Of course she'd use Olive as a cover, a guise, a good fucking excuse. The pressure is back in her chest, tightening like a vice, and she looks up at Dom and expects to see a dawning of recognition, of distrust or realisation, but Dom doesn't look anything of the sort. With his hair ruffled, and still smelling of sleep, he's never looked younger or more innocent, and Olive suddenly finds it hard to imagine him as the boy who trashed the city house with her all those days ago.

'Yeah,' Olive says. ''Course. Just she borrowed something the other night that I need.'

The lie feels weak, even to her, but Dom believes it. He holds the door open a little wider, enough that Olive could steal beneath his arm if she wanted and go inside.

'I can grab it for you, or you can. She won't care.'

Olive looks back out over Lux's front yard, to her abandoned bike, the slumped new road. Across the street a jogger pants, stops to adjust her headphones, her chest flushed pink. Olive shakes her head.

'No, it's okay. I'll get it from her another time.'

Dom stares at her then, a glimpse of suspicion on his face for the first time, and fuck you, she thinks. Fuck Lux for this. He lifts his hand to tap his fingers against the doorframe, looking out over her head, and then back down at her.

'She'll be home later tonight, if you wanted to swing round then.'

'No,' she says. 'Just tell her I stopped by? Tell her I'll …' she fumbles for the words, but her body aches, her limbs feel heavy, weighed down like stones on her witch's legs.

'Tell her whatever you want,' she settles on, and it's unfair, because those words must ring through Dom's head, but he nods slowly and doesn't close the door until Olive is back on her bike, cycling the long, twisting roads towards home.

O

She goes to the park instead. To the place she knows Jude likes to frequent, the one with the low-slung trees and the view of the shallow river, ducks dipping below the surface and the grass alight with the streetlamps' glow.

It takes her a minute to spot him, in a crowd of fresh-faced boys, playing touch among the fireflies, their long bodies lean and fast, their shirts piled at the side of their makeshift field, while the early-evening light settles hazily around them. She stops, heart in her throat, watching Jude duck below the arm of a friend, his legs pounding the grass as he reaches for the ball, his strong body graceful in a way that still makes her tingle.

He spots her then, slowing across the field to wave lightly at her, and she stupidly waves back. She knows by his grin that he'll come for her after the game, and he does, wiping the pearls of moisture from his forehead with his abandoned shirt as he makes his way towards her.

'Olive Rabbit,' he says, grinning. He drops a hand to her side, then lowers his head, brushing her lips, and she lets him until she doesn't. Until she can't anymore. She stiffens in his arms. He leans back, tilting his handsome head.

'You okay?'

'Are you fucking Lux?'

The words slip out before she can stop them, and Jude blinks down at her, having the courtesy, at least, to flush. He takes a step back, shrugging, throwing his shirt over his shoulder and burying his hands in the pockets of his shorts.

'We're just having fun.'

'Who?' she asks, genuinely curious. 'Her and you, or me and you?'

He shrugs again, glancing back at the field, at where his friends have started to gather, pretending not to watch them, and she can feel her chest tighten, feel the pressure build in her head.

'Do you think about me? Did you ever think about me at all?'

Jude's silence is Olive's answer, and it's not a big deal, she reminds herself, because academically she knows it isn't. Jude is just a boy, after all, and boys only matter for a handful of moments, but this doesn't make her feelings for Jude unravel inside her any quicker.

She leans back, staggers, maybe, tries to clear her throat, tries not to care. 'See you at work, I guess,' she says, and Jude waves her a pleasant, friendly goodbye.

○

She's not expecting Benjamin to be standing alone in the front yard of the Dockens' house when she goes to pick him up, but there he is, backpack firmly in place and his long arms folded almost defensively across his chest.

She pulls over and leans across the car seat to push open the passenger door, and is surprised when Benjamin only waves briefly back at the house before climbing in.

'Everything okay?' she asks, and Benjamin nods, leaning down in the car seat, tearing off his backpack and twisting it around to his lap. The ride home passes in near complete silence, the only sound the subdued chatter of talkback hosts interviewing a politician about refugee reform. It's not until they're parked on the kerb that Delia turns around in her seat, looking curiously at her son.

'Did you have a fight?' she asks, because it's all she can think of. She's so used to having to pull Benjamin from Poppy's octopus grip these days that the distance between them feels a little strange.

'No.' He wrinkles his nose. 'I don't think so.'

Delia opens her mouth to say something, anything, but Benjamin continues.

'Her mum is sick.'

'What?'

'Really sick. Like, I think she might be dying.'

The evening light cuts through the glass behind Benjamin's head, the glare making Delia squint and put a hand over her eyes. If Benjamin notices, he doesn't react, his eyes downcast, something tight in the set of his features, as if he's deep in thought. Delia hunts for words of comfort in her head but comes up short. The idea of this little girl experiencing what Delia has only recently experienced is unimaginable and too imaginable all at once.

'We talked about it,' Benjamin says, his narrow shoulders lifting. 'Only a little. And then I just held her hand, like she held mine at Grandma's thing. I think it helped, but I'm not sure. I don't know what helps.'

'I don't think anybody does,' Delia replies, tilting her body closer towards him. She reaches for his chin, wants him to look at her, but he doesn't.

'And I felt bad,' he says. 'Because she's been so good. She's been better than all my favourite things. With her, I don't need Spectacular Man anymore because I am him, and I want to be that for her too, but I don't know how. So I left him with her, Spectacular Man, but that feels weird too.'

She cups Benjamin's cheek, smooths her thumb across his skin, and revels more than she cares to admit in the way Benjamin leans into her touch.

'It's hard sometimes, when things we used to need so much are suddenly not as needed.'

Benjamin pauses, his eyelids fluttering shut.

His lashes are so long. Have they always been this long?

'Do you think Charlie will ever be here for real again?'

There's a lie stuck to the roof of her mouth like taffy, but it won't lift, won't sink down to her tongue, so she tells the truth instead.

'I hope so, but I don't know.'

'I've talked less to him lately,' Benjamin says, frowning. 'I don't know why. I think I'm mad at him.'

'Why are you mad at him?'

'Because he's always been so special, and he never told me. I tell Charlie everything, but he kept secrets. Like the way you keep secrets.'

Sometimes, between heartbeats and inhales, she sees a man in Benjamin. Strong jawed and tall, just like his father. A certain firmness that makes her reel back. It's so unexpected but somehow not unfamiliar. It's a man's look, she decides, not a boy's. Its suddenness shocks her. Of course it would never be him to vanish, she thinks.

Of course it wouldn't be him.

'I don't mean to keep secrets,' she says, and Benjamin shrugs, pulling away from her.

'But you do.'

With that, he opens the passenger door and climbs out, walking through their yard up towards the house. Delia watches, tries to gather up her tired senses, and finally follows. She's still fumbling with her keys when she glances up to see Olive sprawled on the steps, her eyes closed and her shirt pulled up, exposing her tanned belly to the first glimmer of starlight.

'Forget your keys?' she asks, and Olive blinks lazily down at her, the bags beneath her eyes dark and heavy. Benjamin steps around her, letting himself into the house, and Delia goes to follow him, only for Olive to stop her.

'Who's Bo?'

Delia stills, and she looks up to see that Benjamin's frozen too, his gaze fixed ahead, his back rigid.

'What?'

Beneath her, Olive reaches into the back pocket of her jeans and holds up a crumpled slip of paper. Only it's not a bit of paper at all, it's a photograph, creased. Something in Delia's chest lurches.

'Is this a two-pronged attack?' she asks, mouth dry, but Benjamin won't turn around, and Olive is slowly standing up on the step behind her.

'Who the fuck is Bo, Delia?'

The silence is heavy for a second, two, until Delia looks at Olive's creased face, her desperate, hunted eyes, and says, 'Bo was my sister. She drowned. That's it.'

And it is, mostly. Bo had disappeared one fateful afternoon in one of the driest summers on record. They had searched for her for weeks on end, and it wasn't until the rain that things had changed. The city had been easy pickings for a flash flood, after all, one that flew over highways and swallowed houses. Delia had watched from her bedroom window as the river had unmoored itself from its narrow station and evolved into something entirely new. Gone was the place where she'd drop Poohsticks with her sister, and suddenly Brisbane had become the River City it had always been known as.

By the next summer, the drought had found them again. The leaves had browned and curled on every arthritic eucalyptus branch and the river had become little more than a dusty bed. It was only then that a scrappy group of boys, hunting for shed python skins and insect carcasses, had unearthed the mangled bones of Bo Rabbit.

Delia, only fourteen at the time, had watched her stoic mother lose her mind in the space of an afternoon. She wonders then if she'd have gone the same way had Charlie's bones been discovered like that too.

Olive doesn't shift, doesn't turn to look at her, and the ghost of a hand touches Delia's back, and god, she hopes it's Charlie, or Bo, or at least someone who might love her in this awful, blundering moment.

'Why didn't you tell us about her?'

Delia shrugs.

'What's there to tell?'

It was the wrong thing to say, probably, given the split-open look her daughter gives her.

'What's there to tell,' Olive echoes, her voice hollow, and she turns and disappears into the house.

You could've handled that better.

'I'm getting a little tired of unsolicited advice from the invisible boy,' Olive says, fumbling around in her dresser for clean clothes. It takes her a minute to find something she wants to wear, to shove aside the underwear, the cigarettes, the ratty bras she's long grown out of, and finally grab a singlet. She pulls it over the top of her clothes, then yanks her old shirt out from underneath it before bothering to look at the swift scribbles of Charlie's pencil on his floating pad of post-it notes. She can feel herself tremble, her throat tighten, can't unsee Dom's face, or Mindy's, or Jude's, or even her mother's from minutes ago.

She grabs the photograph from the back pocket of her jeans again, unfolds it and rubs a thumb across the smiling face of Bo Rabbit. Her mother's sister. Her drowned aunt. She folds it tightly again, placing it carefully into her dresser drawer.

It's not like you ever listen anyway.

The note is held in front of her face, so she can't escape it, and she plucks it from the air, scrunches it up and tosses it onto her dresser as well, a neat shadow for the picture of Bo.

'And yet here we are again,' she says dryly, grabbing a cigarette and dropping heavily onto her bed. 'Go talk to Banjo. He might want your words of wisdom a little more than me.'

Olive takes a drag, letting the smoke fill her mouth and leave her nose, until the heat from the inhale battles the heat outside of her, and her aching chest loosens just a touch. She reaches for her phone, pulling up a new message to Lux and typing with frantic fingers *did you fuck Jude before or after my grandma died?* before deleting it, then, after a second, leg twitching, retyping it and hitting send.

She tosses her phone down on the bed, rubs roughly at her

face. Looking sideways, she catches a glimpse of a sequined dress – the one she'd borrowed from Lux weeks ago.

I don't think mum means to keep secrets. I think she just doesn't know how to talk to us about this stuff.

Olive plucks the note from the air and throws it away, almost feeling Charlie's huff of frustration, but she doesn't care.

'You really will defend whatever she does, huh?' she says, and when she hears the pen scribbling again she jerks upright, grabs it and the pad of paper and throws them across the room, then slams back down on the bed. It's only a few seconds later that she hears her laptop boot up, and quick, efficient typing. She sees an open Word document, and *Olive Hazel Rabbit: maturity personified* typed large across the screen.

'You know maybe I've got other shit happening in my life,' Olive hisses back. 'Maybe we can't all be home every day, faking our own disappearances, for what, Charlie? The attention? Did you not get enough of that? Do you like playing the omni-fucking-present being? Because guess what, kid, maybe you're not even real. Maybe we made you up, maybe we're dreaming. Maybe you really are nothing at all.'

The air shudders, she feels it, and then the words he's typed are deleted, and the keys start dipping again, typing *fuck you fuck you fuck you fuck you* over and over until they fill pages and pages and Olive is on her feet, ripping the laptop from Charlie's invisible hands and throwing it at the wall, watching the machine split in half as it crashes to the floor.

'What do you want from me?' she yells, and she feels

Charlie retreating, and if she closes her eyes she can see it, that dumb, startled look he gets whenever anyone raises their voice. Charlie's no good with conflict, with the gritted teeth of the women in this house. No one is anymore.

Maybe it's Charlie's fingers at her wrist. Maybe it's nothing at all.

She screams then, howls, and when the door is pushed open, Delia on the other side, Olive doesn't stick around. She grabs her backpack, her phone, her tin of weed and her cigarettes, and, impulsively, Lux's dress, and she splits.

24

He hears the crash, then Olive's bedroom door opening across the hall, and he peers through the doorway in time to see Olive tearing out, their mother on her heels. He watches them retreat, watches them leave the house, and then makes tracks of his own, slipping into his sister's room and taking stock. He's rarely allowed in here, and sure, he didn't exactly get permission, but he figures it doesn't matter, not in this moment at least.

He sees the laptop first, broken in two on the floor, and then the stack of Charlie's post-it notes hovering in the air. Olive's room stinks, of the festering rotten fruit that coats her O'Malley's uniform, and souring alcohol and cigarette smoke, and a smell he's pretty sure is weed. Her clothes are scattered across the floor, along with her bedsheets and ashen notebooks, untouched beyond the brief few months of uni she did last year.

His gaze is still travelling across the room when Charlie moves a note into his line of vision.

She didn't want to talk, that's all.

'You mean she didn't want you to talk back.'

Charlie's lack of a reply is as much a confirmation as Benjamin needs. He sits down on the edge of his sister's bed, surveying the damage and waiting for his brother to sit beside him. The mattress suddenly sags, and Benjamin looks sideways at the empty space and sighs.

'You don't always have to defend her, you know.'

He's met with silence again, and it's enough to make him sigh more deeply, flop back onto his sister's bed. The air is almost wet in here, maybe outside too, but Benjamin can't be sure. Can't summon the energy to find out, or even to recall the events of the afternoon, if it had been this damp then, his hand gripping Poppy's so tightly he couldn't feel anything else.

Guess we won't find out about the bolt from the blue after all.

'What do you mean?' Benjamin says, frowning, and he feels Charlie grip his head, push it gently to the side so that Benjamin feels a splash of warm rainwater colliding with his cheek through the open window.

O

Her mother doesn't follow her for long, which is really the best Olive can hope for. Moving quickly and aimlessly, she knows she needs to find somewhere fast. Knows she needs *something*, no matter what it is.

She swings by the bottle shop, grabs a couple of tallboys, then swings through a party somewhere in the eastern suburbs, buys pills from a local, and darts out. It's then that the storm breaks.

Thunder first, a grumble, sounding through the chest of the suburb, and then the rain starts, a dribble, a drool, and then shattering, sudden and relentless. It soaks her hair, her clothes, coats her skin in relief. The birds start, magpies and galahs, cockatoos and ibises, a flurry in the street, flying open-beaked into it. The plants lurch too, each blade of grass, each leaf, every wilted flower seeming to turn towards the sky, open itself up and breathe.

Olive, though, needs shelter.

And there's only one place she can really go.

The house is larger than she remembers. Vast and empty, a shell of a thing, and she tries not to think ill of it as she pushes in through the broken door, clutching her bag to her chest. The rain is coming through the shattered windows, splattering across the floor, leaving everything musty, damp and tired. Olive steps across it all, runs her fingers along the splintered wood that she and Dom and Lux beat down. She traces the images and patterns they wallpapered this place with, and, when she gets to the rabbit Lux drew for her, she punches her fist into it, letting the painted wood cut her knuckles, her blood leaving streaks of red.

She surges forwards again, hits it again and again, revelling in the sudden starkness of the pain, at all her wastefulness. She stumbles off, holding her bloodied fist to her chest until it stains her shirt so badly she takes it off, shrugging into the sequined dress instead and wrapping her hand in her shirt. She keeps walking until she finds the bathroom, tries to turn on the tap, but no water comes out, and so she crouches down to the cupboard below, tearing it open, unsure what she's even looking for, but there's nothing there except a bandaid wrapper, a pair of scissors and a few dirty cotton buds.

Leaning back up, she catches a glimpse of herself in the mirror, a battered, beaten mess, her lipstick smeared across her face like it's been split, her eyes dull and her bloodied hand leaving stains at her chest and neck. She looks at that dusty blonde hair, and it's not dark like Charlie's, it's not dark like her mother's, like her secret aunt's, no, it's fairer even than her father's, and in the moment she hates it. Hates the way it dresses her up and tells her – tells her—

With a hiss she crouches down again, grabs the scissors from beneath the sink and, with a trembling hand, cuts straight through her hair. A shaky gasp escapes her lips as she looks at her reflection in the smoggy mirror, her hand raised, clutching a chunk of damp hair, and fuck it, she thinks, lifting the scissors again. Fuck it.

She hacks it all off, every inch of her sweet hair, letting it fall about her in the bowels of this ugly, wasted home. When she's done she crouches on the floor, takes another pill, another swig from a tallboy. She drinks until her mouth is fizzing with the chemical reaction, with the weight of this moment, and all the things she wishes were better.

God, she wishes *she* was better. A better daughter, sister, friend.

If she was—

If she was—

She pounds her cut fists into the side of her head, until all she can smell is the metallic scent of iron at her temples.

There's a bang. The sound of a door being forced open, the

frenetic sound of the storm outside, and Olive drops to the floor, eyes wide and wild as a voice calls her name somewhere in the distance. She recoils from it. The noise is too loud, warping at her ear drums, and it's not until the body stands in the doorway that Olive realises it's Mindy.

'*Fuck*,' she says, crouching down at Olive's side. Mindy's hands check her head, rubbing at the blood smears before refocusing on Olive's broken knuckles. 'What have you done to yourself, Rabbit?'

'I fucked up,' Olive sniffs, her head lolling back, and Mindy hums in agreement.

'Come on, my car's out front.'

She reaches a hand around Olive's waist, pulling her up, and it's all Olive can do not to collapse against her.

'I hate this,' she mumbles, and Mindy pushes at her temple.

'What, Olive? What do you hate?'

But Olive isn't sure what she hates. Just everything – about herself, about this moment, about her life. She hates everything, until she doesn't anymore, and that's too hard to say.

'How'd you even know I was here?'

'Lux sent me a message. She was worried about you. She told me you'd probably be here.'

Olive blinks, but the house is wobbling, blurring above her, and her head drops as her legs collapse beneath her.

She doesn't hit the ground though, not with Mindy's arm around her waist, and she stares at the long ribbons of her fair hair splayed across the tiles, and she's not sure what she expects, what she wants from Mindy. Not sure what she wants from anything. She lets her eyes slip shut and tries to still her thrumming nerves.

'Olive,' Mindy hisses above her, shakes her, maybe, Olive doesn't know, and then Mindy gasps.

There's a knock on the door, and Delia answers it to be met with a girl she only half recognises, a girl Olive works with, and she opens the door further out of curiosity.

The girl stands aside as if for some big reveal, and Delia looks – of course she *looks*, searches the vast nothingness behind her like it might reveal something. All there is is air, though, and the slanting rain, wetting her floorboards.

And then.

She can't explain it. Not truly. The strange malformedness of the space. The way it seems to give, to make room for some great nothing, and Delia's breath catches in the back of her tender throat.

'Olive,' she says, and the girl grimaces, pressing into the wall, letting Delia stumble forwards, her knees crashing to the floor, her hands desperately reaching, searching, for the shape of her invisible daughter. 'Oh, *Olive*.'

The air recoils, but Delia won't let it, not again, and oh, is this what November meant about not being finished? She inhales, pulls at the air, feeling it shift beneath her fingers, feeling it tug forwards, into her, until her daughter's weight settles at her chest, until she feels a stiffening neck, flesh stitching itself beneath her fingers like the makings of a fantasy. Like a spell brought to life through sweat and vomit, beneath the desperate hands of a mother, and really, Delia thinks wryly, have they ever really existed in anything but?

'Okay,' the girl says somewhere above them. She steps away from the wall, drops a hand to Olive's disappearing-reappearing shoulder. 'Feel better, yeah?'

She sends Delia a quick, uncertain nod before ducking down the stairs, and right, Delia thinks, *right*.

'Come on, then.'

She pulls Olive's body down the hallway, letting her daughter's shoes catch in the floorboard creases and slip off. She pulls her past her room, past her brothers', past her own, and into the bathroom. She heaves her over the side of the bath, into the empty tub, and half turns the faucet away as she starts to run the water.

'You're okay,' Delia says, watching her daughter fade in and out of view against the porcelain tub. 'You're okay.'

Olive hiccups, and she's there again, vomit caked in the sequins of her dress, her hair cut, her cheeks flushed pink, and she looks up at Delia, her eyelashes damp with tears.

'I know you hate me,' Olive grumbles, trying to shift herself up. 'I know you—'

She slips, sliding heavily back down into the tub, her feet leaving bloody smears on the base, her back surely set to bruise by morning. Delia reaches out, and she means to smooth back her daughter's new hair, means to pull her to her breast, like a kind mother with a weepy child, but Delia has never been a kind mother. She pulls a washer from the shelf and leans forwards, jerking Olive's vomit-crusted dress from her frail form, ridding her of it. She reaches down, scrubbing at Olive's already-raw skin, willing it into reality, wishing the invisibility away. She wants it gone. She wants to see her daughter, her son, her mother, her sister. Wants to pin these people like butterflies to a board, hold their wings down and never stop seeing them.

Can you draw someone from memory?

If she has anything to say about it, she'll never have to. Not Olive.

Not Charlie. Not anymore.

Delia grunts, pulling Olive into her chest, scrubbing the night from her back, washing her daughter's skin so clean it pinks. Until it reddens raw, and the bruises blossom beneath her touch.

'You're a brat,' Delia says. 'But I love you, and I want you to feel better. I'm sorry I couldn't make you.'

Olive's crying now, pressing her head into the cold, hard rim of the bathtub. 'I don't feel like anything,' she says. 'I don't—'

She heaves, and Delia washes her harder, warms the water, pushes her hand down her daughter's hair.

'I love you,' she says again, because it's all she can. 'Whatever it is you're going through, it's you and me, okay? It'll always be you and me.'

And is that what Bo needed to hear?

Is that what Delia needed? All those years ago when they'd found Bo's bones?

Is that what her mother needed at the end?

Delia doesn't know, but she files the question away for another time, training her attention back on her weeping daughter, washing her like this is a baptism or a way home – like she's some tired sinner finding her way back into the arms of something sacred. Until she smells not like sweat and weed and blood, but just of soap and maybe a smell that's all her own. Delia sees her sister, playing coyly at the edge of the schoolyard, and she sees her mother, withdrawn but steady-handed, and she sees her daughter – every spitfire inch of her.

She sees herself – just herself, whatever that might be.

'I know I'm a brat,' Olive says, finally lifting her gaze, and Delia's heart catches somewhere between her ankles and her throat. 'But please don't leave me on my own anymore.'

There is no longer hair to shield her, no blonde cape, nothing to hide her daughter's desperate, earnest look, and instead it's just the two of them, visible, pretending they know each other.

No, Delia thinks.

Knowing that they don't, and choosing this anyway.

'Oh, baby,' Delia says lightly, cupping her daughter's jaw. 'You're stuck with me. My magic daughter. Your magic brothers. We're the Rambunctious, Riveting Rabbits, aren't we?'

'Rabbits,' Olive says uncertainly, burrowing her head into her mother's arm. 'I guess.'

O

He can hear Olive crying, her feet squeaking on the base of the bath, while the desk chair turns round and round in front of their computer. Like a record skipping – or, at least, how

Benjamin's always imagined a record skipping to sound.

'It'll be okay,' Benjamin says, over the howl of the storm outside. It's quiet for a moment, and then Charlie types.

You don't know that.

'I do,' Benjamin says.

Past evidence is not on our side.

'Things can change,' he says, because they can, because they *do*, and then, remembering Poppy's words all those weeks ago, he adds, 'nothing's just one thing.'

Because maybe this is how things *become* more than one thing. How they grow and change and discover new parts of themselves.

Charlie's quiet for a minute or two, and the only sound between them is Olive's sobbing and their mother's soothing tones. Benjamin drops his legs down onto the bed. He thinks about Olive, then Poppy again, then Grandma, then Bo, then he shakes the thoughts clean from his head. He doesn't think any of it'll help right now.

She's mad at me.

'Olive?' Benjamin folds back against the wall. 'She's always mad at everyone.'

No. She's usually just mad at herself. I think mum is. Mad at me, I mean.

Benjamin's brow furrows.

'Why do you think that?'

I think she's mad about all of it.

Benjamin considers this, rolling back into the bed. Outside the rain is thickening. Pouring down like cream from a jar, leaving everything damp and cool. He pulls up the hem of his shirt, coaxing air up there.

'We're all mad at you for all of it,' Benjamin says, because they are, and maybe that's okay. 'Maybe it's okay to be mad at people you love, because being mad means you care, and maybe when someone you love is mad at you, it makes you try more to be better.'

He says this out loud, and Charlie's quiet for another moment, before suddenly he types:

It was nice to be missed.

'What?'

That's why I let you think I was gone instead of invisible.

'That's really bad,' Benjamin tells him, and Charlie types:

I know.

Benjamin doesn't reply to that, and Charlie doesn't elaborate, and after a moment Benjamin lies down on the bed and lets his eyes close. Focuses on the sounds of the rain outside and the splash of the bath inside, on *right now*. He folds his hands over his chest and doesn't look up again until he hears the rapping of fingers on the computer keys.

Do you remember when I used to take care of you?

Benjamin pauses. He looks down at his schoolbag, still propped against the door, and he thinks of Spectacular Man, but he's with Poppy now, taking care of her instead. He rolls over to face the spot where he knows his brother is.

'You're my brother,' he says, the words sure and certain on his heavy tongue. 'We take care of each other.'

'*I love you*,' Charlie says, his voice ringing through the quiet, and Benjamin's heart hammers in his throat, he sits bolt upright, and, however briefly, sees the line of a jaw and a flash of braces, but the image is gone before he can hold it.

'I love you too.'

25

After she strips Olive of her sequined dress and her stinking bra and undies – after she washes her clean of the vomit and the blood and the sweat – Delia finishes the job Olive started.

She cuts her hair.

It's been so long since she's done it, and she can't help but feel a pull in her at the loss of Olive's sleek hair, the dusky sunset blonde, so foreign from Delia's own. Most of it, of course, is gone. Lost to wherever Olive has been, wherever it was she bloodied her fists and her skin and her bones and her voice. There are only torn-up fragments left, occasional swatches of colour covering the pale canvas of her daughter's skull.

She cuts what she can before grabbing her electric razor and finishing the job, taking Olive's locks down to a static buzz. She's barely finished before Olive is rubbing her hands over it, feeling it, getting a sense of it. She doesn't look pleased, but she doesn't look displeased either.

'Thanks,' she says, and Delia puts the razor away, grabbing a towel to wrap up Olive's skinny body.

'Sure,' Delia replies with a shrug, the rim of the bathtub

leaving a painful imprint against the curve of her arse. She adjusts her seat.

'It looks good,' she adds, because it does. Olive has the soft features and the big eyes to pull it off, the odd sort of effervescent energy Delia knows she had in her own youth, in those lost and trying years, and she feels a twitch of unease at the realisation. She's glad she said it, though, when Olive smiles, something small and open and unexpected. Her daughter turns from her, pressing her face into the side of the porcelain tub.

'Can I ask you a question?' Olive says into the tub, stumbling over the words, and Delia nods, pulling the towel up over Olive's body like a blanket. 'What was she like? My aunt, I mean.'

'Like you and Charlie. Invisible. And she died. I told you that.'

'That's not what I asked.'

Olive looks at her then, properly, the bags beneath her eyes heavy, her expression careful. Cautious. The door cracks open behind her, just a little wider, and she doesn't have to look to know that Benjamin and Charlie are in the hallway, listening.

'What was she like?'

Delia pauses, heart in her throat.

What was Bo like?

(Can you draw someone from memory?)

O

Bo Rabbit was what the teachers at school called a smart cookie. She could recite her times tables faster than you could ask them of her, and the alphabet backwards, and later was the star of their high-school debate team.

She could argue.

Man, could she argue.

She had such a bad overbite their dad used to say it was from all the piss and bluster she'd spout, fast as her mouth could manage. She was quick-tempered and quick-witted, and somehow able to diffuse situations as quickly as she could ignite them. She wasn't pretty exactly – not like Delia always was, but there was something in the look of her that ensnared their parents' friends, rivals and boys alike. As if she knew something about the world that you didn't, which, Delia supposes now, she did.

Bo knew how to read the book of their mother, how to open her at any page, as if she'd written the story herself, and Rosie never quite knew Bo, but it never seemed to matter. Delia had heard once that a parent has a soulmate in a child, but not in children, and Bo and Rosie were like nothing Delia had ever known. A partnership, more than that. A part of each other. A secret, coded unit that Delia had never been able to infiltrate, but then Delia and Bo had been that way too. They'd been something else. Secrets swapped in dens made of sheets and dining-room chairs and shared looks over family dinners. They'd been fights over dolls and boys and books and space, and weepy make-ups after fights and little kindnesses and races through the park in the dark. They'd saved a bird once, and after they'd released it it had followed Bo, loved her, like everybody else. It hadn't mattered that they'd both saved it, because Bo was something that Delia, for all her pretty, girlish looks and her drawings and her teenage frustrations, was not. Bo was Bo Rabbit, who gave and took and withheld, and was with Delia from the very start of her life, and left it unfairly, and too early.

She tells Olive all of this, and her sons too, who stand silently in the hall and listen to their mother share stories of the aunt they will never know. And there's something in the telling of it all, something in the words that feels like finding a precious thing you'd forgotten you ever had.

Benjamin doesn't sleep well.

It's not really because of Olive, or Charlie, or Mum, or even Aunt Bo, but rather it's the sound of the rain, which rumbles throughout the night, beating against their tin roof like a game of Jacks. He ends up leaving his bedroom window open and getting Charlie to help him push his bed out from the wall, and they both lie on it, letting the rain hit their foreheads and dampen their skin. Or, at least, he thinks it dampens Charlie's. He reaches out, touches it, and finds whatever's there, though invisible, wet.

He's woken by the sun yawning through the open curtains, the rain now a light trickle, a glow leaving everything humming. He sits up in the bed, feels around for Charlie, whose motionless body indicates he's still asleep, then stretches and pads across the hall.

He's not sure he could tell you why. If it's because of the night before, or all the nights before, or even watching Poppy with her sisters, but right now Benjamin wants his sister, and so he steals into her room like a ghost.

He's surprised to find Olive half awake, sprawled in faded pink-striped pyjamas on her bed, the sheets tangled between her legs like Benjamin knows his so often are. She smells not like the cigarettes he's used to, but instead faintly of their mother's rosemary soap and satsuma-scented shampoo, which is funny, really, given all of Olive's hair is gone.

'What do you want, Banjo?'

He shrugs, scuffing his feet against the floorboards. The rain's stopped, the drought broken, but the air still feels wet, even to the touch. Buttery, almost. He waits for Olive to tell him to leave, but she doesn't. Instead he's shuffling in the doorway, and Olive's awake but not up, and it takes a minute for him to think of what to say, and when the words come they're not what he expects.

'Can I touch it?' he asks, and Olive blinks blearily up at him, her blue eyes damp.

'What?'

'Your head.'

Olive rolls her eyes, but she leans forwards all the same, off the edge of the bed, tilting her chin down to her chest. He walks over, tentative at first, pressing only the blunt tops of his fingers there and then flattening them down so the joints press too. It's not soft like he'd maybe expected, rather it's staccato. Beneath his hands Olive's body seems to sag, to droop further, her breathing evening, and Benjamin pulls back.

'What do you think?' Her voice is muffled against the mattress, the words spilling down into her own skin instead of up towards his, and Benjamin shrugs.

'It's cool,' he says, and Olive smiles a little shyly at him. 'Did it hurt?'

'Oh, come on, Banjo. You've had a haircut before.'

And he has, but he shrugs anyway, shifting his weight between his feet.

'Not like this, I don't think.'

Olive doesn't say anything for a long time, and Benjamin doesn't either. He leans forwards a little to press his bare kneecaps to the soft side of her mattress, but not enough to weigh it down. Outside a bird calls, a magpie or a dove, something with a deep, melodic tone, and he looks out through Olive's window at nothing.

'You're a weird kid, you know that?'

Benjamin just shrugs.

'Yeah.'

'I'm sorry I'm such an arsehole to you.'

He grins at that, looking back at where the door has cracked open again, enough for a body, Charlie's, to slip through.

'You usually make up for it.'

'Not as much as I should.'

Benjamin considers that, turning over her words, her tone. He thinks about all the anger in her, and then he thinks about all the anger in Poppy, and maybe Jodi too, and his mother, and his grandmother, and in all the women he knows, and he knows there are good reasons for it, that things aren't easy for them in a way he might never really understand.

So he says 'I'm sorry' instead, and Olive closes her eyes, tears pearling at the corners, and he thinks about folding his body over hers like he would as a little boy, and hugging her.

'It's okay,' she says. 'At least Spectacular Man and the Invisible Boy have my back, huh?' She says it just over his shoulder, at Charlie, and Benjamin pauses, leaning back into the bed.

'And Benjamin and Charlie too,' he adds, and Olive grins like he's never seen her grin before, an expression he'll keep in the treasure chest of his head forever, then drops her head back down to the mattress.

'And Benjamin and Charlie too,' she says.

○

The afternoon chases the morning with a bright-skied downpour, and it leaves Olive lazy and languid, files down the edge of her hangover.

She stretches, watching through her bedroom window as Benjamin dashes across the grass towards Charlie's telescope, which is moving gently and purposefully beneath Charlie's invisible hands. The thought makes her look down at her own, wish herself away again, like she did last night, but her skin stays present, as if painted in midair, an immovable thing.

She can hear her mother a few rooms over, hear the clamour in her bedroom, the easel being jerked across the floor, brushes dropped in pots of dirty water, the shift of her mother's heavy body against the groaning floorboards. The walls in this house really are too thin.

Her phone buzzes, vibrates against her mattress, and she picks it up to find a message from Lux.

Mindy get you home okay?

Olive reads it twice, licks her teeth.

Yeah. Meet me at Minnippi?

An ellipsis appears, indicating typing, but no message arrives, not for minutes (hours, it feels like). Olive's aching fingers twitch for a cigarette, a joint, for a full-moon pill or a breadcrumb trail of powder. For piss-weak wine or rusty spirits.

I can be there in 20.

○

It was only yesterday that she saw Jude at the park, that he made clear her weight in his life, but it somehow feels like a million years ago. The memory will hold, she's sure, grip at the hem of her life like the cobbler's peg now clutching the bottom of her jeans. But she hopes others will too, the better ones, like of the way he'd held her here, of watching Charlie at the lookout, every inch of him, as he babbled about stars and tree frogs, or of Benjamin, turning upside down on the flying fox, his cape billowing out behind him.

The rain has lulled, but it's left the river fuller than Olive's seen it in years. Waterbirds wade by the edges, preening their sleek feathers and ducking their heads beneath the stream, disappearing and reappearing at will.

She shakes her head, sniffs, gropes for her phone in her pocket. She's about to text Lux, to tell her where she is, when—

'Love the look,' a voice says behind her, light and warm. 'Very Furiosa.'

Olive runs a hand over her head, feeling the bristle beneath her fingernails. She gestures as if to grab a handful, but finds there's nothing to grab. Lux looks like she usually does – better than usual, if anything, her sharpness startling in the clean light of the day, her hair long, recently washed, her cheeks pinked from blush or burn.

'I needed a change,' Olive replies with a shrug, dropping her arm, and Lux nods slowly, gaze stretching over the park.

'Change can be good.'

Olive pauses, tries to remember the script she'd written in her head for this moment. The dialogue that would see her strong-jawed and firm-footed to Lux's wavering concessions, her apologies, her forfeit. Only Lux isn't offering any of them. Not yet.

'Why did you fuck him?'

Lux pushes her fingers to her mouth, chews a fingernail, looks at Olive and then away just as quickly.

'I don't know.'

'Why couldn't you be there for me? With Charlie and with Jude and with my mum? Why couldn't you just ... I needed you, I think.'

'You could've said.'

'Friends shouldn't have to say.'

'Sometimes they do.'

Olive fumbles for the words.

'What are we? Are we friends?'

Lux startles, reeling back, her hand dropping. It's the most honest reaction Olive thinks she's ever gotten from her.

'Of course we're friends.'

Olive opens her mouth to reply, but no words come out. She's not even sure she knows what a friend is.

'I'm not responsible for your unhappiness,' Lux says, and

Olive looks up in surprise, taking in the harsher lines of Lux's face, her wet lips and serious expression.

'I know that.'

'I don't think you do. You blame other people for it, but it's on you. You can't put all your shit onto everyone else.'

Above them, a pelican soars through the air, the wide set of its wings casting shadows across the grass. It flies out to the river, angling down to glide across the surface, beak parting as it dives for fish. Olive watches it instead of Lux, because maybe it makes it easier to let go now of the anger, the annoyance, the blame. 'I don't mean to,' she says instead, and she hears Lux shuffle, step a little closer and then back again.

'I know. I do it too sometimes. I think it's hard. To be unhappy, and not know how to fix it.'

Beyond the pelican, a swamphen wanders through the reeds towards the water. It wriggles its long red legs before resting its body on the water's surface, floating easily downstream.

'Whatever.' Lux shuffles her feet. 'I'm not trying to be a cunt. I just …'

She sighs, shaking her head, and Olive looks back to see her leaving imprints in the muddy floor of the playground, wet dirt and grass caking to her shoes. Even after the rain the park looks thirsty, the trees barren and the grass pale, shades of yellow and green, wilting in the sun instead of turning towards it. This summer has been stupid hot, but Lux is still in her oversized black sweater and jean shorts that lose themselves beneath its ratty hem. She'll do anything to get her legs to look even longer than they already do, and Olive's reminded of daddy-long-legs with their tight, compact bodies and endless limbs.

Lux is the one who won't look at her now, and that's okay, Olive thinks, turning to leave. She doesn't have to.

She's halfway back across the park when Lux suddenly calls her name, and Olive turns to see her small form, narrow in the distance. 'I *am* sorry. For all of it.'

Olive cups her hands around her mouth and calls back, 'Okay.'

And then she goes home.

26

November is sitting cross-legged on her patio, a bowl of diced cantaloupe in her lap and a cup of tea by her knee. One of her daughters, the smaller one, is hiding behind the railing bolted to the front steps of the house, her small, chubby hands curled around it and her eyes wide with anticipation. Her sister is a few feet away, climbing muddy-footed out of the bushes, her thick, curly hair tossed back. There's a bright plum bruise blossoming at the side of her mouth and another, fading, just below her elbow.

The afternoon is oddly cool for this early stage of the new year, not enough for a cardigan or coat, but enough to be a welcome reprieve from the clenched-fist heat of the last few weeks.

November's bruised daughter wails, the sound cutting through the quiet, and November's on her feet, cursing as she almost knocks her tea over, but the girl is fine.

'You okay?' Delia calls, and November turns back to look at her, waving a hand out in resignation so that Delia grins, resting back against the steps of her house. She ends up lighting a cigarette, slender fingers propping it up in one hand, a glass of wine in the other, and she inhales, lets her lungs fill up with the thick, black taste. The grass is still heavy with water, sodden and clumped with flecks of mud from the beating overnight rain. She hadn't managed to salvage her laundry in time and so a few of her art smocks, her dress from her mother's funeral and Olive's O'Malley's uniform hang there still, dripping from the line. It's been forever since she's felt this sort of dampness in her skin and beneath her toes, and it comes like a relief, a salve to a sunburnt land.

Behind her the door slides open with a whine, the metal runners desperate for an oiling and the saturated wood of the house swollen.

'Hey,' Ed says, sliding the door shut behind him and dropping down beside her on the step. 'Thought you quit.' They're too close like this, legs touching, the stairway too narrow.

She shrugs. 'I quit, I take it back up, I quit. Nature of addiction, etc.' She holds the cigarette out, looks at it. 'These were in Olive's drawer. I'll put the packet back empty.'

He's looking out over the garden, which has gone to shambles since he moved out, overgrown and patchy from the lack of weeding and watering. It must be killing him to see it like this. She remembers when they were young and pregnant and she'd sit out here and draw while he gardened, his shirt off and his body thick with dirt, and how she'd wanted to lie beneath him in the garden bed, on sheets of soil and pillows of herbs. She wonders if she'll ever stop wanting to make love to him, to paint themselves together with their sweat and their saliva and everything else.

'Olive pulled a Charlie last night,' Delia says, tapping the ash from the end of her cigarette. Ed's head spins quickly around to face her.

'What?'

'Poofed,' Delia says, then reconsiders. 'Not really a poof, more like someone was tuning a radio. In and out. My mother did it too for me, a few days before she died. She said Bo could do it too.'

Ed doesn't reply to that, not right away, and Delia resists the urge to look at him. Instead she watches their children – Benjamin and Olive and still-invisible Charlie, lurching around the legs of his telescope, fucking around with the instrument.

'Can you? Tune in and out, I mean?'

Delia rolls the words in her mouth, tastes them, before shrugging.

'I don't know. I've never tried.'

'I'm glad you don't,' he fumbles with the words. 'Know, I mean. I'm glad you don't know. That you never felt you needed to.'

But that's not true really, she thinks. There are moments she's felt invisible, but maybe it just wasn't enough, or wasn't in the same way, or maybe she just always felt like she had people she was responsible for – her mother, Ed, her children. That it didn't matter if sometimes they didn't see her, because they needed her.

'I quit my job,' she says, because she has, and she relishes in the surprised look Ed gives her.

'What brought that on?'

'I made a couple of mistakes, and I was trying to work out why I made them, and I'd given the uni too many reasons to fire me. I'm going to paint for a while. I have enough saved to keep me going for a bit. I'll see what happens.'

They sit in the quiet for another moment before Ed leans backwards on the step and says, 'Do you know when I realised I was in love with you?'

Delia raises an eyebrow at him and purses her lips. He's looking at her with a small, sly grin and the wine is warm and sloshing inside her skull and there's something loose in her that lets her entertain him.

'You are full of surprises at the moment.'

He shrugs, his shoulders relaxed. He pulls off his tie suddenly, undoes the top button of his pressed suit shirt, and she glances down at herself, wearing one of the ones he left behind. It hangs off of her like she's eighteen again and this is their afterglow, except this shirt is paint covered now, flecked with charcoal and primer.

'Try and guess,' he says.

'Am I to suppose it wasn't the first time you told me? Because that was at the Ekka the year after high school. On the Ferris wheel.'

He wrinkles his nose at that, lets his head loll to the side. 'No, that was when you told me. I couldn't not reply, and there was no escaping the high point of a Ferris wheel.'

Go figure, she thinks. 'Before or after?'

'What?'

'Did you love me before or after that?'

'After.'

'When Olive was born, then.'

'No,' he says, then, taking mercy, 'but close. It was while you were pregnant, just far enough along that we were thinking we'd have to tell people because my friends kept asking when you were going to wise up and dump me.'

Delia snorts, takes another sip of her wine, lets it unfold on her tongue like a blanket.

'I came home from uni and you were asleep on the couch watching *Star Trek* in one of my shirts and you had … you had this expression on your face like you were totally happy. Like you weren't overthinking it for once, and I remember thinking that I wanted you and only you for the rest of my life, and then I put a blanket over you and went and studied for an exam I don't even remember while you drooled on my couch.'

Delia laughs, her expression soft and warm, and she says, 'And forever turned into twenty-one years.'

He shrugs. 'When I was nineteen, twenty-one years was forever.'

She smiles, properly this time.

'You should paint,' he says. 'You should do things that make you happy because you deserve that and I want you to have it. I want you to have everything you want, and I don't want to be the reason that you hold back anymore, and the kids shouldn't be either. They're arseholes, they don't deserve that. They don't deserve you.'

Delia is worn out, and she knows that she looks it, but she thinks that for the first time she looks how she looked then – with her fingers perpetually marked with charcoal or chalk or drying paint, a time when Ed would climb so close to her, inside of her, that he would come out covered in it too. He used to joke that she was full of the stuff, and that if someone cut her open all they'd find would be art supplies, like paint ran in her veins instead of blood, and she bled brushstrokes, and her heart beat only to the sound of artists. He'd grin as he said it, voice pulsing out *Mo-net, Mo-net, Mo-net.*

'I left Vanessa. After your mother's funeral. I told her on the way home.'

Delia groans.

'Ed.'

'I really do love you.'

Delia sighs, has a drink.

'I need more than love now. I need to swim forwards, not just stick around treading water while you swim laps around me. We're not kids anymore.'

'I'm not asking you to tread water. I guess what I'm asking is if we can just see what happens.'

She looks at him and thinks of all the ways she loves him and the new imperfect perfect life she's found without him. When she doesn't reply, he stands up, brushing down his pants and walking out through their yard, squeezing Benjamin's shoulder as he goes. And she should let him leave, she should, but she reels back and calls out.

'Ed!'

He turns on the spot to look at her. His hair is greying at the temples. How long has it been greying? Was it like that when he left her? His eyes are big, have always been big. Brown. And somehow they're not like any of theirs – not bright like Olive's baby blues (so much like Bo's), or twinkling like Charlie's green ones (so much like her own), or dark like

Benjamin's. Ed's eyes are entirely his own – like murky creek water, and they've always made her feel like she is standing in one. Alone. Bare. Just her.

'Del,' he says, nearly a question, and she sighs around the words in her throat and then he leaves her, but not without a parting call to the kids.

'Love the hair!'

Olive flips him off.

○

Her father leaves like he always does, and from the vantage point of the trampoline Olive watches her mother watching him.

If their yard had seemed wild before, it's positively primitive now – overgrown and lush from rain and twitching with the wild creatures that call it home. Olive looks past it all to her brothers, still hovering around Charlie's telescope, boyish explorers on a backyard expedition.

She drops heavily onto the trampoline, stretching her legs against the damp mat, revelling in the warm slickness of it.

'What are you guys looking at, anyway?' she asks.

'Planetary huddle,' Benjamin replies. 'It's supposed to be tonight.'

Olive makes a noise of acknowledgement in the back of her throat, looking up towards the house at her mother still sitting on the steps, at the path that her father just made as he left. Takes in the strong shape of her, and she looks away, but it's too late.

Her mother's standing up and heading towards them.

'Why don't we all stay out tonight, then,' Delia says, looking between them. 'We could camp. We have the tent in the garage. The air mattress.'

Benjamin and Charlie both buzz with excitement, and Olive follows, watching as they all uncurl the tent and the mattress, hose the dust and cobwebs and insect carcasses from it and brush it clean. It takes them a few hours to finish. To get it up and moving, and when they're done their mother orders pizza, and they eat it on the damp grass outside before piling into the tent to go to sleep.

The boys are snoring softly – or at least she assumes Charlie is – when she turns over, sleepless, to find her mother's eyes fixed on her.

'What?' Olive asks, and Delia just shrugs.

'Just thinking about you.'

Olive wrinkles her nose, and Delia laughs lightly, rubbing a hand over her forehead, her lips curled in thought.

'Do you feel any better?'

'Than last night? Sure.'

Delia hums gently, like she'd meant something else, but Olive's not sure what, and then before she can stop herself she starts to talk.

'I always thought I knew what I wanted,' Olive says. 'And that I knew what sort of woman I wanted to be, but then I grew up, and I'm not her at all. I'm just – *me.*'

Because that's the thing. She was supposed to be at uni, she was supposed to make new friends, get a better job, she was supposed to be *something*, and too often she just doesn't feel like anything at all.

There's a twitch to her mother's lips, the young streaks of grey in her hair luminous below the light of the half-slung moon visible through the mesh overlay of the tent.

'There's no one sort of woman to be,' her mother says. 'You're going to fuck up in your life – if you believe nothing else I say, believe that – and you're never going to feel like you know what's going on, and you're going to hurt in ways you can't explain, that are so unique to you that sharing them will feel like giving somebody something in a different language, or passing them a knife, or both, but that's okay. That's just what growing up is.'

Olive leans backwards.

'Did you always know that you wanted to paint?'

'Yes,' Delia says. 'But it's okay that you don't know what you want. We don't have to be the same. We don't have to understand every part of each other. I never understood my mother, but I don't think that's what love is. Love isn't knowing every thought or feeling or secret, or even liking someone, it's just this thing in your gut and in your bones that says this person is mine and I'm theirs, at least a little, and maybe I'm mad at them, but I'd pull out my bones and give them to them if that's what they needed. You. If that's what *you* needed.'

Olive's crying now, can feel the wet swell of tears dribbling down her cheeks, and she swipes at them, sniffs, gives up. She shakes her head.

'I'm so angry, and I don't know why. There's just something in me that feels like a fire and I don't know whether to snuff it out or fan the flames, so I do neither and then it catches and it catches on everything I do and on everyone I talk to and it ruins everything. I hate it, but that's just what it is.'

Her jaw clenches.

'I feel bad a lot. More than I think I'm supposed to.'

'I know,' her mother whispers, pulling her in close. 'I see you. We'll figure it out. It's you and me, it'll always be you and me.'

'You and me,' Olive repeats, voice hoarse, and she feels her mother then, her paint-slick hands at her waist, at her back, pulling Olive so tightly against her chest she almost can't breathe, and there's a minute of shaking, trembling nothing before Olive wraps her arms around her mother's waist too and doesn't dream of letting go.

The rain starts again sometime after Olive and Mum fall asleep, pattering down on the roof of the tent, echoing in the dingy stretch of space. It brings the pulsing hoots of tawny frogmouths with it, and the chatter of the nighttime birds, the stranger chorus of the wild.

Benjamin sits up on the air mattress, ducking quickly so as not to hit his head on a part of the tent ceiling sagging with rainwater. It's growing heavy already, and he's not sure how well it'll hold. He glances down to see his mother and Olive, sharing the better half of the mattress, their limbs entangled, their mouths open, like they fell asleep mid-word, mid-conversation, mid-something. He grins and turns, grappling in the open air, waiting for the thud that means his hand has met Charlie's, but no matter where he reaches, he doesn't hit a thing.

Benjamin frowns.

'Charlie?' he whispers, but there's no reply. No ruffle of air, no pressure on his shoulder, his wrist, his cheek.

'Charlie?' he says, louder this time, and Olive groans beside him, rolls over on the mattress, and he quickly falls silent.

The rain's getting louder again, thick, heavy. He can smell it in the air. He looks out through the plastic window of the tent towards the darkness beyond, back up towards their house, and, after only a moment's hesitation, unzips the door and steps out into the rain.

It takes his eyes a moment to adjust, to get used to the misty glow of the moon above them, to take in the wild look of their yard, and the shatter of rain. The insects have escaped it at least, hidden beneath the cover of grass and foliage, beneath the low-hanging branches of the jacarandas and poincianas. Birds huddle there as well, and Benjamin watches their ruffled feathers even as his pyjamas soak through with rain.

He's not sure what makes him look, not really, but his gaze slips back to Charlie's telescope, and his heart stops.

Standing over the instrument, dressed only in one of Mum's art smocks, the hem dripping at his knees, is Charlie. He rotates the dial, fixes the lens, mouths words to himself that Benjamin can't hear across the distance of their yard. He takes a step forwards, then another, slowly, as if Charlie is a wild animal or a mirage, something fleeting and ephemeral and perhaps not really here at all.

He stops just a few steps in front of him, and it's only then that Charlie's eyes rise to meet his. He smiles his toothiest smile.

'Hi,' Charlie says, voice scratchy from disuse, and Benjamin grins back.

'Hi.'

Charlie stills, heartbreakingly thin, his lemur eyes dull, his lips pink and chapped. He looks somehow exactly the same and not a thing like himself, and it startles Benjamin, how Charlie in the flesh seems like something foreign.

'Y'know, there's something different about you tonight,' Charlie jokes, holding a hand up to his eyes, shielding them from the pelt of the rain, and Benjamin giggles.

'You too. New shirt?' he asks, and Charlie laughs, his eyes crinkling at the corners as he tugs at the neck of the smock.

'Yeah, figured it was time for a change.'

An owl hoots somewhere in the distance, frogs bleat, the night settles warm around them, and behind them Delia and Olive sleep in their tent, and for the first time in a long time Benjamin thinks not of his dad or Poppy or school or anything, but just this moment. Just them. Just this.

'You want to help?' Charlie asks, interrupting Benjamin's thoughts, resting a hand on the body of his telescope, smiling his crooked smile.

Benjamin couldn't say no even if he wanted to.

Acknowledgements

A huge and endless thank you to the people at Penguin Random House who made this dream a reality, in particular Meredith Curnow and Melissa Lane, who helped me tell this story better. Their editorial work is all over this finished book, and I'm forever grateful for their feedback and care, as well as all the lessons they taught me that I know I'll take beyond this story and onto the next.

Thank you too to my agent, Alex Adsett, who leapt on board this train with both feet and offered essential advice and support, and to all the creative institutions and the people within them who saw promise in this story and supported it: the team at the Katharine Susannah Prichard Writers' Centre, the Queensland Literary Awards, and Tin House. This book wouldn't be half of what it is without the people who gave me the space, time and guidance to develop it, and I am forever grateful for that.

I'm also grateful to Brisbane's vibrant writing scene, which took me in and built me up and continues to challenge and inspire me, even from across state lines. Stacey Clair, Lara Shprem, Angela Slatter, Meg Vann, and Peter M. Ball in particular, and extra special thanks goes to my partner in crime, Aimée Lindorff, whose championing, listening ear, advice and occasional slap-upside-the-head have meant more to me than she could ever possibly know.

Thank you to my current team too – the wonderfully magical cohort at Polyglot Theatre, who've celebrated every step of the publication journey with me and whose companionship and embrace during 111 days of lockdown was a gift: Erica Heller-Wagner and Kath Fyffe in particular.

And there are so many friends I want to mention too who helped in big ways, small ways, and ways they didn't even realise were helping. Emma and Steve Hewitt, Meagan Vella, Hayley Sargison, Ellen Newcombe, Natasha Rogers, Christopher Hackett, Kate Hough, Jill Martin, Holly Leong and Jerod Duenas. Special shout-outs go to Emma Haig, who never stopped believing in me, even when I struggled to believe in myself – you're one of my soul mates, and I love you forever – and to Megan Fajardo and Meg Lalley too – our friendship is newer than many, but being able to talk to you both about writing and about this book has been its own sort of magic. You're two of the best cheerleaders and sounding boards out there, and your thoughtfulness and patience have meant so much to me over the last eighteen months.

Thank you too, of course, to my family – Mark Overett, Maddy Overett, Chase, Kai and Hudson Dingle, and Sally and Chris Rodda, but especially my mother, Cathy Rodda, and brother Alexander Overett, who have been there through the highs and lows of this project, and have always given me the room to write, edit, vent and celebrate in equal measure. I love you a lot.

And finally, no thanks at all to Oreo the cat, who did his level best to make sure this book never got finished.